6/21

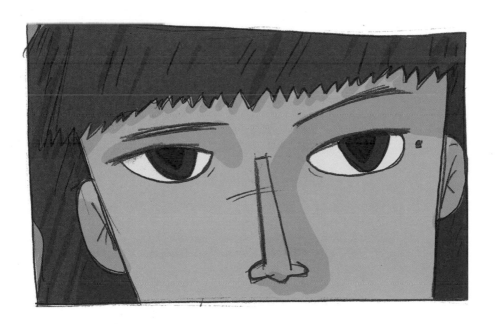

FOR THE REAL-LIFE NERA,
IRMA KAREN.

ONION SKIN © 2021 EDGAR CAMACHO

Published by Top Shelf Productions, an imprint of IDW Publishing, a division of
Idea and Design Works, LLC. Offices: Top Shelf Productions, c/o Idea & Design
Works, LLC, 2765 Truxtun Road, San Diego, CA 92106. Top Shelf Productions®,
the Top Shelf logo, Idea and Design Works®, and the IDW logo are registered
trademarks of Idea and Design Works, LLC. All Rights Reserved. With the
exception of small excerpts of artwork used for review purposes, none of the
contents of this publication may be reprinted without the permission of IDW
Publishing. Printed in China.

IDW Publishing does not read or accept unsolicited submissions
of ideas, stories, or artwork.

Editor-in-Chief: Chris Staros.
Edited by Leigh Walton.
Design by Nathan Widick.
Translated by Edgar Camacho.

Originally published in Mexico as *Piel de cebolla* by Fondo Editorial Tierra
Adentro and Instituto Queretano de la Cultura y Artes.

ISBN: 978-1-60309-489-4   24 23 22 21   4 3 2 1

Visit our online catalog at topshelfcomix.com.

ONION SKIN

SKIN

EDGAR CAMACHO

Top Shelf
PRODUCTIONS

PART ONE

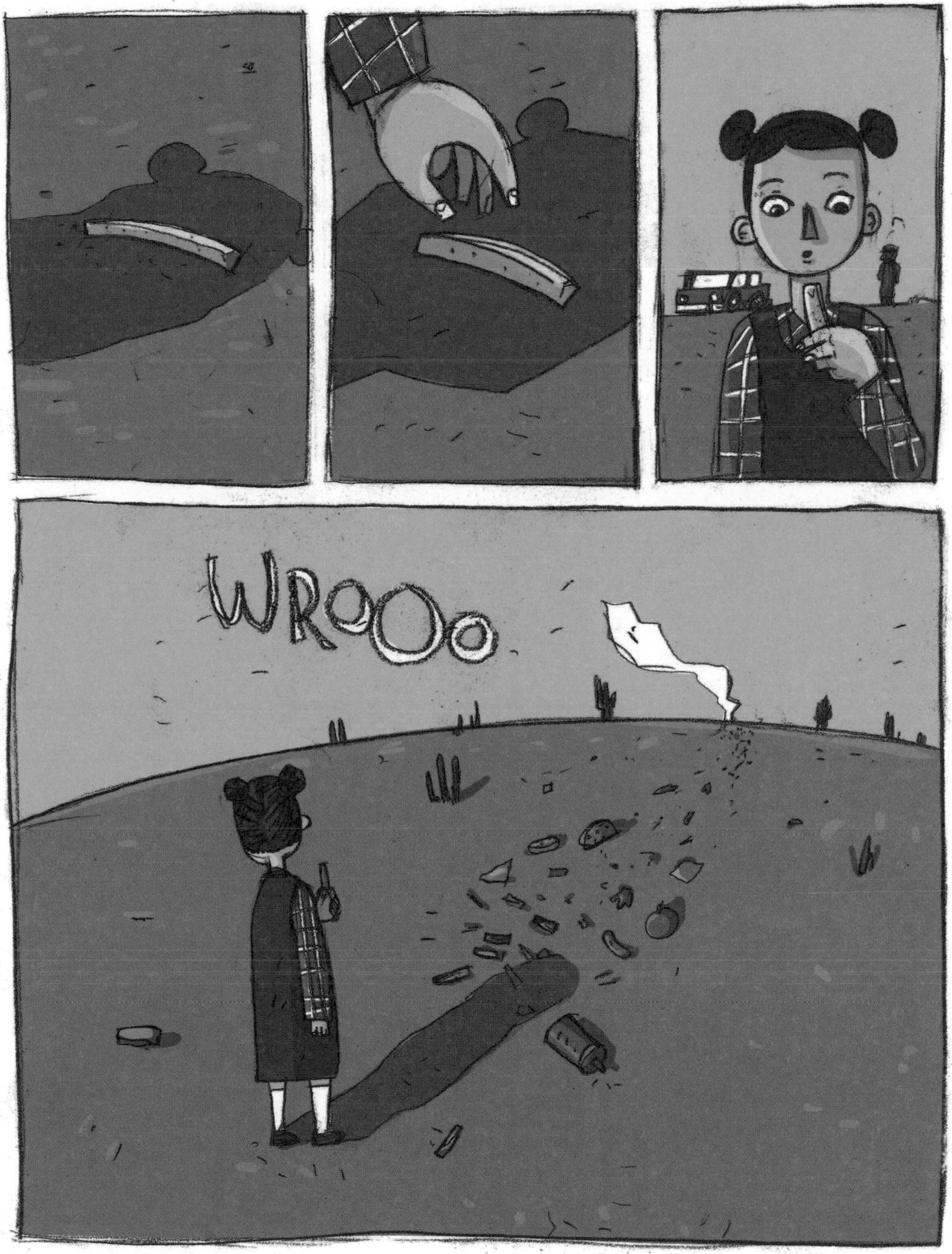
WROOOO

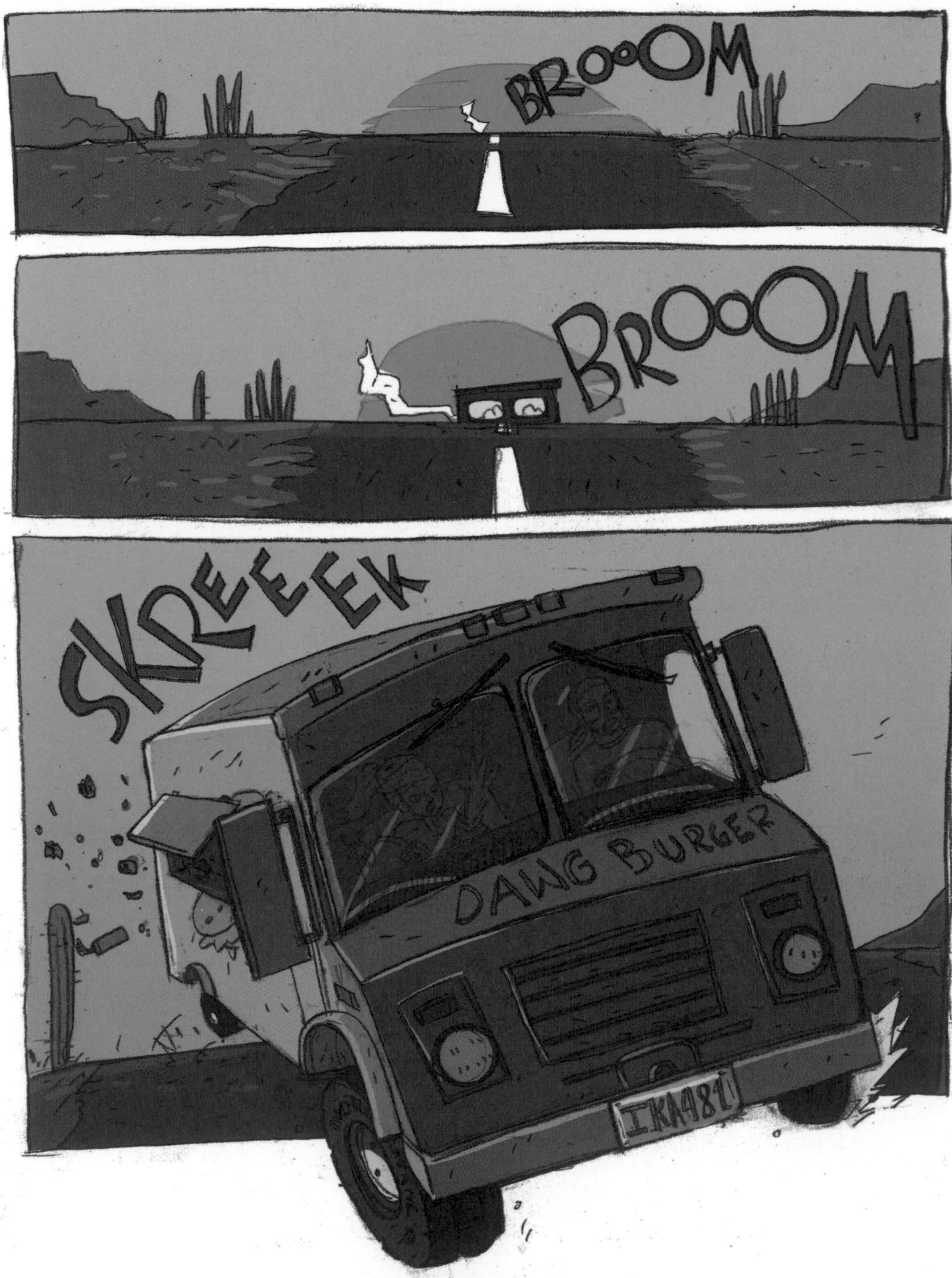
BROoOM
BROoOM
SKREEEK
DAWG BURGER
IKA981

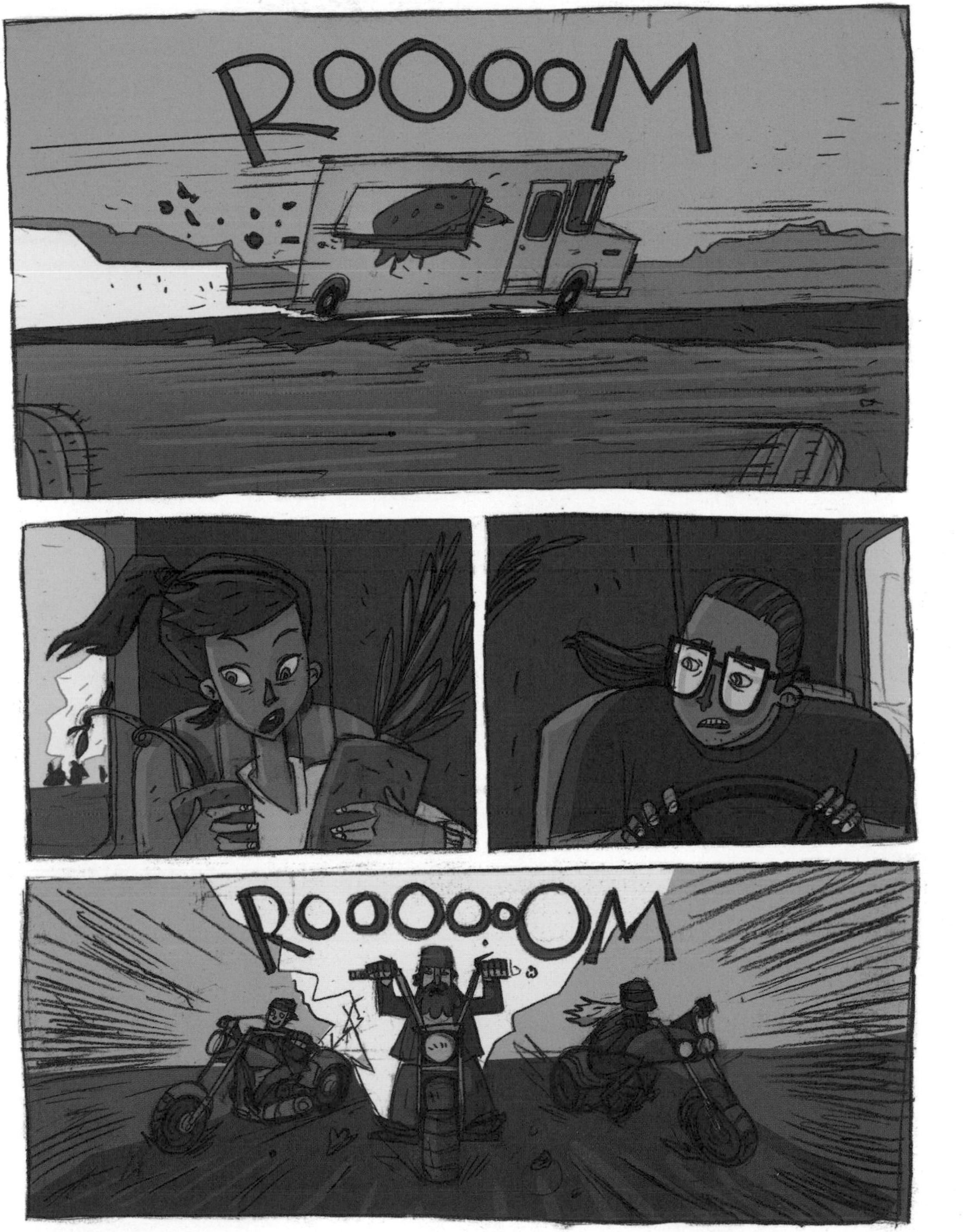
ROOOoOM
ROOOO·OM

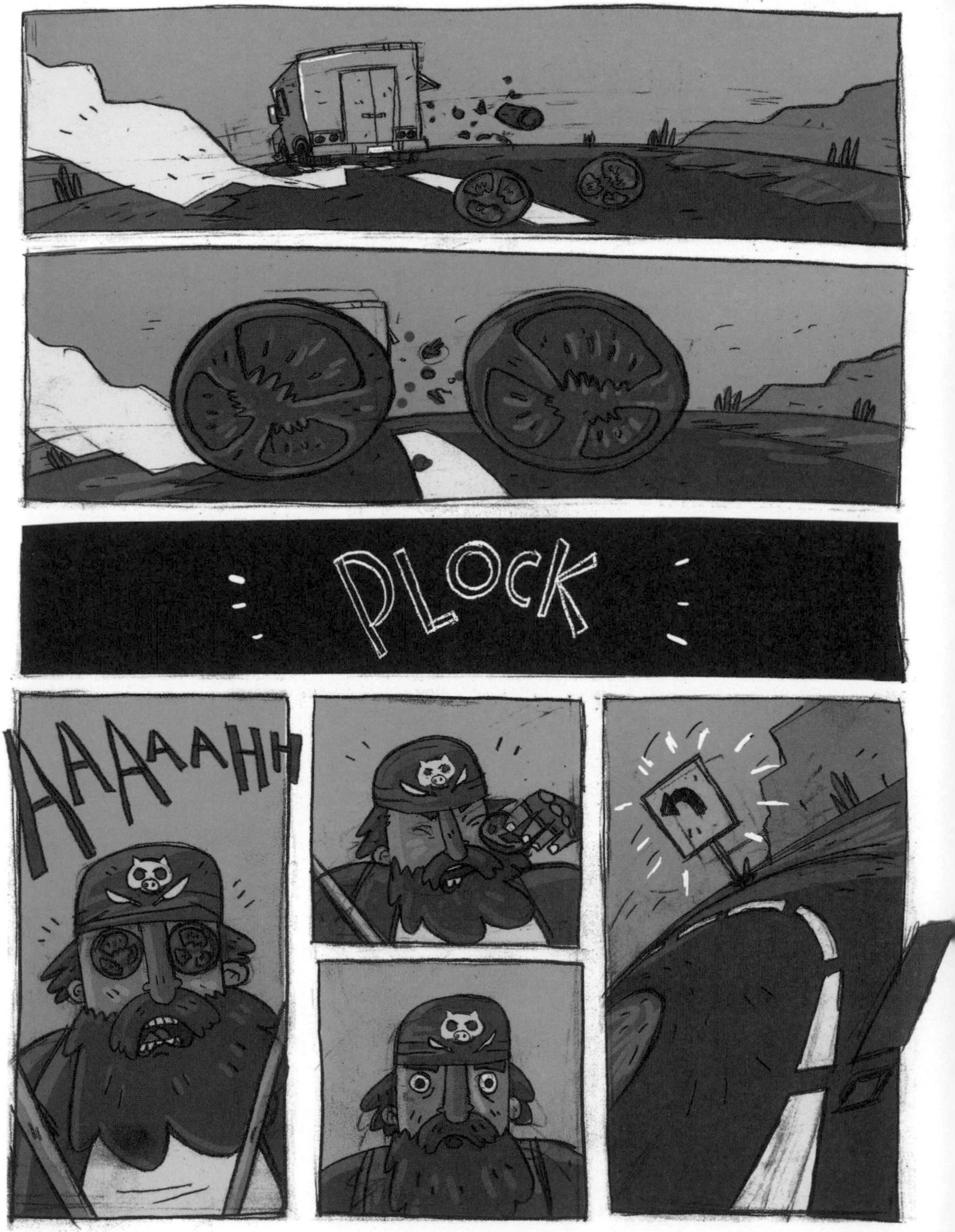
PLOCK
AAAAAHH

SKREEEK

SKRRRRREK

EEEEEE

AAAAAAHH

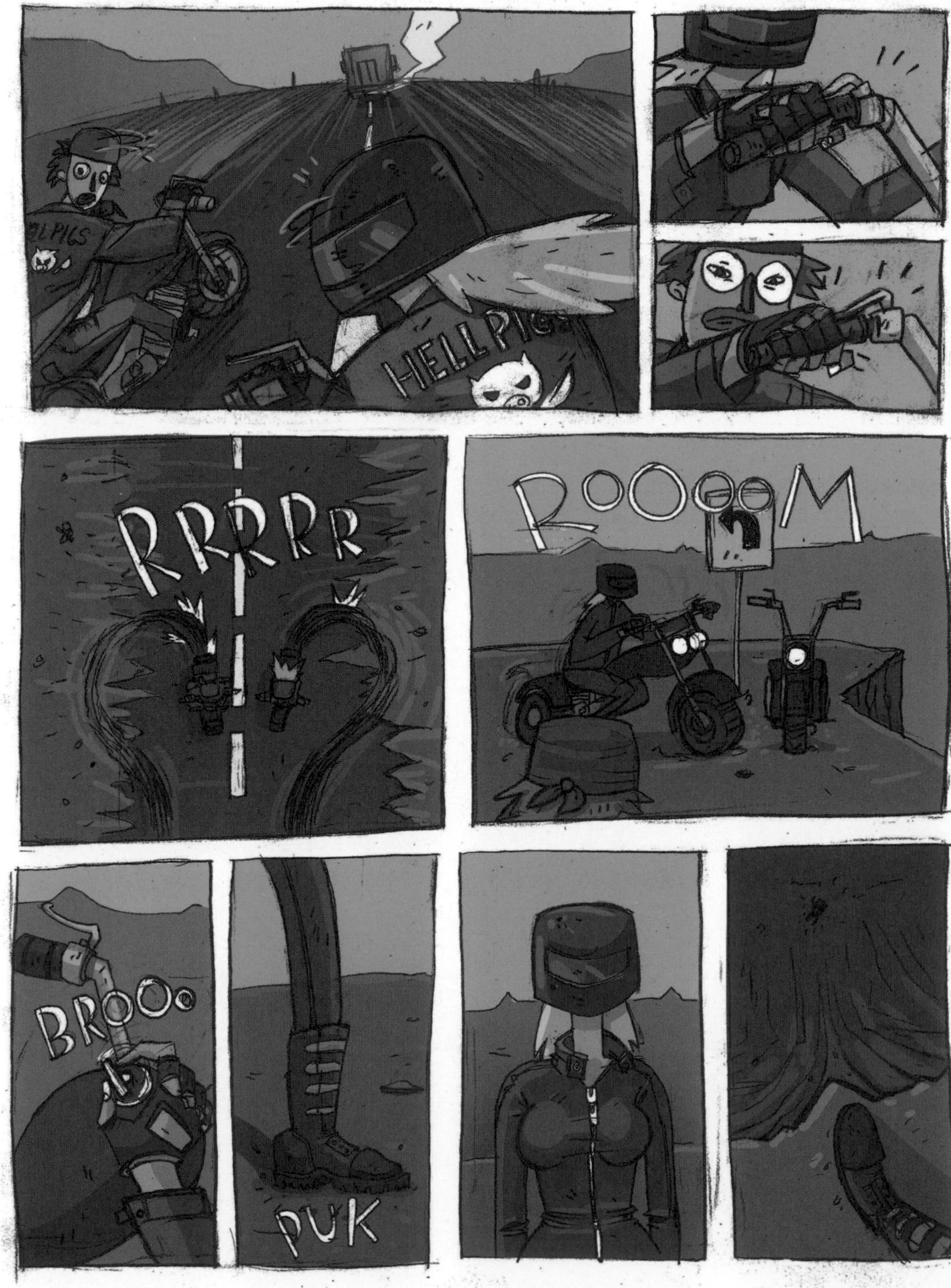

LL PIGS
HELLPIGS
RRRRRR
ROOOOOM
BROOo
PUK

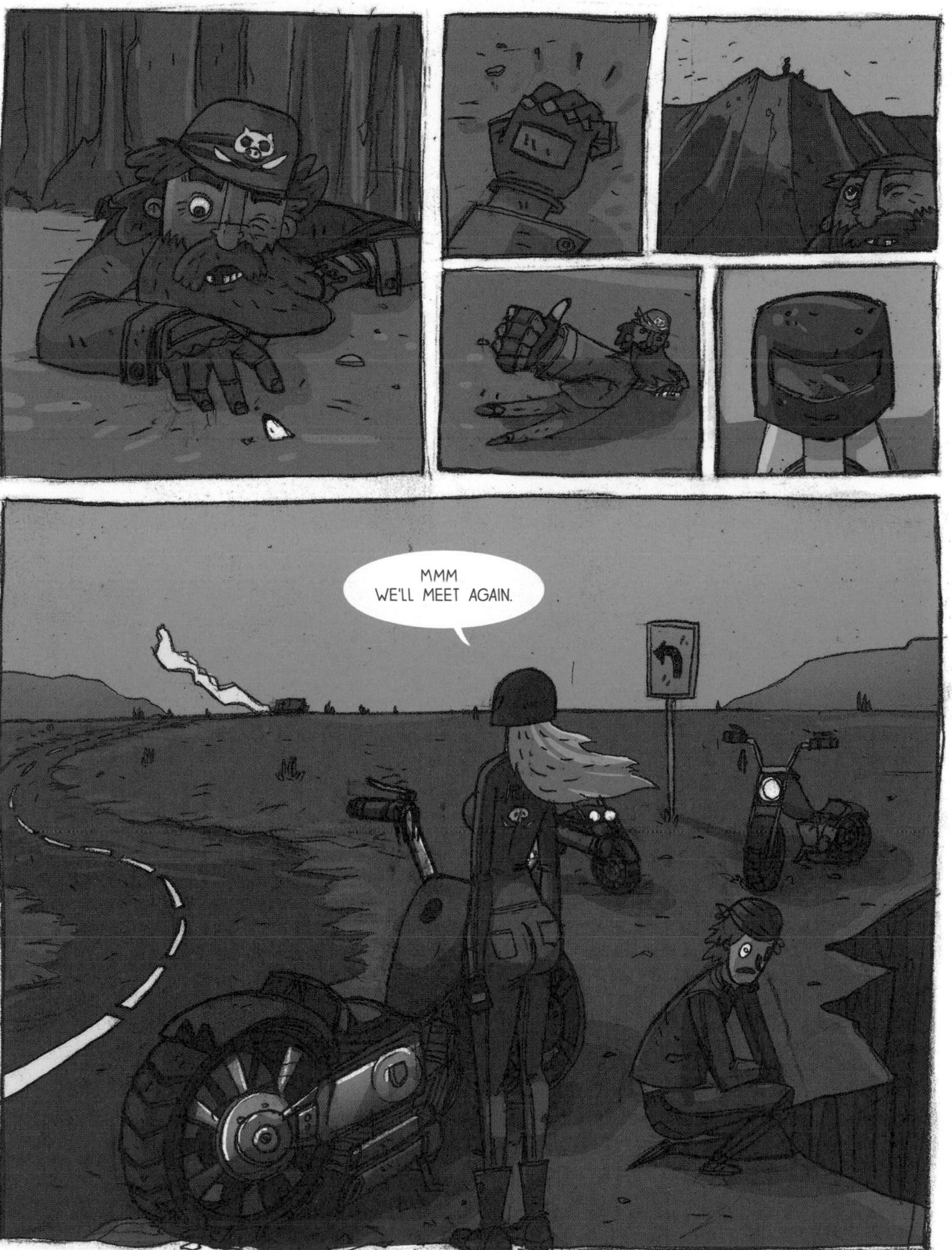
MMM
WE'LL MEET AGAIN.

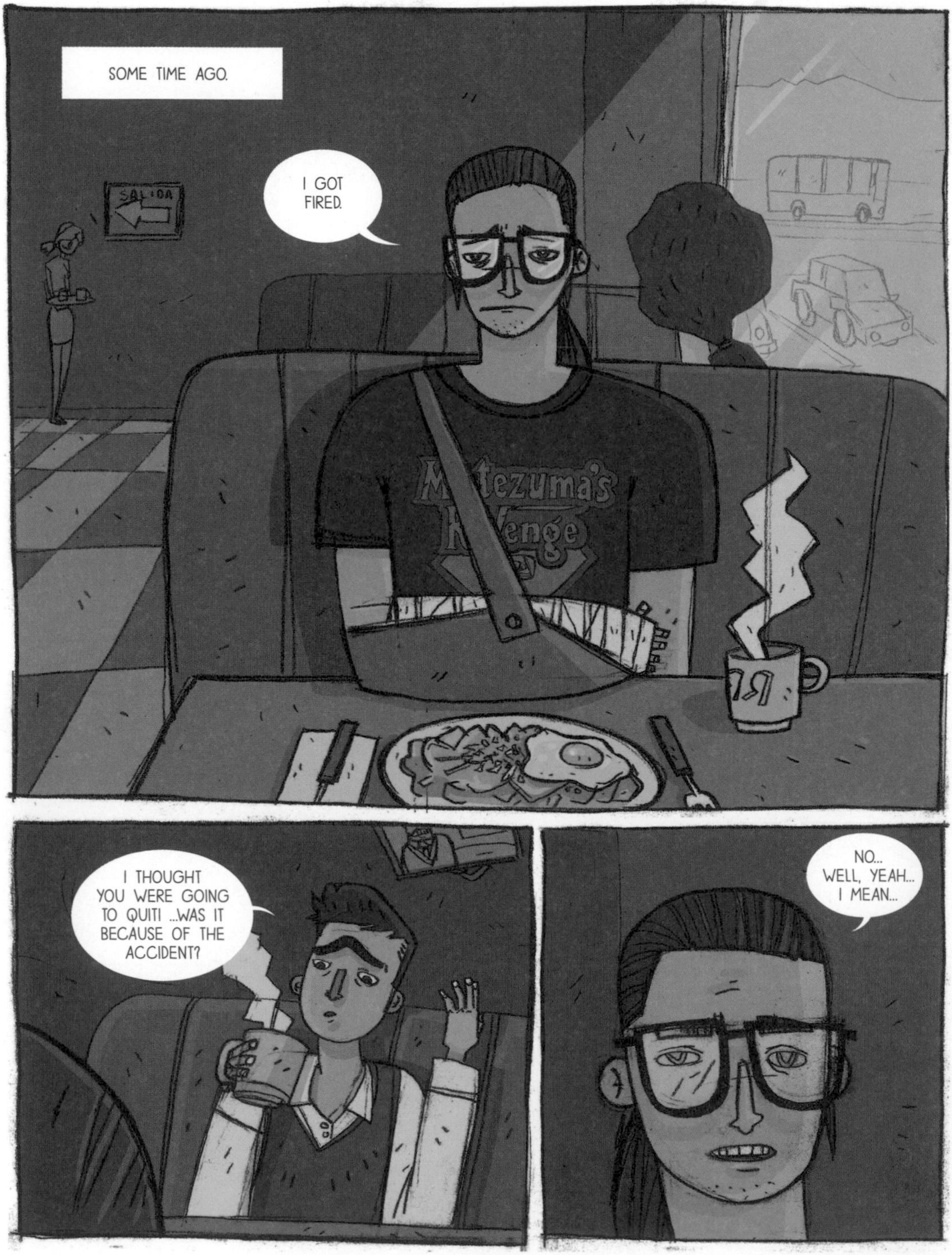
SOME TIME AGO.
I GOT FIRED.
I THOUGHT YOU WERE GOING TO QUIT! ...WAS IT BECAUSE OF THE ACCIDENT?
NO... WELL, YEAH... I MEAN...

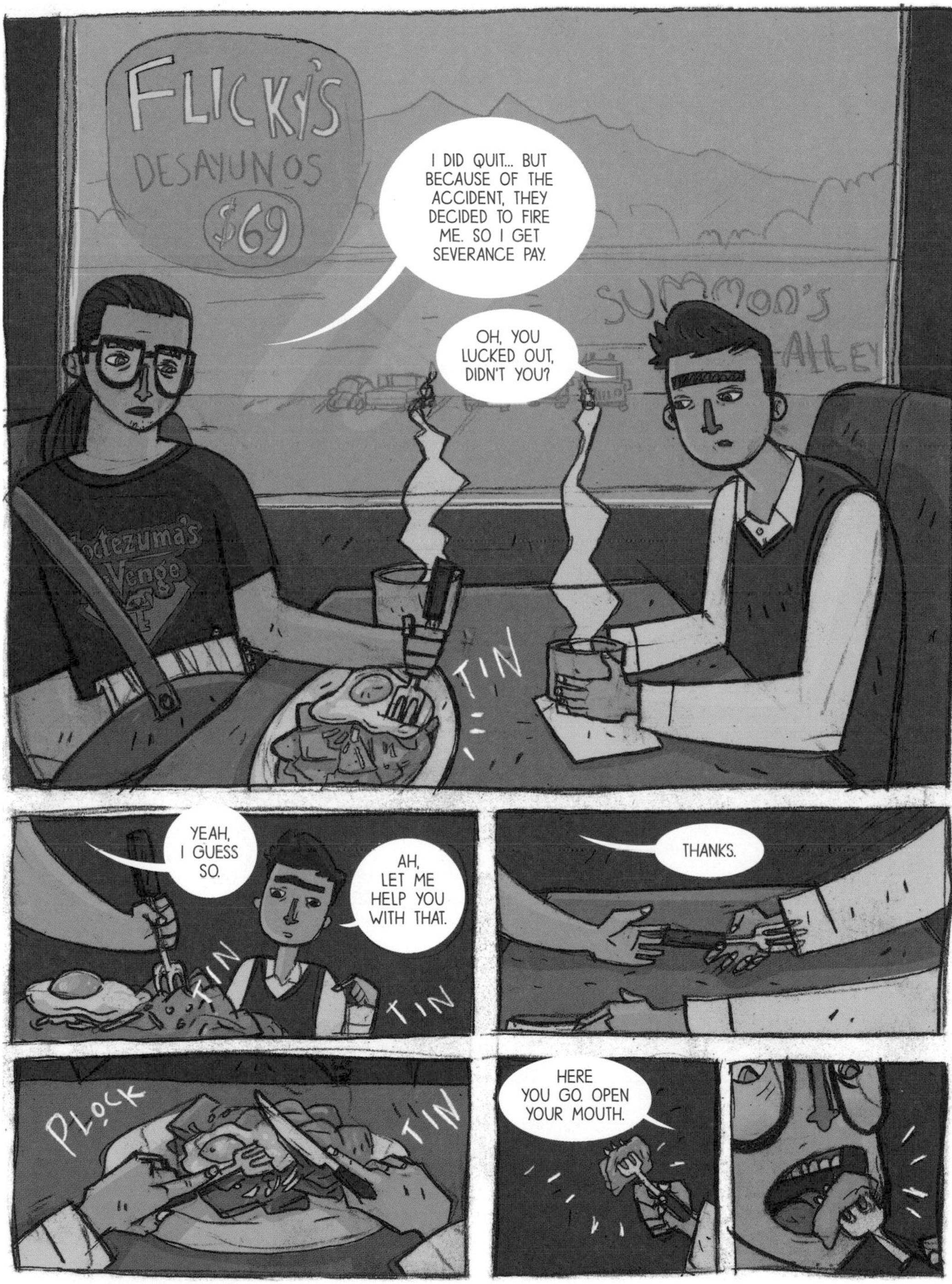
FLICKY'S
DESAYUNOS
$69
I DID QUIT... BUT BECAUSE OF THE ACCIDENT, THEY DECIDED TO FIRE ME. SO I GET SEVERANCE PAY.
SUMMON'S
ALLEY
OH, YOU LUCKED OUT, DIDN'T YOU?
Moctezuma's Venge
TIN
YEAH, I GUESS SO.
AH, LET ME HELP YOU WITH THAT.
TIN
TIN
THANKS.
PLOCK
TIN
HERE YOU GO. OPEN YOUR MOUTH.

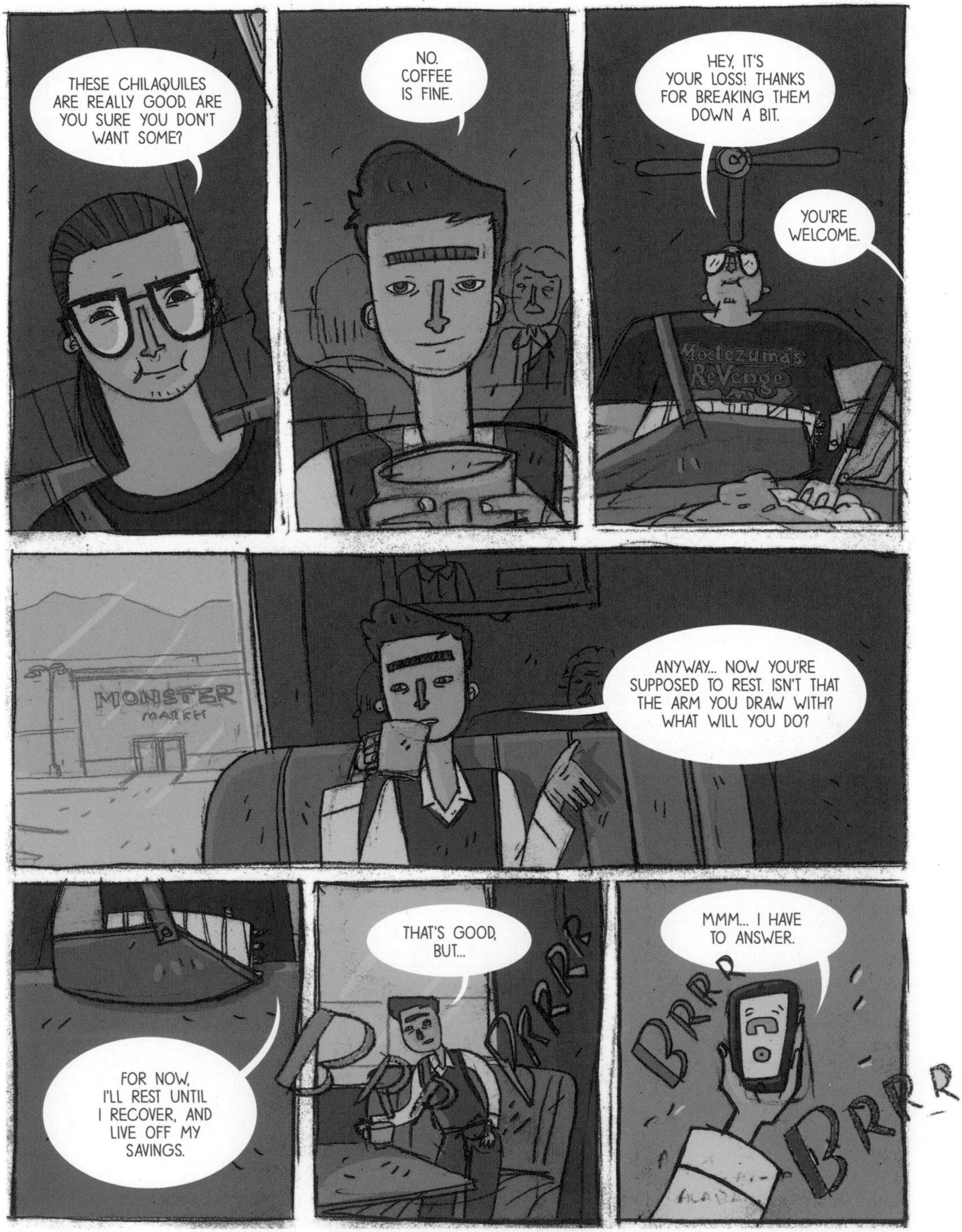
THESE CHILAQUILES ARE REALLY GOOD. ARE YOU SURE YOU DON'T WANT SOME?
NO. COFFEE IS FINE.
HEY, IT'S YOUR LOSS! THANKS FOR BREAKING THEM DOWN A BIT.
YOU'RE WELCOME.
Moctezuma's ReVenge
MONSTER
ANYWAY... NOW YOU'RE SUPPOSED TO REST. ISN'T THAT THE ARM YOU DRAW WITH? WHAT WILL YOU DO?
FOR NOW, I'LL REST UNTIL I RECOVER, AND LIVE OFF MY SAVINGS.
THAT'S GOOD, BUT...
BRRRR
MMM... I HAVE TO ANSWER.
BRRR
BRRRR

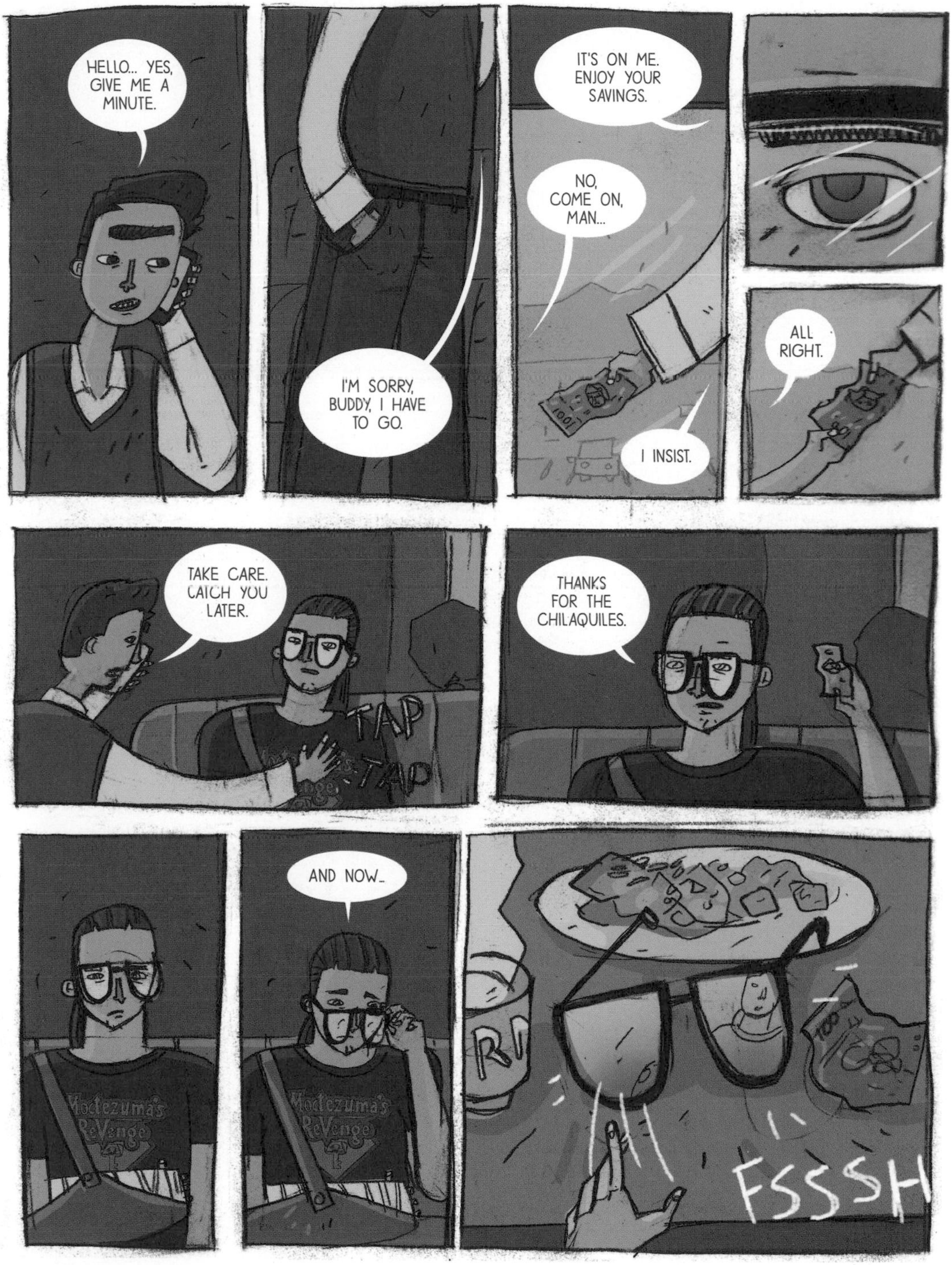
HELLO... YES, GIVE ME A MINUTE.
I'M SORRY, BUDDY, I HAVE TO GO.
IT'S ON ME. ENJOY YOUR SAVINGS.
NO, COME ON, MAN...
I INSIST.
ALL RIGHT.
TAKE CARE. CATCH YOU LATER.
TAP TAP
THANKS FOR THE CHILAQUILES.
Moctezuma's ReVenge
AND NOW...
FSSSH

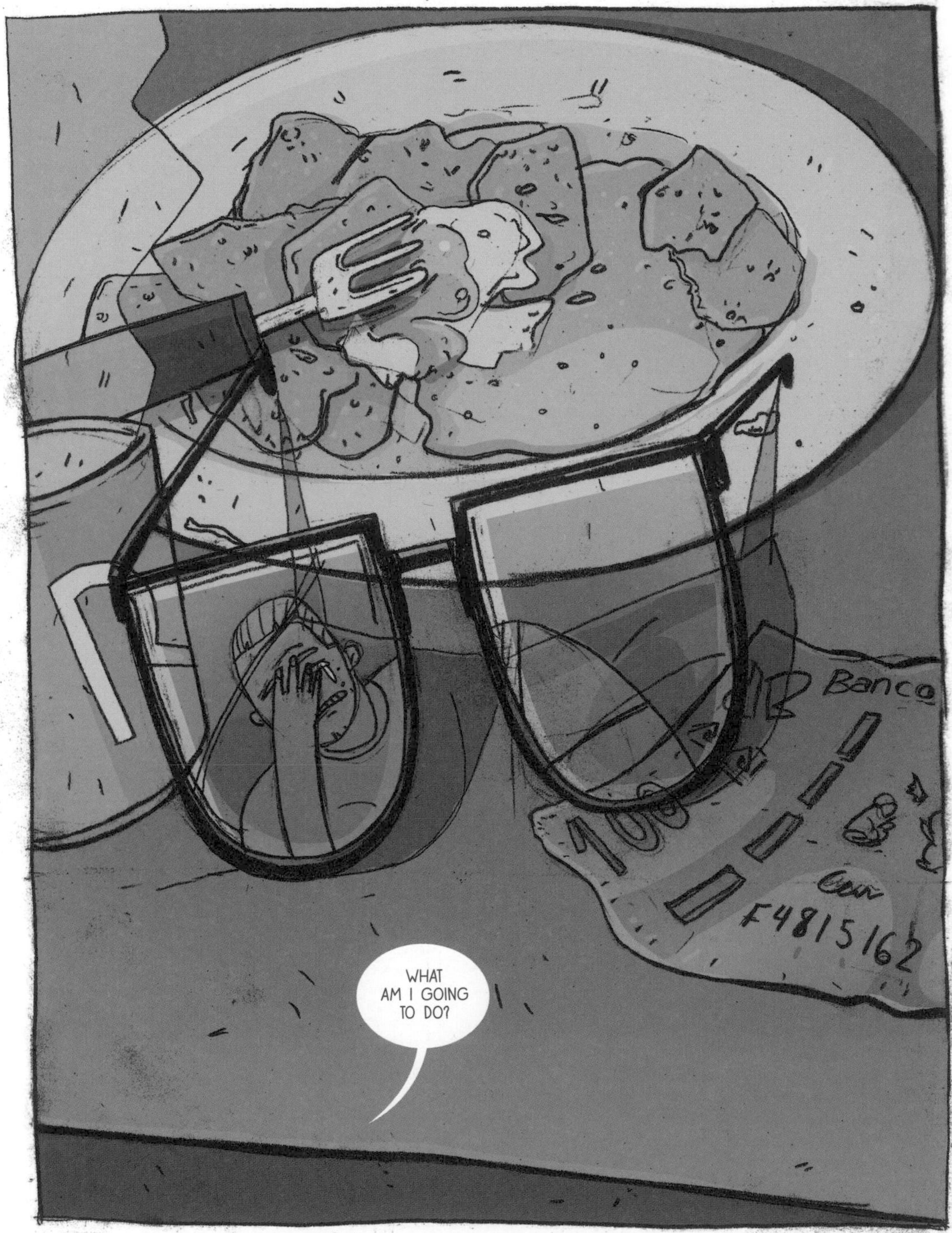
Banco
F4815162
WHAT AM I GOING TO DO?

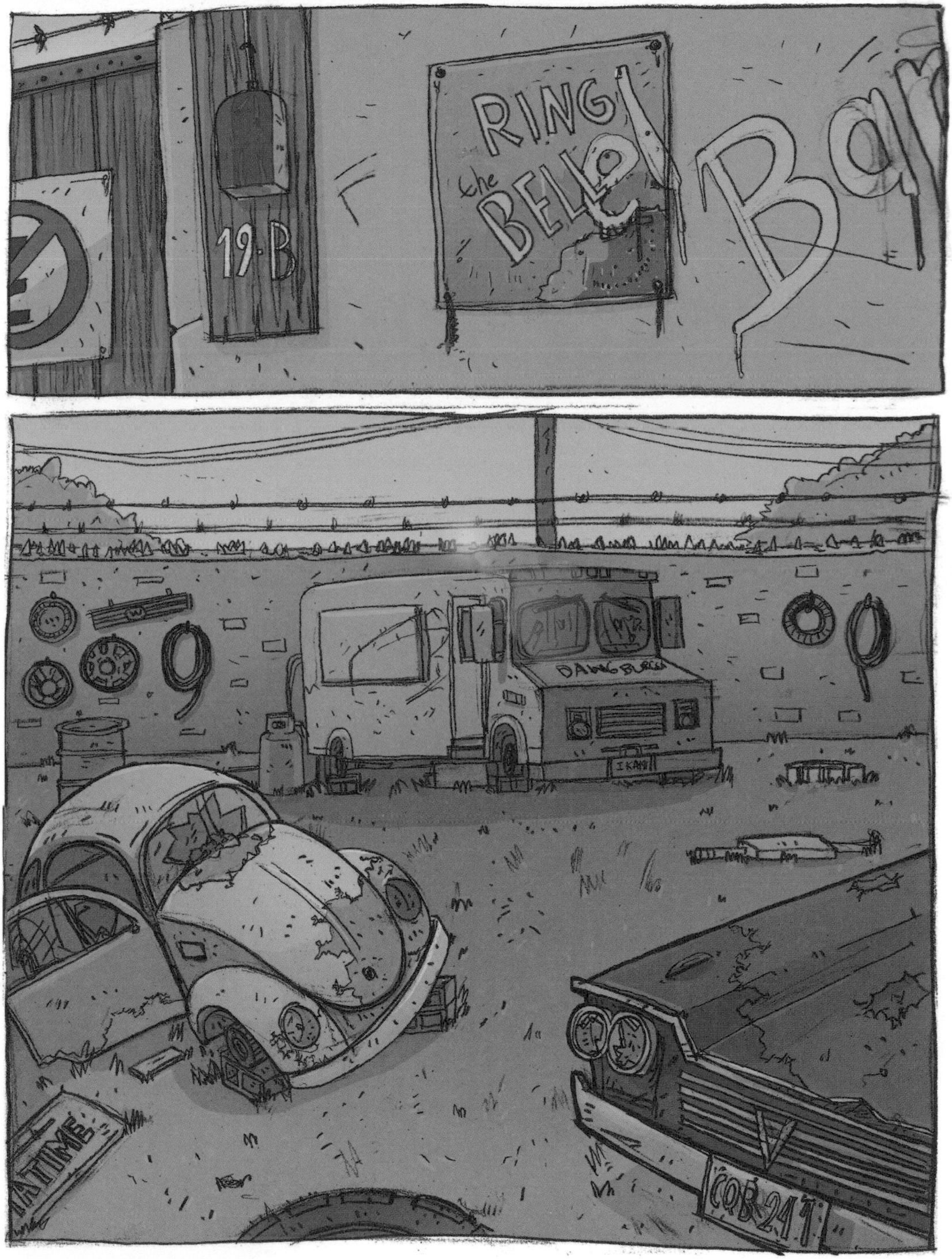
19-B
RING the BELL
COB 241

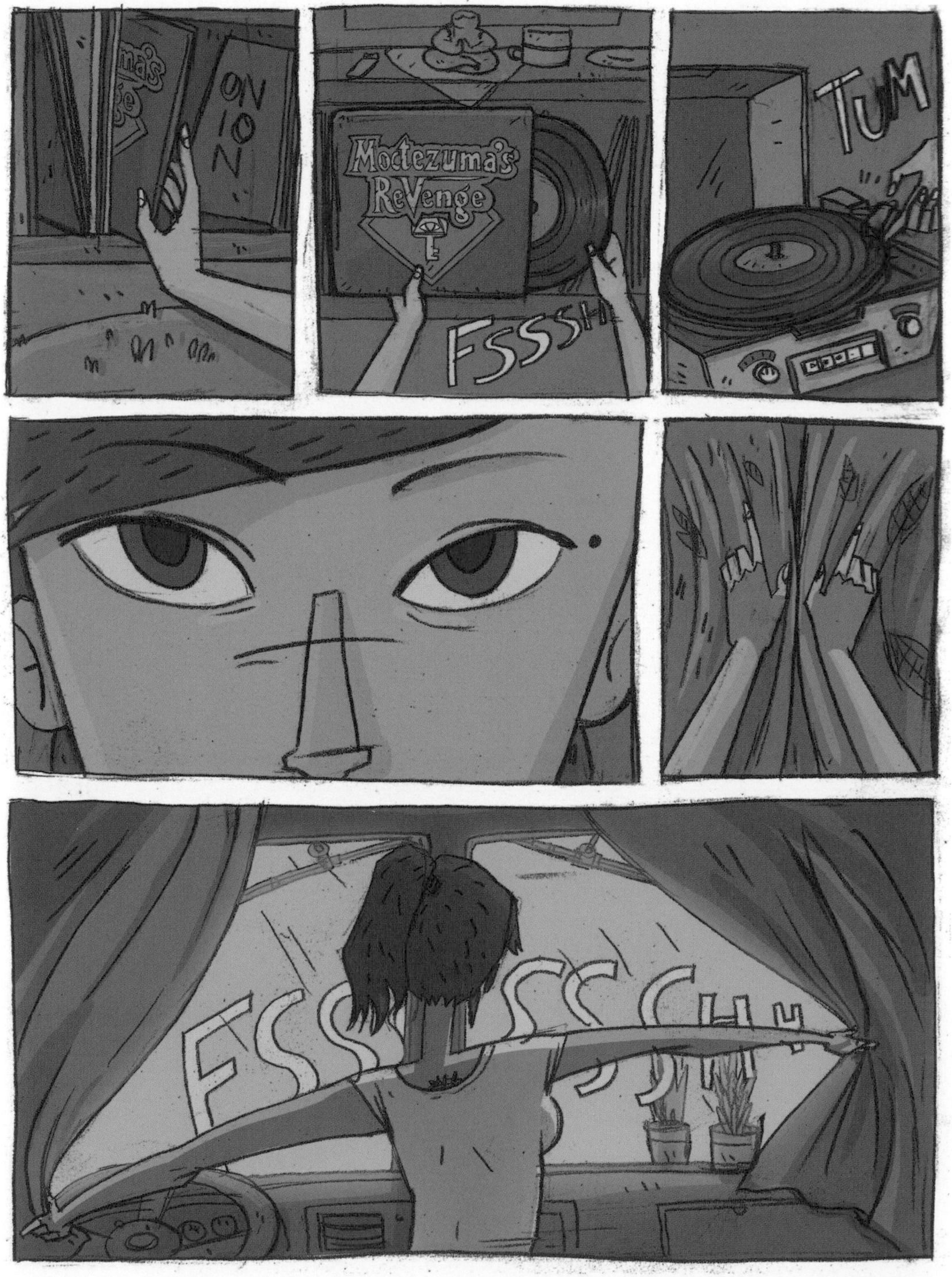
ONION
Moctezuma's ReVenge
FSSSH
TUM
FSSSSSSHH

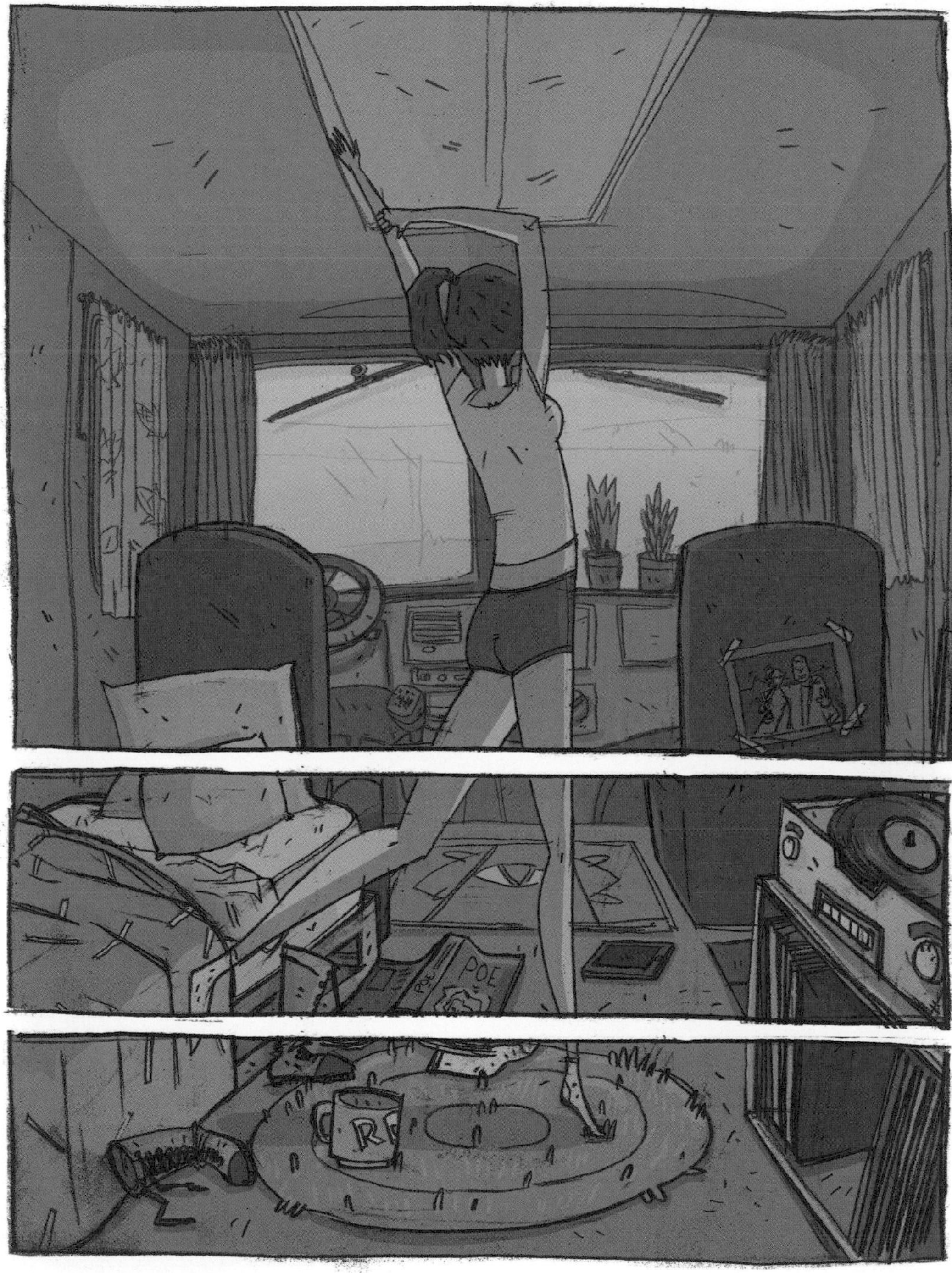
POE
POE

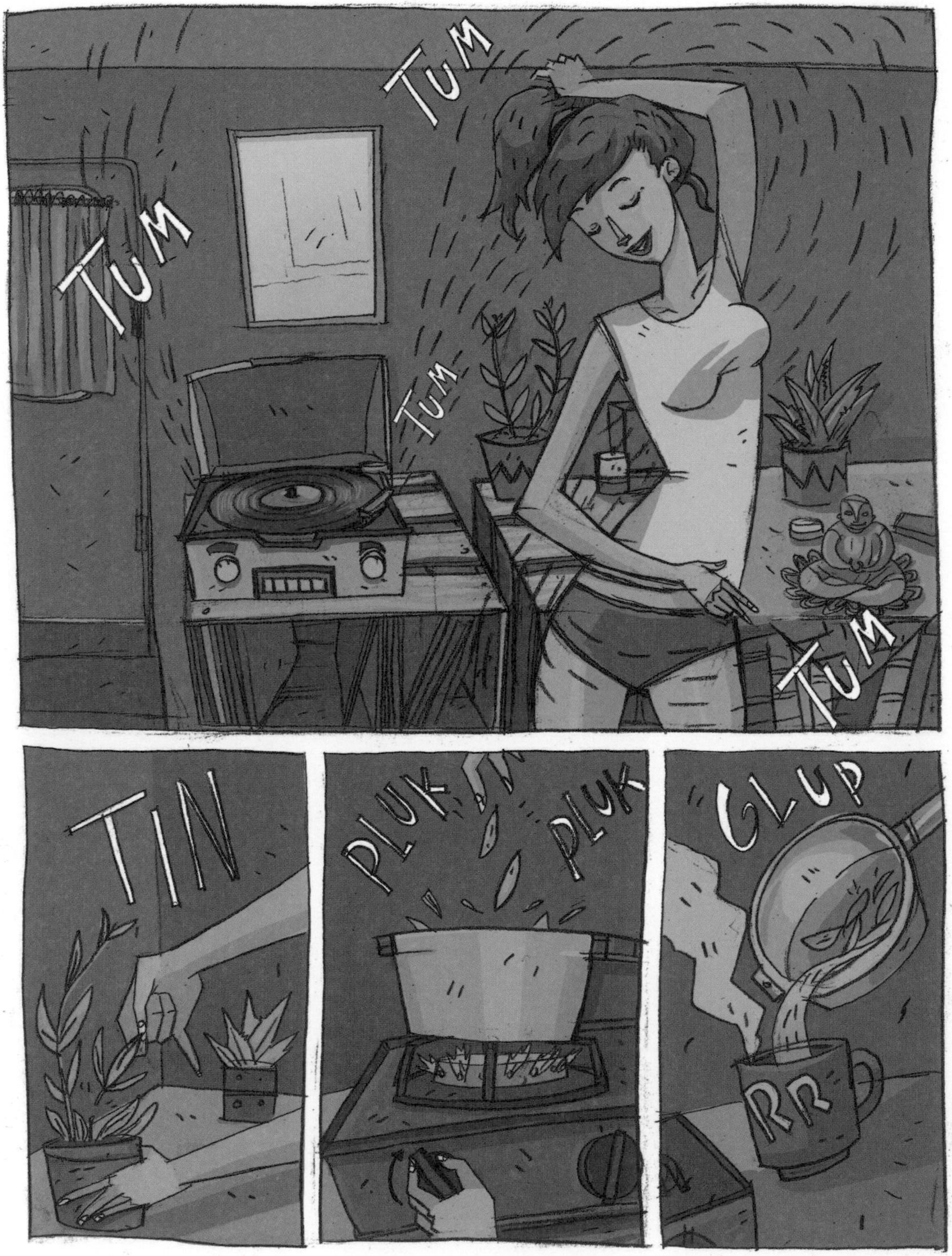
TUM
TUM
TUM
TUM
TUM
TIN
PLUK
PLUK
GLUP
RR

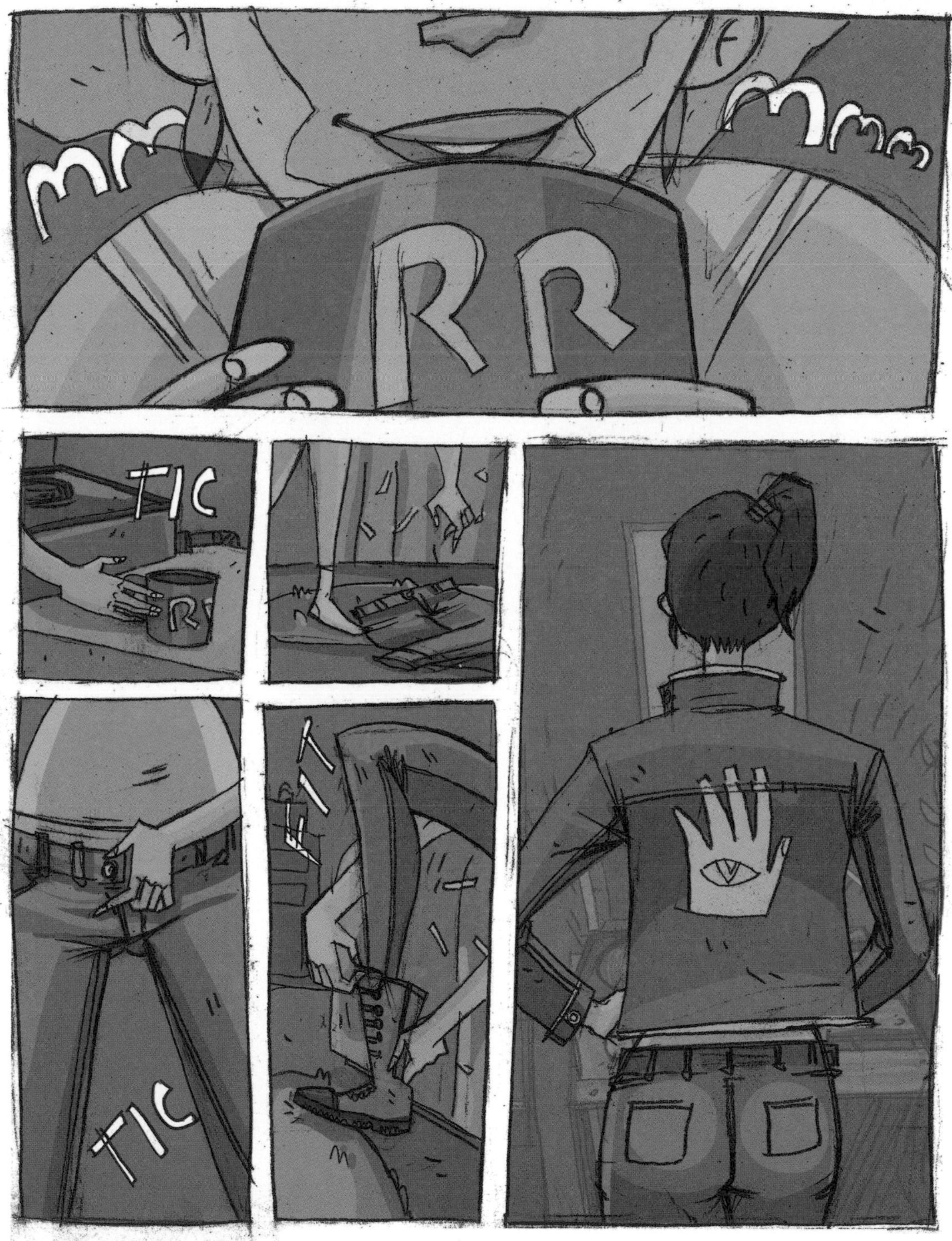

mmm
mmmm
TIC
TIC

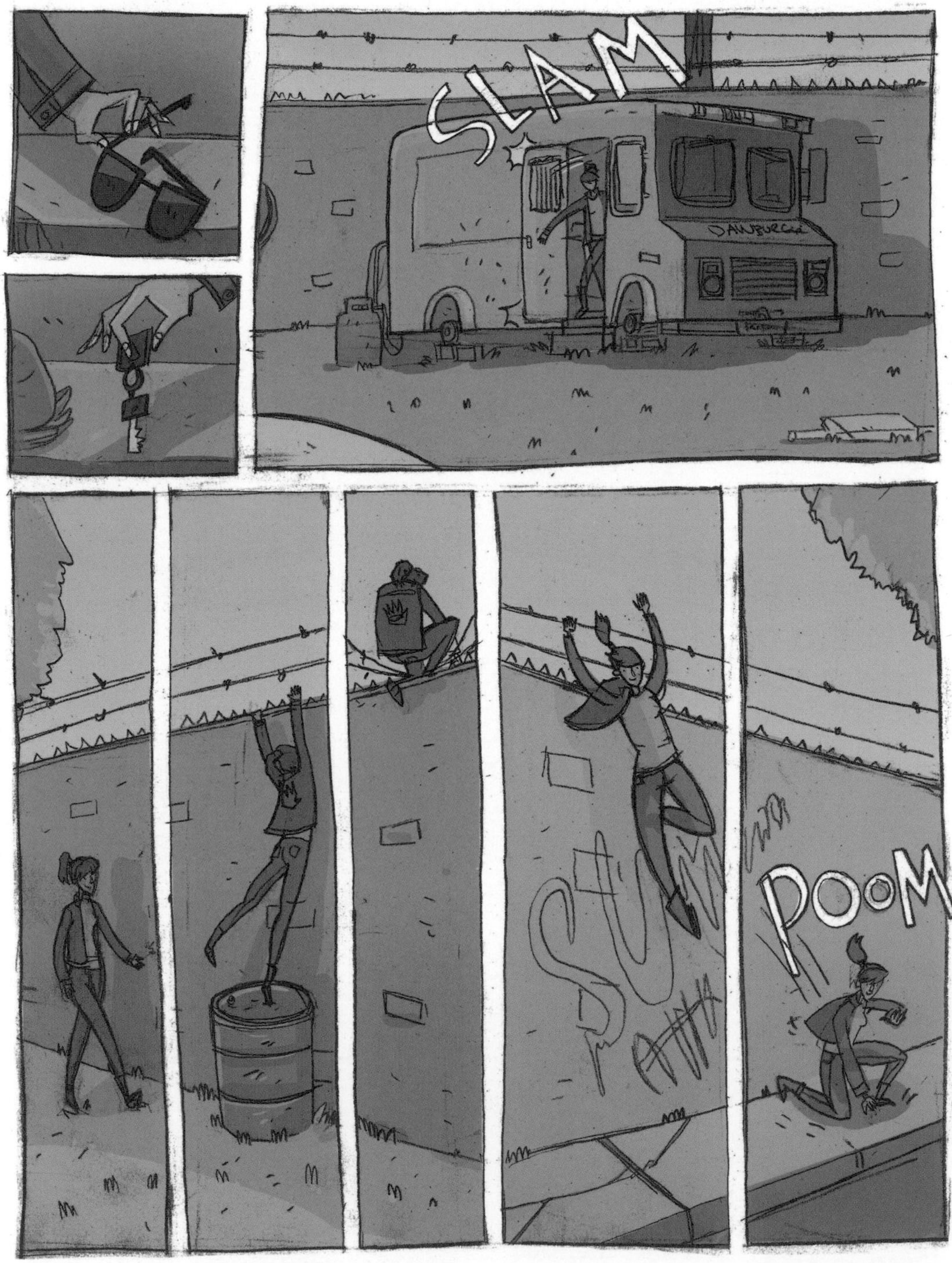
SLAM
POOM

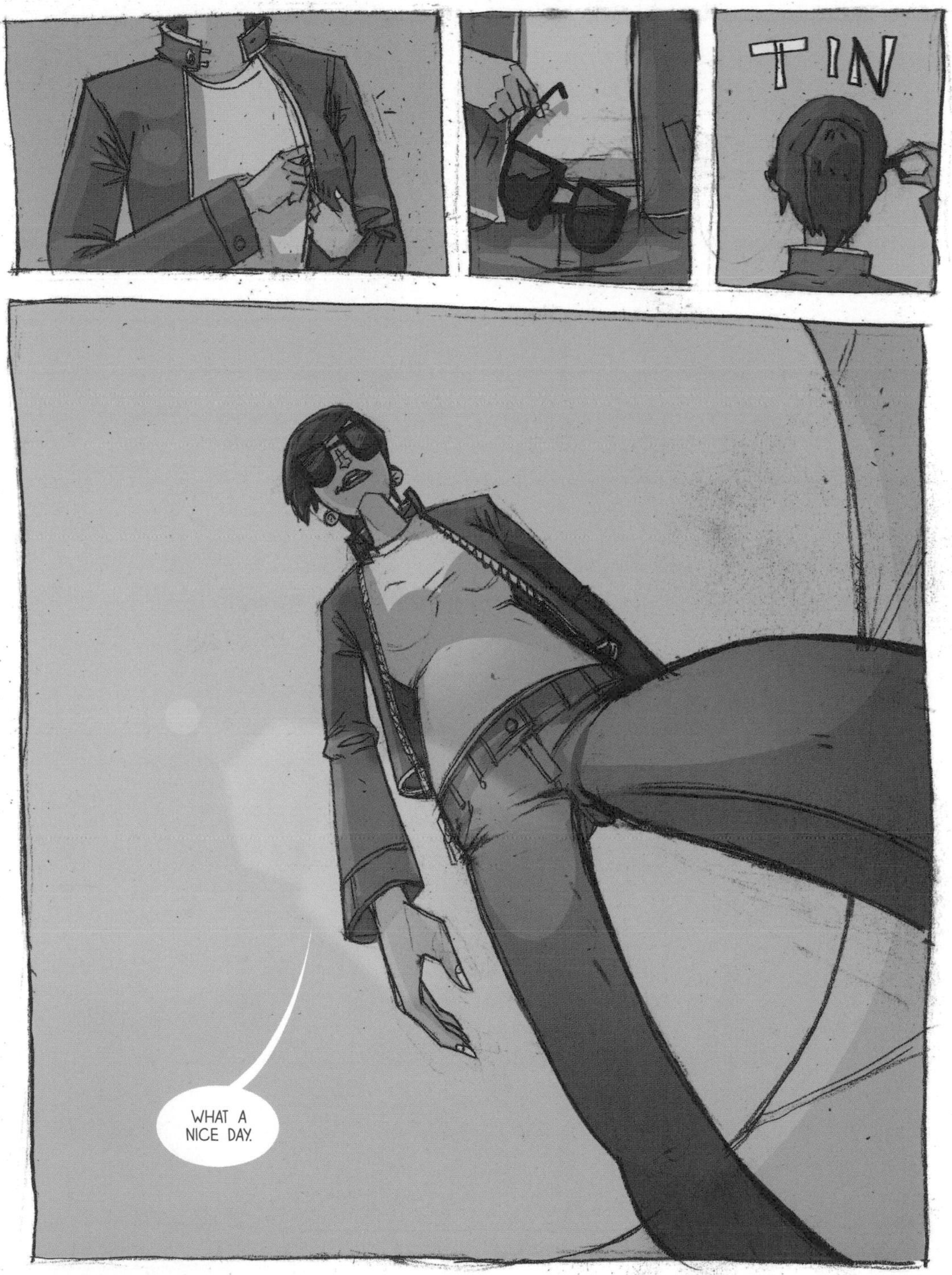
TIN
WHAT A NICE DAY.

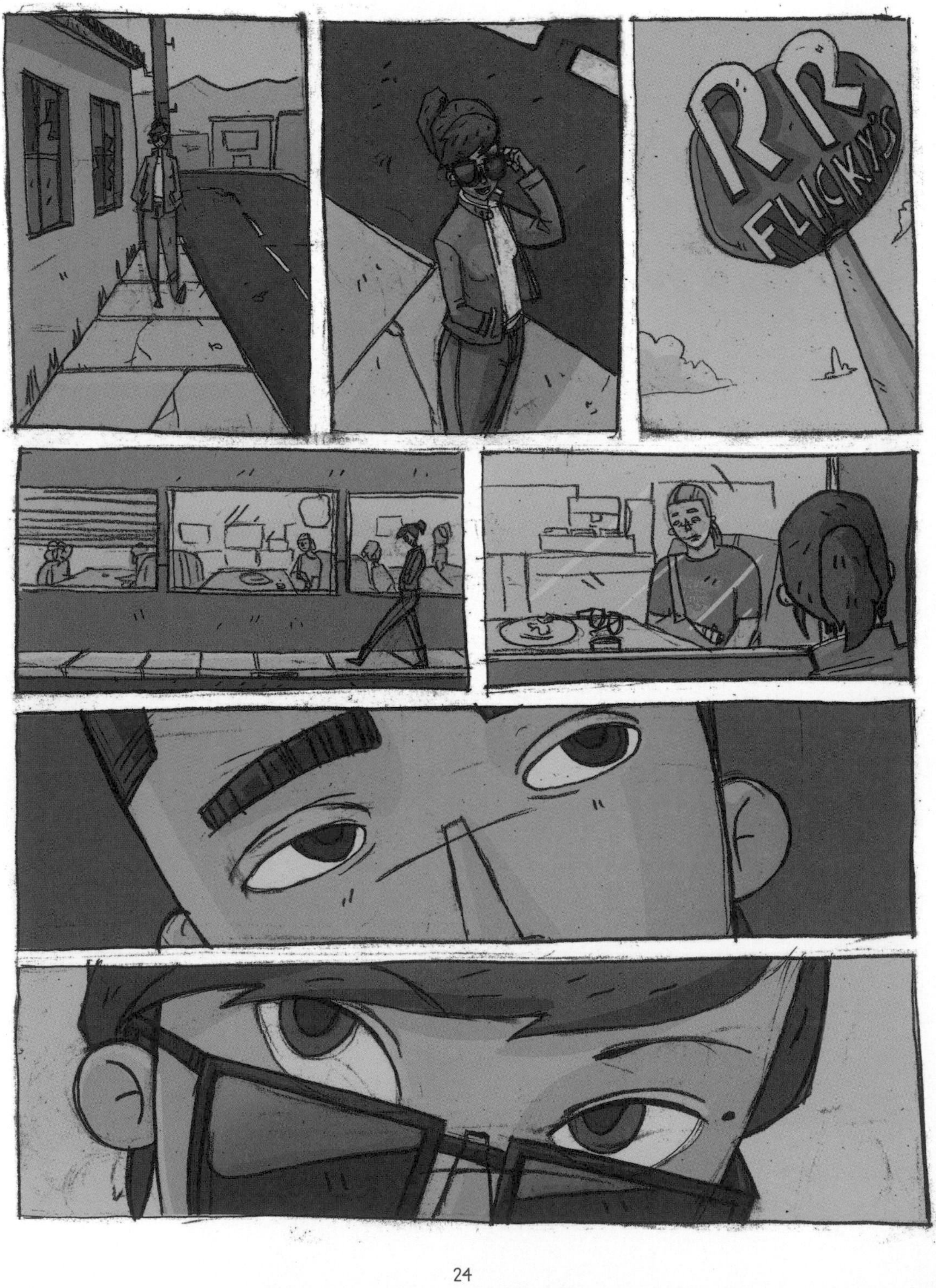
RR
FLICKY'S

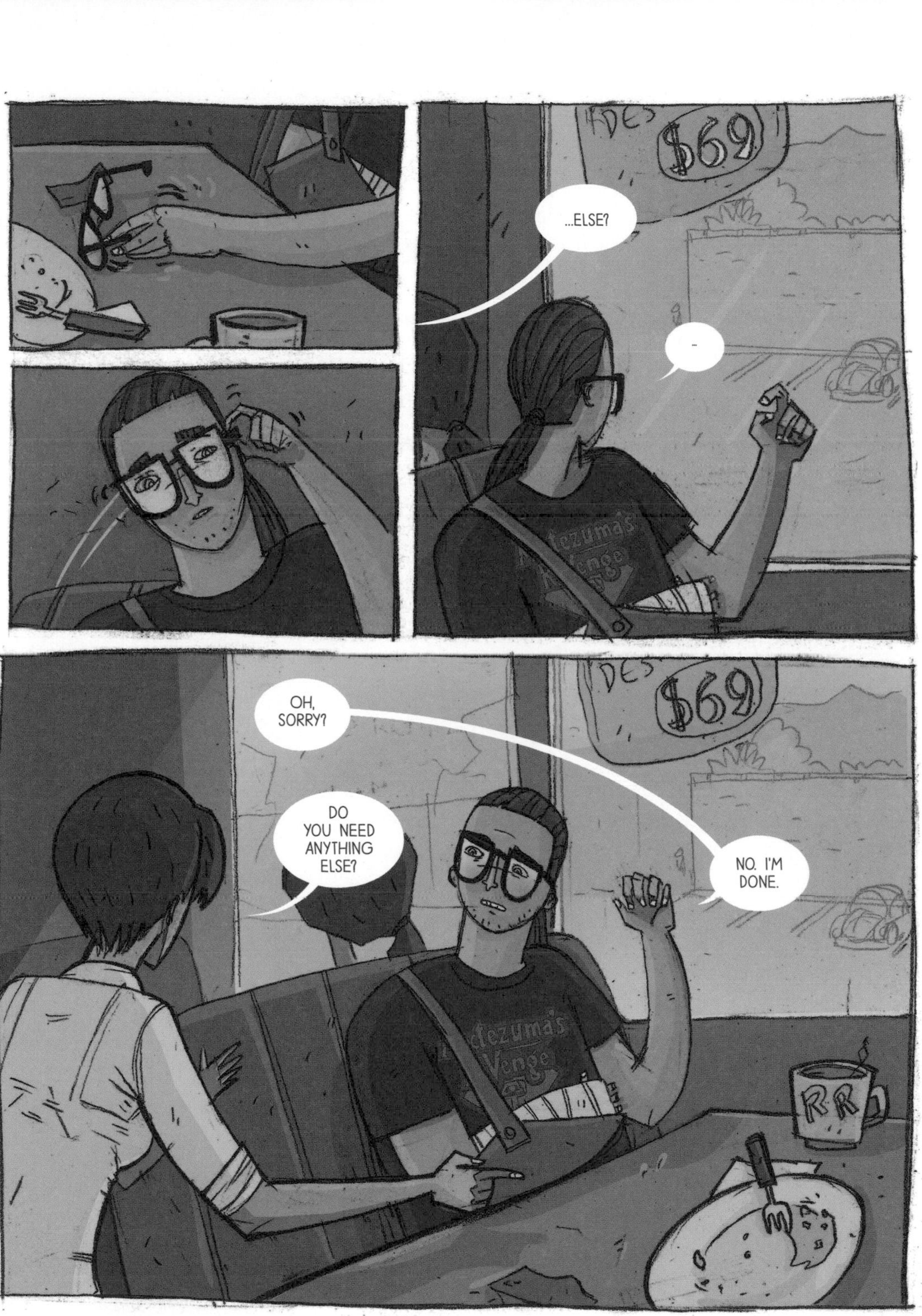
...ELSE?
..
OH, SORRY?
DO YOU NEED ANYTHING ELSE?
NO. I'M DONE.

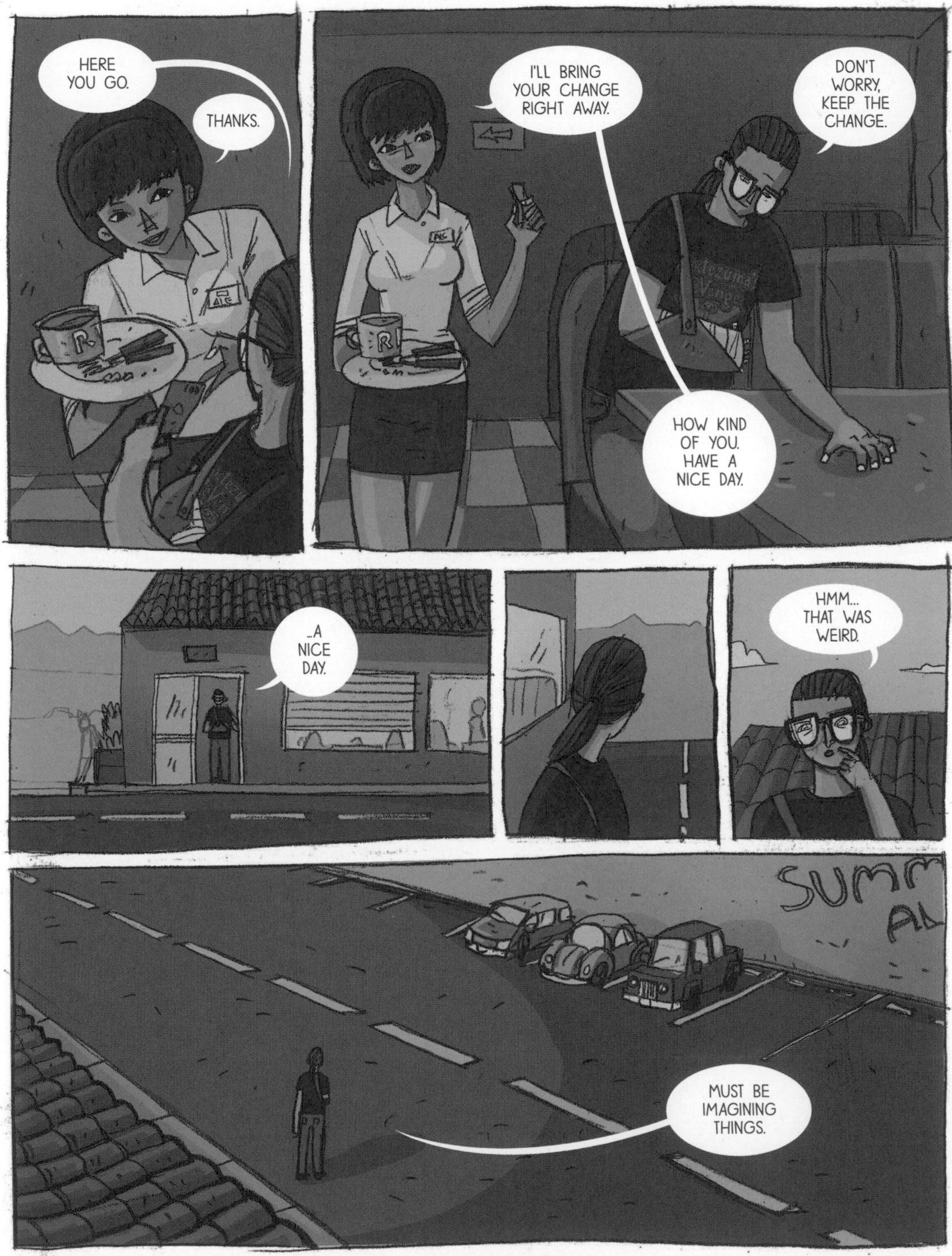
HERE YOU GO.
THANKS.
I'LL BRING YOUR CHANGE RIGHT AWAY.
DON'T WORRY, KEEP THE CHANGE.
HOW KIND OF YOU. HAVE A NICE DAY.
...A NICE DAY.
HMM... THAT WAS WEIRD.
MUST BE IMAGINING THINGS.

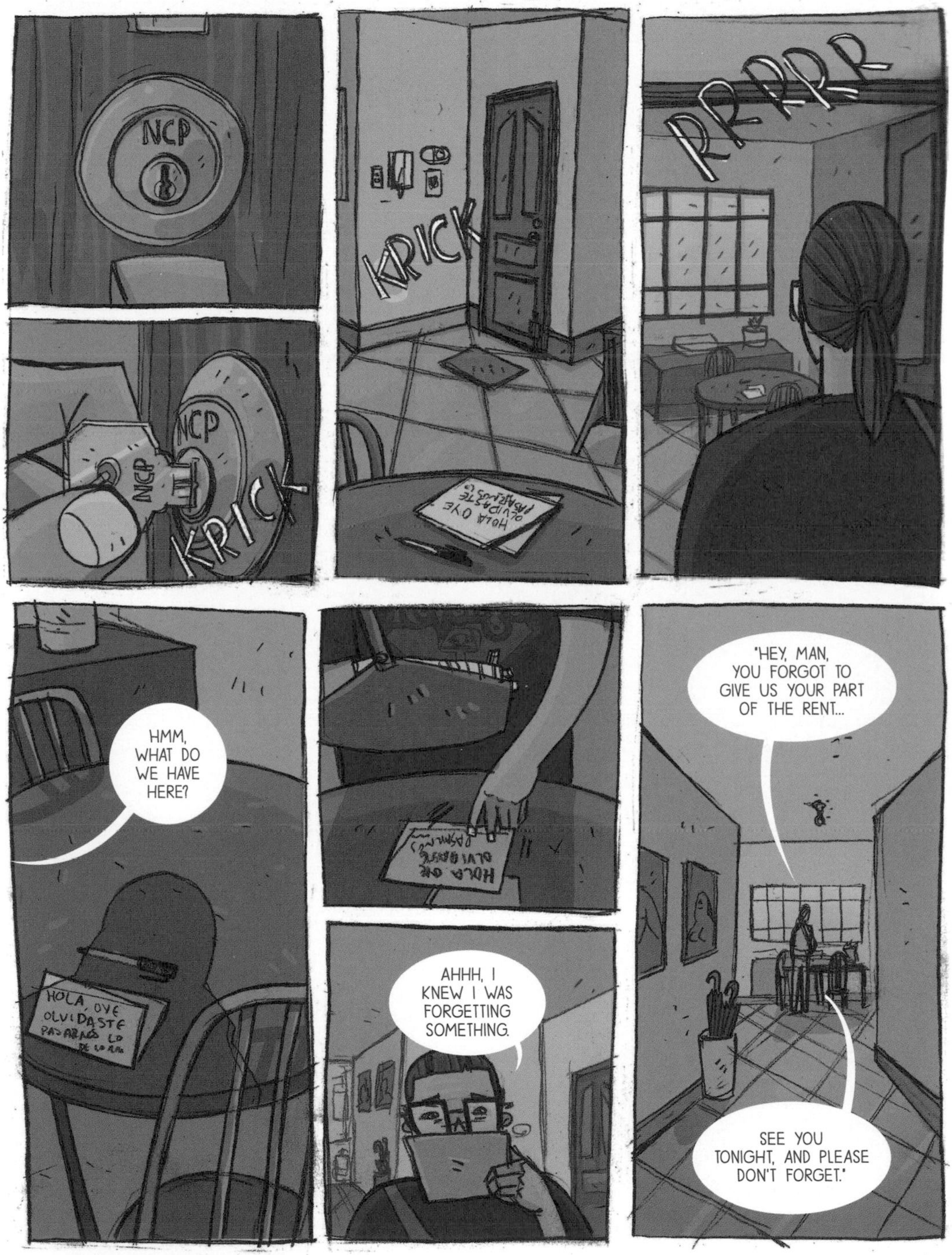

NCP
NCP
NCP
KRICK
KRICK
RRRRR
HMM, WHAT DO WE HAVE HERE?
AHHH, I KNEW I WAS FORGETTING SOMETHING.
'HEY, MAN, YOU FORGOT TO GIVE US YOUR PART OF THE RENT...
SEE YOU TONIGHT, AND PLEASE DON'T FORGET.'

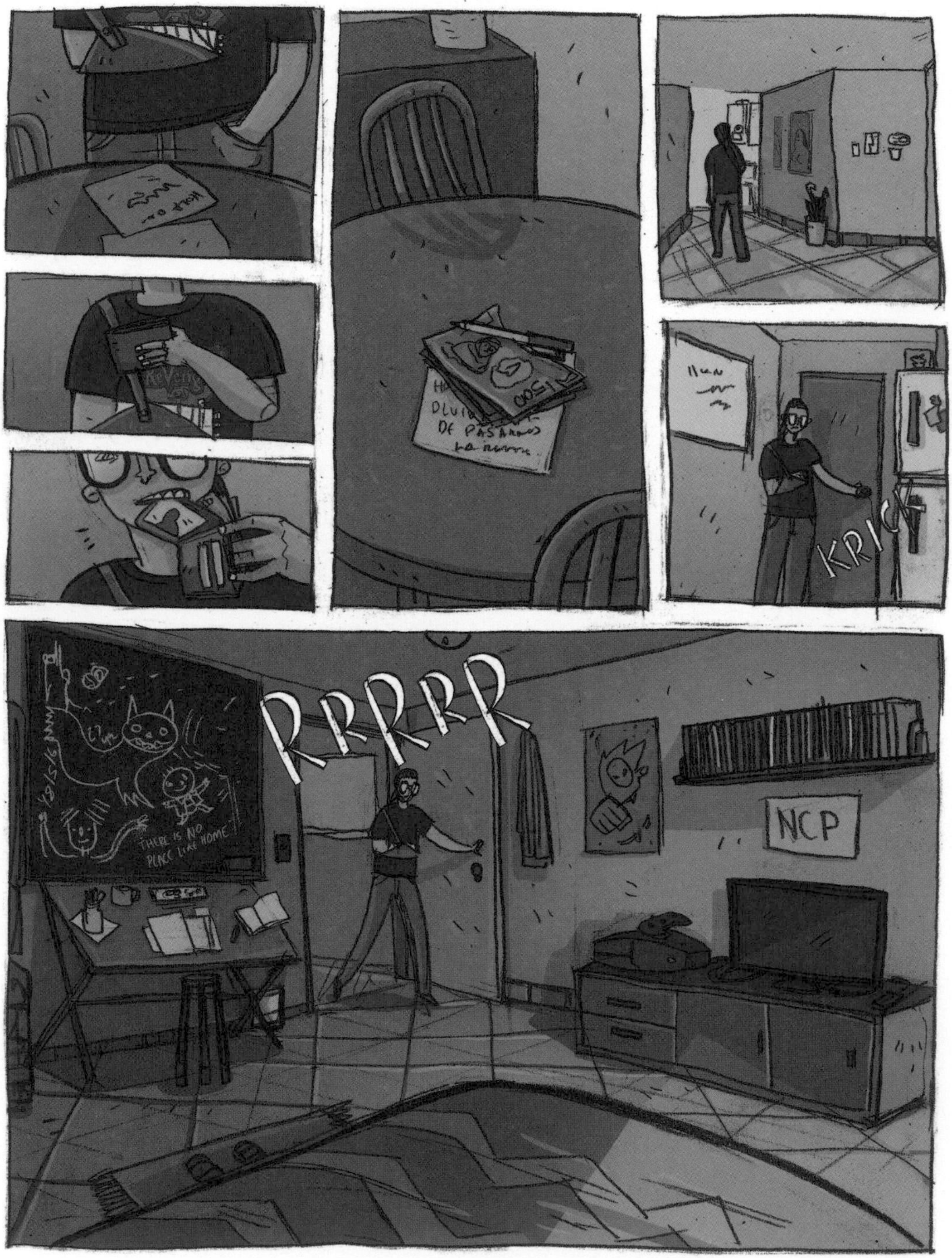
1500
DE PASAROS
KRICK
RRRRR
THERE IS NO PLACE LIKE HOME
NCP

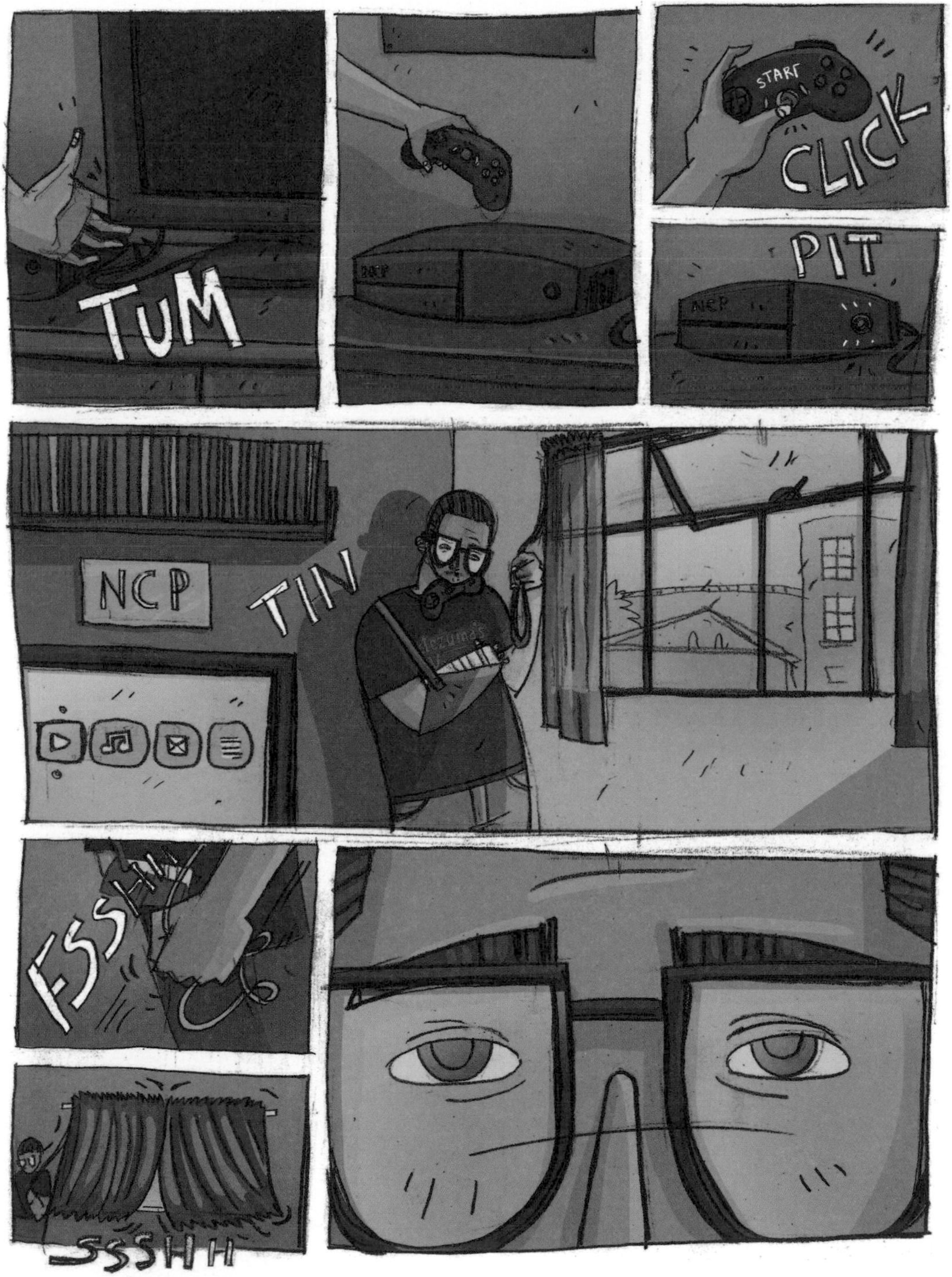
TUM
START
CLICK
PIT
NCP
NCP
TIN
FSSHH
SSSHH

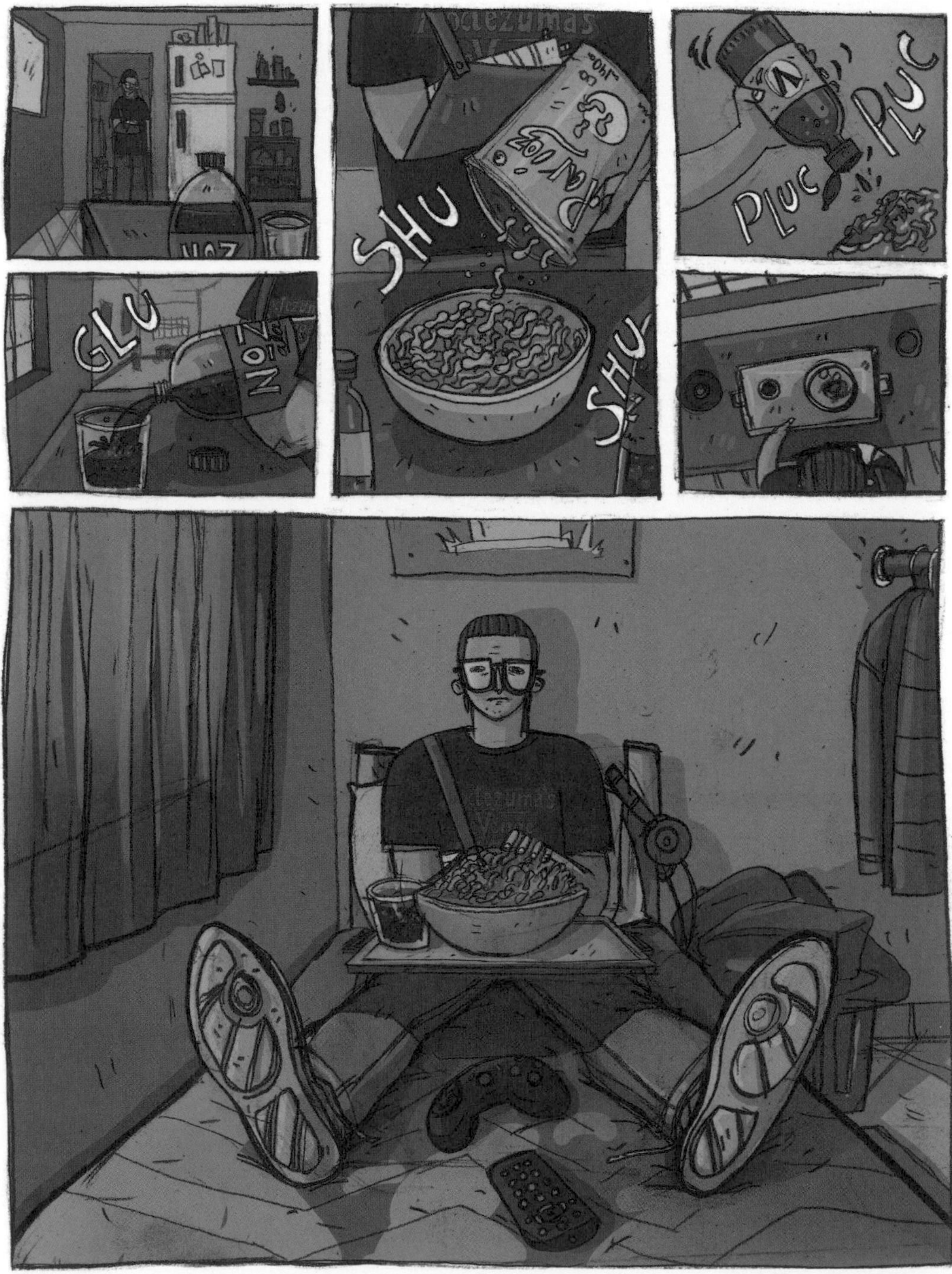
SHU
SHU
PLUC
PLUC
PLUC
GLU

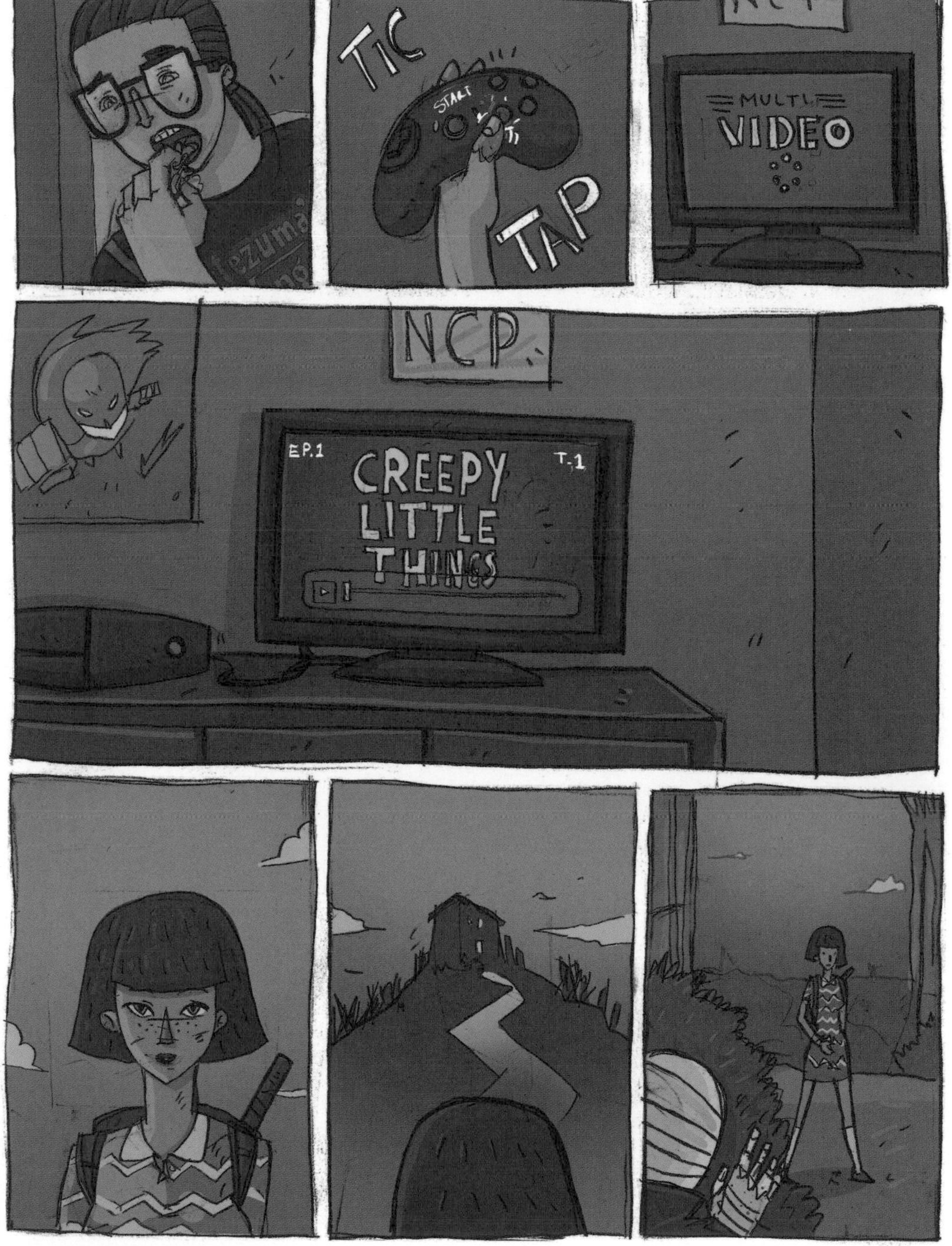
TIC
START
TAP
NCP
MULTI
VIDEO
NCP
EP.1
T.1
CREEPY
LITTLE
THINGS

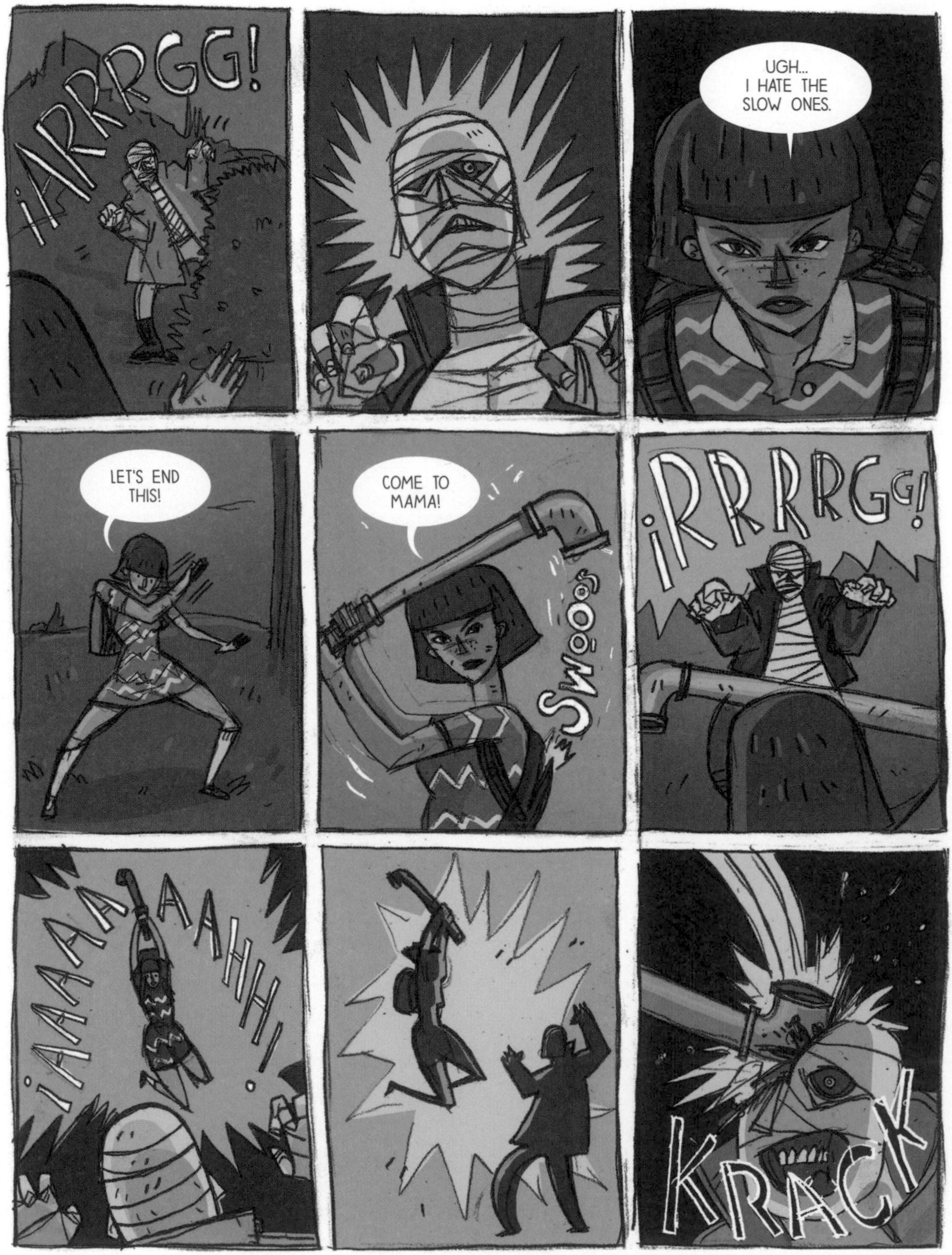

¡ARRRGG!
UGH... I HATE THE SLOW ONES.
LET'S END THIS!
COME TO MAMA!
SWOOOSH
¡RRRRGG!
¡AAAAAAAHHH!
KRACK

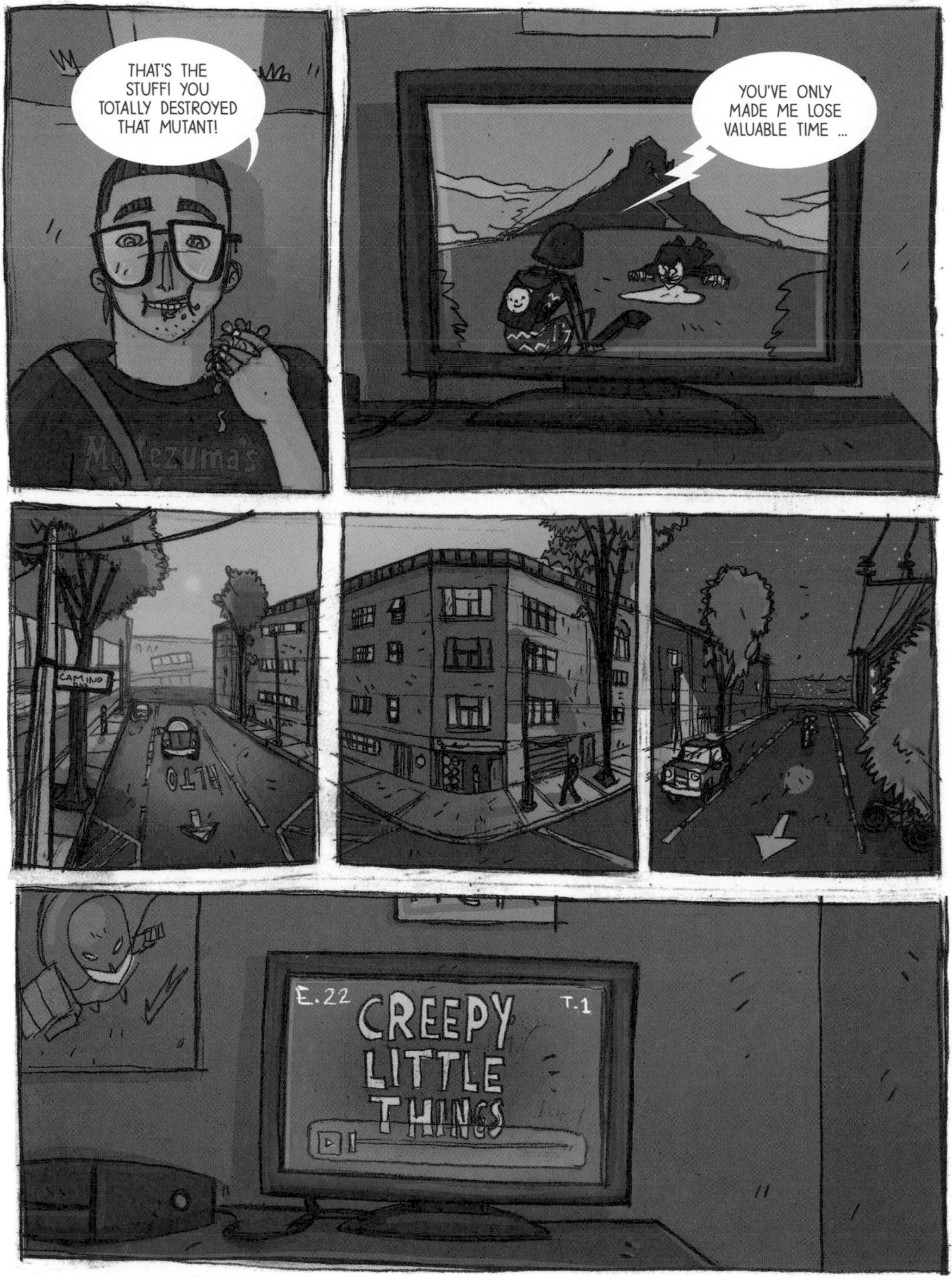
THAT'S THE STUFF! YOU TOTALLY DESTROYED THAT MUTANT!
YOU'VE ONLY MADE ME LOSE VALUABLE TIME ...
CAMINO
ALTO
E. 22
T. 1
CREEPY LITTLE THINGS

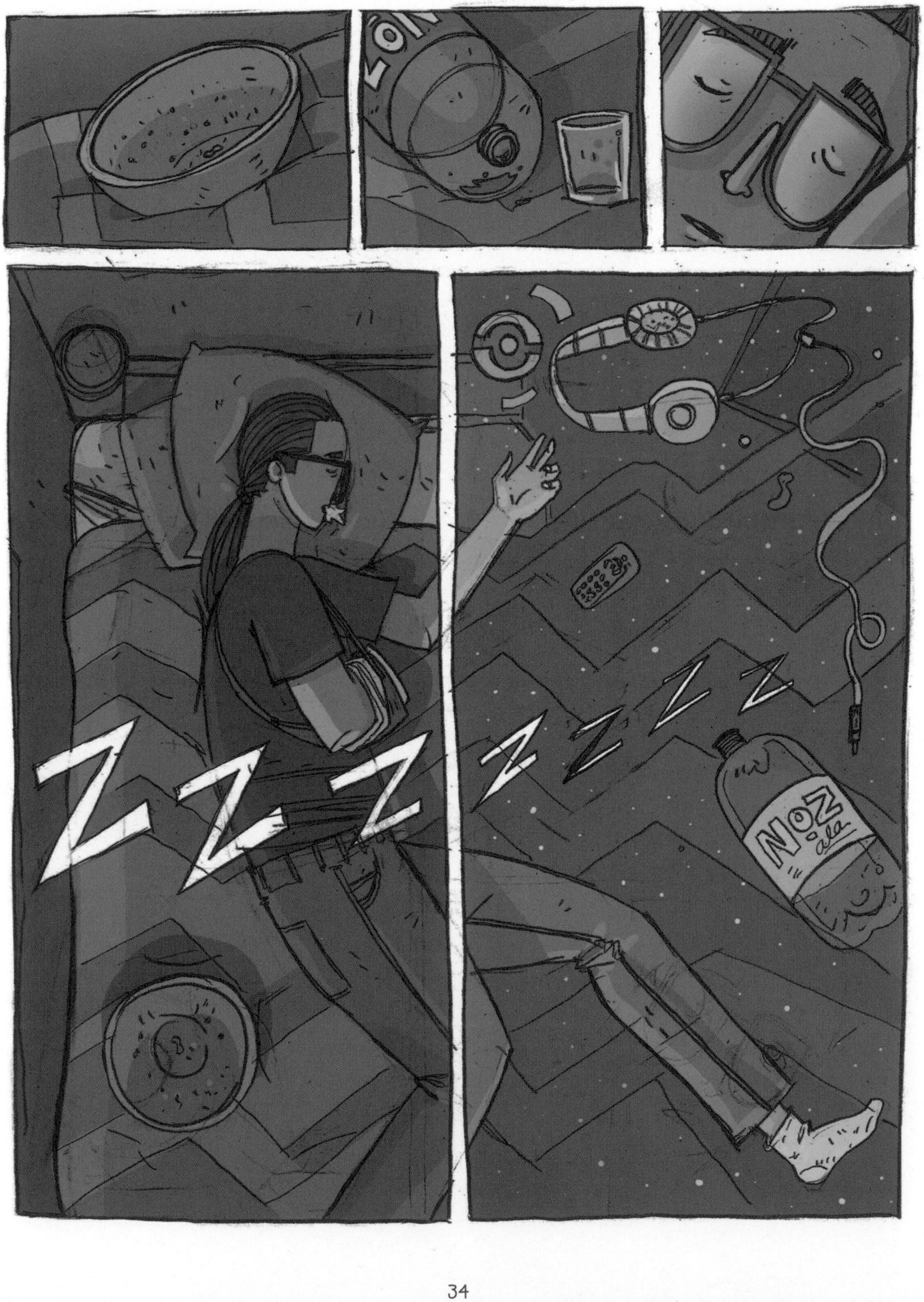
Z Z Z Z Z Z Z Z
NOZ

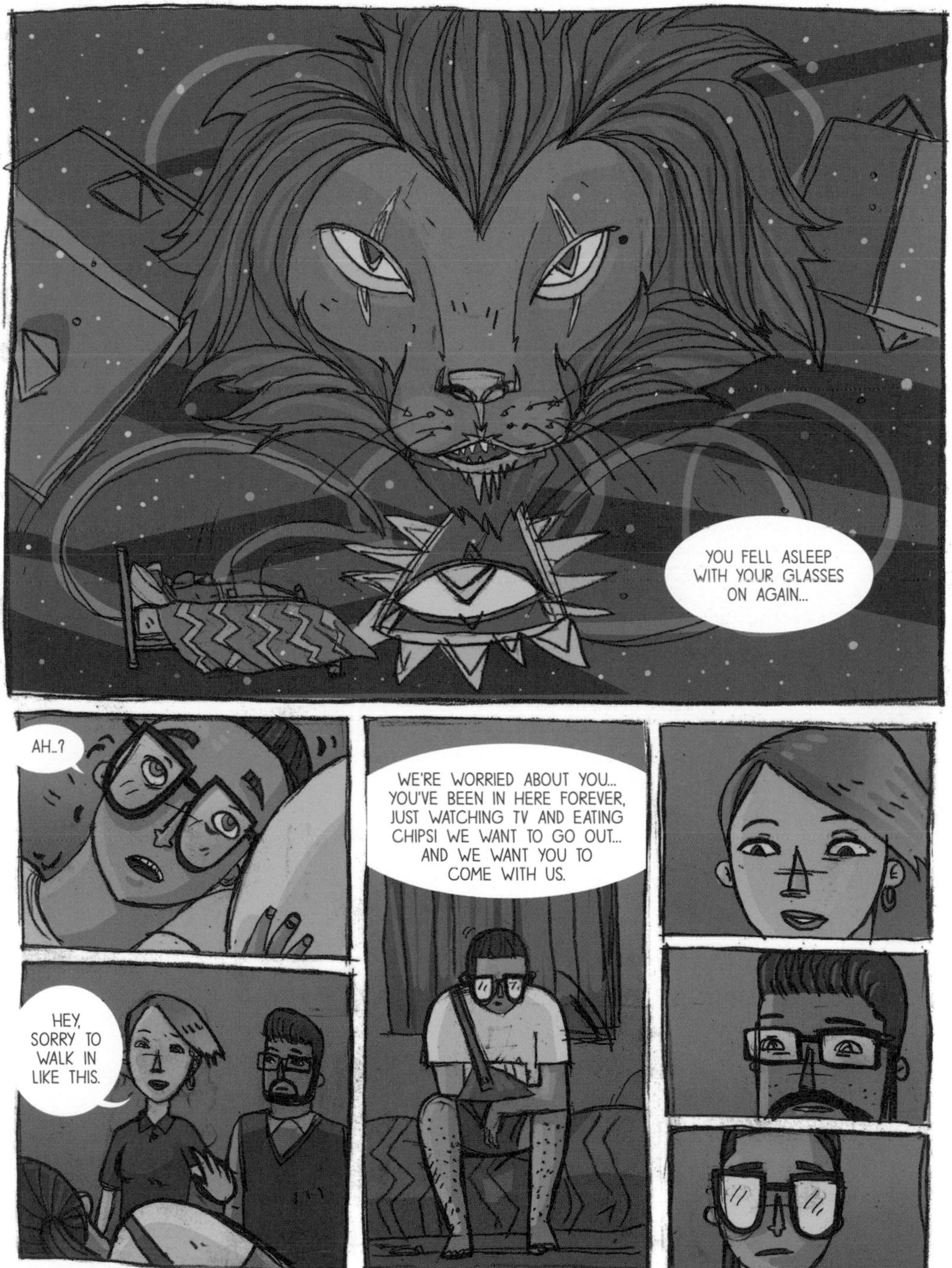
YOU FELL ASLEEP WITH YOUR GLASSES ON AGAIN...
AH..?
HEY, SORRY TO WALK IN LIKE THIS.
WE'RE WORRIED ABOUT YOU... YOU'VE BEEN IN HERE FOREVER, JUST WATCHING TV AND EATING CHIPS! WE WANT TO GO OUT... AND WE WANT YOU TO COME WITH US.

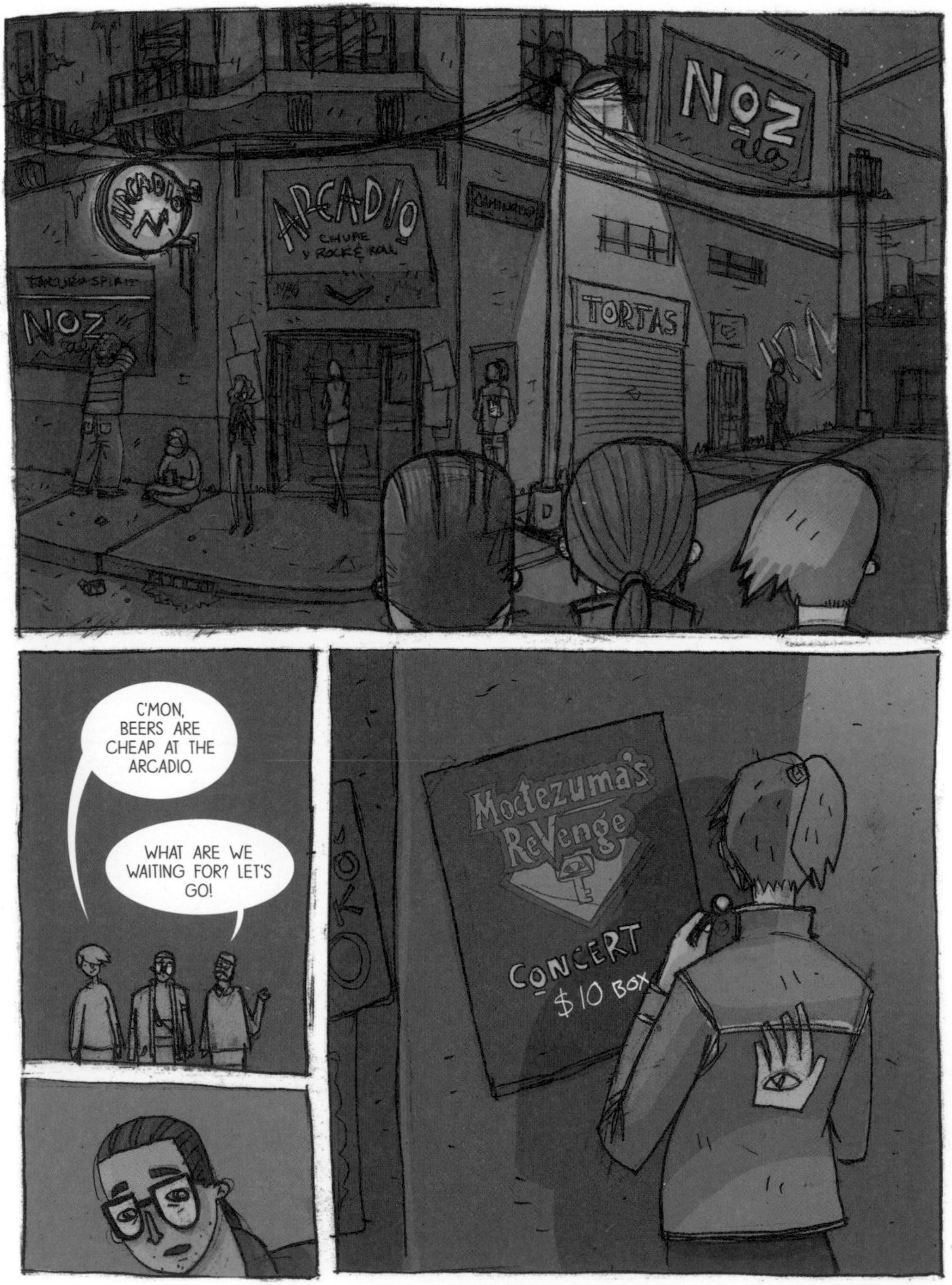
ARCADIO
NOZ
TORTAS
C'MON, BEERS ARE CHEAP AT THE ARCADIO.
WHAT ARE WE WAITING FOR? LET'S GO!
Moctezuma's ReVenge
CONCERT
$10 BOX

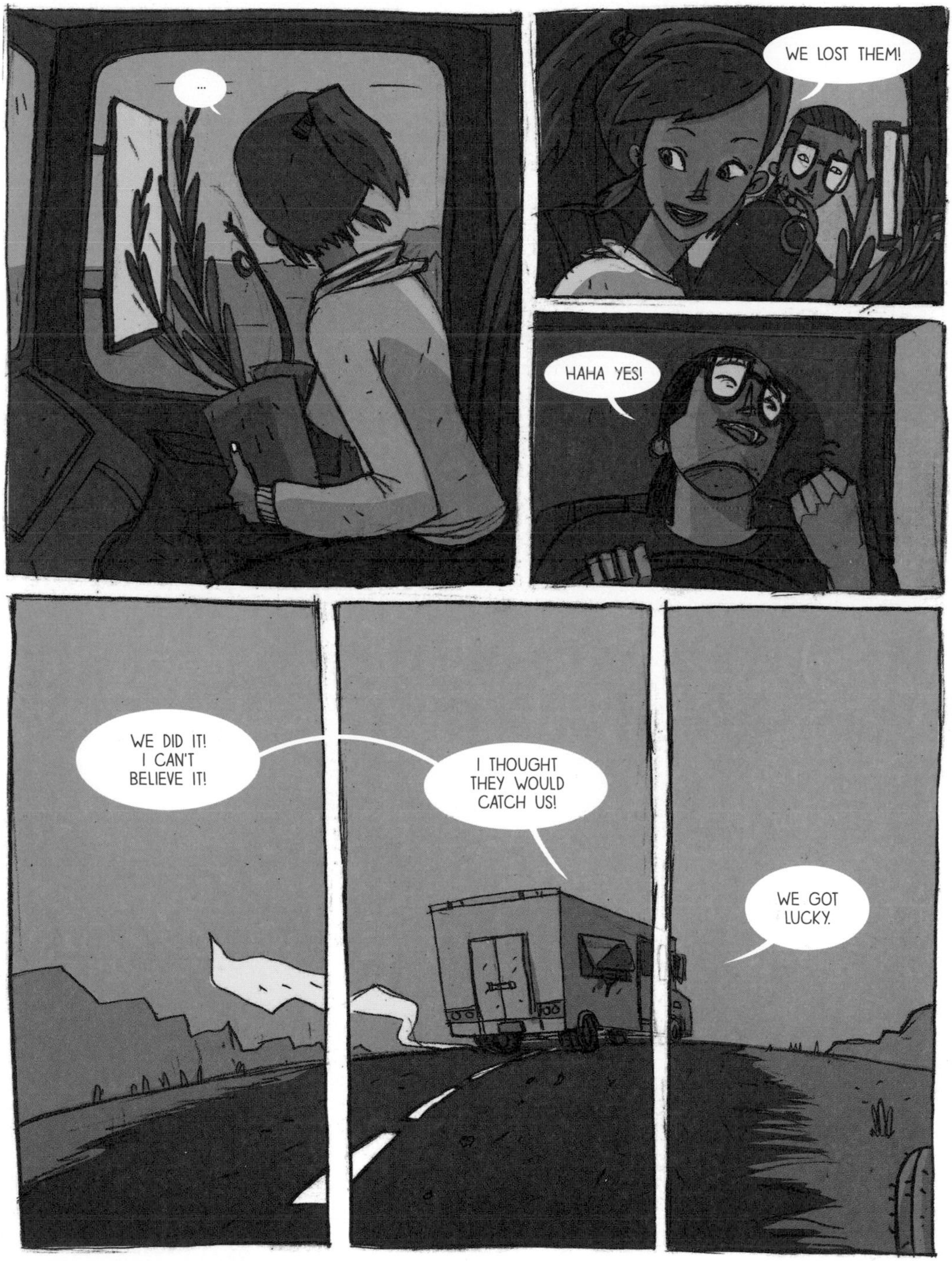
...
WE LOST THEM!
HAHA YES!
WE DID IT!
I CAN'T
BELIEVE IT!
I THOUGHT
THEY WOULD
CATCH US!
WE GOT
LUCKY.

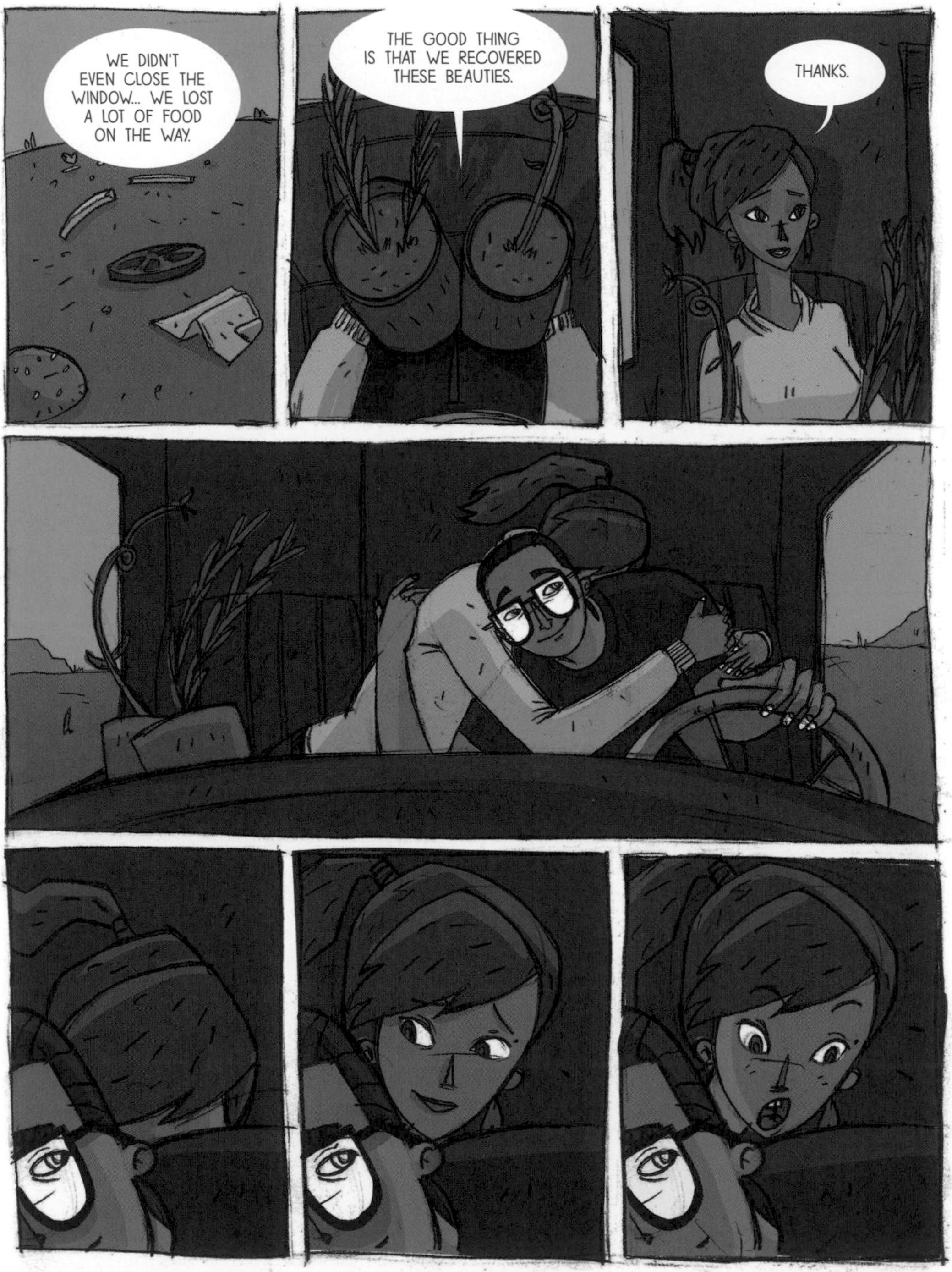
WE DIDN'T EVEN CLOSE THE WINDOW... WE LOST A LOT OF FOOD ON THE WAY.
THE GOOD THING IS THAT WE RECOVERED THESE BEAUTIES.
THANKS.

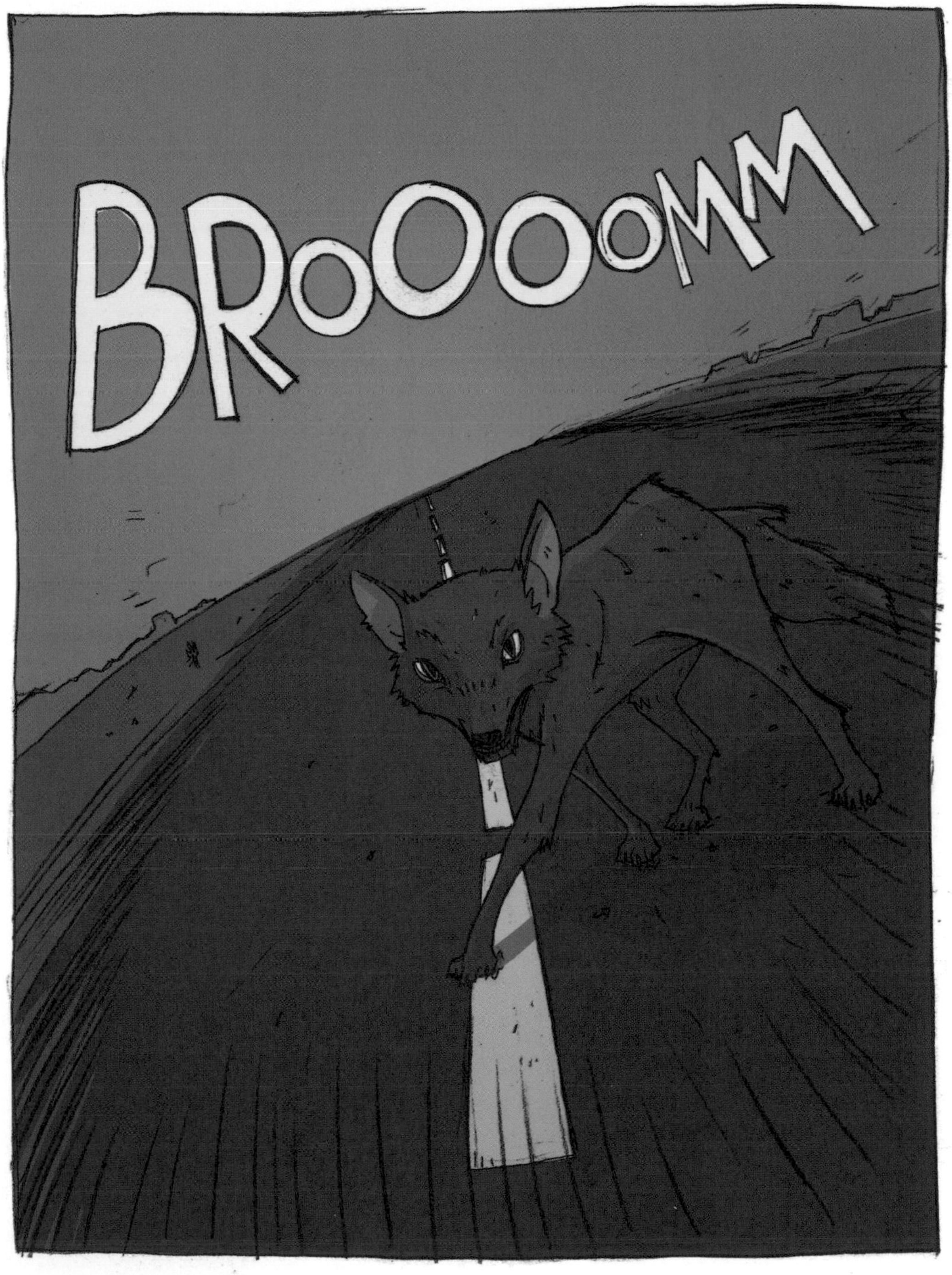
BROOOOMM

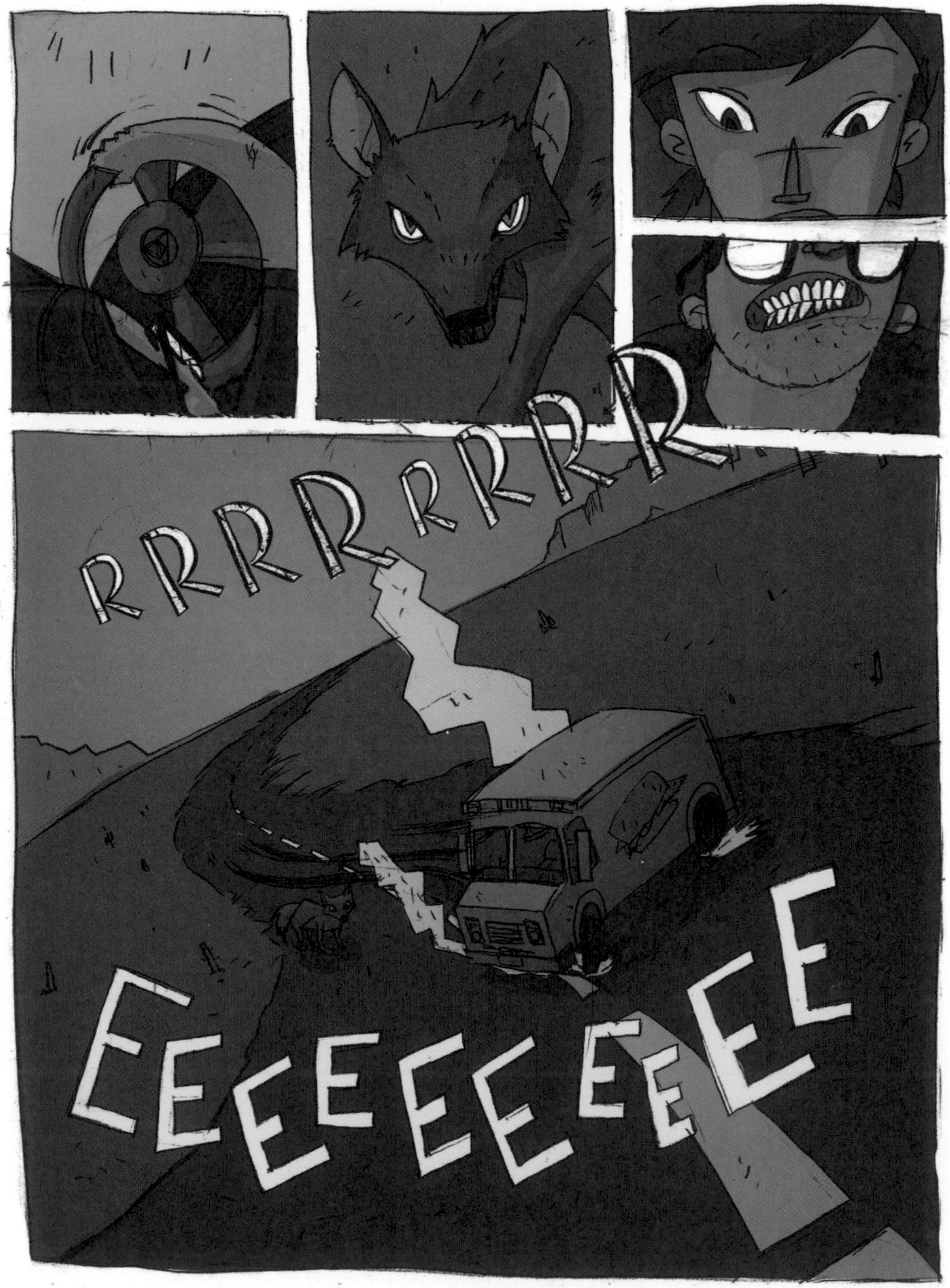
RRRRRRRRRR
EEEEEEEEEE

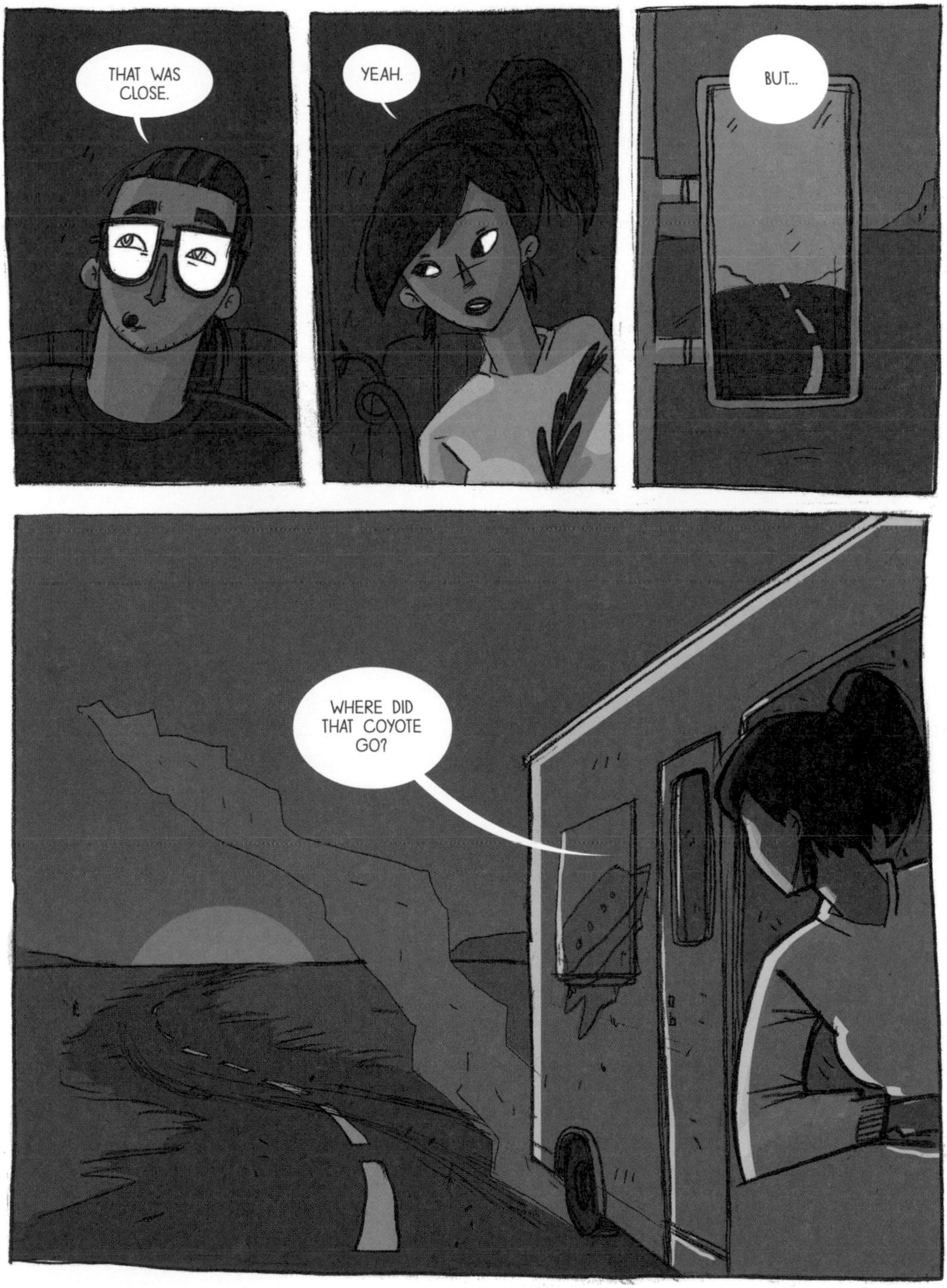
THAT WAS CLOSE.
YEAH.
BUT...
WHERE DID THAT COYOTE GO?

PART TWO

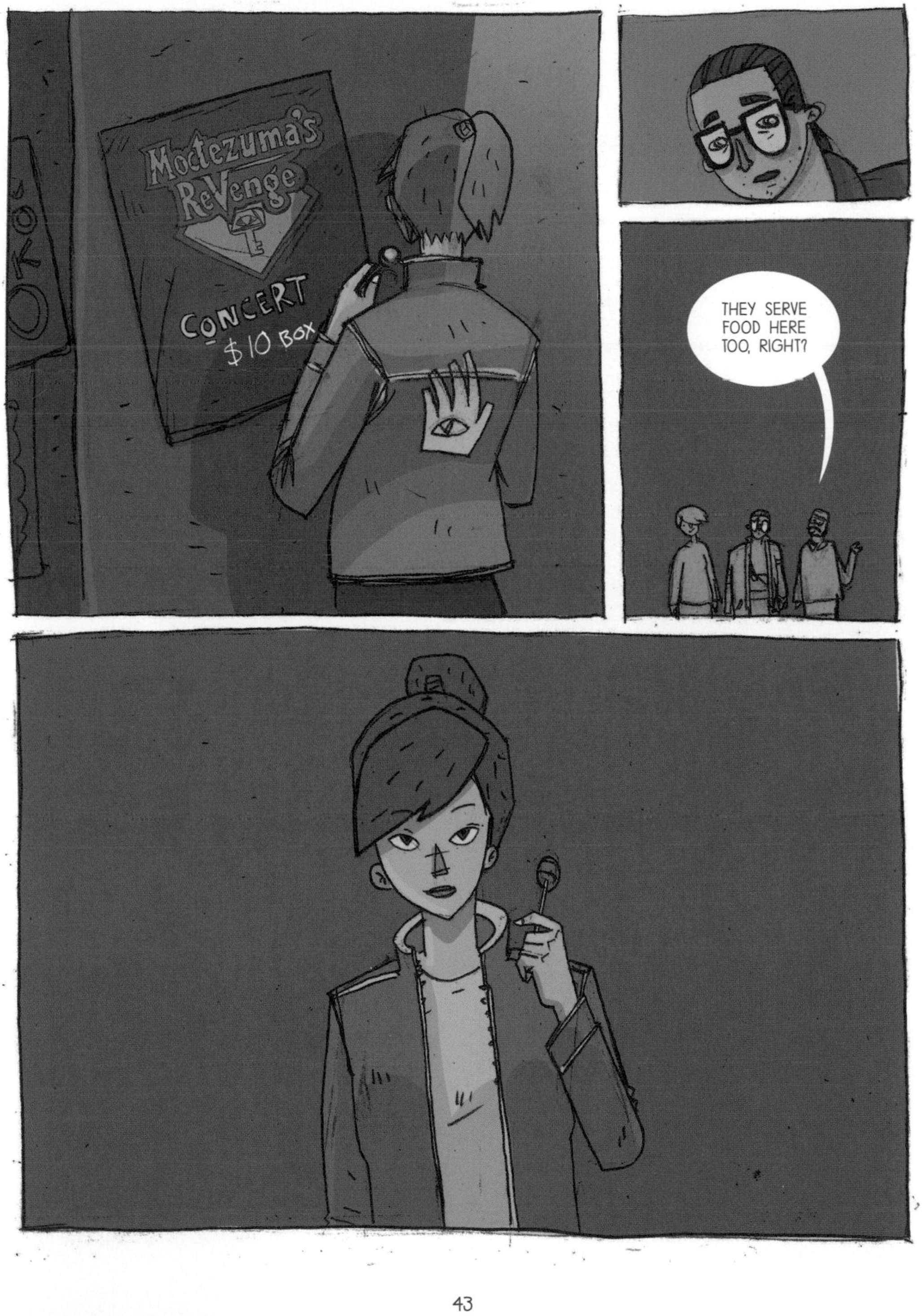
Moctezuma's Revenge
CONCERT
$10 BOX
THEY SERVE FOOD HERE TOO, RIGHT?

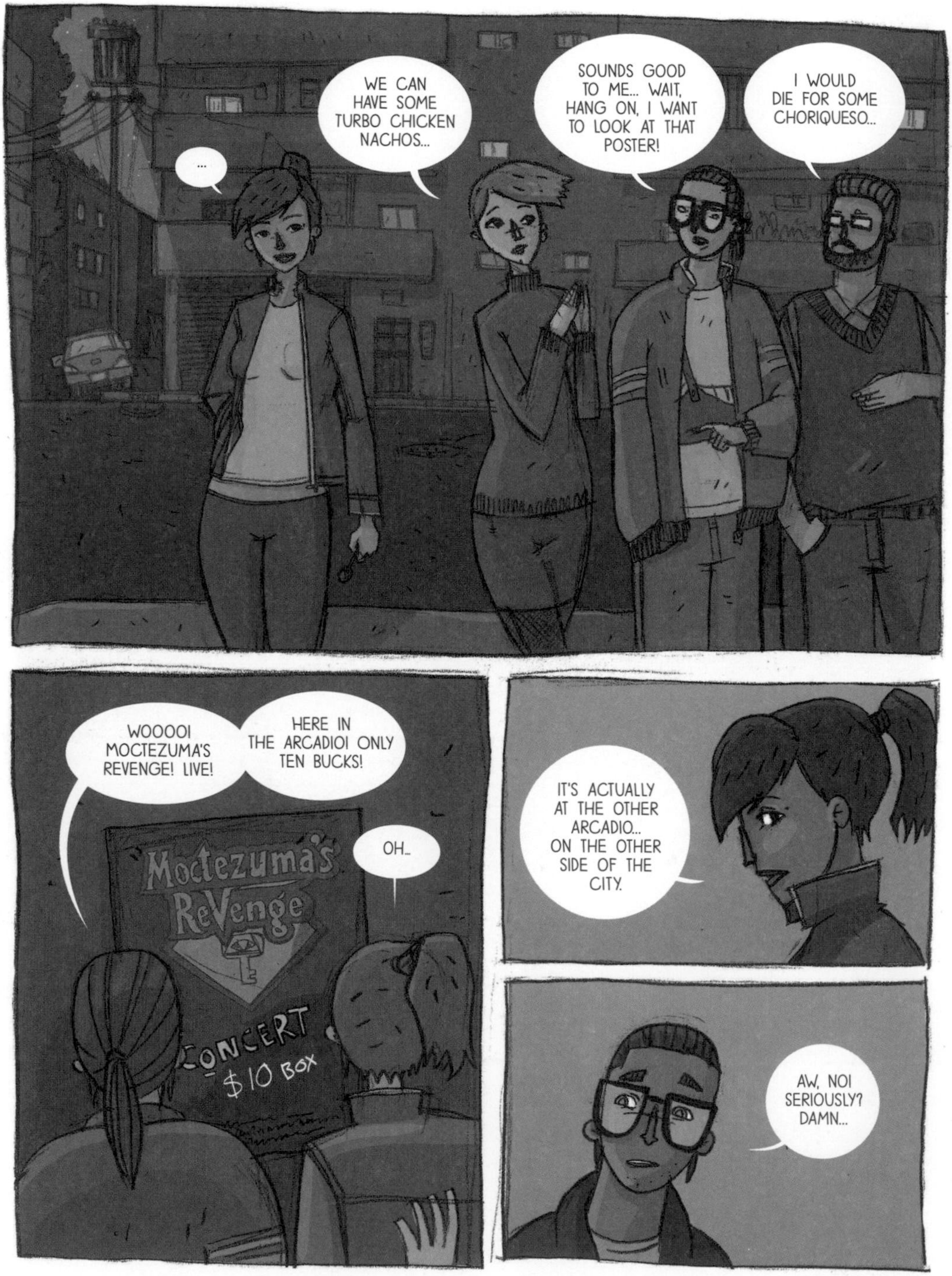
...
WE CAN HAVE SOME TURBO CHICKEN NACHOS...
SOUNDS GOOD TO ME... WAIT, HANG ON, I WANT TO LOOK AT THAT POSTER!
I WOULD DIE FOR SOME CHORIQUESO...
WOOOO! MOCTEZUMA'S REVENGE! LIVE!
HERE IN THE ARCADIO! ONLY TEN BUCKS!
Moctezuma's ReVenge
CONCERT
$10 BOX
OH...
IT'S ACTUALLY AT THE OTHER ARCADIO... ON THE OTHER SIDE OF THE CITY.
AW, NO! SERIOUSLY? DAMN...

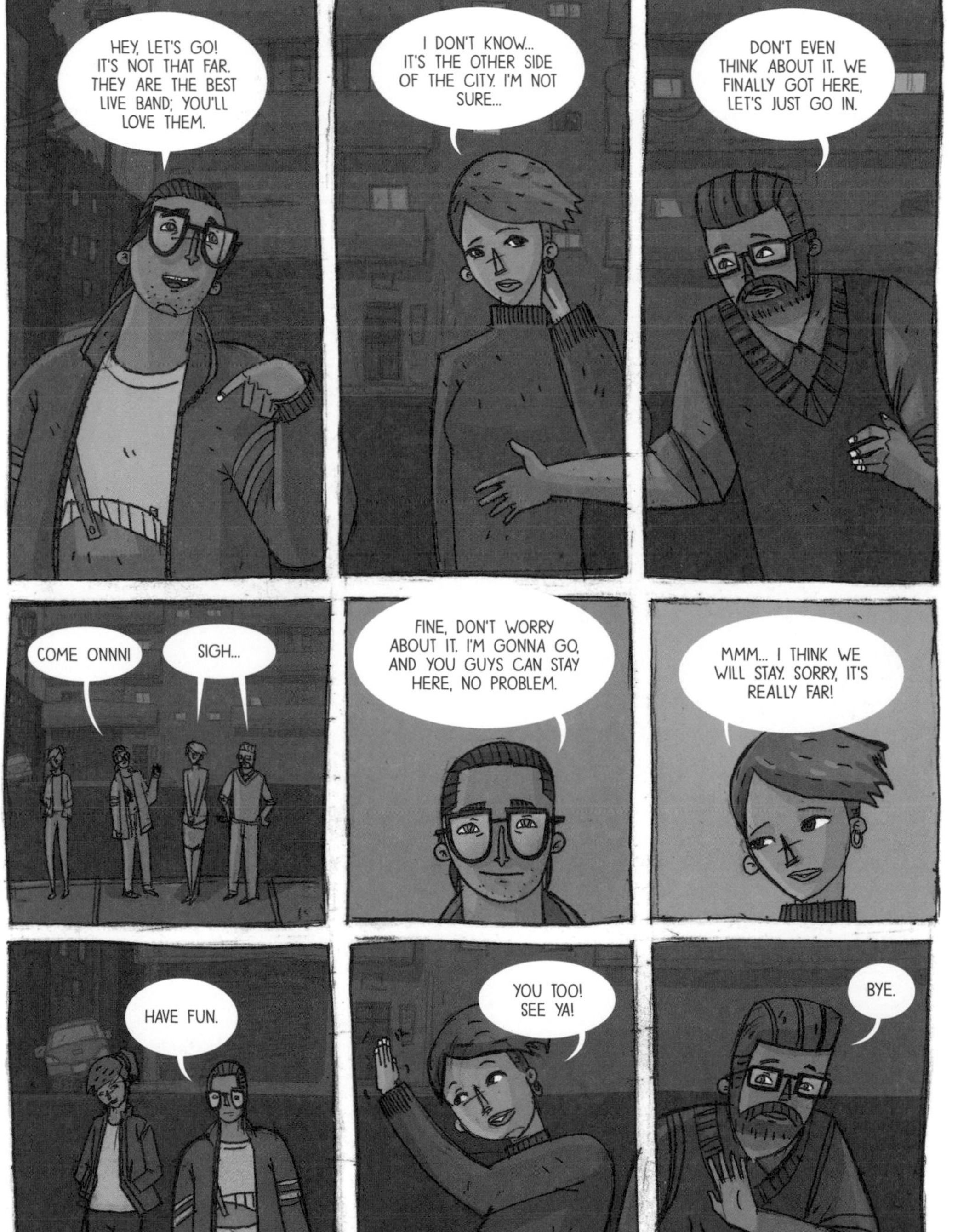
HEY, LET'S GO! IT'S NOT THAT FAR. THEY ARE THE BEST LIVE BAND; YOU'LL LOVE THEM.
I DON'T KNOW... IT'S THE OTHER SIDE OF THE CITY. I'M NOT SURE...
DON'T EVEN THINK ABOUT IT. WE FINALLY GOT HERE, LET'S JUST GO IN.
COME ONNN!
SIGH...
FINE, DON'T WORRY ABOUT IT. I'M GONNA GO, AND YOU GUYS CAN STAY HERE, NO PROBLEM.
MMM... I THINK WE WILL STAY. SORRY, IT'S REALLY FAR!
HAVE FUN.
YOU TOO! SEE YA!
BYE.

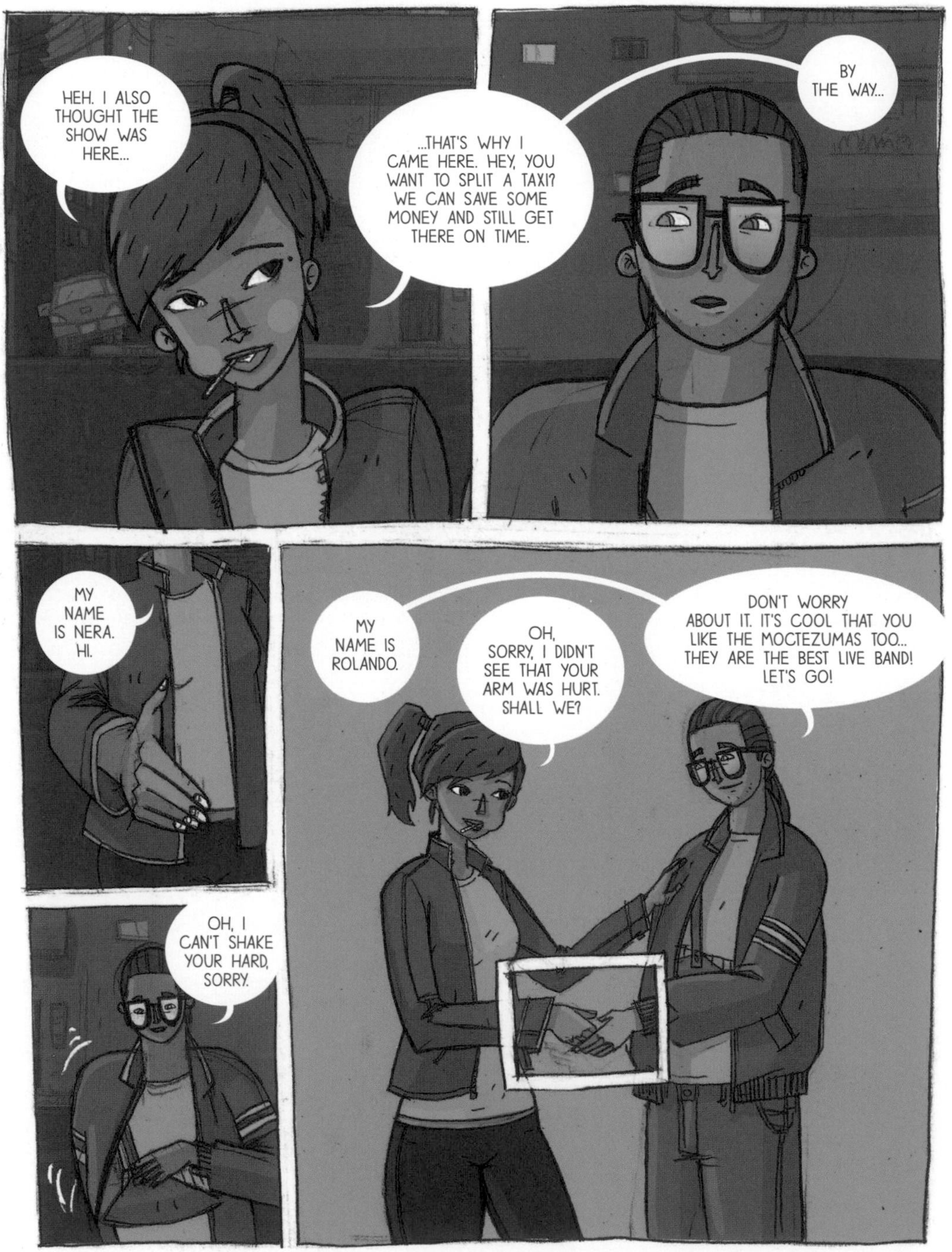
HEH. I ALSO THOUGHT THE SHOW WAS HERE...
...THAT'S WHY I CAME HERE. HEY, YOU WANT TO SPLIT A TAXI? WE CAN SAVE SOME MONEY AND STILL GET THERE ON TIME.
BY THE WAY...
MY NAME IS NERA. HI.
OH, I CAN'T SHAKE YOUR HARD, SORRY.
MY NAME IS ROLANDO.
OH, SORRY, I DIDN'T SEE THAT YOUR ARM WAS HURT. SHALL WE?
DON'T WORRY ABOUT IT. IT'S COOL THAT YOU LIKE THE MOCTEZUMAS TOO... THEY ARE THE BEST LIVE BAND! LET'S GO!

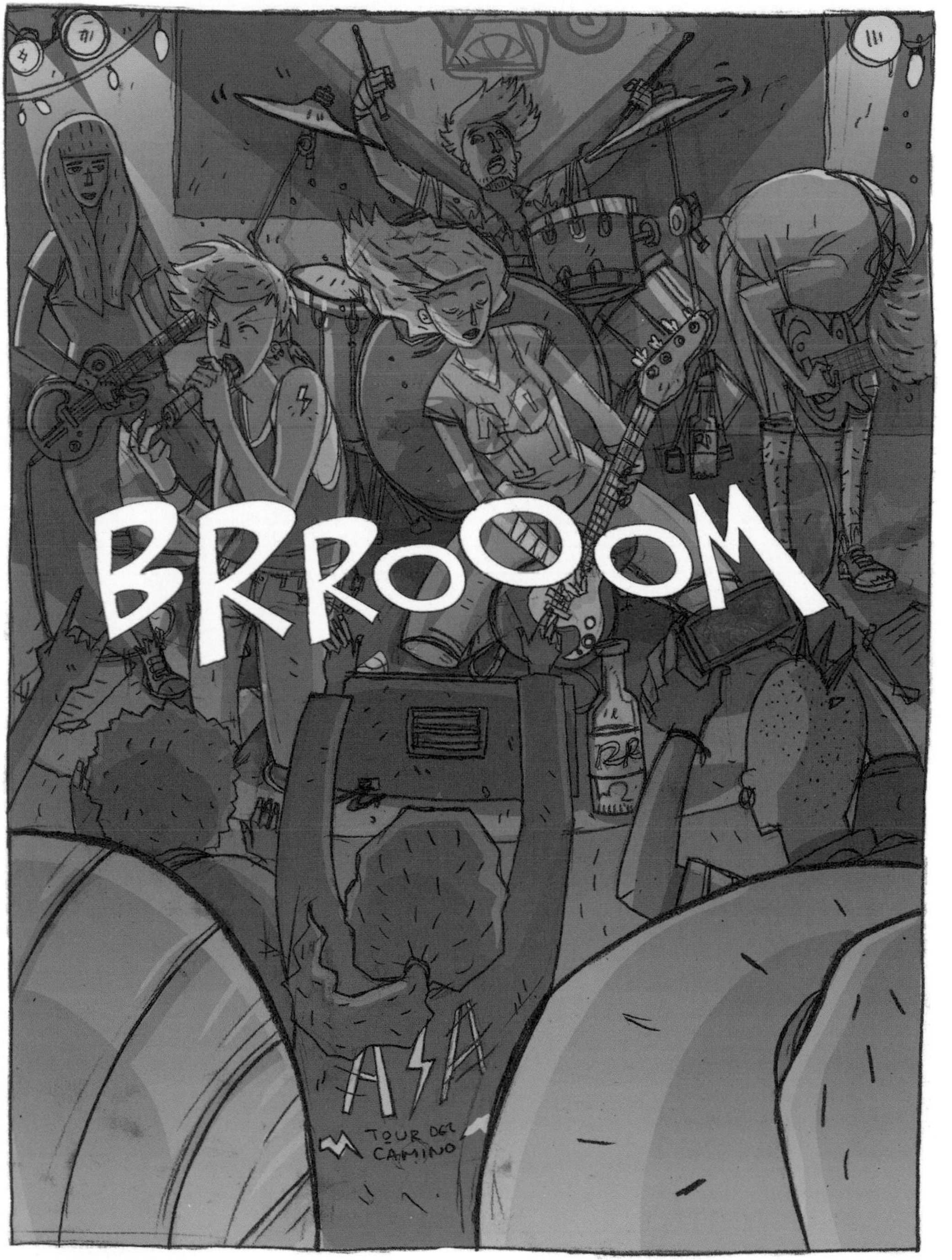
BRROOOM
ASA
TOUR DEL CAMINO

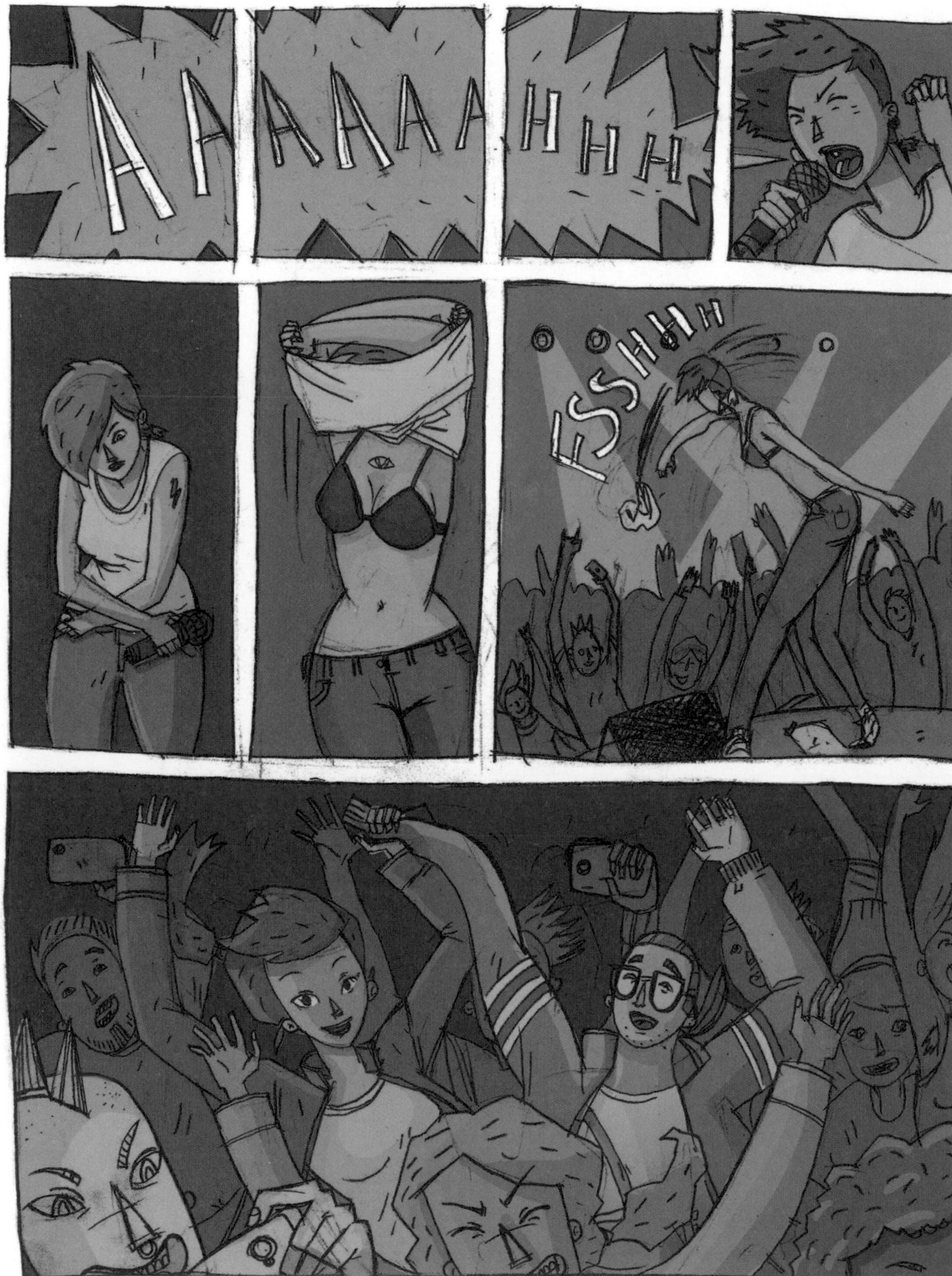
AAAAAAHHHH
FSSHHHH

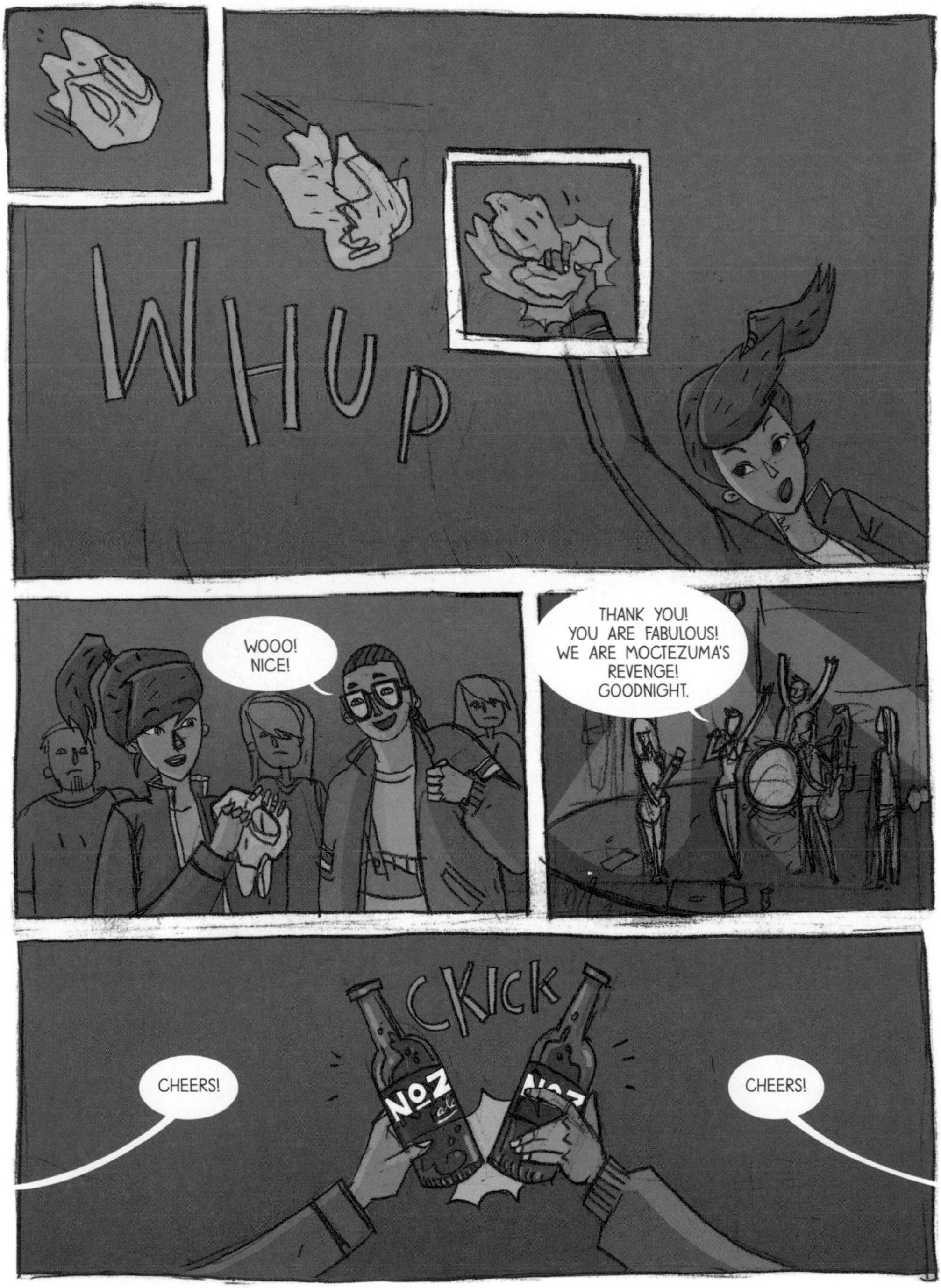
WHUP
WOOO! NICE!
THANK YOU! YOU ARE FABULOUS! WE ARE MOCTEZUMA'S REVENGE! GOODNIGHT.
CKICK
CHEERS!
NoZ
CHEERS!

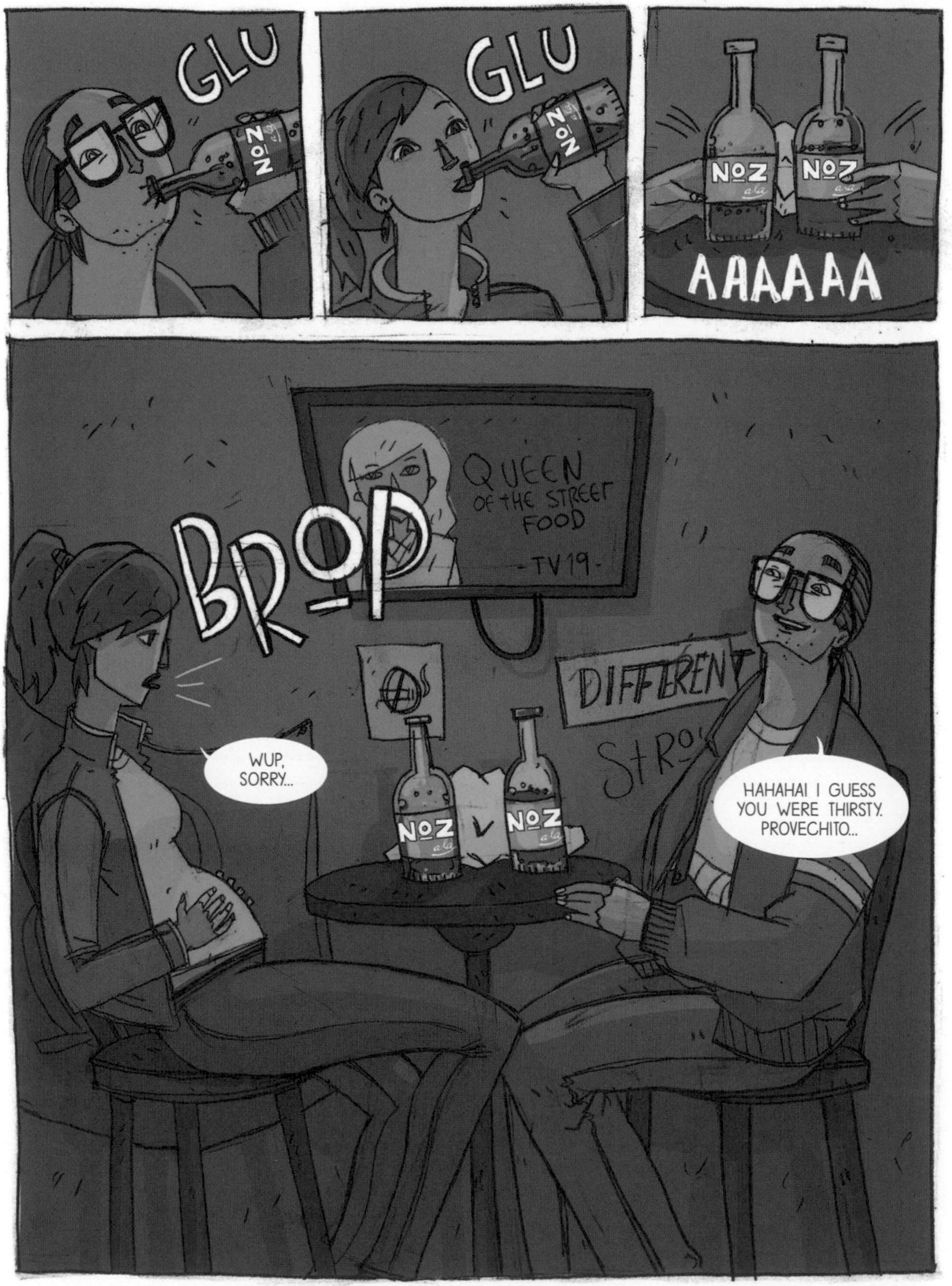
GLU
GLU
NoZ
AAAAAA
QUEEN OF THE STREET FOOD
-TV19-
BROP
WUP, SORRY...
DIFFERENT
HAHAHA! I GUESS YOU WERE THIRSTY. PROVECHITO...

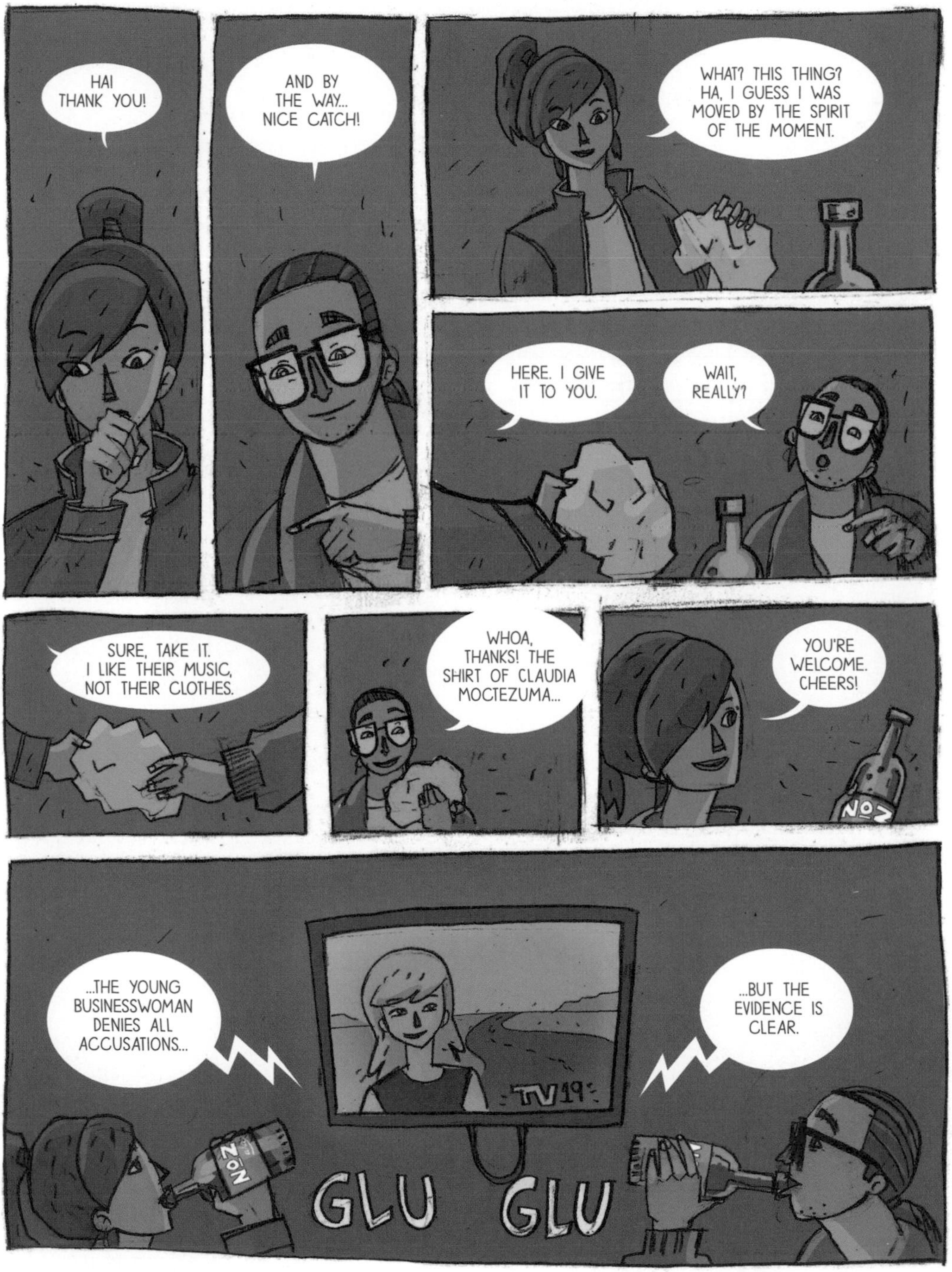
HAI
THANK YOU!
AND BY THE WAY... NICE CATCH!
WHAT? THIS THING? HA, I GUESS I WAS MOVED BY THE SPIRIT OF THE MOMENT.
HERE. I GIVE IT TO YOU.
WAIT, REALLY?
SURE, TAKE IT. I LIKE THEIR MUSIC, NOT THEIR CLOTHES.
WHOA, THANKS! THE SHIRT OF CLAUDIA MOCTEZUMA...
YOU'RE WELCOME. CHEERS!
No7
...THE YOUNG BUSINESSWOMAN DENIES ALL ACCUSATIONS...
TV19
...BUT THE EVIDENCE IS CLEAR.
GLU GLU

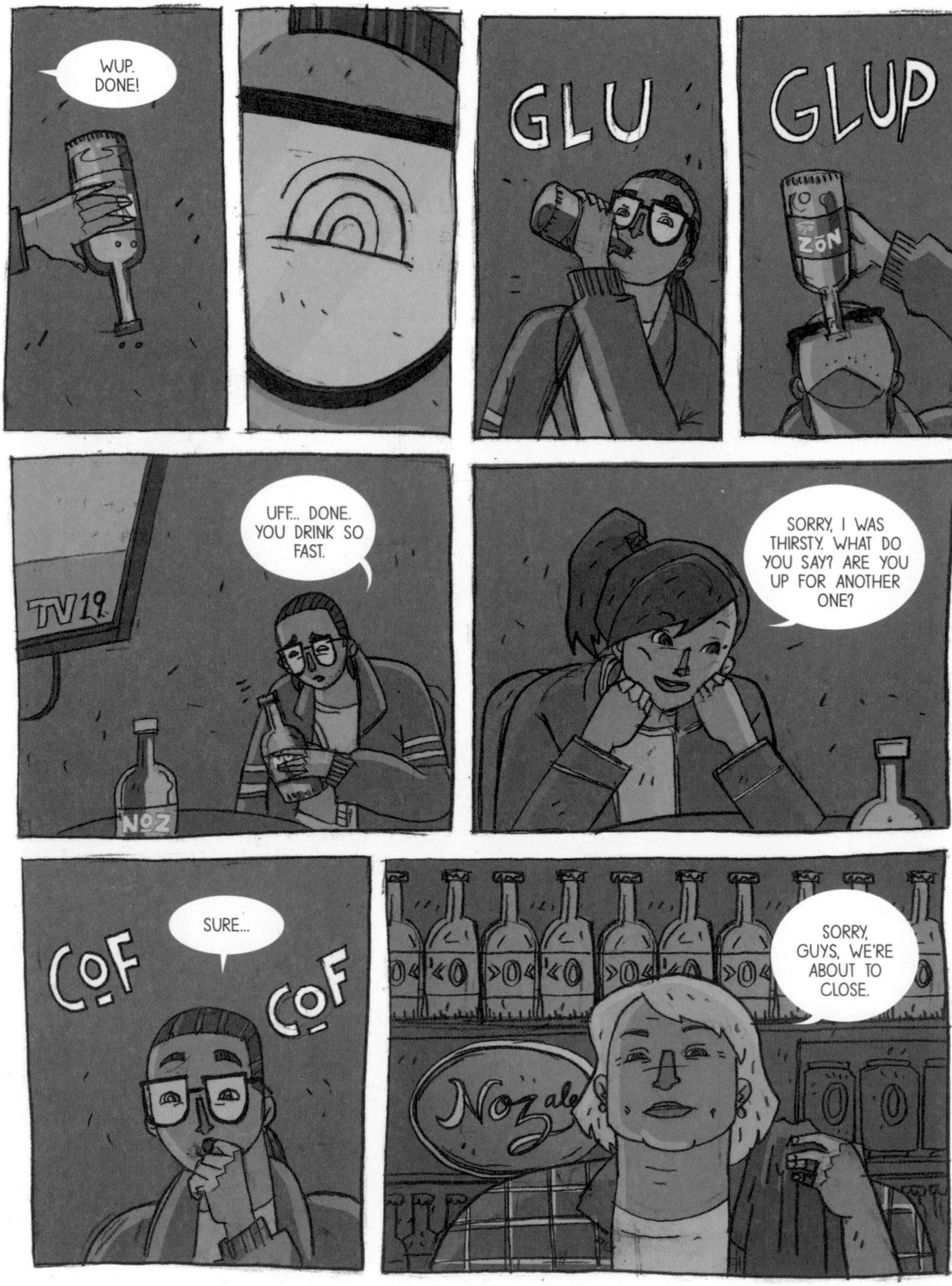
WUP. DONE!
GLU
GLUP
ZON
TV19
UFF... DONE. YOU DRINK SO FAST.
NOZ
SORRY, I WAS THIRSTY. WHAT DO YOU SAY? ARE YOU UP FOR ANOTHER ONE?
COF
SURE...
COF
SORRY, GUYS, WE'RE ABOUT TO CLOSE.
Noz ale

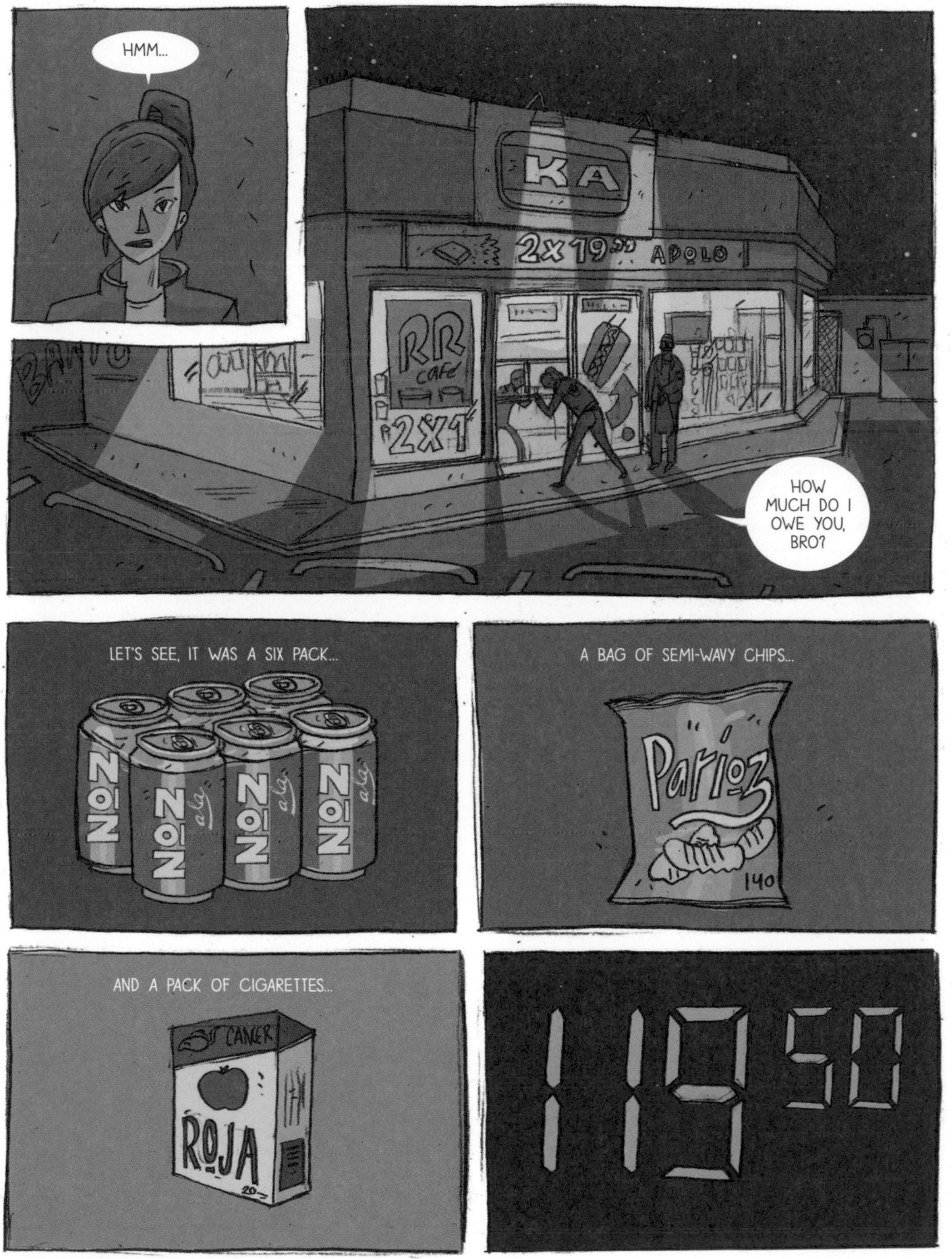
HMM...
KA
2x19.99 APOLO
RR café 2x1
HOW MUCH DO I OWE YOU, BRO?
LET'S SEE, IT WAS A SIX PACK...
NOZ ala
A BAG OF SEMI-WAVY CHIPS...
Parioz
140
AND A PACK OF CIGARETTES...
CANCER
ROJA
20
119.50

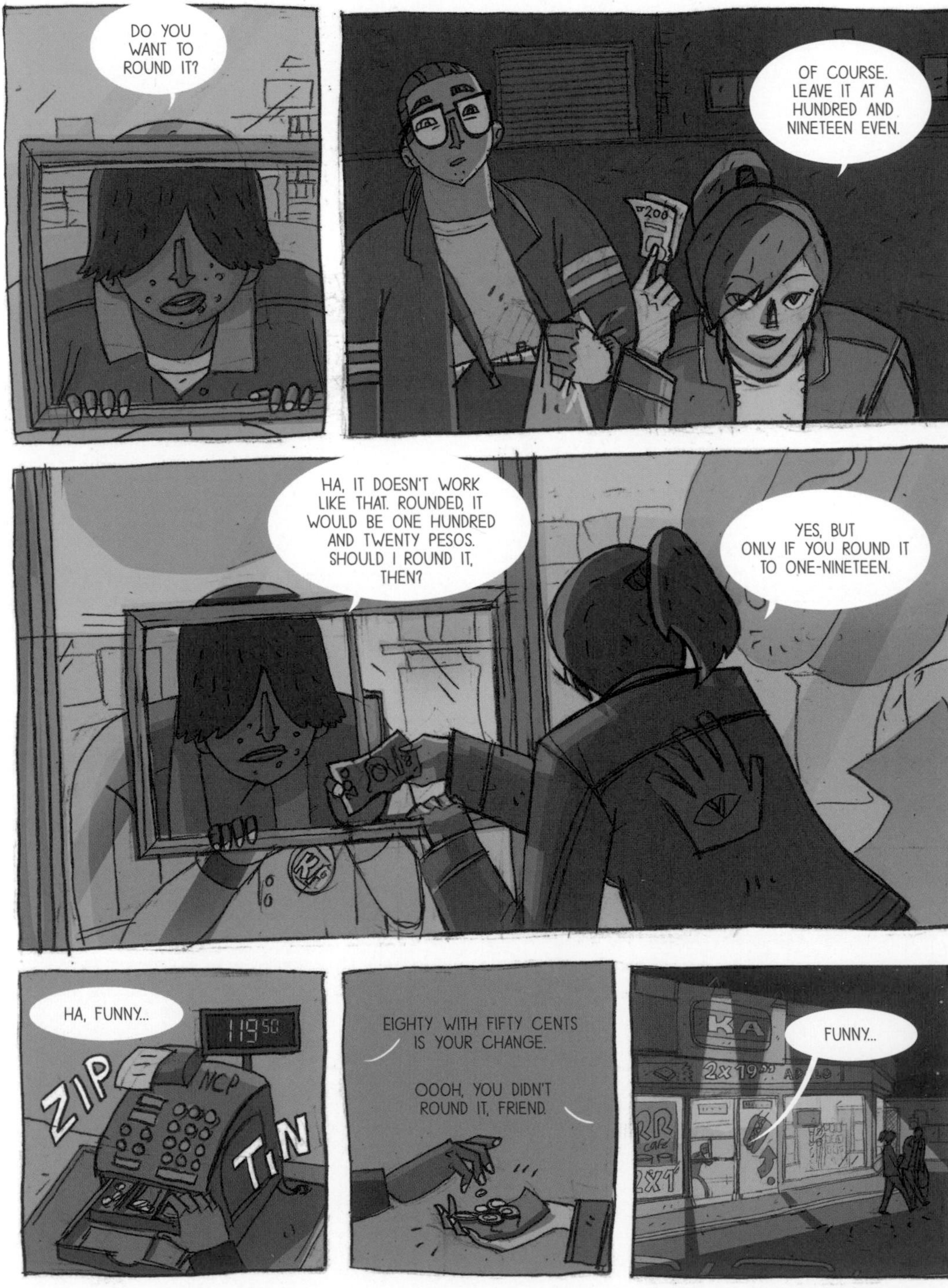
DO YOU WANT TO ROUND IT?
OF COURSE. LEAVE IT AT A HUNDRED AND NINETEEN EVEN.
HA, IT DOESN'T WORK LIKE THAT. ROUNDED, IT WOULD BE ONE HUNDRED AND TWENTY PESOS. SHOULD I ROUND IT, THEN?
YES, BUT ONLY IF YOU ROUND IT TO ONE-NINETEEN.
HA, FUNNY...
ZIP
TIN
EIGHTY WITH FIFTY CENTS IS YOUR CHANGE.
OOOH, YOU DIDN'T ROUND IT, FRIEND.
FUNNY...

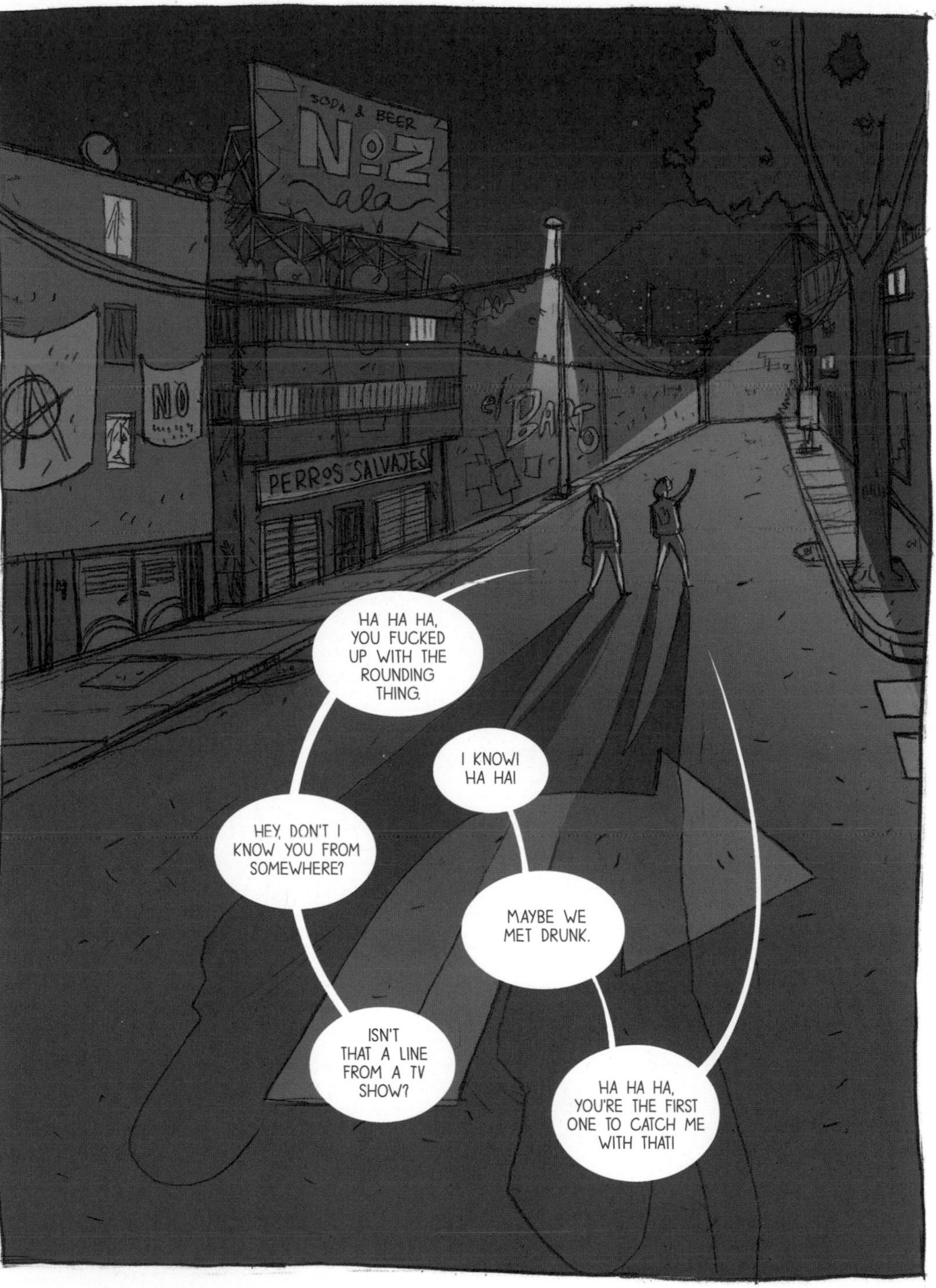
SODA & BEER
NO
PERROS SALVAJES
HA HA HA, YOU FUCKED UP WITH THE ROUNDING THING.
I KNOW! HA HA!
HEY, DON'T I KNOW YOU FROM SOMEWHERE?
MAYBE WE MET DRUNK.
ISN'T THAT A LINE FROM A TV SHOW?
HA HA HA, YOU'RE THE FIRST ONE TO CATCH ME WITH THAT!

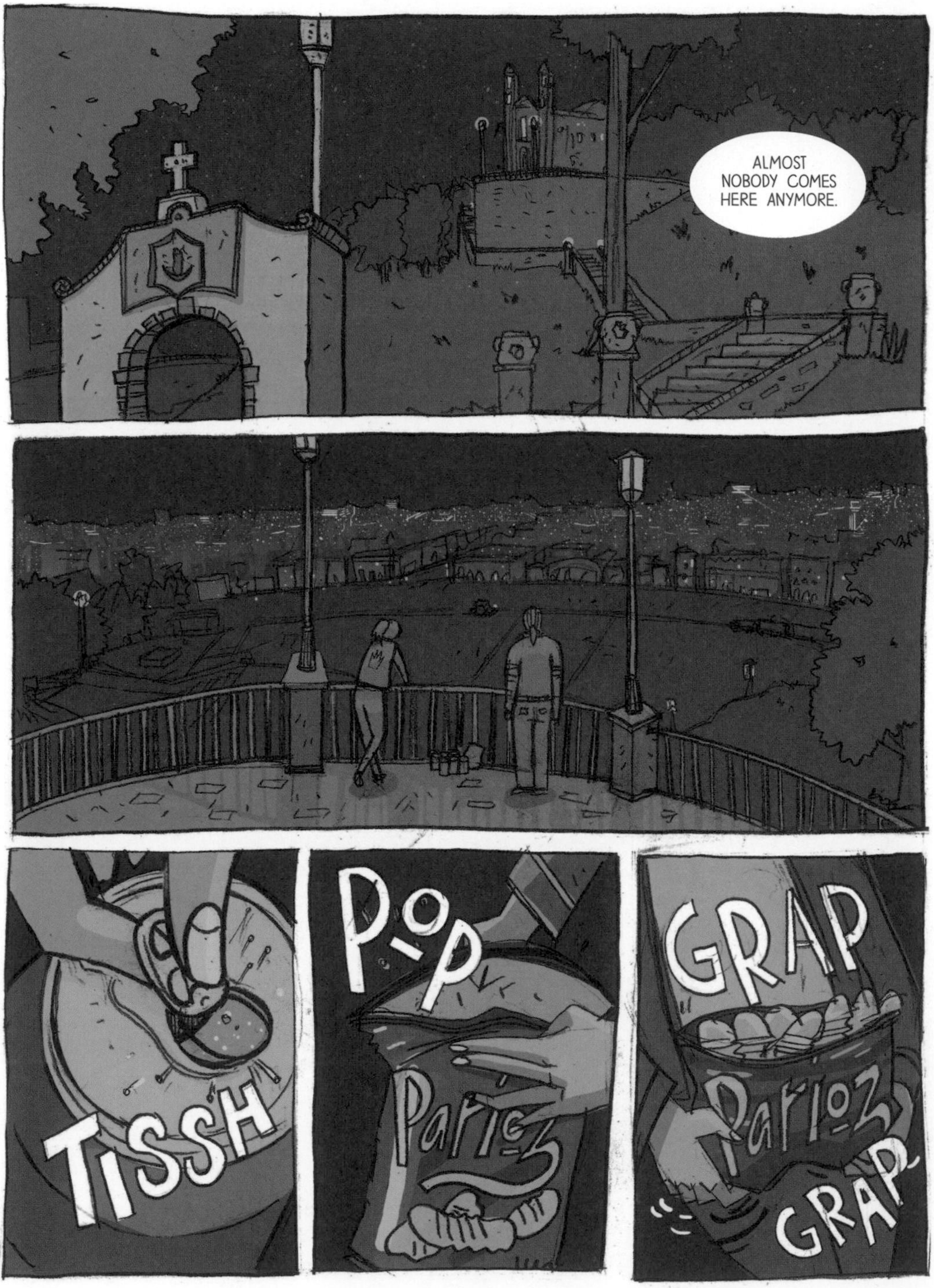
ALMOST NOBODY COMES HERE ANYMORE.
TISSH
POP
Parioz
GRAP
Parioz
GRAP

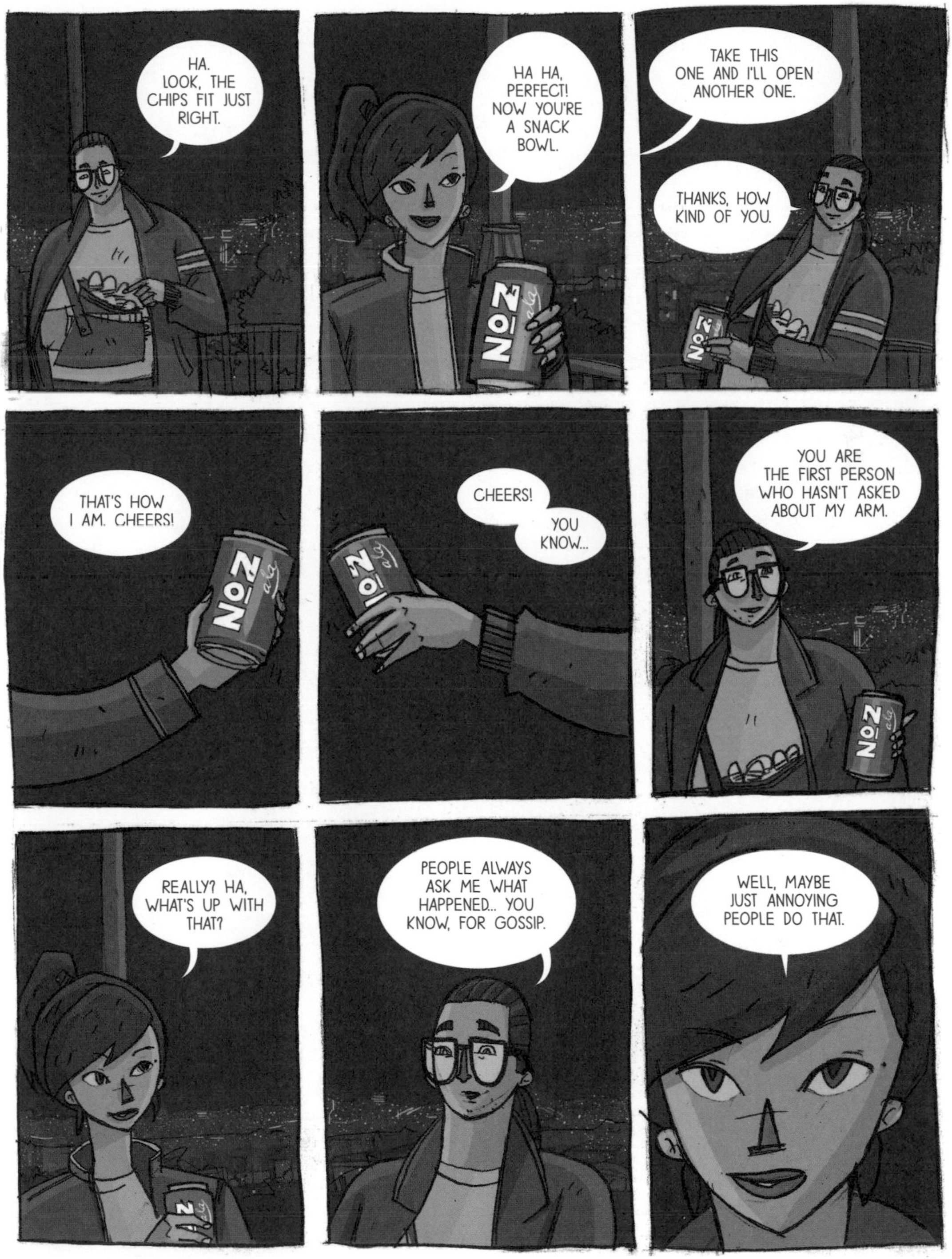
HA. LOOK, THE CHIPS FIT JUST RIGHT.
HA HA, PERFECT! NOW YOU'RE A SNACK BOWL.
TAKE THIS ONE AND I'LL OPEN ANOTHER ONE.
THANKS, HOW KIND OF YOU.
THAT'S HOW I AM. CHEERS!
CHEERS!
YOU KNOW...
YOU ARE THE FIRST PERSON WHO HASN'T ASKED ABOUT MY ARM.
REALLY? HA, WHAT'S UP WITH THAT?
PEOPLE ALWAYS ASK ME WHAT HAPPENED... YOU KNOW, FOR GOSSIP.
WELL, MAYBE JUST ANNOYING PEOPLE DO THAT.

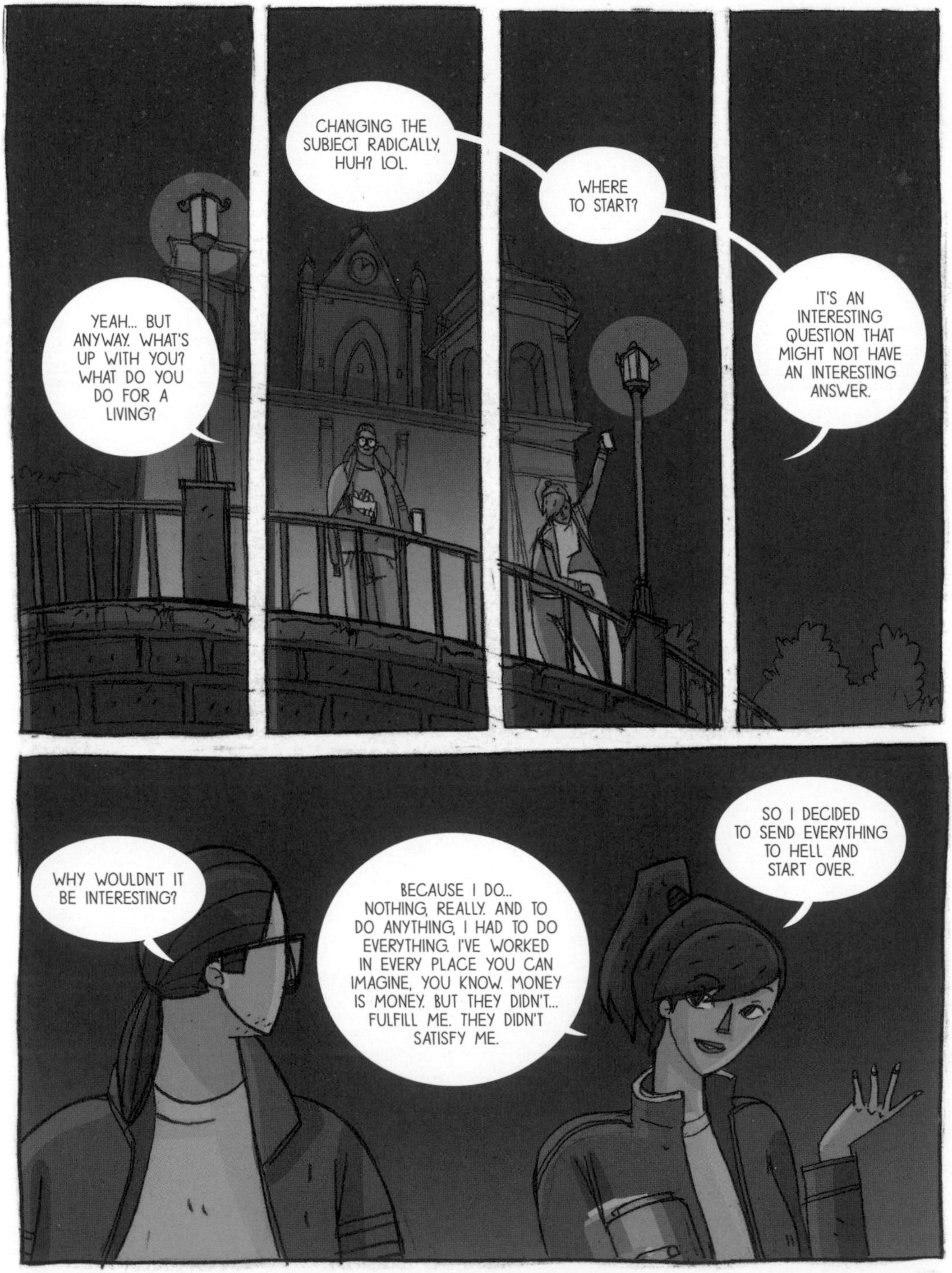
YEAH... BUT ANYWAY. WHAT'S UP WITH YOU? WHAT DO YOU DO FOR A LIVING?
CHANGING THE SUBJECT RADICALLY, HUH? LOL.
WHERE TO START?
IT'S AN INTERESTING QUESTION THAT MIGHT NOT HAVE AN INTERESTING ANSWER.
WHY WOULDN'T IT BE INTERESTING?
BECAUSE I DO... NOTHING, REALLY. AND TO DO ANYTHING, I HAD TO DO EVERYTHING. I'VE WORKED IN EVERY PLACE YOU CAN IMAGINE, YOU KNOW. MONEY IS MONEY. BUT THEY DIDN'T... FULFILL ME. THEY DIDN'T SATISFY ME.
SO I DECIDED TO SEND EVERYTHING TO HELL AND START OVER.

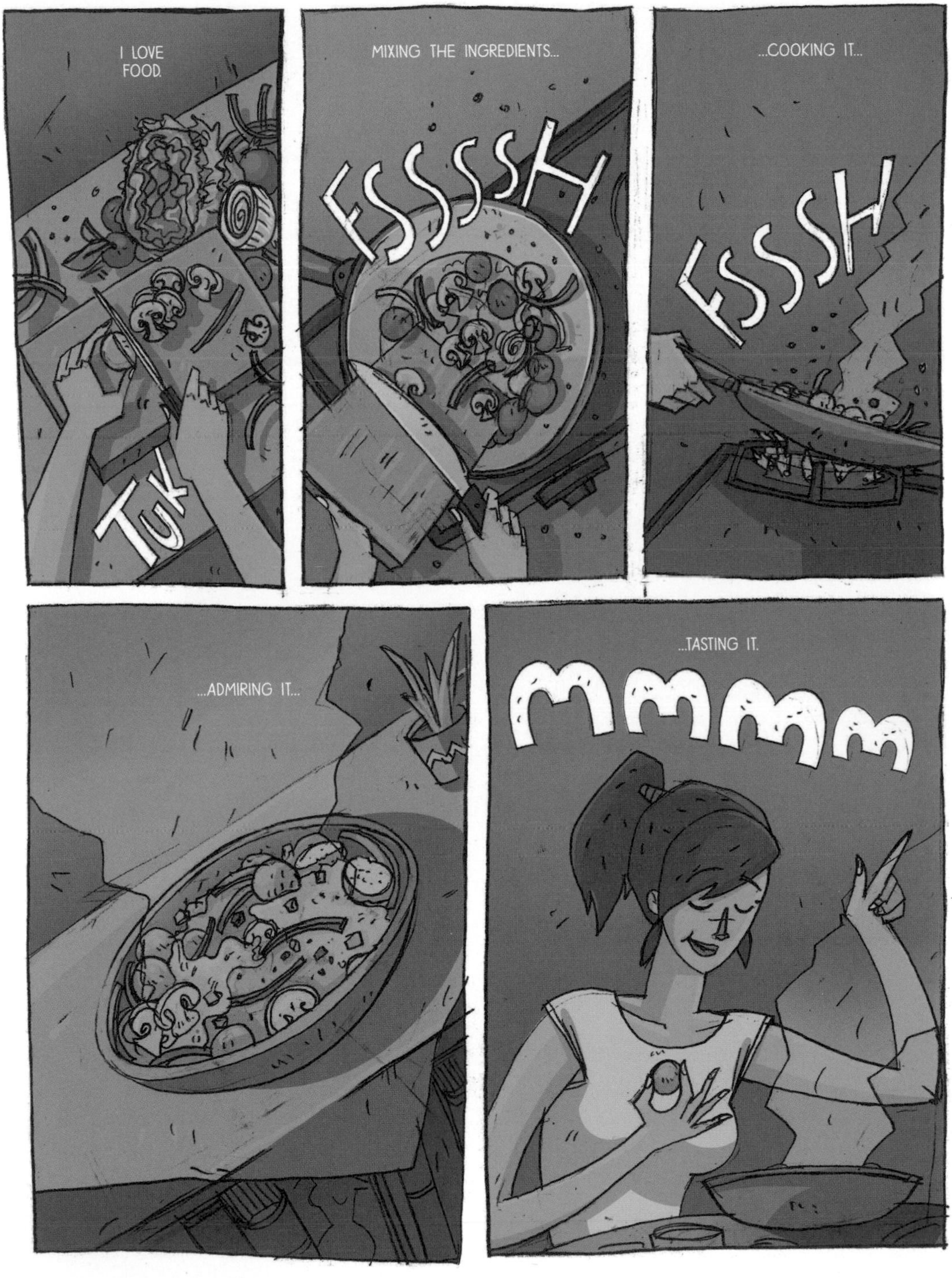
I LOVE FOOD.
TUK
MIXING THE INGREDIENTS...
ESSSSH
...COOKING IT...
ESSSH
...ADMIRING IT...
...TASTING IT.
MMMM

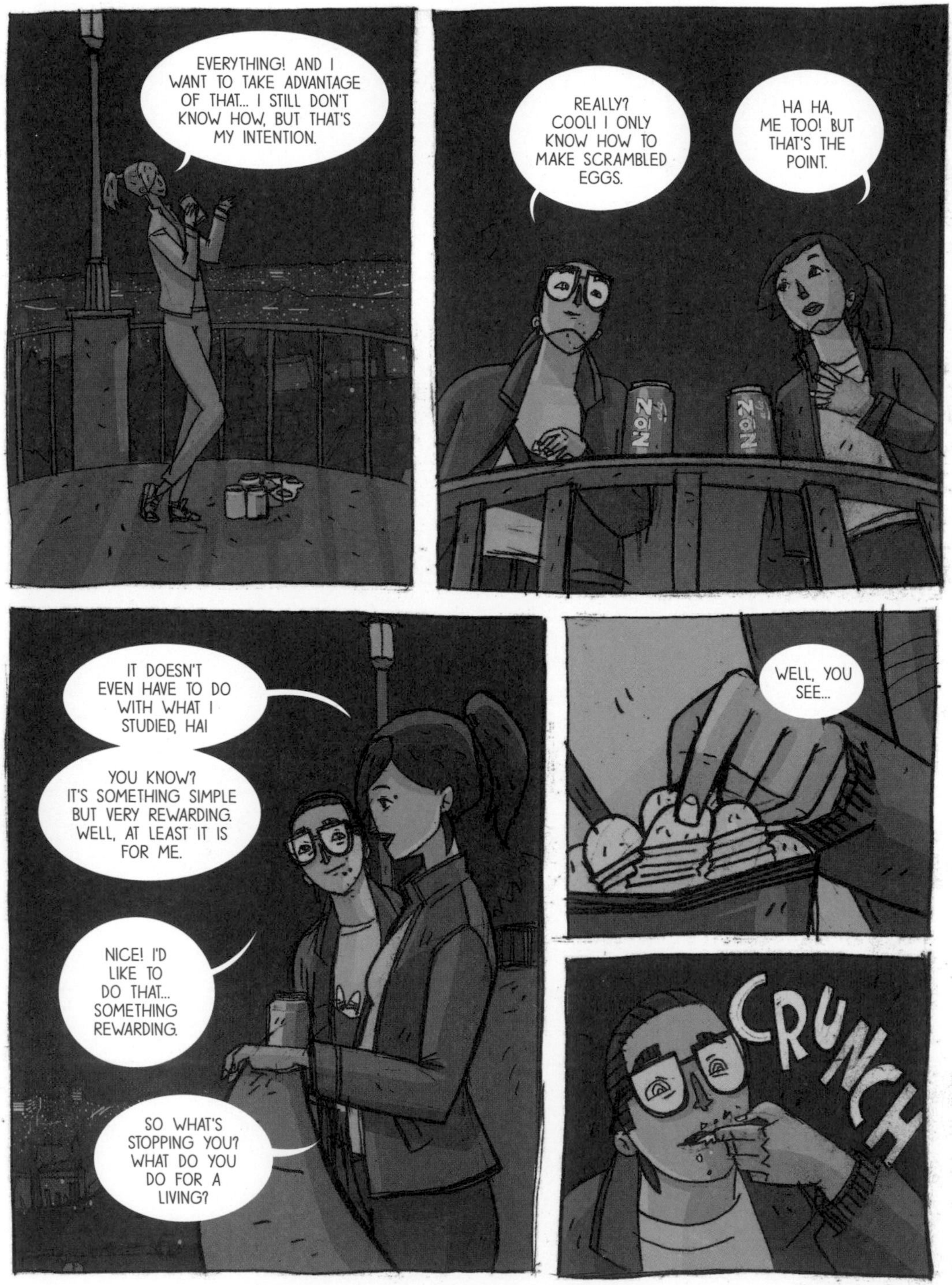
EVERYTHING! AND I WANT TO TAKE ADVANTAGE OF THAT... I STILL DON'T KNOW HOW, BUT THAT'S MY INTENTION.
REALLY? COOL! I ONLY KNOW HOW TO MAKE SCRAMBLED EGGS.
HA HA, ME TOO! BUT THAT'S THE POINT.
ZON
ZON
IT DOESN'T EVEN HAVE TO DO WITH WHAT I STUDIED, HAI
YOU KNOW? IT'S SOMETHING SIMPLE BUT VERY REWARDING. WELL, AT LEAST IT IS FOR ME.
NICE! I'D LIKE TO DO THAT... SOMETHING REWARDING.
SO WHAT'S STOPPING YOU? WHAT DO YOU DO FOR A LIVING?
WELL, YOU SEE...
CRUNCH

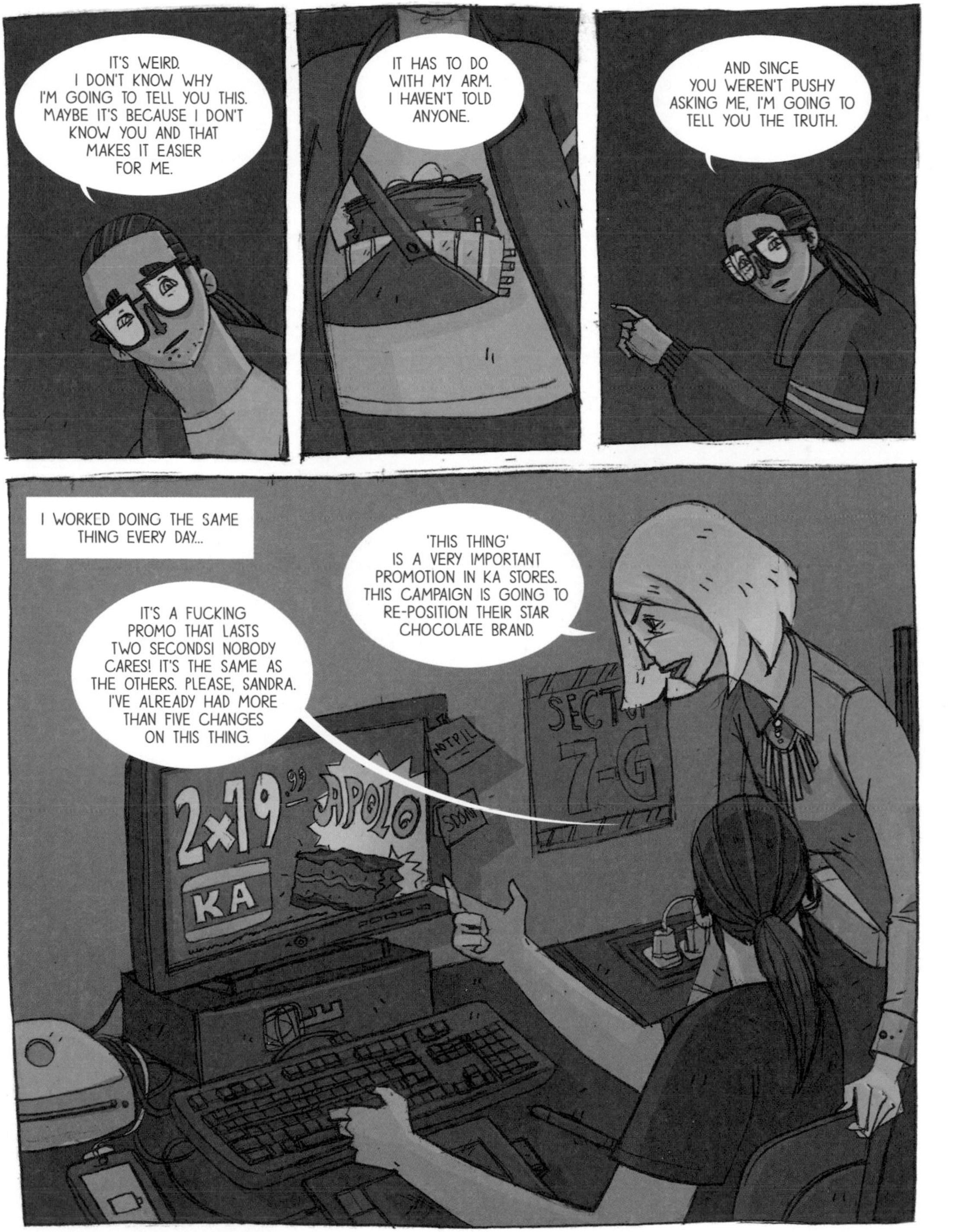
IT'S WEIRD. I DON'T KNOW WHY I'M GOING TO TELL YOU THIS. MAYBE IT'S BECAUSE I DON'T KNOW YOU AND THAT MAKES IT EASIER FOR ME.
IT HAS TO DO WITH MY ARM. I HAVEN'T TOLD ANYONE.
AND SINCE YOU WEREN'T PUSHY ASKING ME, I'M GOING TO TELL YOU THE TRUTH.
I WORKED DOING THE SAME THING EVERY DAY...
'THIS THING' IS A VERY IMPORTANT PROMOTION IN KA STORES. THIS CAMPAIGN IS GOING TO RE-POSITION THEIR STAR CHOCOLATE BRAND.
IT'S A FUCKING PROMO THAT LASTS TWO SECONDS! NOBODY CARES! IT'S THE SAME AS THE OTHERS. PLEASE, SANDRA. I'VE ALREADY HAD MORE THAN FIVE CHANGES ON THIS THING.
2x19.99
APOLO
KA
7-G

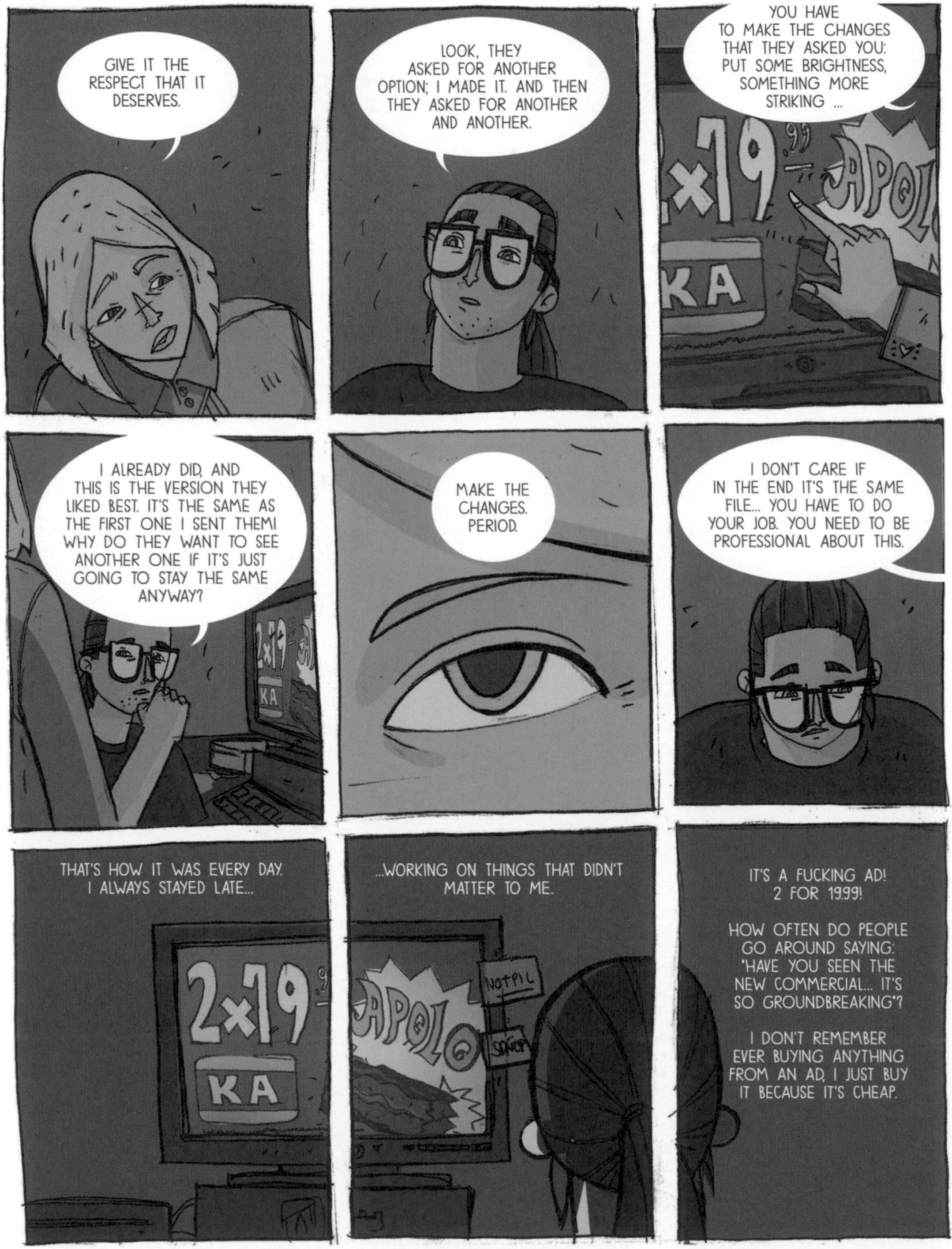
GIVE IT THE RESPECT THAT IT DESERVES.
LOOK, THEY ASKED FOR ANOTHER OPTION; I MADE IT. AND THEN THEY ASKED FOR ANOTHER AND ANOTHER.
YOU HAVE TO MAKE THE CHANGES THAT THEY ASKED YOU: PUT SOME BRIGHTNESS, SOMETHING MORE STRIKING ...
2×19.99
KA
I ALREADY DID, AND THIS IS THE VERSION THEY LIKED BEST. IT'S THE SAME AS THE FIRST ONE I SENT THEM! WHY DO THEY WANT TO SEE ANOTHER ONE IF IT'S JUST GOING TO STAY THE SAME ANYWAY?
MAKE THE CHANGES. PERIOD.
I DON'T CARE IF IN THE END IT'S THE SAME FILE... YOU HAVE TO DO YOUR JOB. YOU NEED TO BE PROFESSIONAL ABOUT THIS.
THAT'S HOW IT WAS EVERY DAY. I ALWAYS STAYED LATE...
2×19.99
KA
...WORKING ON THINGS THAT DIDN'T MATTER TO ME.
APOLO
IT'S A FUCKING AD! 2 FOR 19.99!
HOW OFTEN DO PEOPLE GO AROUND SAYING: "HAVE YOU SEEN THE NEW COMMERCIAL... IT'S SO GROUNDBREAKING"?
I DON'T REMEMBER EVER BUYING ANYTHING FROM AN AD, I JUST BUY IT BECAUSE IT'S CHEAP.

I WANTED TO QUIT, BUT THE TRUTH WAS THAT I WAS VERY AFRAID TO TAKE RESPONSIBILITY FOR MY LIFE.

IT WAS EASIER FOR ME TO BLAME MY PROBLEMS ON SOMEONE OTHER THAN MYSELF.

I DIDN'T THINK ABOUT WHAT I DID, I JUST DID IT.

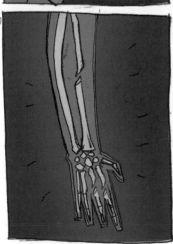

MAYBE I'M EXAGGERATING THE STORY A BIT... DRAMATIZING. HA, MAYBE THE WINDOW WASN'T BROKEN... MAYBE.

THE POINT IS THAT IT WASN'T AN ACCIDENT, BUT I TOLD THEM ALL IT WAS. IT WAS AN EASY WAY OUT.

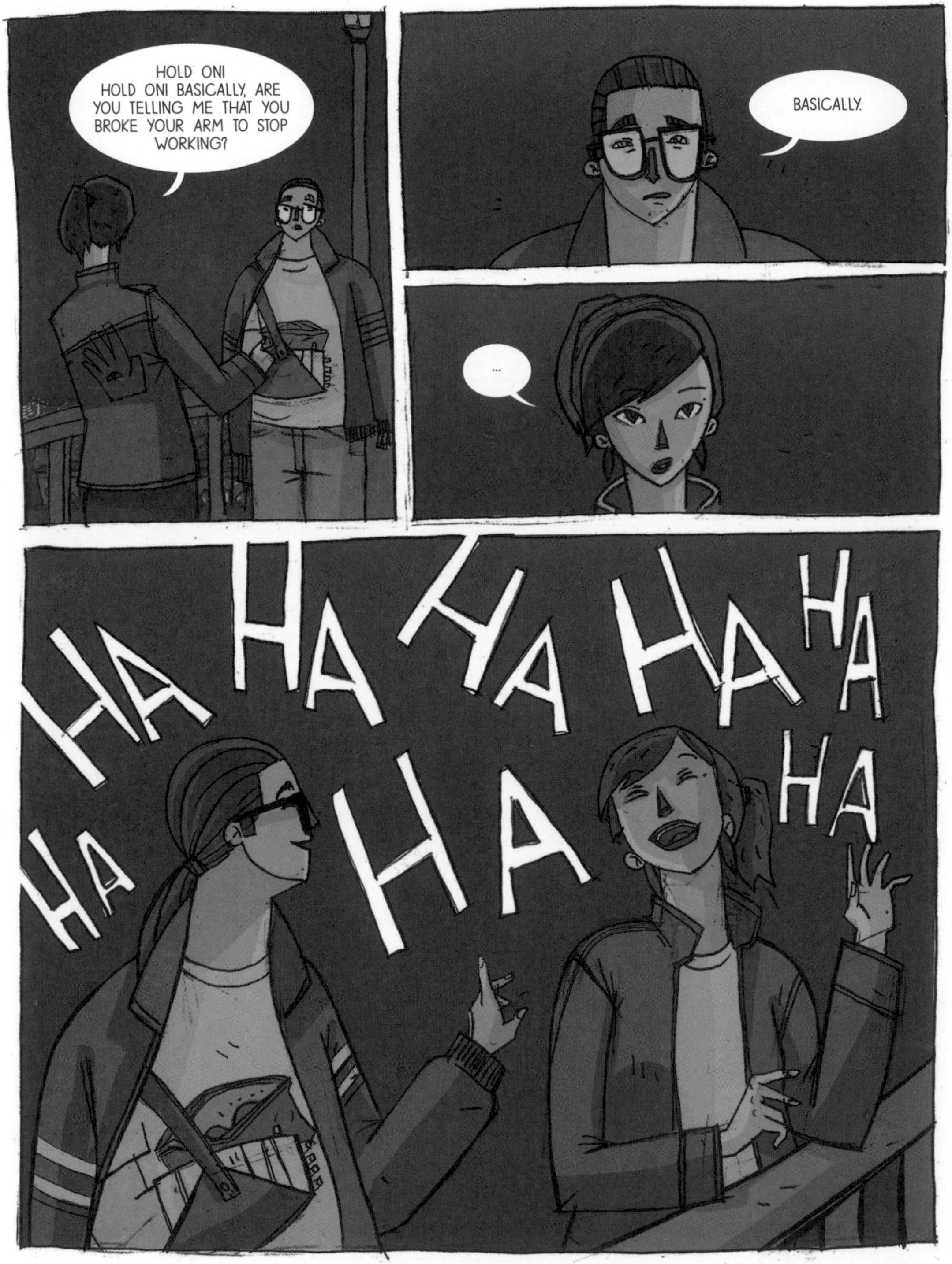
HOLD ON!
HOLD ON! BASICALLY, ARE YOU TELLING ME THAT YOU BROKE YOUR ARM TO STOP WORKING?
BASICALLY.
...
HA HA HA HA HA HA HA HA HA HA HA HA

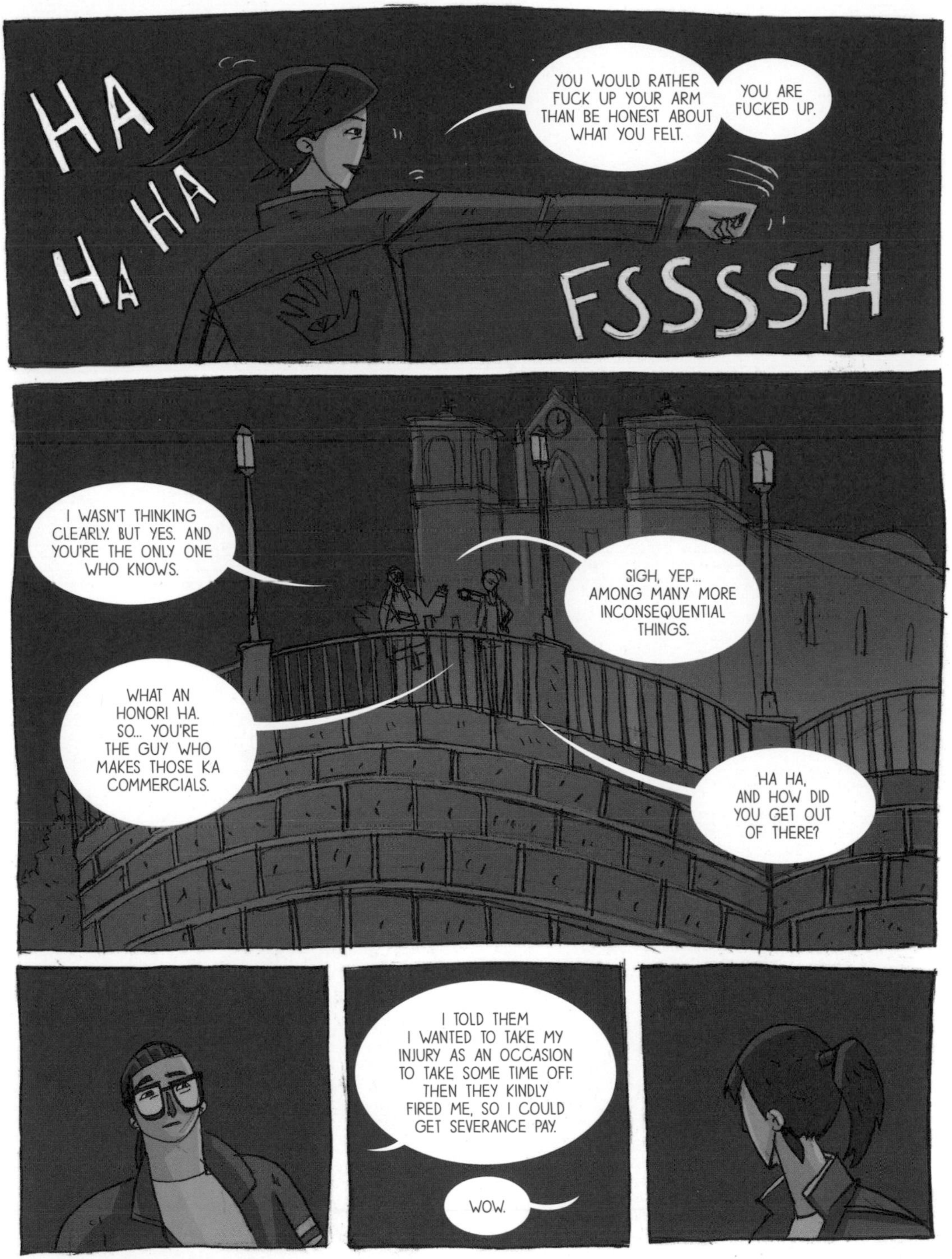
HA HA HA HA
YOU WOULD RATHER FUCK UP YOUR ARM THAN BE HONEST ABOUT WHAT YOU FELT.
YOU ARE FUCKED UP.
FSSSSH
I WASN'T THINKING CLEARLY. BUT YES. AND YOU'RE THE ONLY ONE WHO KNOWS.
SIGH, YEP... AMONG MANY MORE INCONSEQUENTIAL THINGS.
WHAT AN HONORI HA. SO... YOU'RE THE GUY WHO MAKES THOSE KA COMMERCIALS.
HA HA, AND HOW DID YOU GET OUT OF THERE?
I TOLD THEM I WANTED TO TAKE MY INJURY AS AN OCCASION TO TAKE SOME TIME OFF. THEN THEY KINDLY FIRED ME, SO I COULD GET SEVERANCE PAY.
WOW.

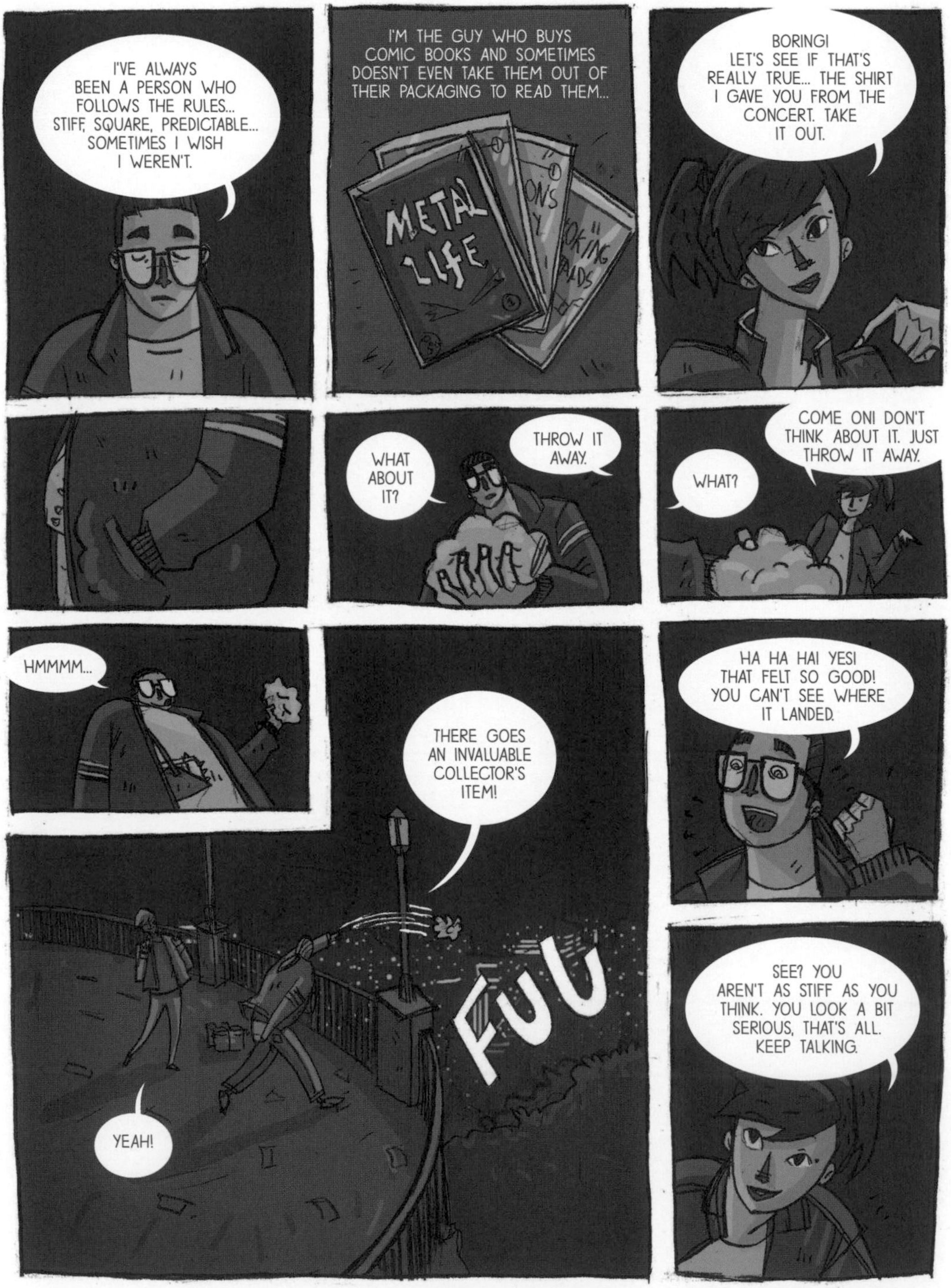
I'VE ALWAYS BEEN A PERSON WHO FOLLOWS THE RULES... STIFF, SQUARE, PREDICTABLE... SOMETIMES I WISH I WEREN'T.
I'M THE GUY WHO BUYS COMIC BOOKS AND SOMETIMES DOESN'T EVEN TAKE THEM OUT OF THEIR PACKAGING TO READ THEM...
METAL LIFE
BORING! LET'S SEE IF THAT'S REALLY TRUE... THE SHIRT I GAVE YOU FROM THE CONCERT. TAKE IT OUT.
WHAT ABOUT IT?
THROW IT AWAY.
WHAT?
COME ON! DON'T THINK ABOUT IT. JUST THROW IT AWAY.
HMMMM...
THERE GOES AN INVALUABLE COLLECTOR'S ITEM!
FUU
YEAH!
HA HA HA! YES! THAT FELT SO GOOD! YOU CAN'T SEE WHERE IT LANDED.
SEE? YOU AREN'T AS STIFF AS YOU THINK. YOU LOOK A BIT SERIOUS, THAT'S ALL. KEEP TALKING.

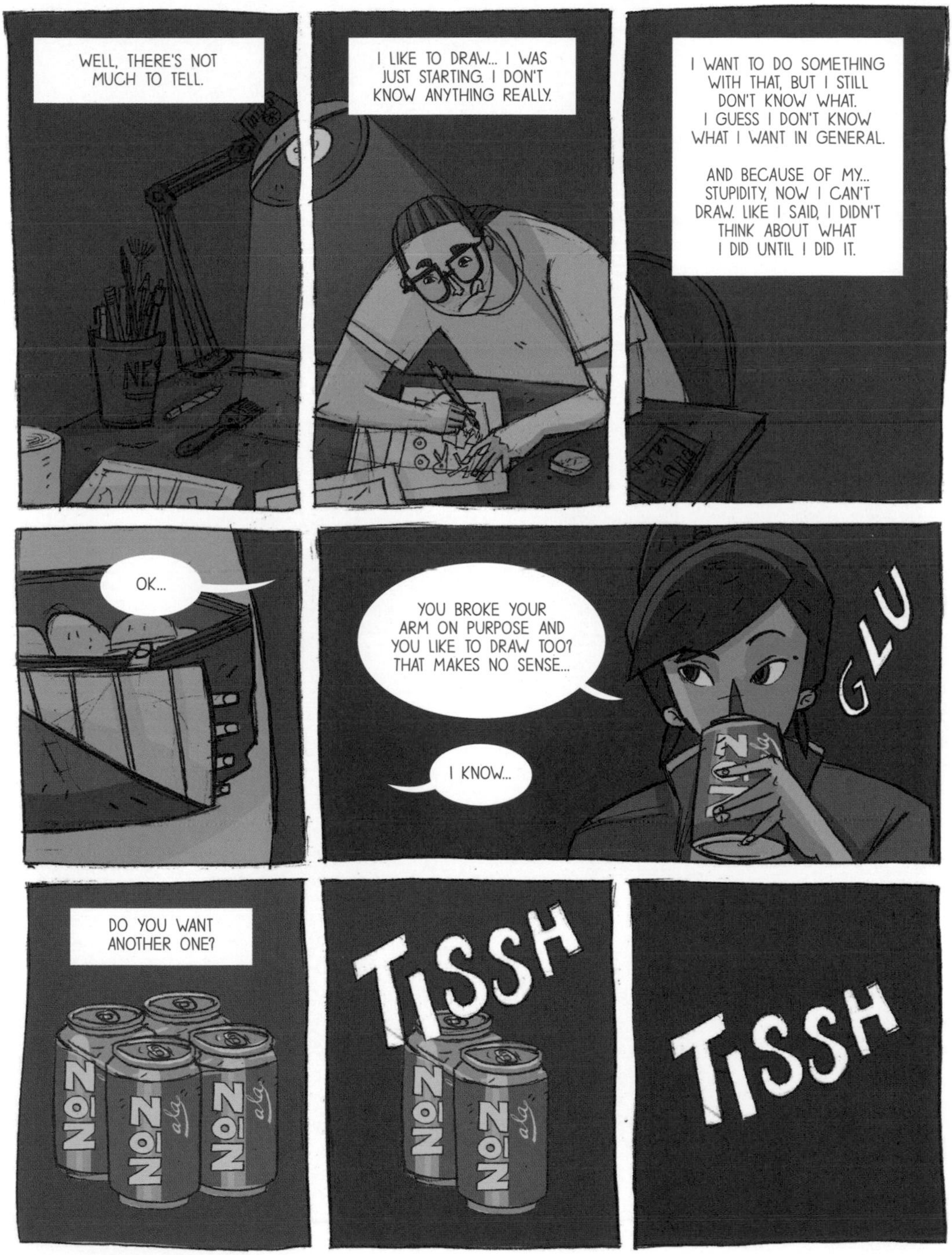
WELL, THERE'S NOT MUCH TO TELL.
I LIKE TO DRAW... I WAS JUST STARTING. I DON'T KNOW ANYTHING REALLY.
I WANT TO DO SOMETHING WITH THAT, BUT I STILL DON'T KNOW WHAT. I GUESS I DON'T KNOW WHAT I WANT IN GENERAL.
AND BECAUSE OF MY... STUPIDITY, NOW I CAN'T DRAW. LIKE I SAID, I DIDN'T THINK ABOUT WHAT I DID UNTIL I DID IT.
OK...
YOU BROKE YOUR ARM ON PURPOSE AND YOU LIKE TO DRAW TOO? THAT MAKES NO SENSE...
I KNOW...
GLU
DO YOU WANT ANOTHER ONE?
TISSH
TISSH

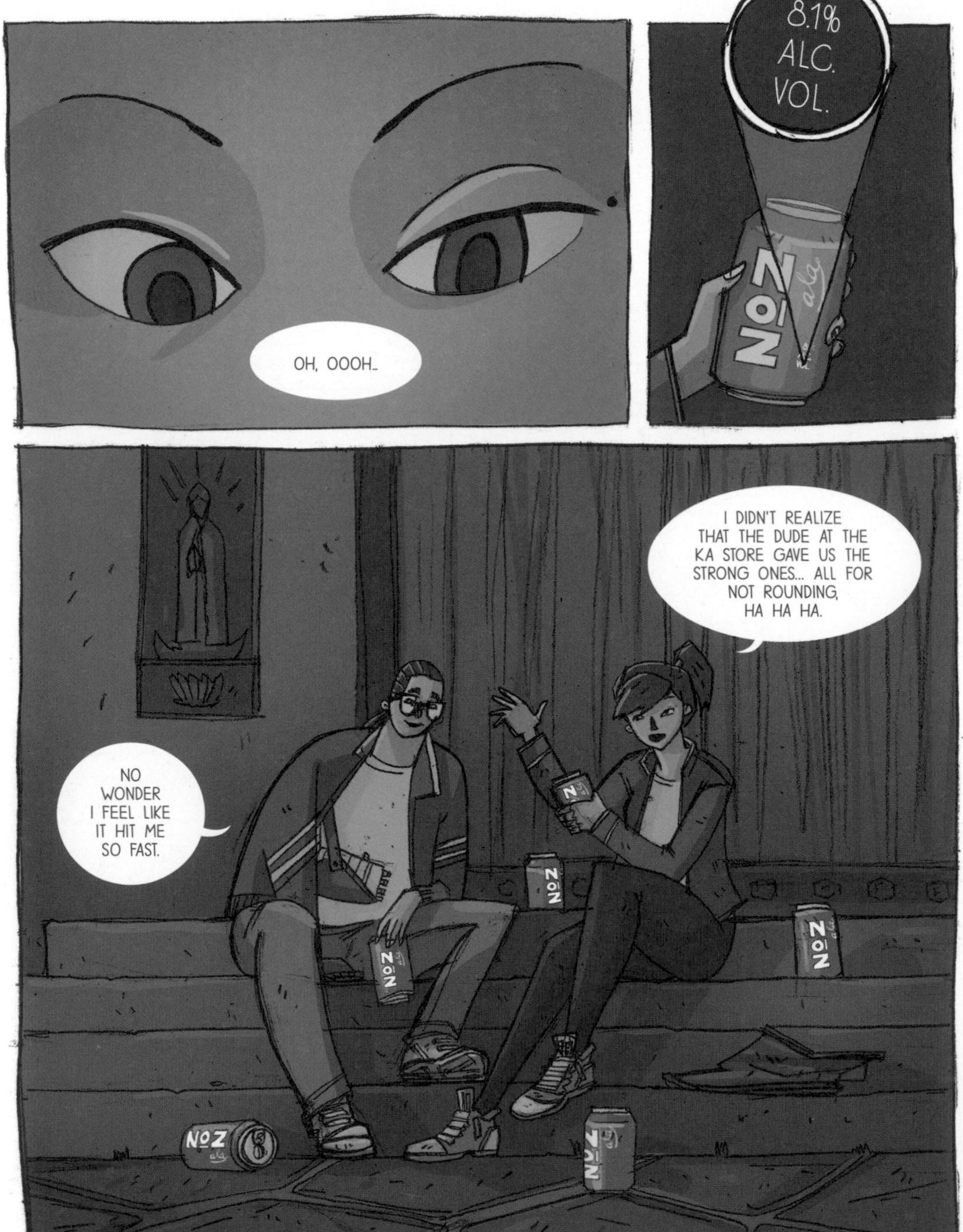
OH, OOOH...
8.1% ALC. VOL.
I DIDN'T REALIZE THAT THE DUDE AT THE KA STORE GAVE US THE STRONG ONES... ALL FOR NOT ROUNDING, HA HA HA.
NO WONDER I FEEL LIKE IT HIT ME SO FAST.

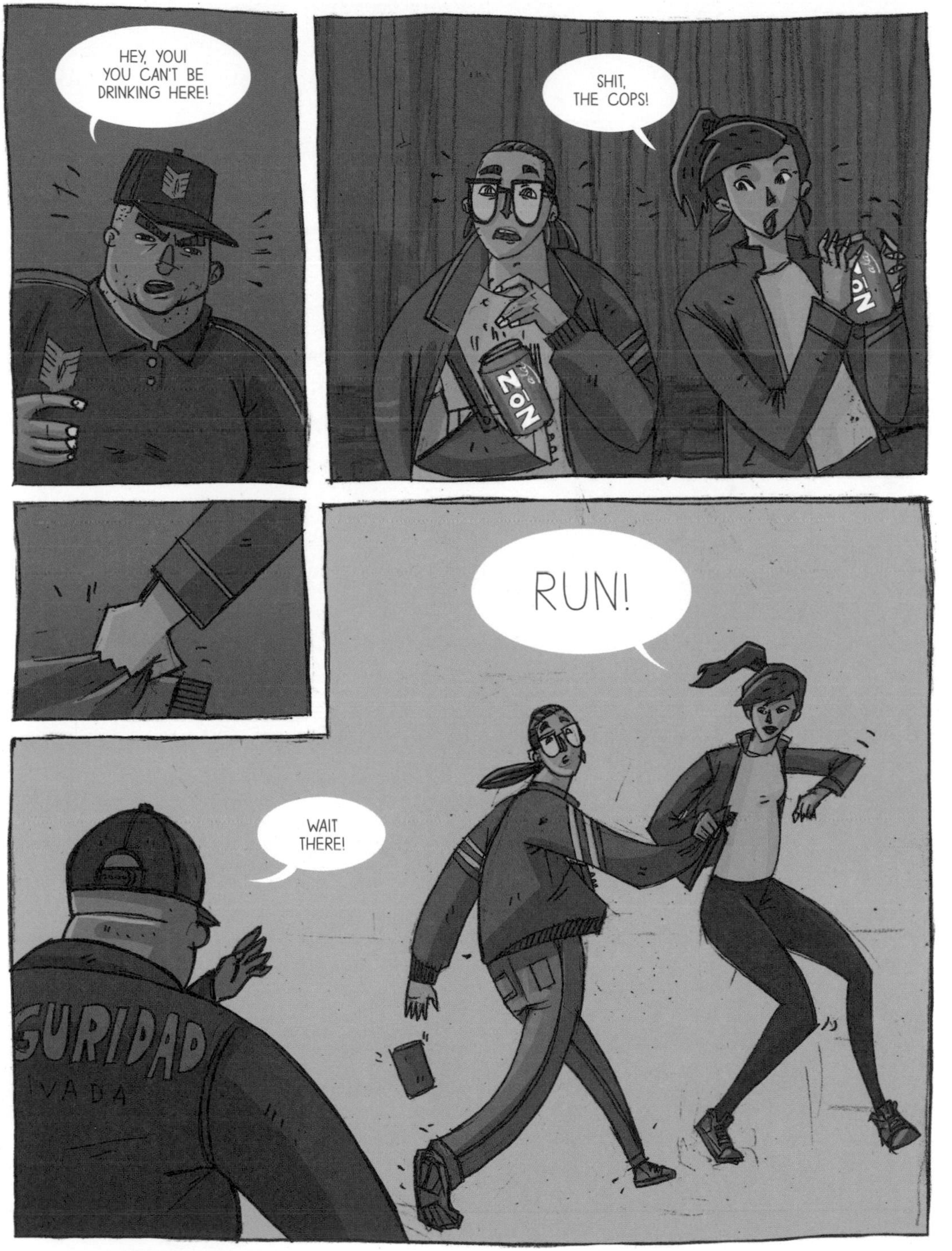
HEY, YOU! YOU CAN'T BE DRINKING HERE!
SHIT, THE COPS!
NoN
RUN!
WAIT THERE!
GURIDAD
VADA

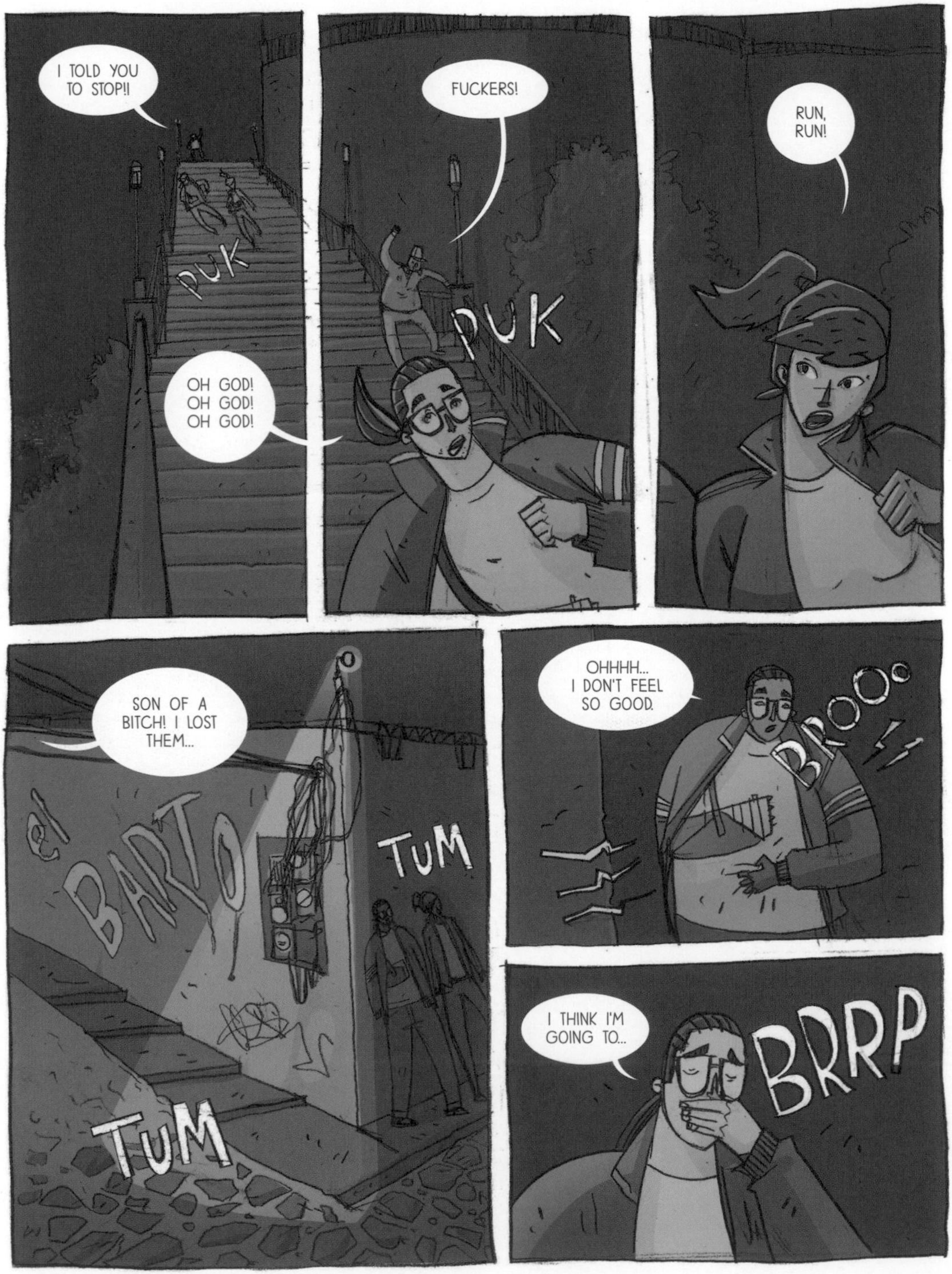
I TOLD YOU TO STOP!!
PUK
OH GOD! OH GOD! OH GOD!
FUCKERS!
PUK
RUN, RUN!
SON OF A BITCH! I LOST THEM...
el BARTO
TUM
TUM
OHHHH... I DON'T FEEL SO GOOD.
BROOo
I THINK I'M GOING TO...
BRRP

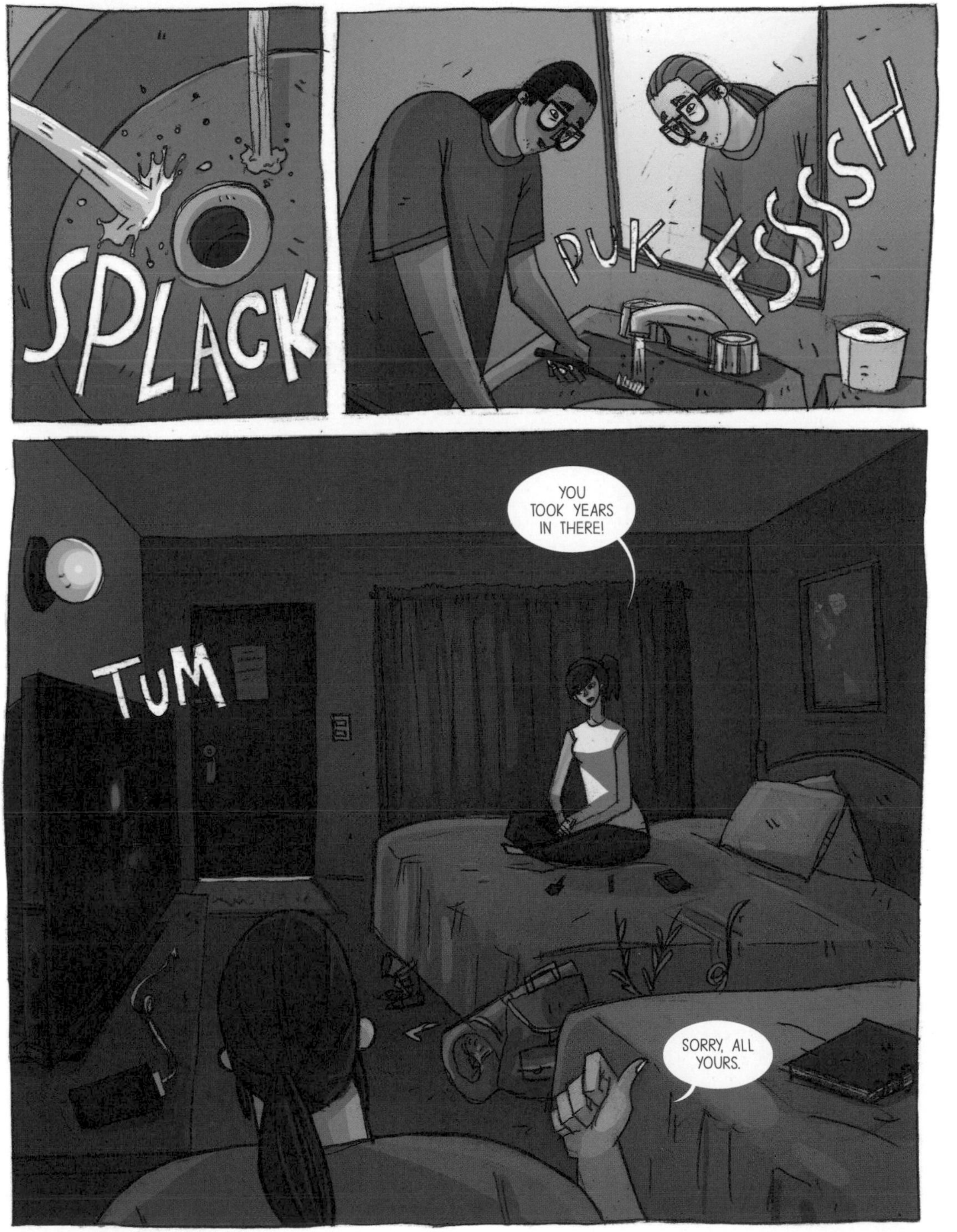
SPLACK
PUK
FSSSSH
YOU TOOK YEARS IN THERE!
TUM
SORRY, ALL YOURS.

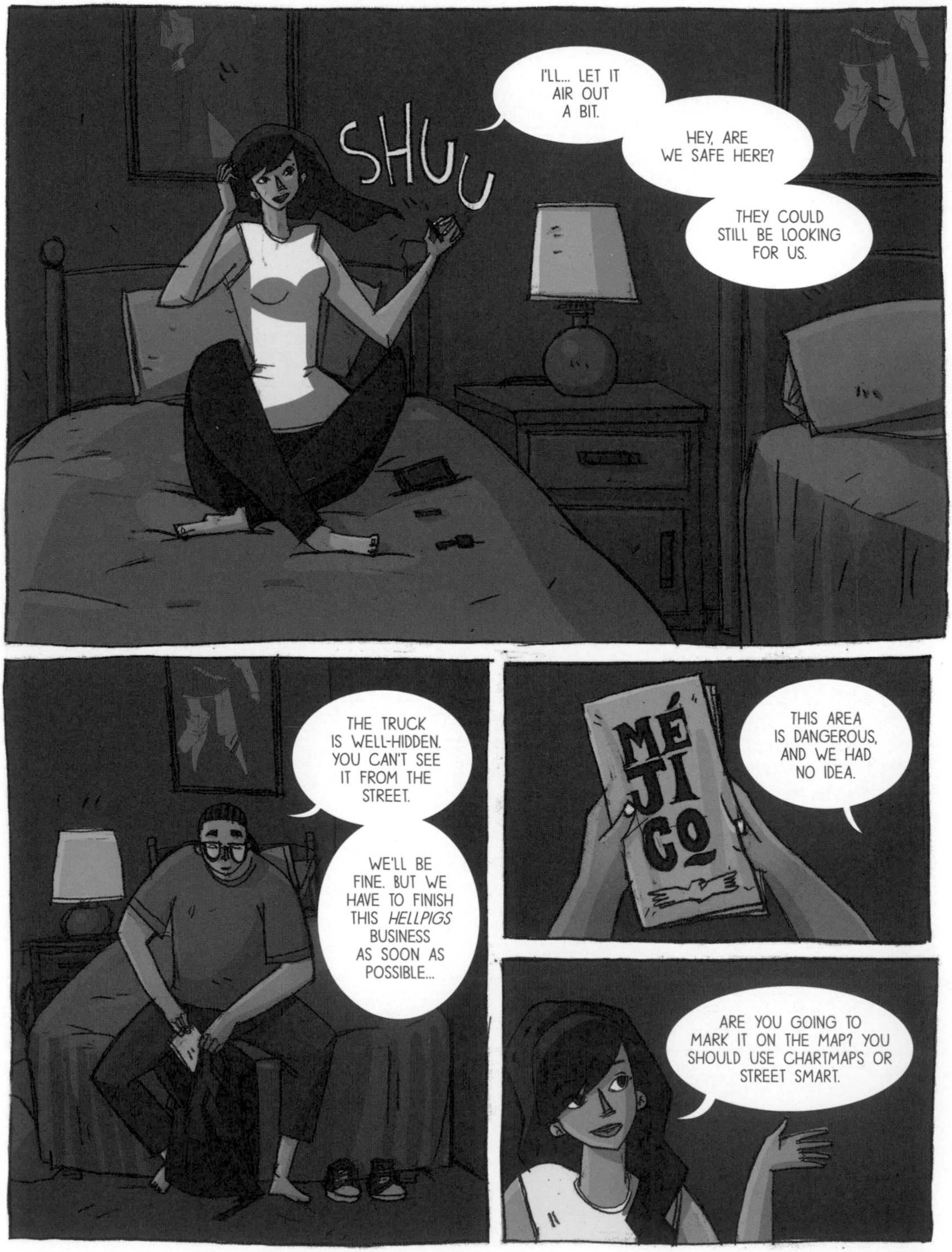
SHUU
I'LL... LET IT AIR OUT A BIT.
HEY, ARE WE SAFE HERE?
THEY COULD STILL BE LOOKING FOR US.
THE TRUCK IS WELL-HIDDEN. YOU CAN'T SEE IT FROM THE STREET.
WE'LL BE FINE. BUT WE HAVE TO FINISH THIS *HELLPIGS* BUSINESS AS SOON AS POSSIBLE...
MÉ JI CO
THIS AREA IS DANGEROUS, AND WE HAD NO IDEA.
ARE YOU GOING TO MARK IT ON THE MAP? YOU SHOULD USE CHARTMAPS OR STREET SMART.

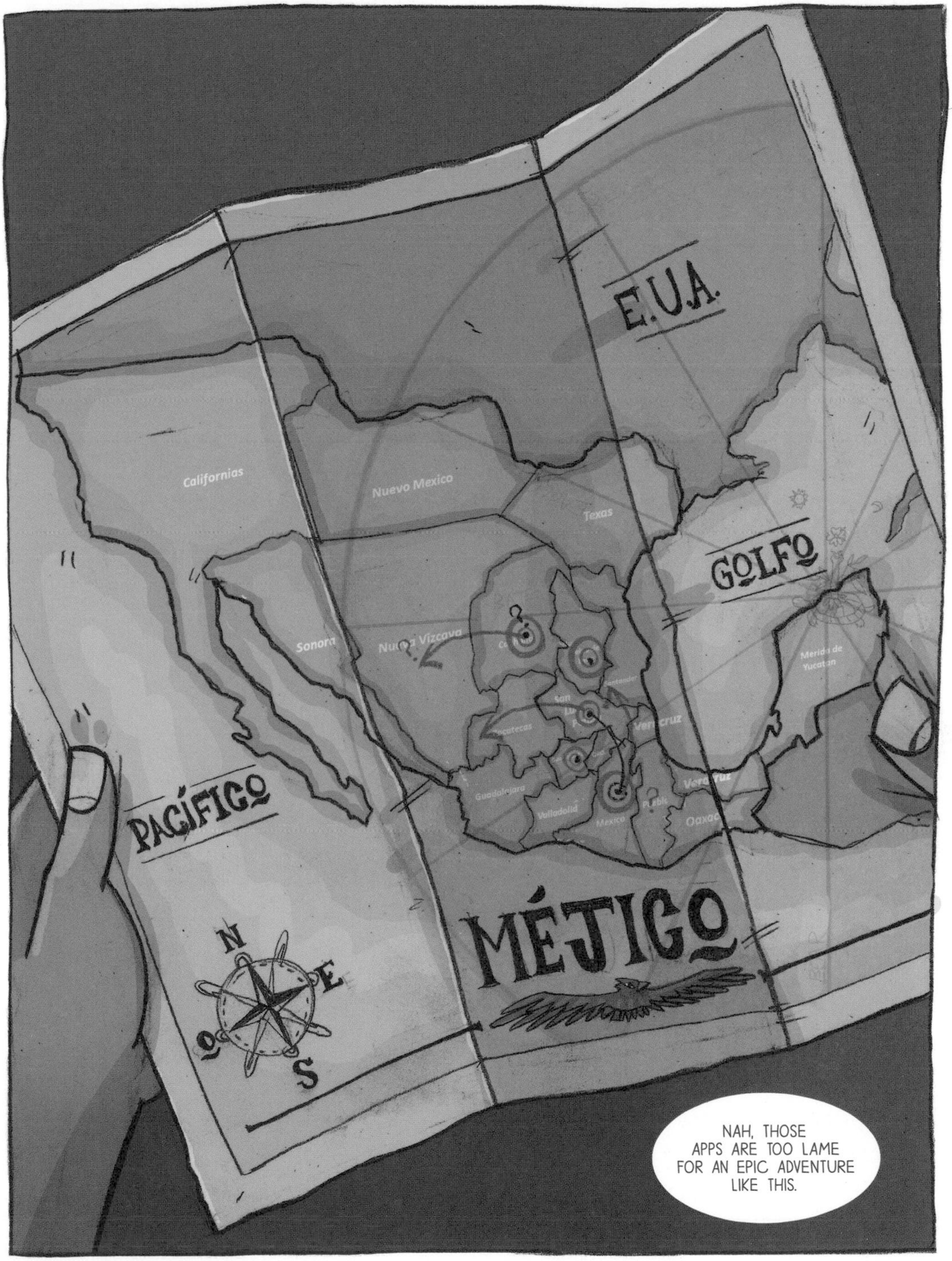
E.U.A.
Californias
Nuevo Mexico
Texas
GOLFO
Sonora
Guadalajara
Valladolid
Mexico
Oaxaca
PACÍFICO
MÉJICO
N
E
O
S
NAH, THOSE APPS ARE TOO LAME FOR AN EPIC ADVENTURE LIKE THIS.

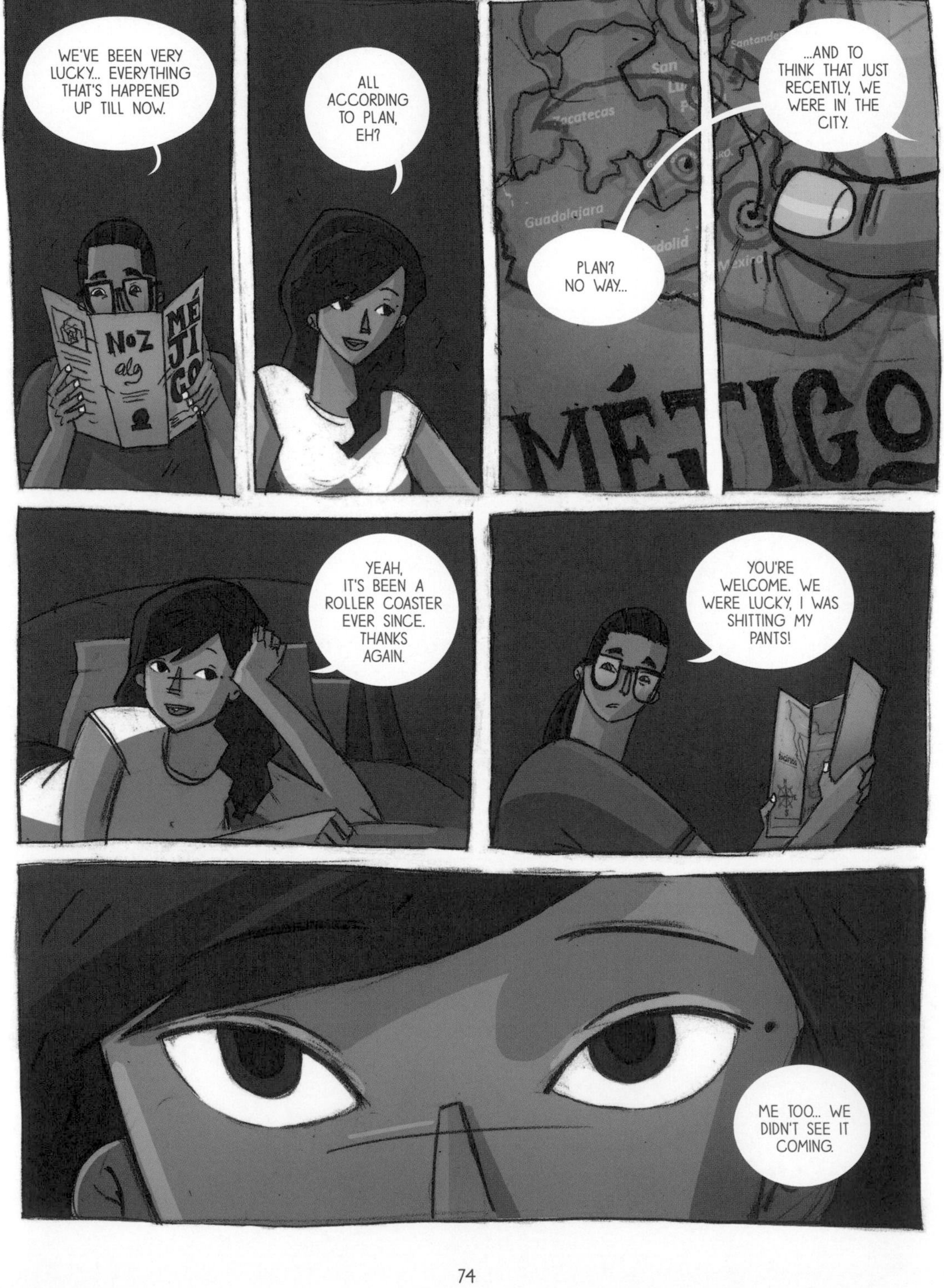

WE'VE BEEN VERY LUCKY... EVERYTHING THAT'S HAPPENED UP TILL NOW.
NoZ alg MÉJIGO
ALL ACCORDING TO PLAN, EH?
Zacatecas
San Lu P
Guadalajara
Santand
PLAN? NO WAY...
...AND TO THINK THAT JUST RECENTLY, WE WERE IN THE CITY.
México
MÉJICO
YEAH, IT'S BEEN A ROLLER COASTER EVER SINCE. THANKS AGAIN.
YOU'RE WELCOME. WE WERE LUCKY, I WAS SHITTING MY PANTS!
ME TOO... WE DIDN'T SEE IT COMING.

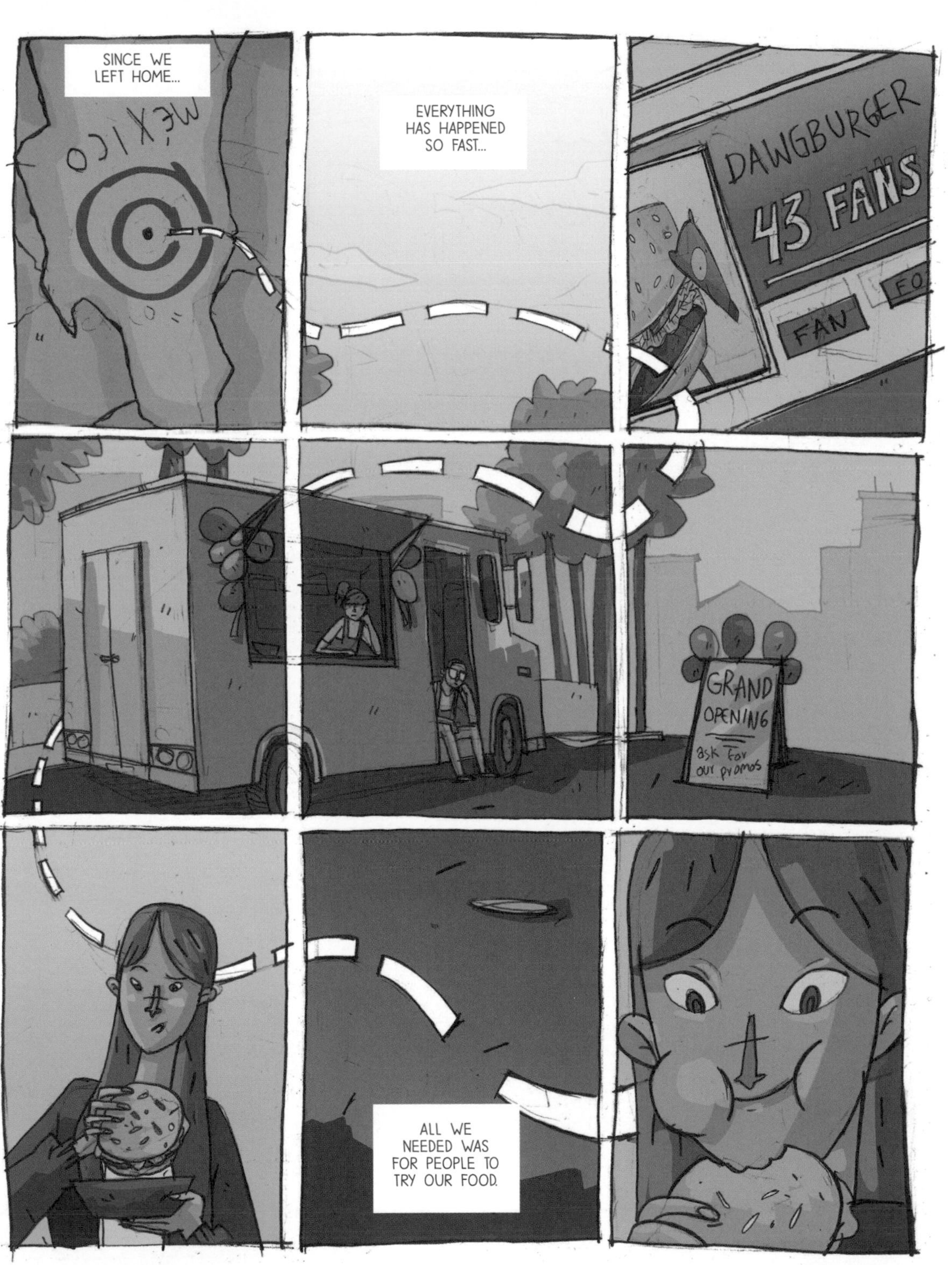
SINCE WE LEFT HOME...
MEXICO
EVERYTHING HAS HAPPENED SO FAST...
DAWGBURGER
43 FANS
FAN
GRAND OPENING
ask for our promos
ALL WE NEEDED WAS FOR PEOPLE TO TRY OUR FOOD.

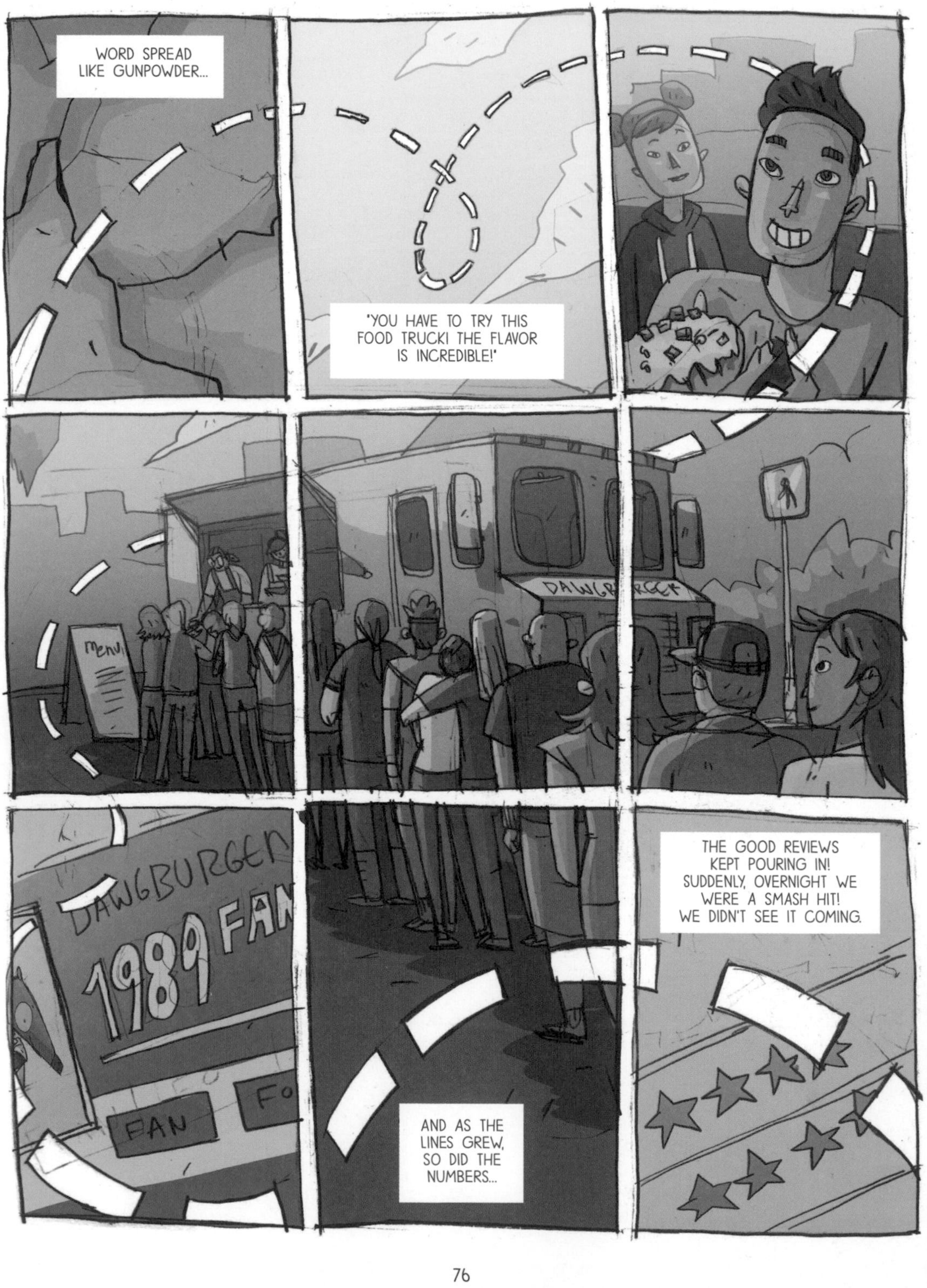
WORD SPREAD LIKE GUNPOWDER...
"YOU HAVE TO TRY THIS FOOD TRUCK! THE FLAVOR IS INCREDIBLE!"
menu
DAWGBURGER
DAWGBURGER
1989 FAN
FAN
AND AS THE LINES GREW, SO DID THE NUMBERS...
THE GOOD REVIEWS KEPT POURING IN! SUDDENLY, OVERNIGHT WE WERE A SMASH HIT! WE DIDN'T SEE IT COMING.

PUK

THEY ALREADY HAD THEIR EYE ON US.

FLICK

WE JUST DIDN'T KNOW IT.

TUM

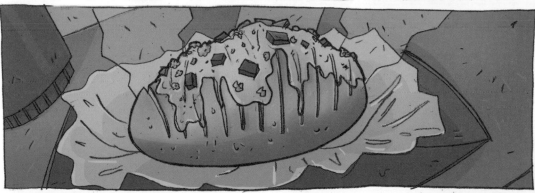

HOW'S ORDER NINETEEN GOING?

IT'S READY. I'M JUST SPICING IT UP.

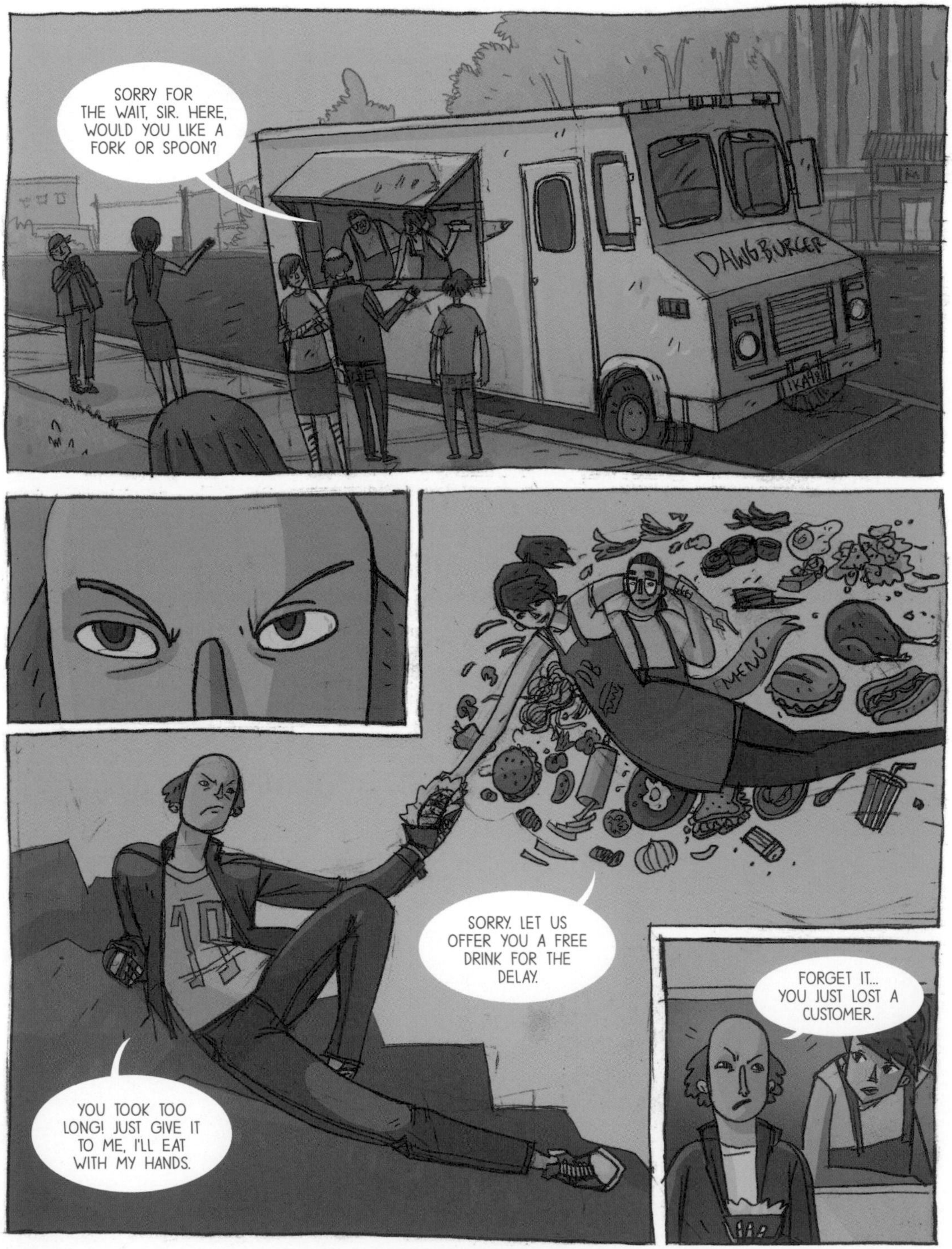
SORRY FOR THE WAIT, SIR. HERE, WOULD YOU LIKE A FORK OR SPOON?
DAWGBURGER
MENU
SORRY. LET US OFFER YOU A FREE DRINK FOR THE DELAY.
YOU TOOK TOO LONG! JUST GIVE IT TO ME, I'LL EAT WITH MY HANDS.
FORGET IT... YOU JUST LOST A CUSTOMER.

randi
LIBROS, CAFE Y +

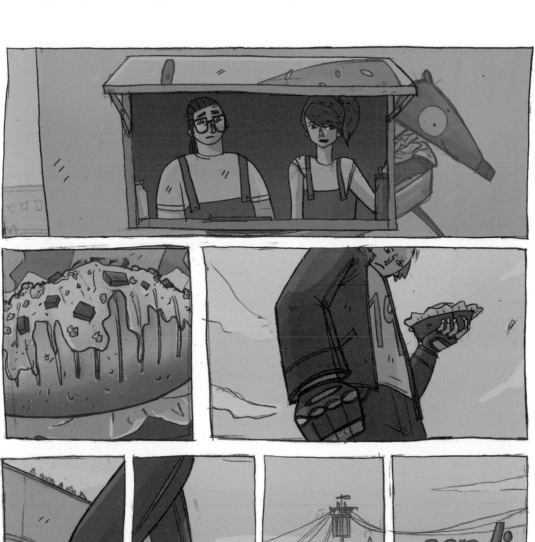

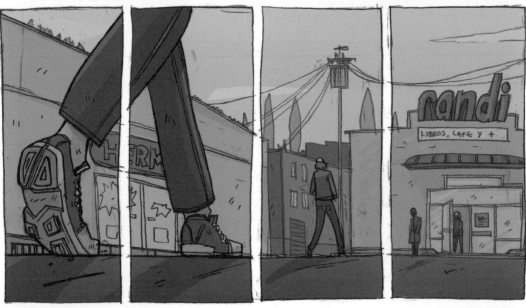

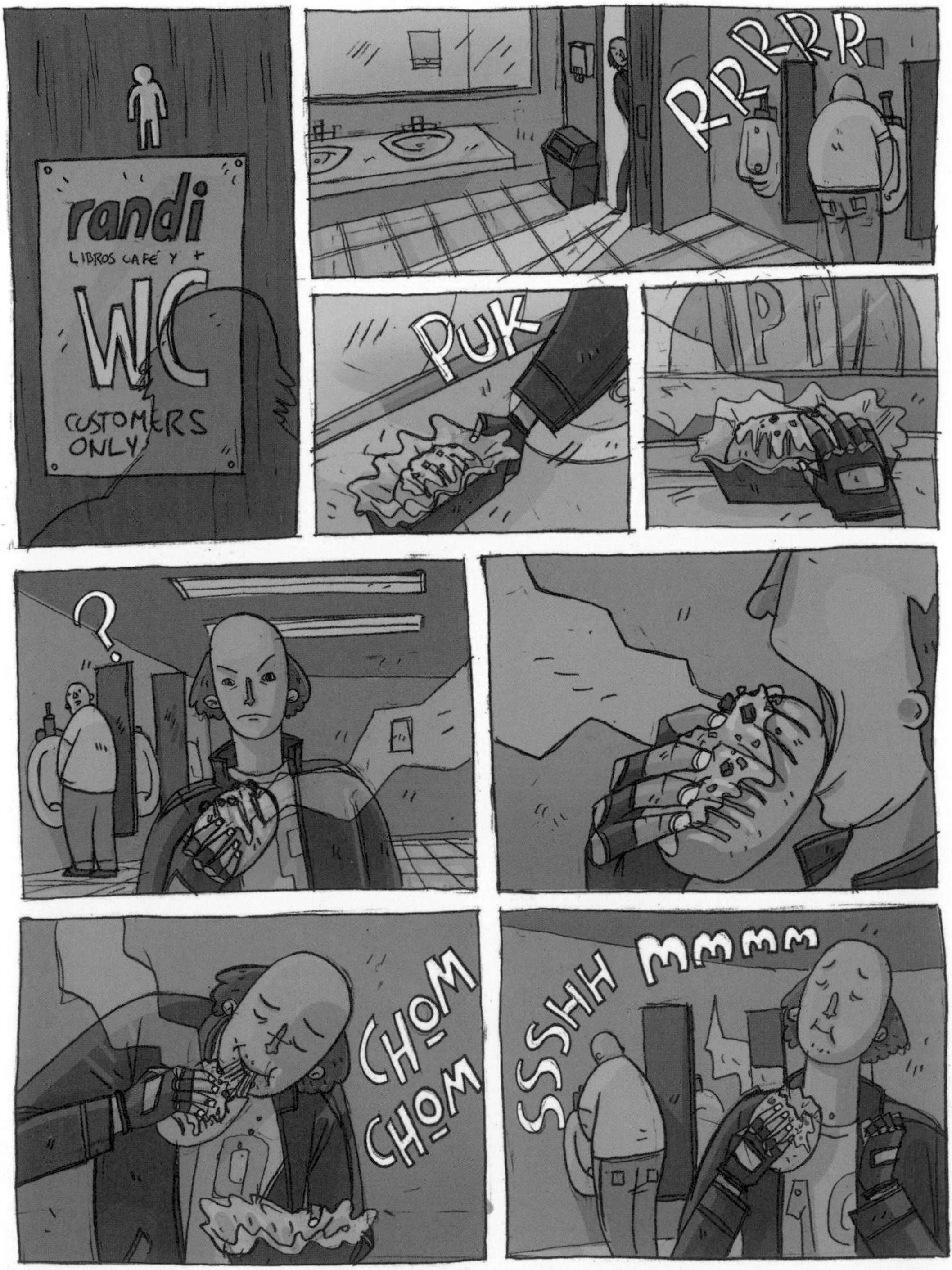
randi
LIBROS CAFÉ Y +
WC
CUSTOMERS ONLY
RRRRR
PUK
PF
?
CHOM CHOM
SSSHH MMMM

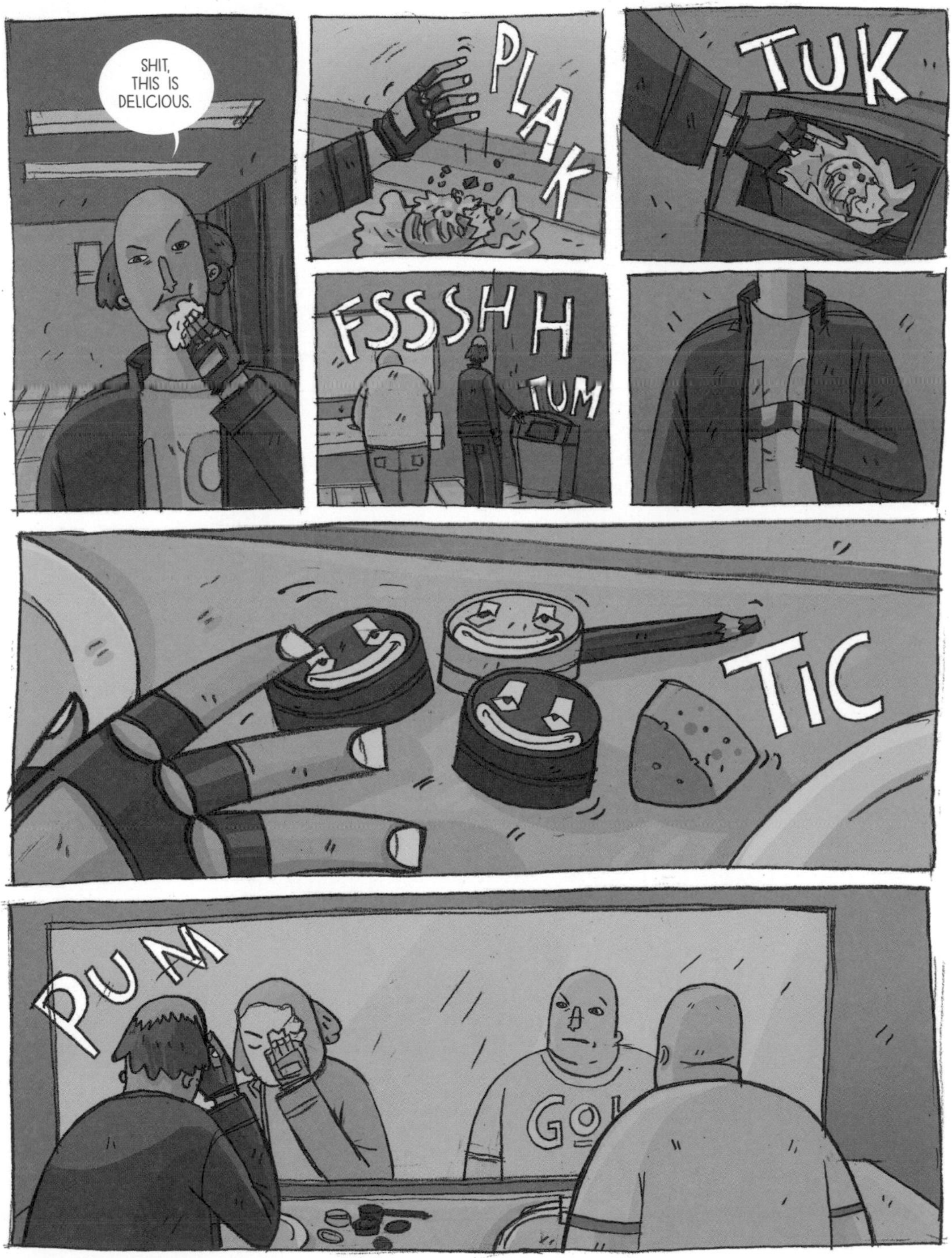
SHIT, THIS IS DELICIOUS.
PLAK
TUK
FSSSHH
TUM
TIC
PUM
GO

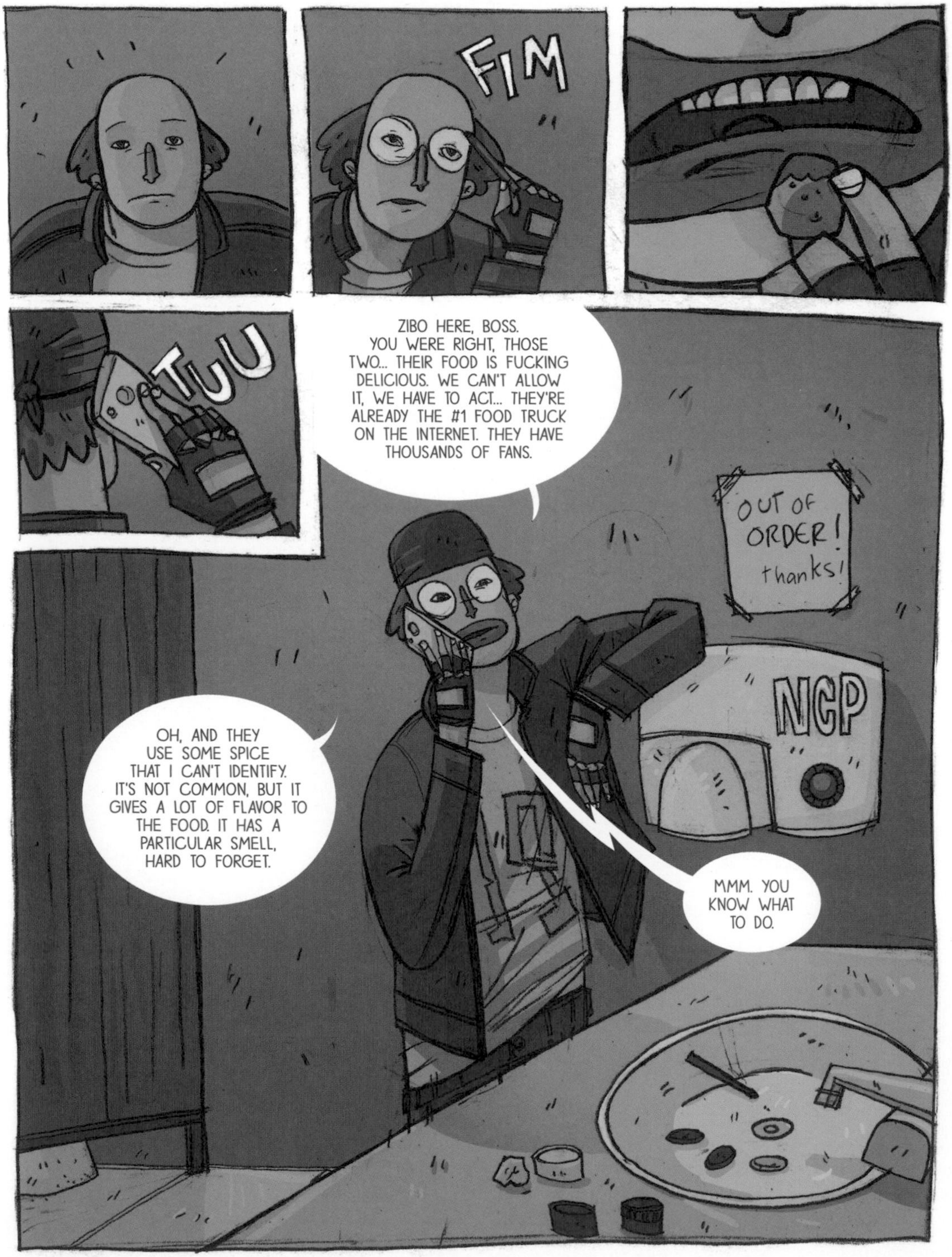
FIM
TUU
ZIBO HERE, BOSS. YOU WERE RIGHT, THOSE TWO... THEIR FOOD IS FUCKING DELICIOUS. WE CAN'T ALLOW IT, WE HAVE TO ACT... THEY'RE ALREADY THE #1 FOOD TRUCK ON THE INTERNET. THEY HAVE THOUSANDS OF FANS.
OUT OF ORDER! thanks!
NCP
OH, AND THEY USE SOME SPICE THAT I CAN'T IDENTIFY. IT'S NOT COMMON, BUT IT GIVES A LOT OF FLAVOR TO THE FOOD. IT HAS A PARTICULAR SMELL, HARD TO FORGET.
MMM. YOU KNOW WHAT TO DO.

PART THREE

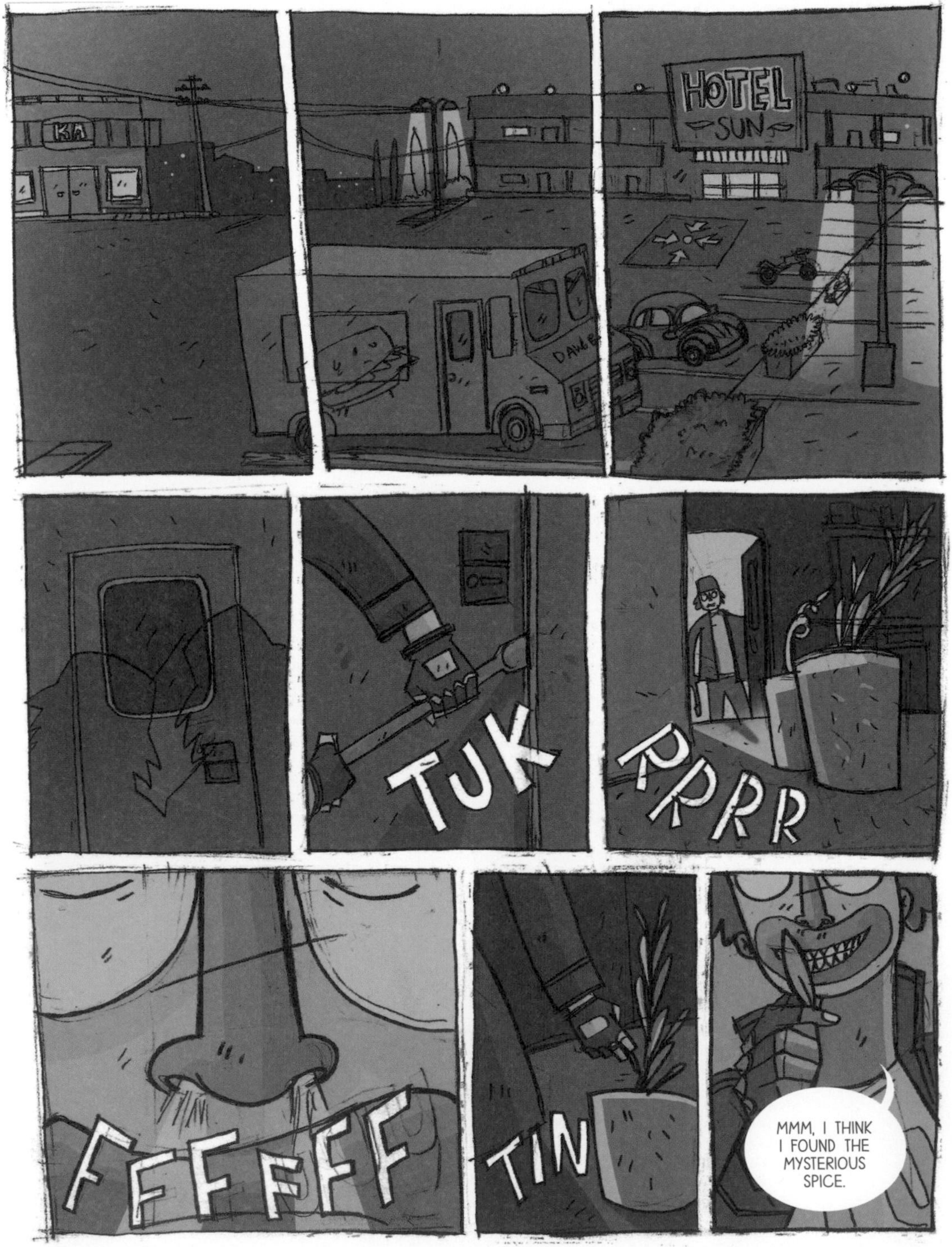
HOTEL
SUN
DAWG
TUK
PRRRR
FFFFFF
TIN
MMM, I THINK I FOUND THE MYSTERIOUS SPICE.

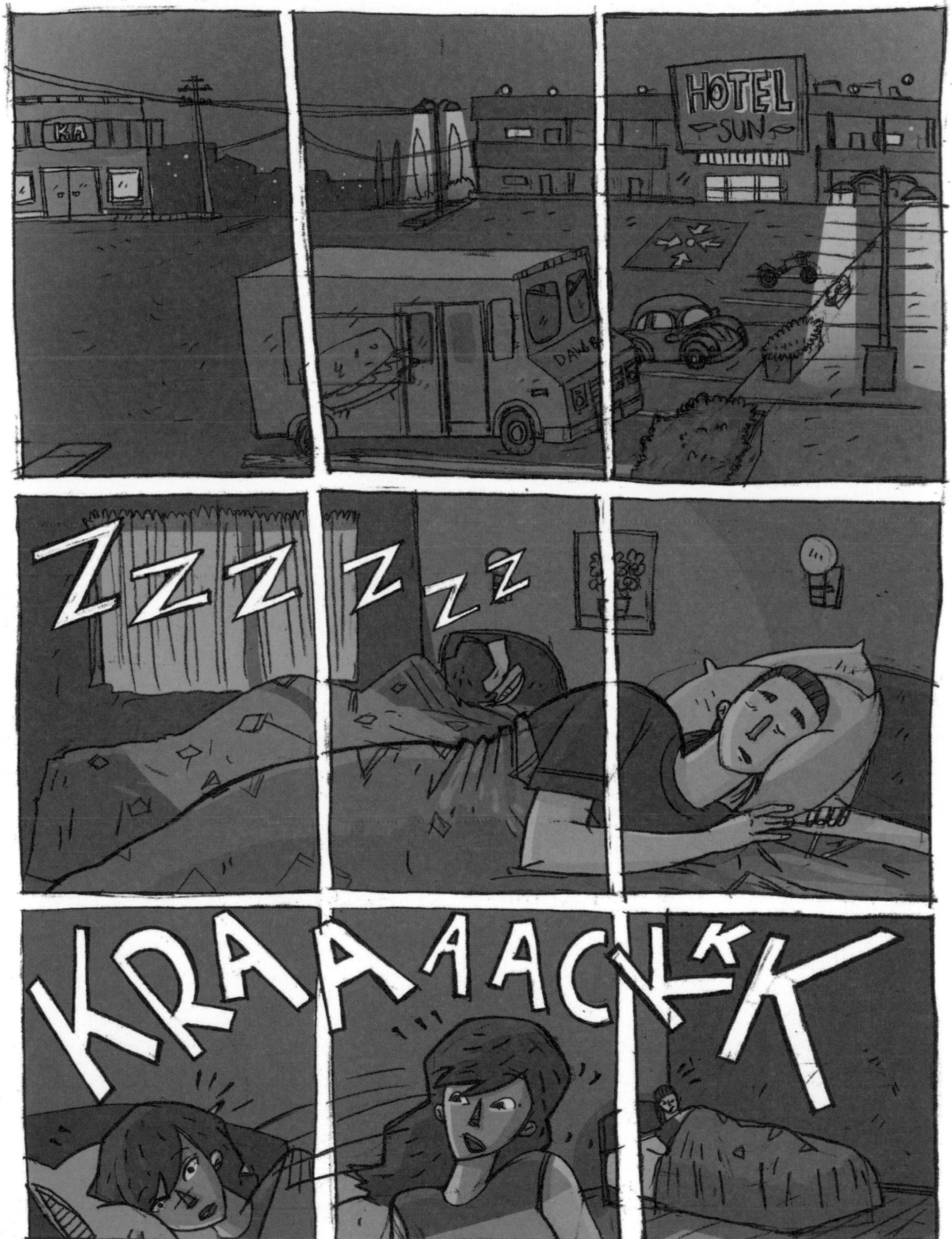
KA
HOTEL
SUN
DAWB
ZZZZZZZ
KRAAAACKKK

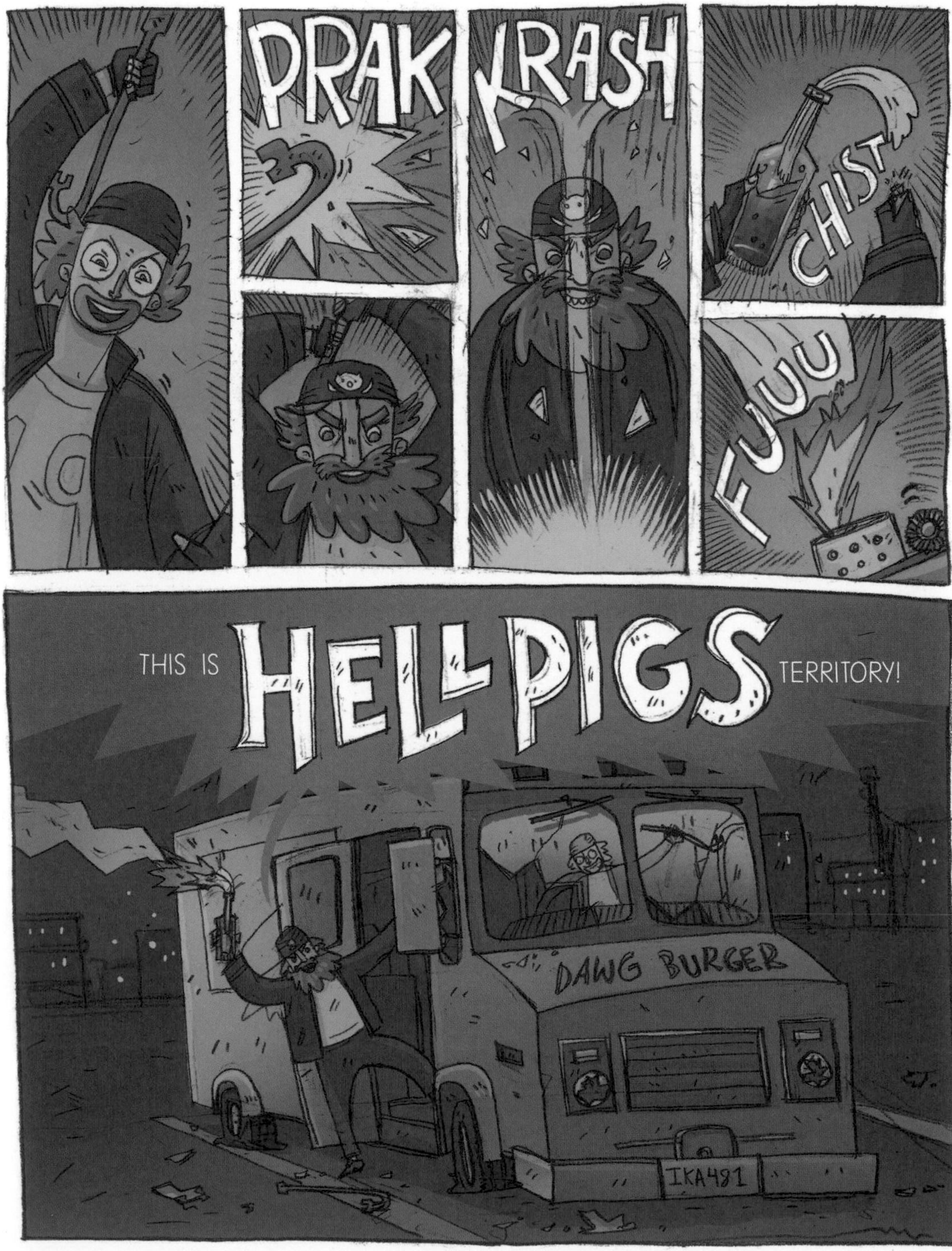
PRAK
KRASH
CHIST
FUUU
THIS IS HELLPIGS TERRITORY!
DAWG BURGER
IKA481

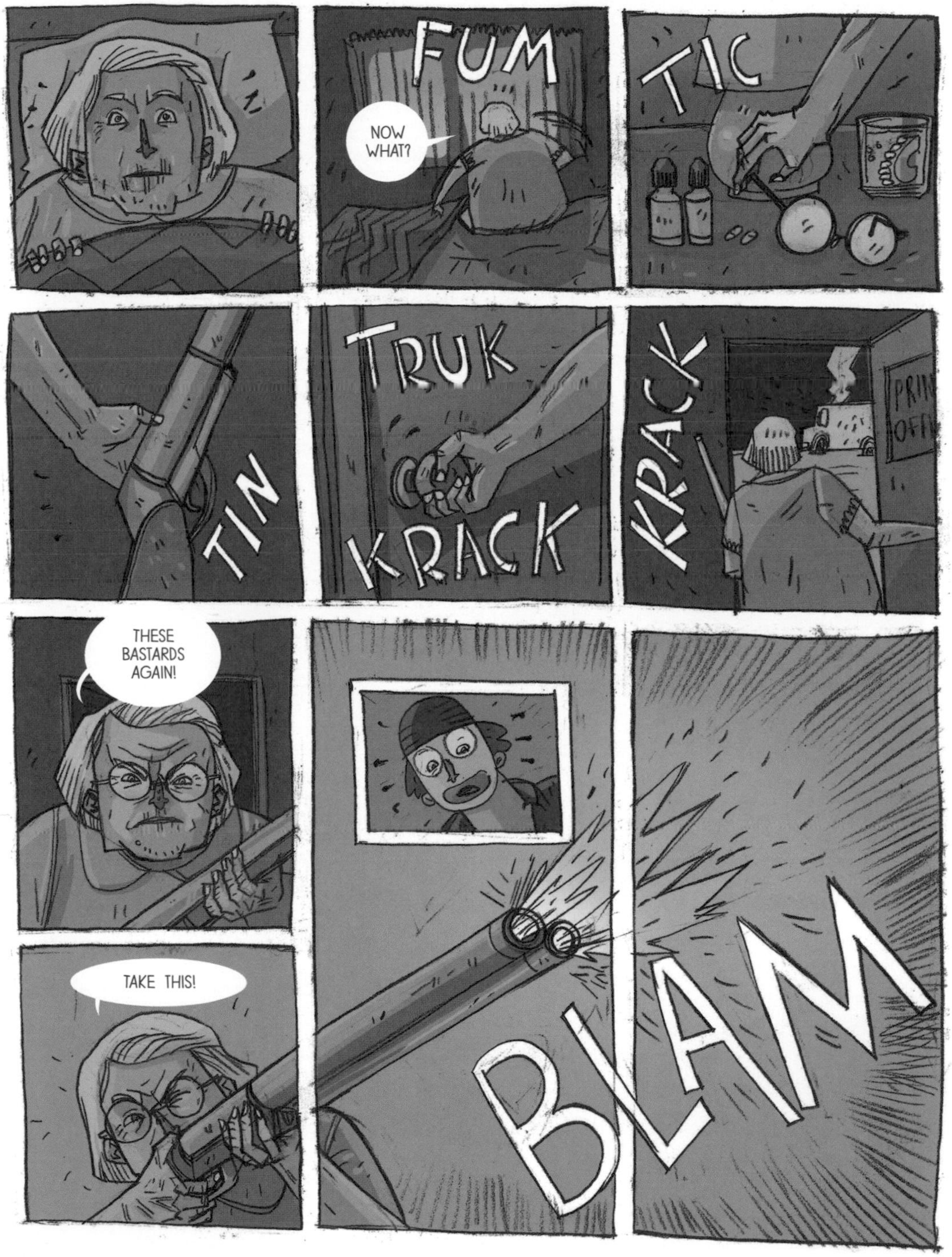
FUM
NOW WHAT?
TIC
TIN
TRUK
KRACK
KRACK
THESE BASTARDS AGAIN!
TAKE THIS!
BLAM

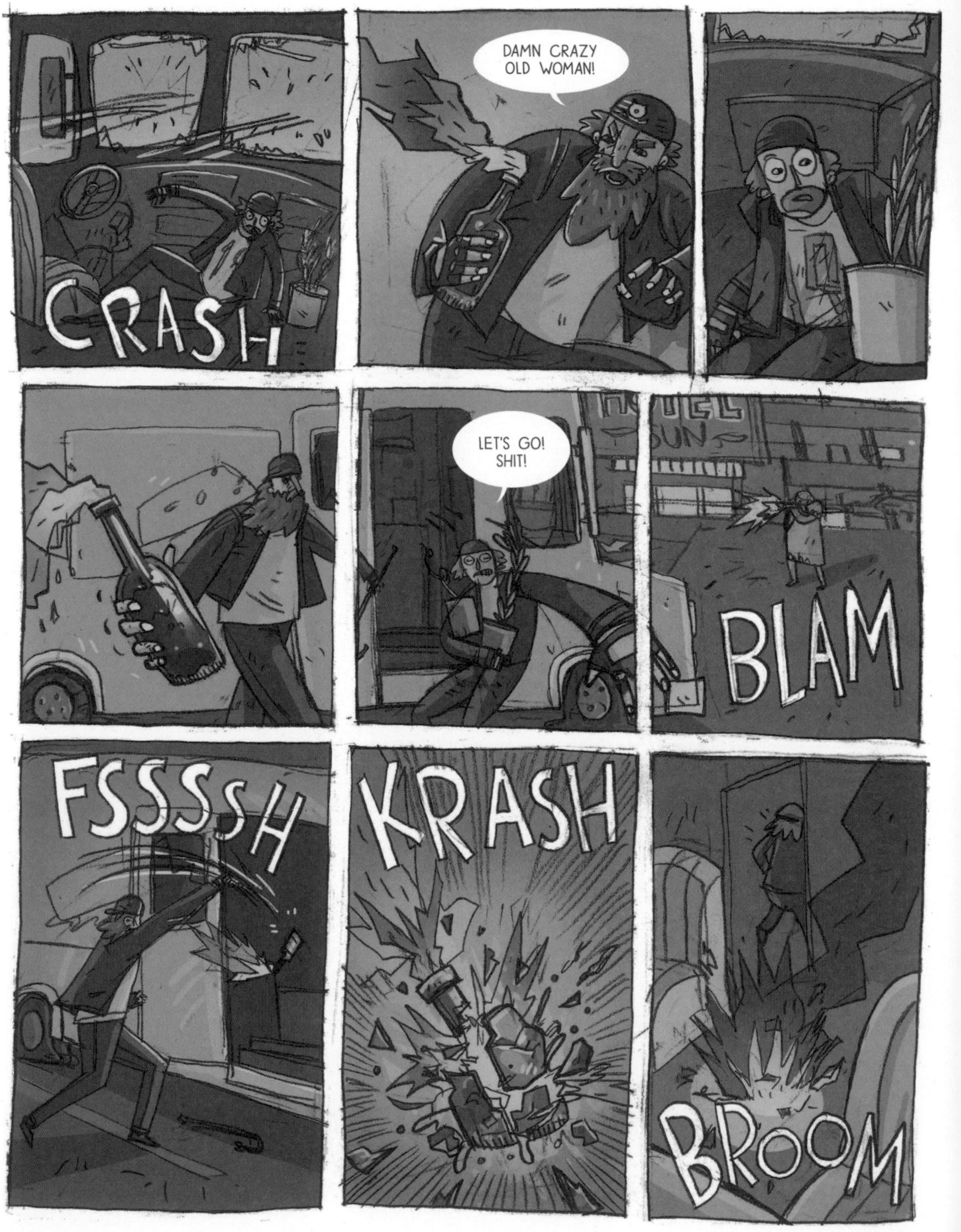
CRASH
DAMN CRAZY OLD WOMAN!
LET'S GO! SHIT!
BLAM
FSSSSH
KRASH
BROOM

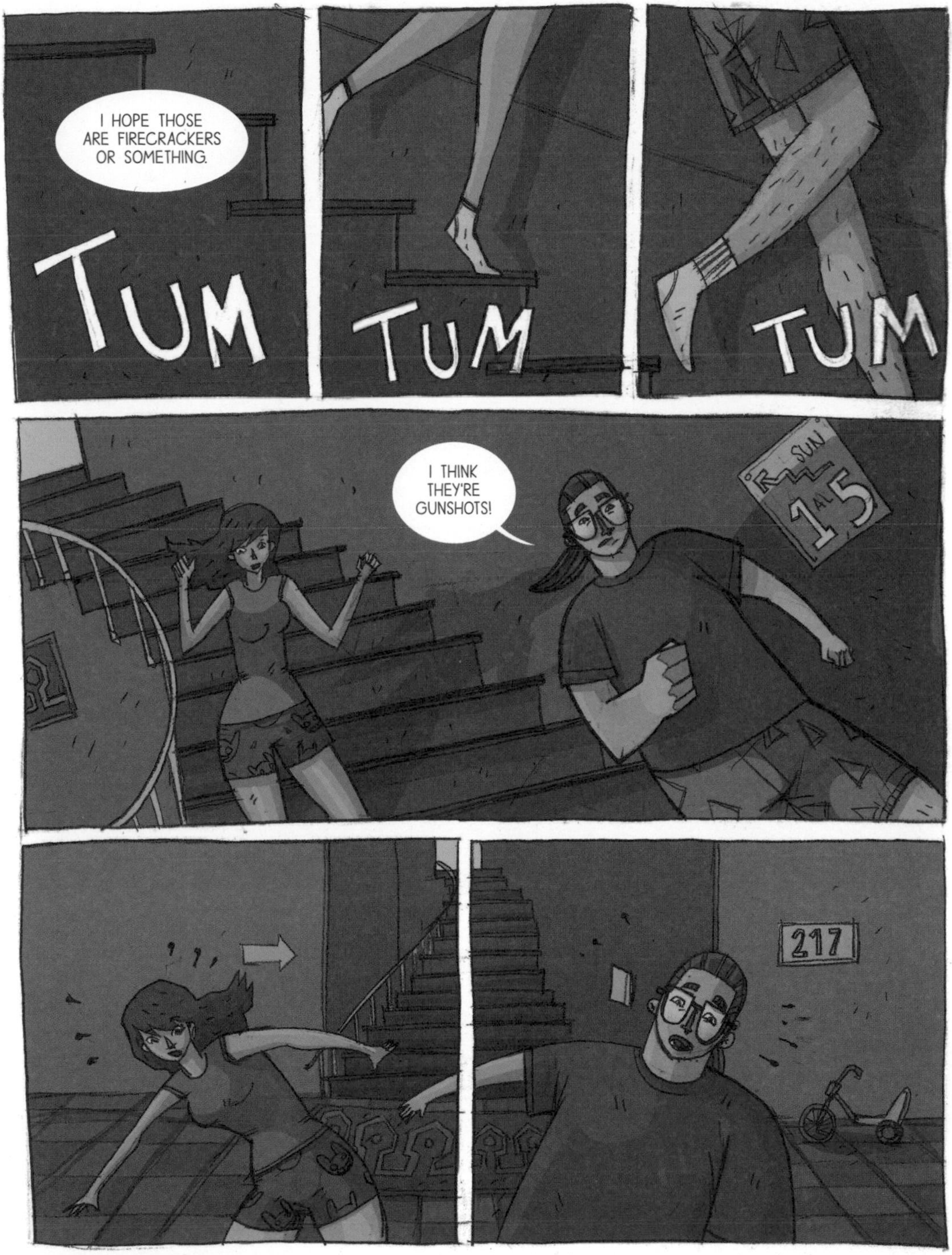
I HOPE THOSE ARE FIRECRACKERS OR SOMETHING.
TUM
TUM
TUM
SUN
1 AL 5
I THINK THEY'RE GUNSHOTS!
217

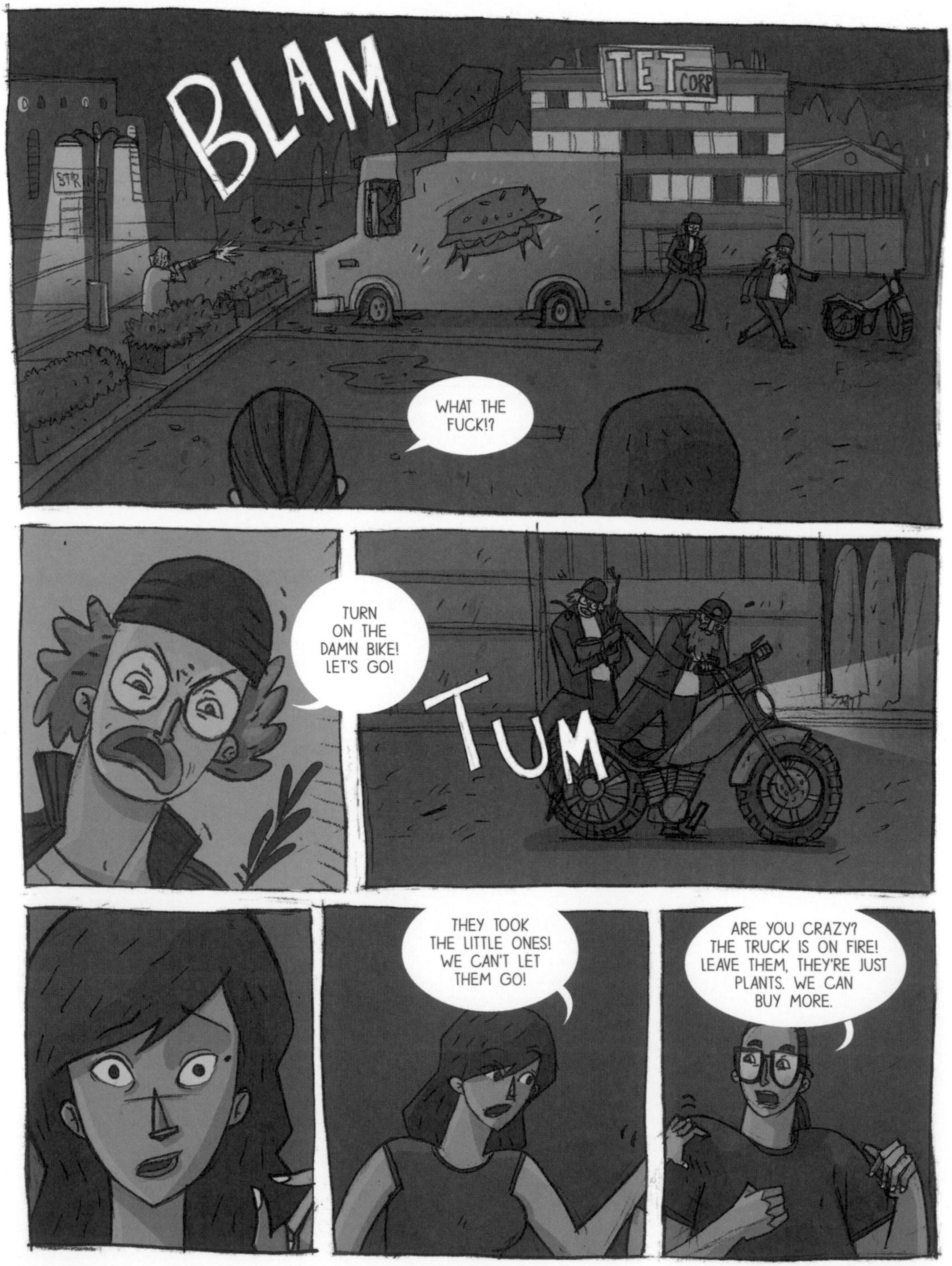
BLAM
TET CORP
WHAT THE FUCK!?
TURN ON THE DAMN BIKE! LET'S GO!
TUM
THEY TOOK THE LITTLE ONES! WE CAN'T LET THEM GO!
ARE YOU CRAZY? THE TRUCK IS ON FIRE! LEAVE THEM, THEY'RE JUST PLANTS. WE CAN BUY MORE.

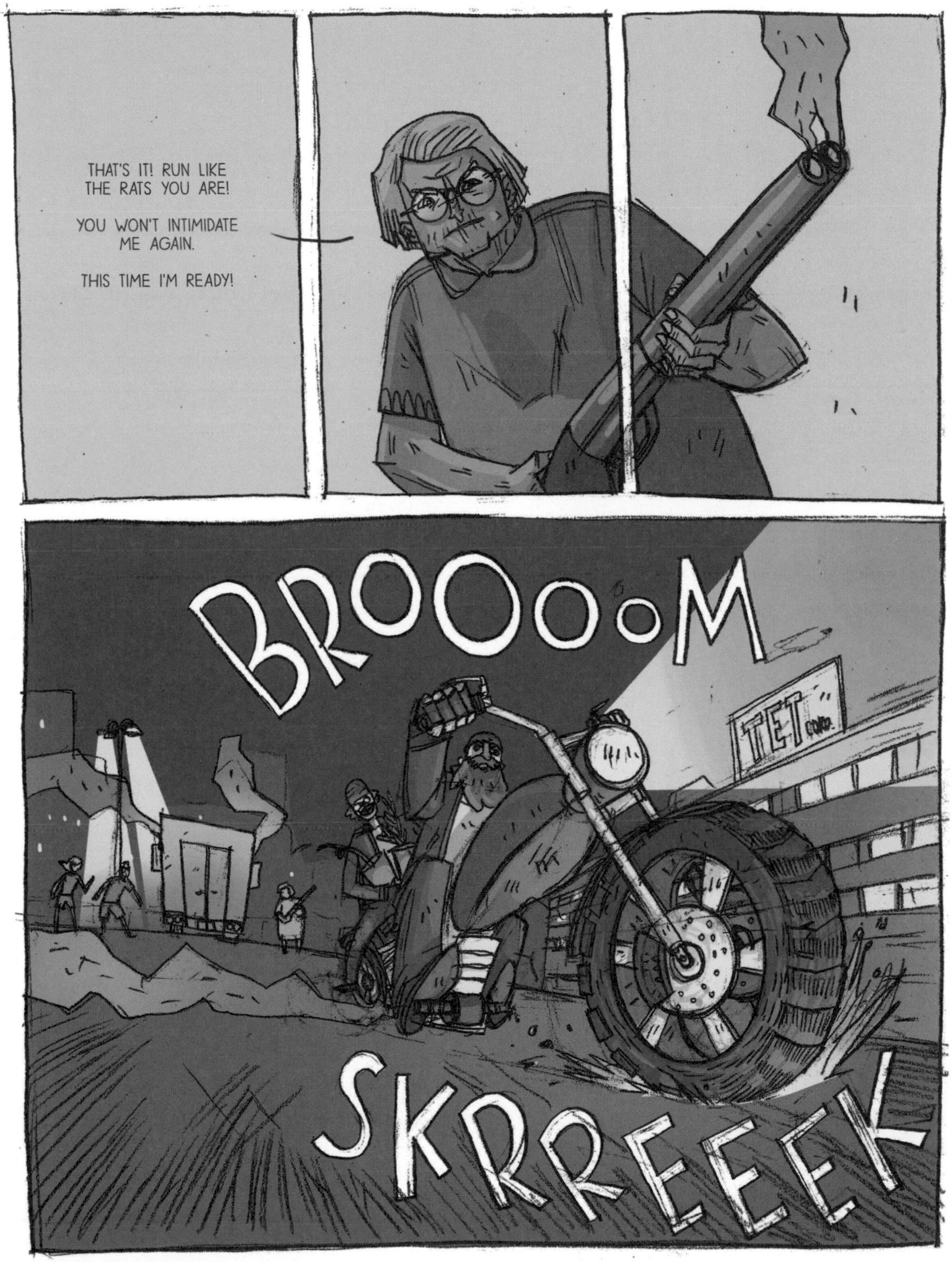
THAT'S IT! RUN LIKE THE RATS YOU ARE!
YOU WON'T INTIMIDATE ME AGAIN.
THIS TIME I'M READY!
BROOOoM
TET
SKRREEEK

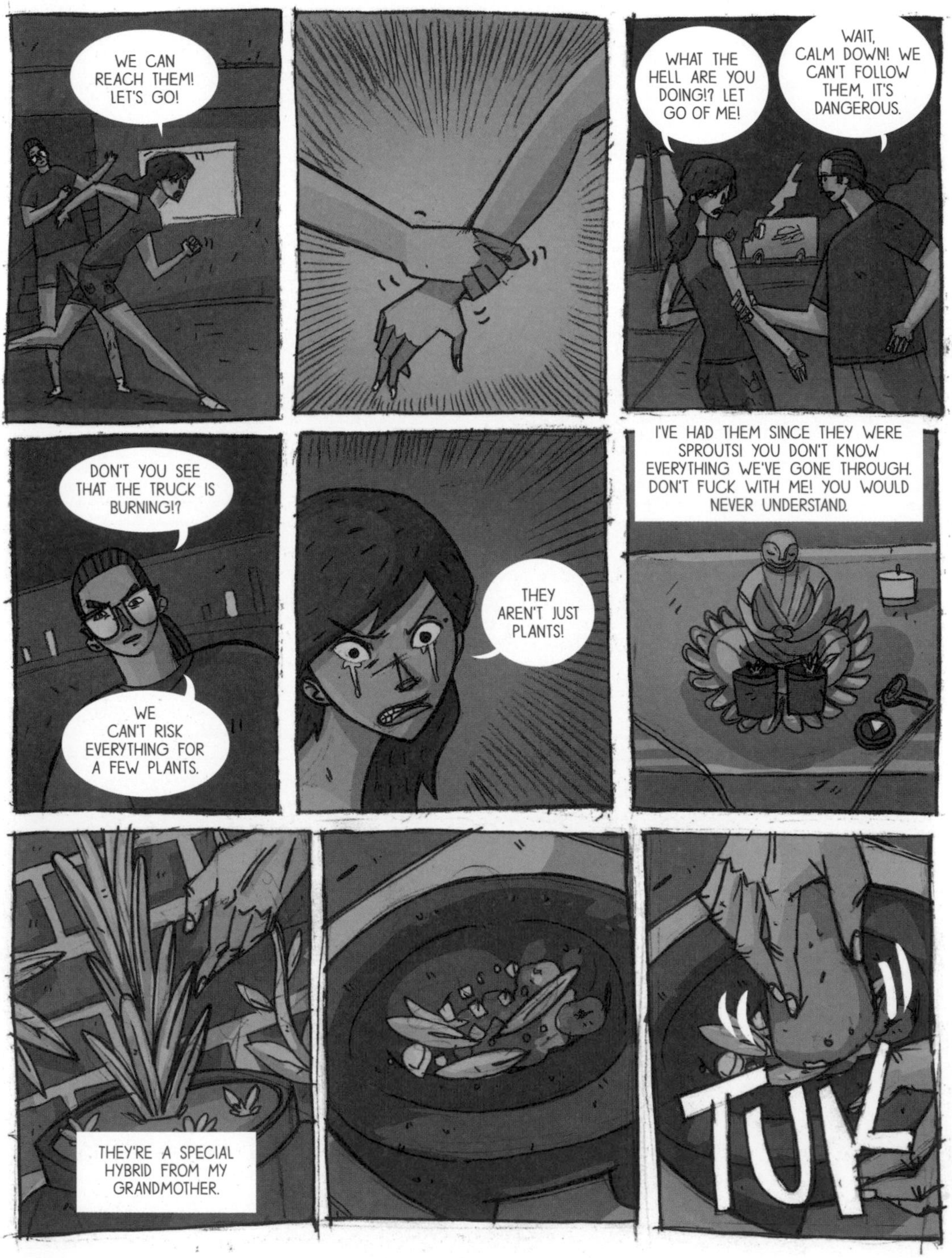
WE CAN REACH THEM! LET'S GO!
WHAT THE HELL ARE YOU DOING!? LET GO OF ME!
WAIT, CALM DOWN! WE CAN'T FOLLOW THEM, IT'S DANGEROUS.
DON'T YOU SEE THAT THE TRUCK IS BURNING!?
WE CAN'T RISK EVERYTHING FOR A FEW PLANTS.
THEY AREN'T JUST PLANTS!
I'VE HAD THEM SINCE THEY WERE SPROUTS! YOU DON'T KNOW EVERYTHING WE'VE GONE THROUGH. DON'T FUCK WITH ME! YOU WOULD NEVER UNDERSTAND.
THEY'RE A SPECIAL HYBRID FROM MY GRANDMOTHER.
TUK

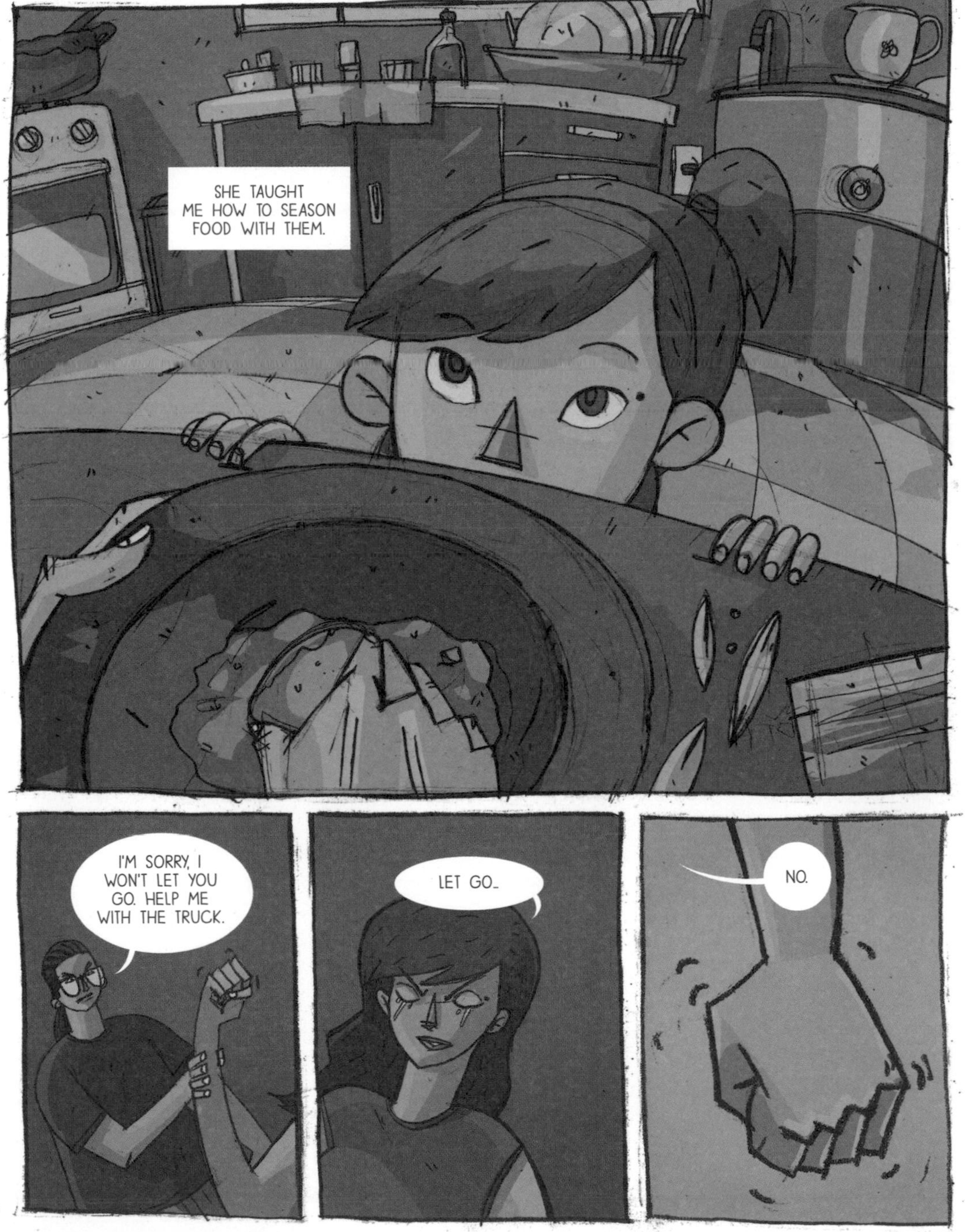
SHE TAUGHT ME HOW TO SEASON FOOD WITH THEM.
I'M SORRY, I WON'T LET YOU GO. HELP ME WITH THE TRUCK.
LET GO...
NO.

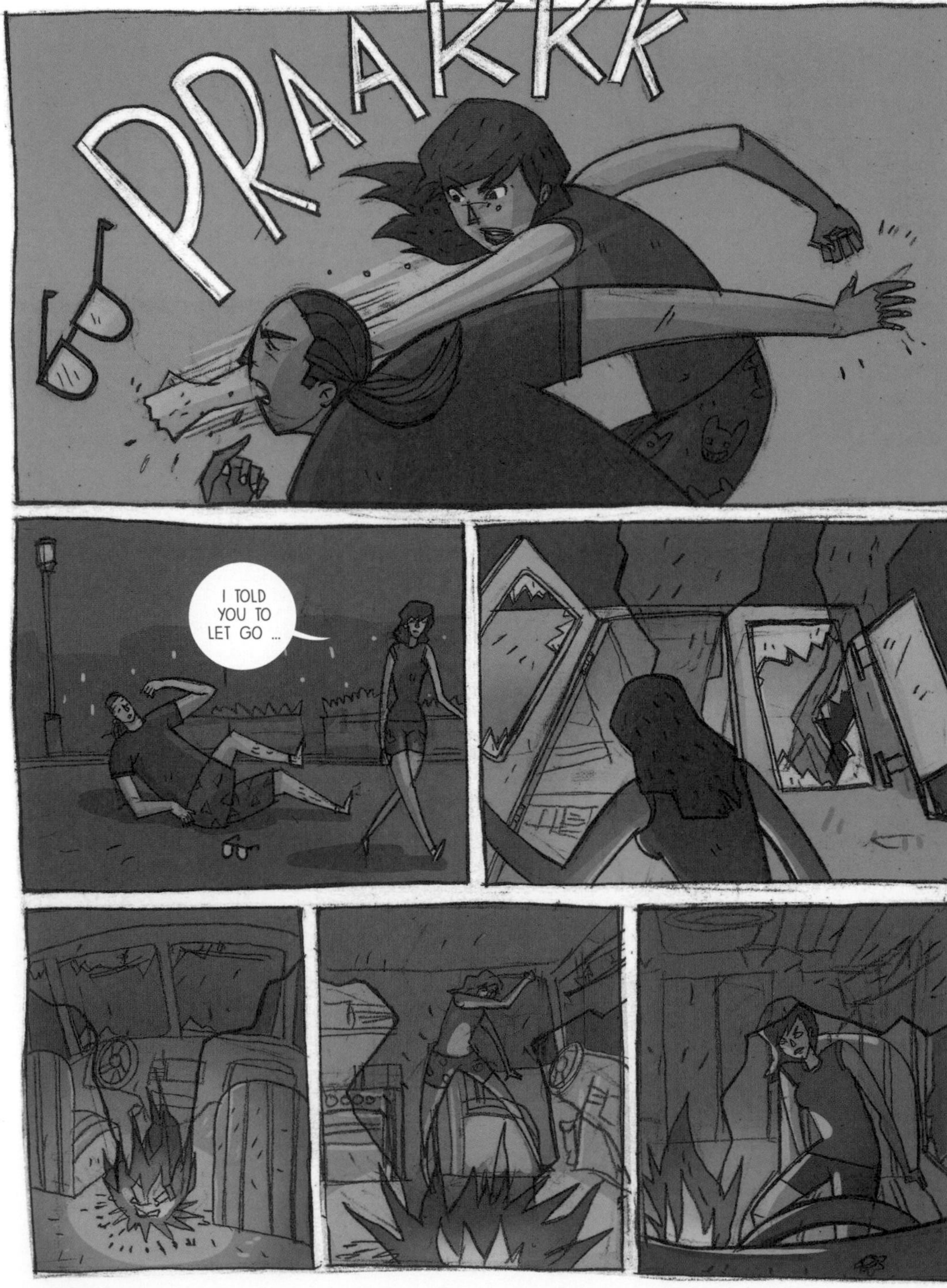
PRAAKKK
I TOLD YOU TO LET GO ...

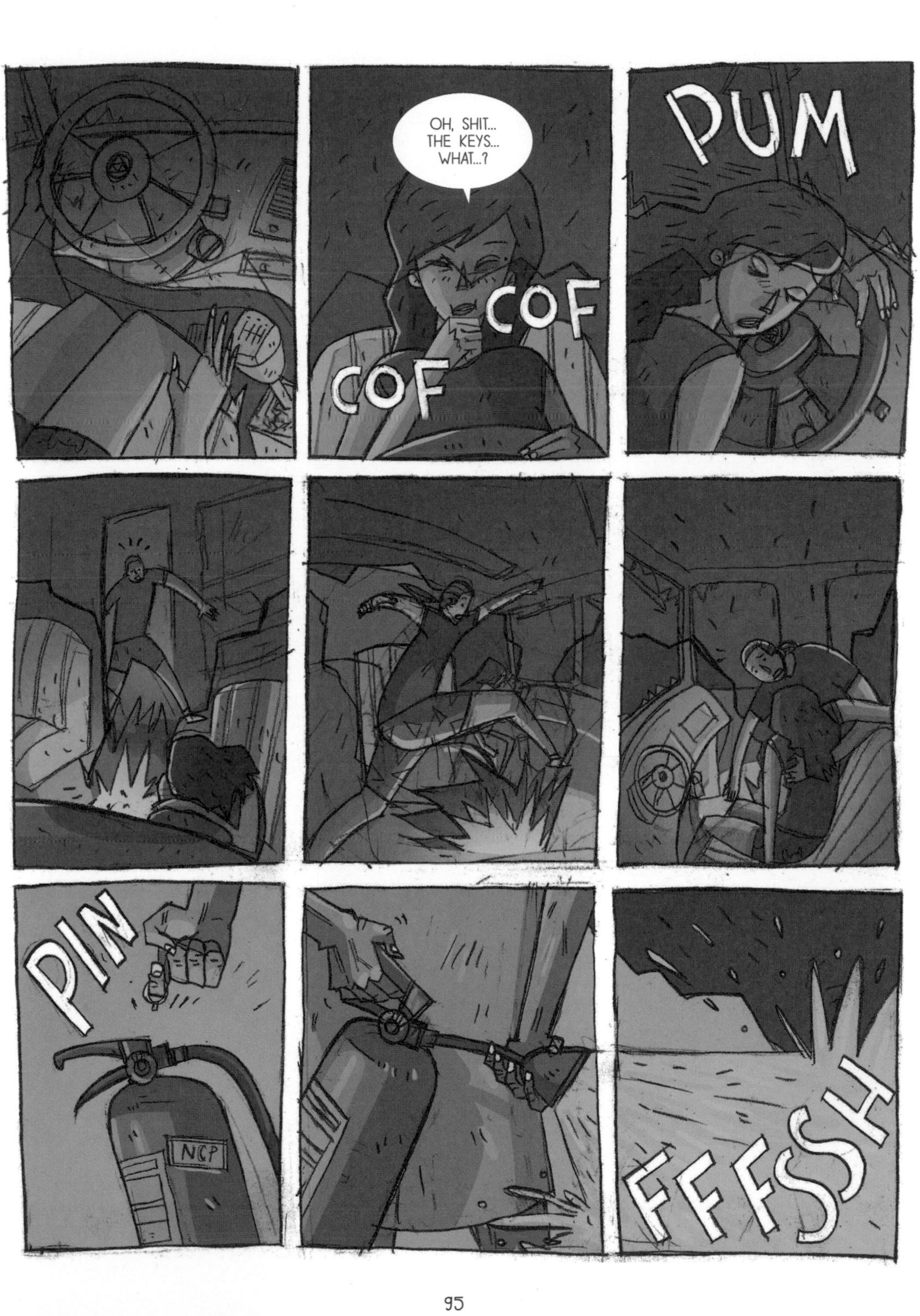
OH, SHIT...
THE KEYS...
WHAT...?
COF
COF
PUM
PIN
NCP
FFFSSH

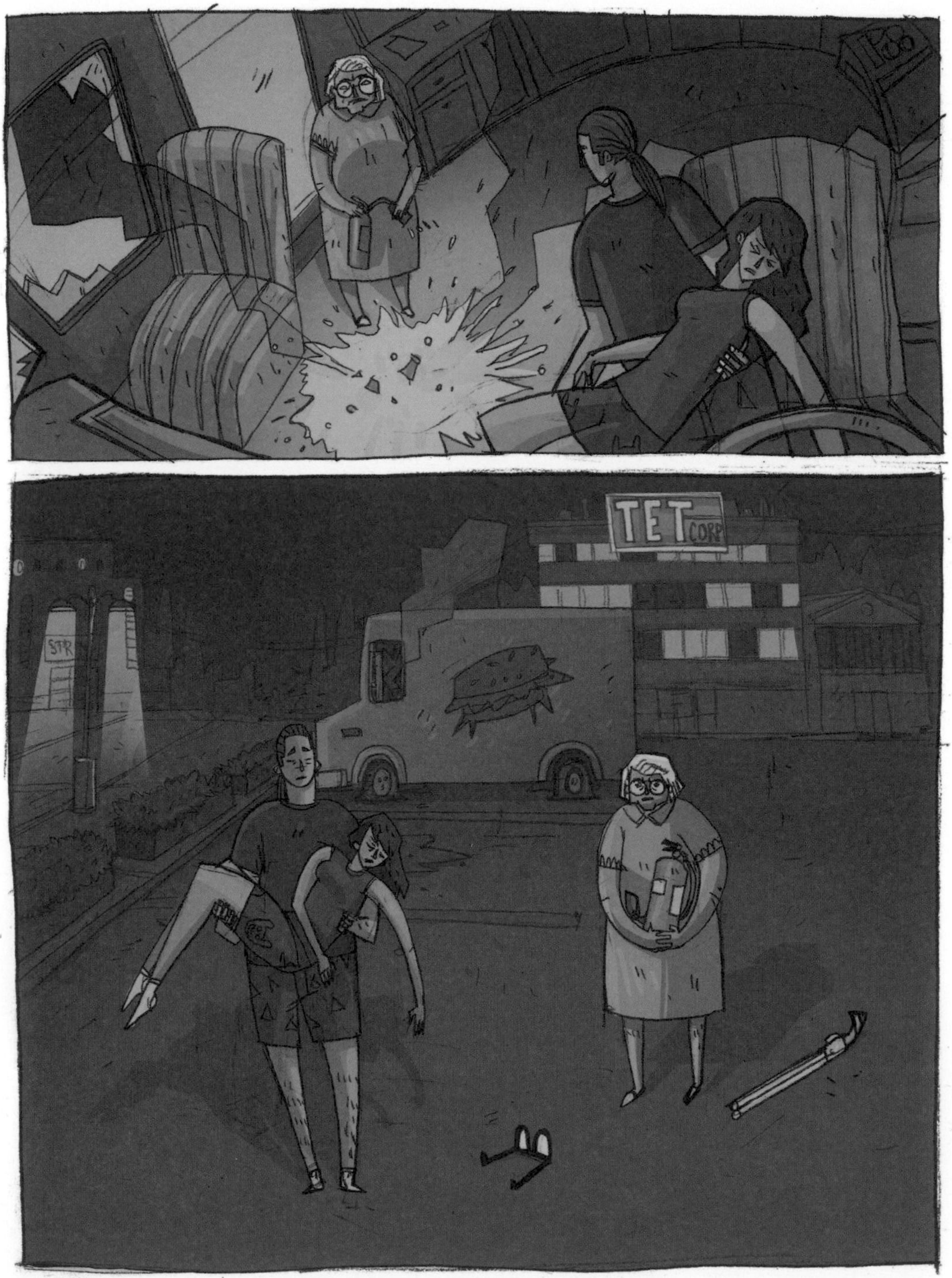
TET CORP

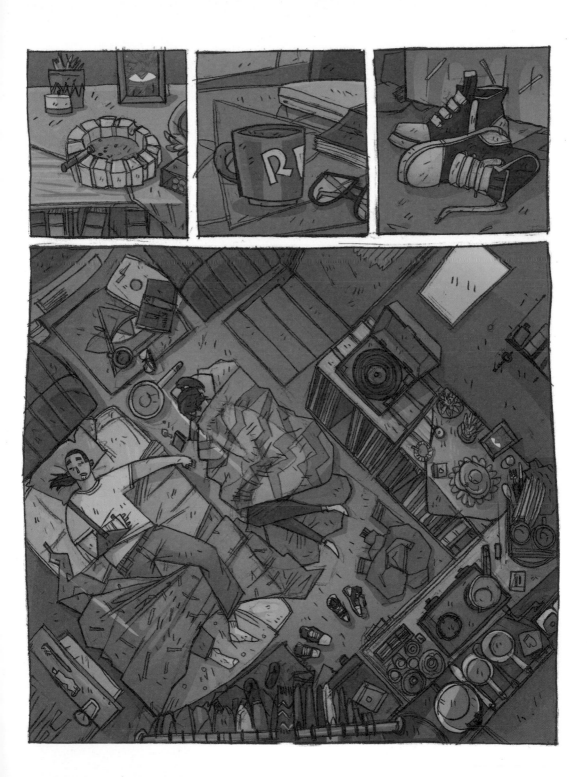

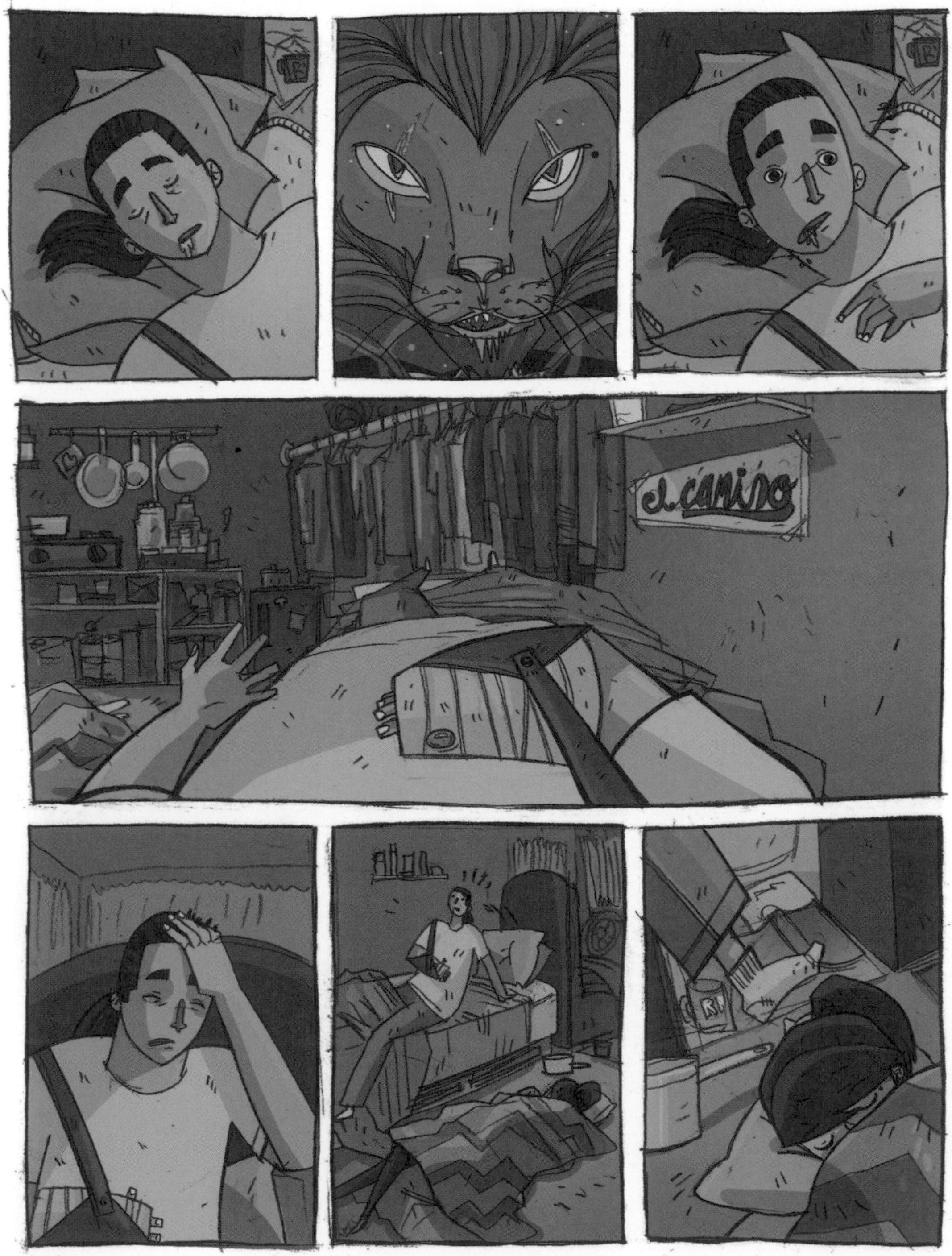
el camino

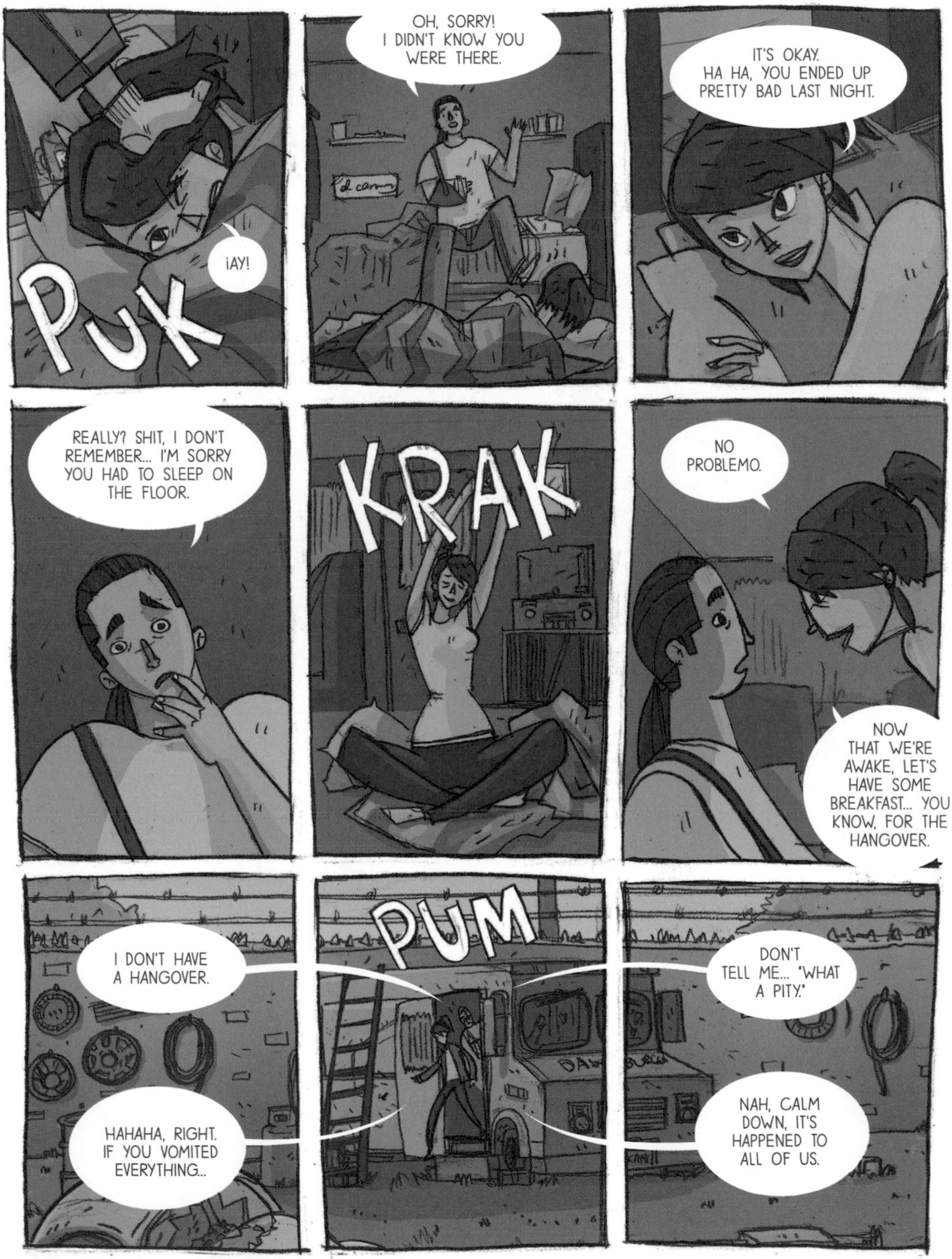
PUK
¡AY!
OH, SORRY! I DIDN'T KNOW YOU WERE THERE.
IT'S OKAY. HA HA, YOU ENDED UP PRETTY BAD LAST NIGHT.
REALLY? SHIT, I DON'T REMEMBER... I'M SORRY YOU HAD TO SLEEP ON THE FLOOR.
KRAK
NO PROBLEMO.
NOW THAT WE'RE AWAKE, LET'S HAVE SOME BREAKFAST... YOU KNOW, FOR THE HANGOVER.
PUM
I DON'T HAVE A HANGOVER.
DON'T TELL ME... "WHAT A PITY."
HAHAHA, RIGHT. IF YOU VOMITED EVERYTHING...
NAH, CALM DOWN, IT'S HAPPENED TO ALL OF US.

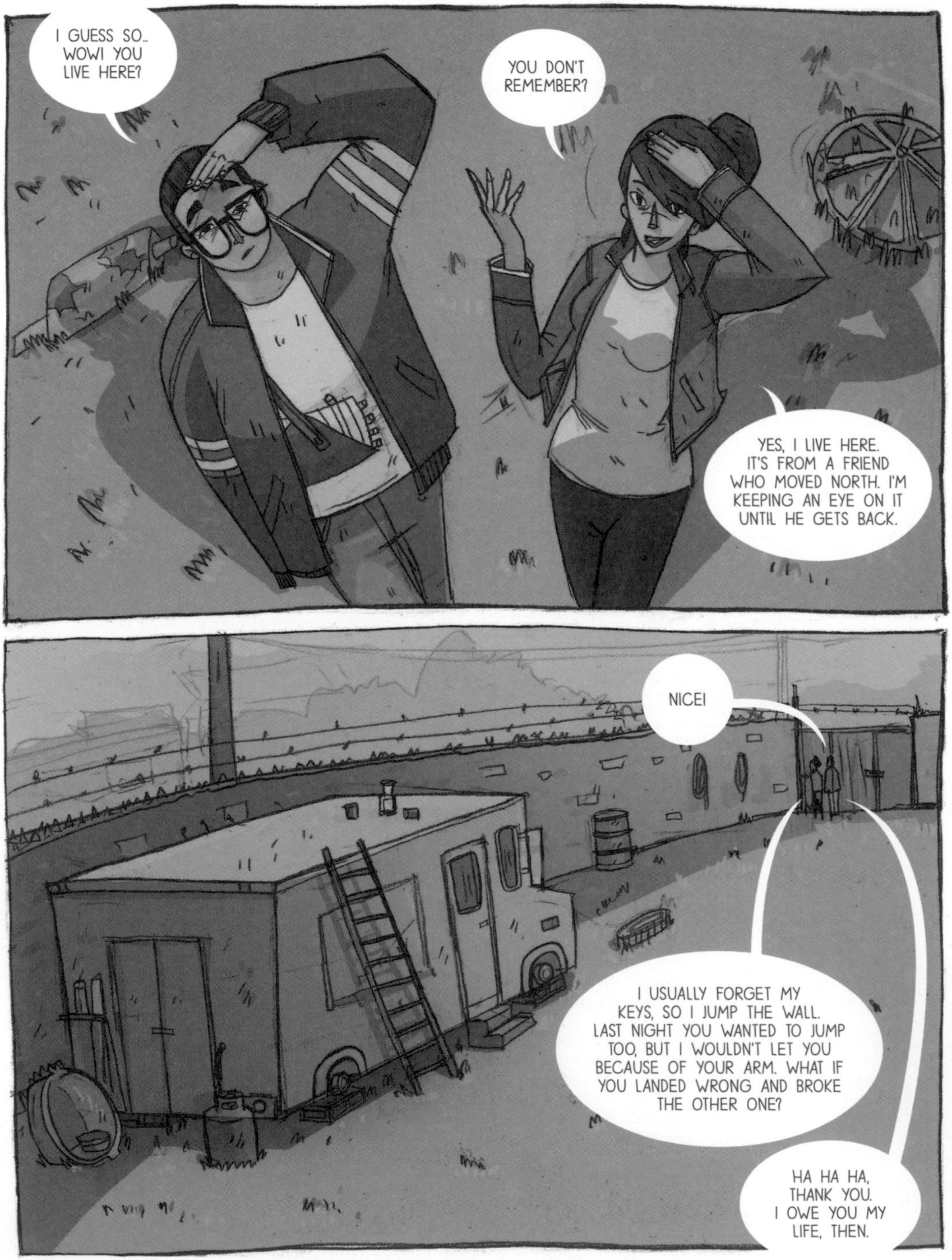
I GUESS SO... WOW! YOU LIVE HERE?
YOU DON'T REMEMBER?
YES, I LIVE HERE. IT'S FROM A FRIEND WHO MOVED NORTH. I'M KEEPING AN EYE ON IT UNTIL HE GETS BACK.
NICE!
I USUALLY FORGET MY KEYS, SO I JUMP THE WALL. LAST NIGHT YOU WANTED TO JUMP TOO, BUT I WOULDN'T LET YOU BECAUSE OF YOUR ARM. WHAT IF YOU LANDED WRONG AND BROKE THE OTHER ONE?
HA HA HA, THANK YOU. I OWE YOU MY LIFE, THEN.

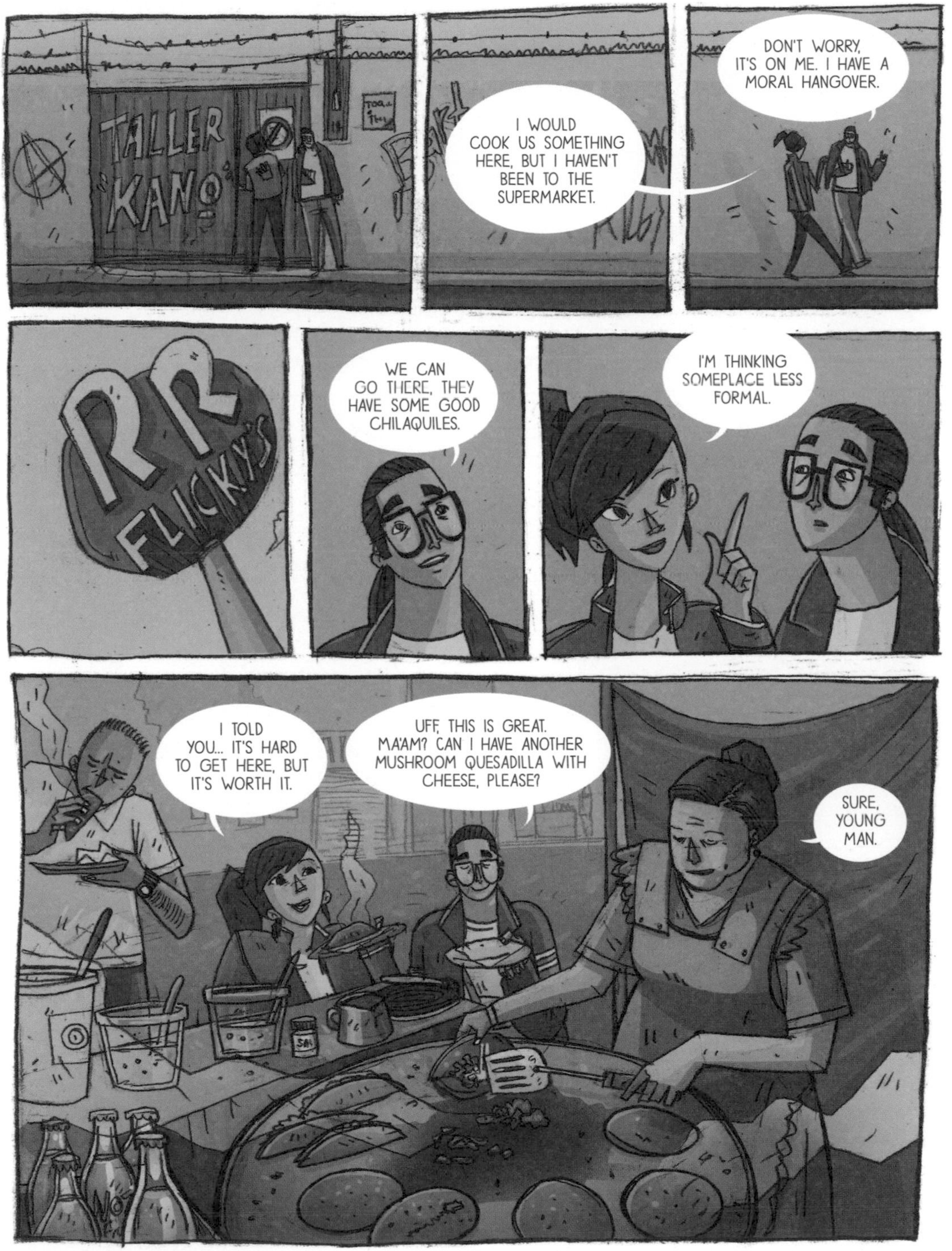
TALLER KANO
I WOULD COOK US SOMETHING HERE, BUT I HAVEN'T BEEN TO THE SUPERMARKET.
DON'T WORRY, IT'S ON ME. I HAVE A MORAL HANGOVER.
FLICKY'S
WE CAN GO THERE, THEY HAVE SOME GOOD CHILAQUILES.
I'M THINKING SOMEPLACE LESS FORMAL.
I TOLD YOU... IT'S HARD TO GET HERE, BUT IT'S WORTH IT.
UFF, THIS IS GREAT. MA'AM? CAN I HAVE ANOTHER MUSHROOM QUESADILLA WITH CHEESE, PLEASE?
SURE, YOUNG MAN.

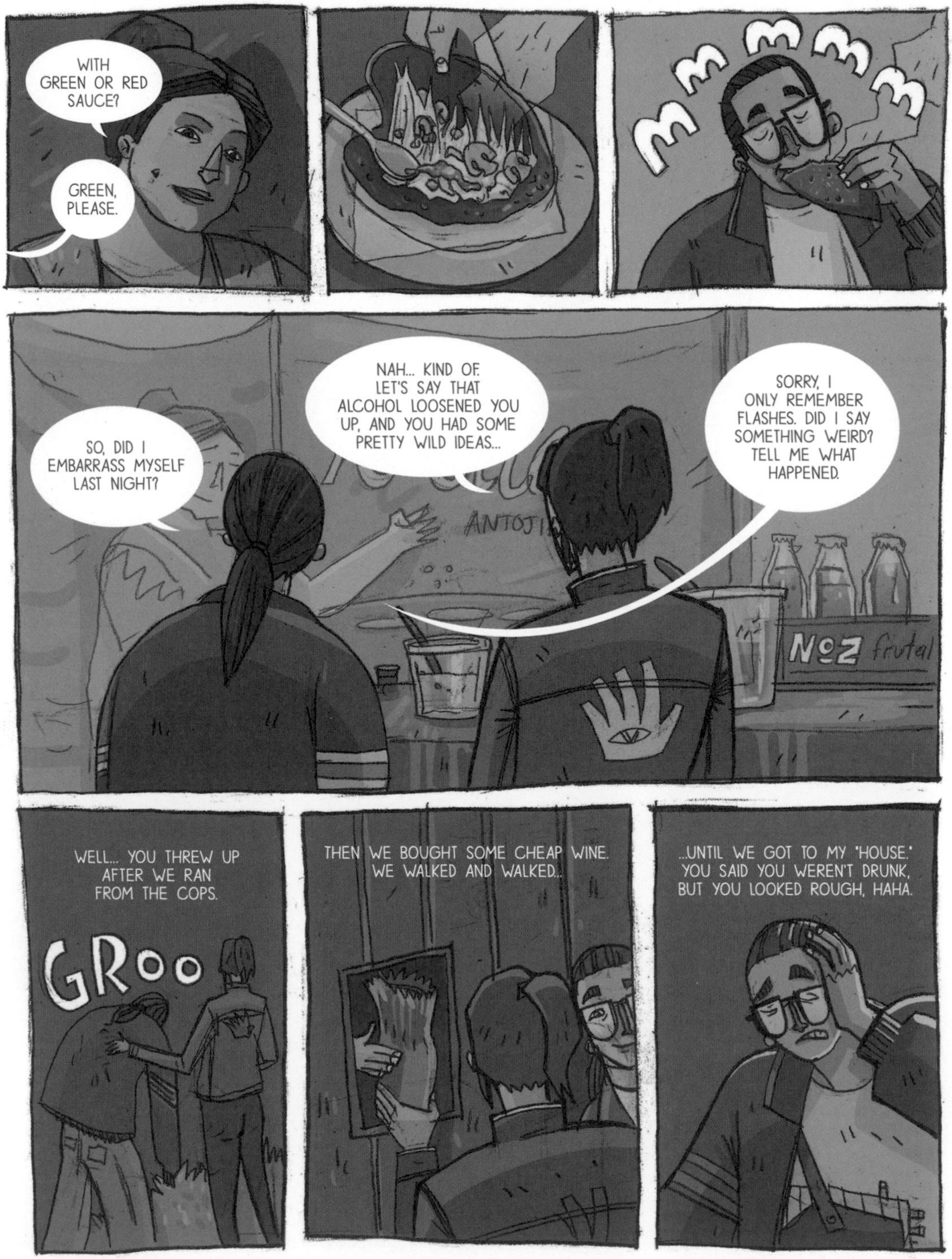
WITH GREEN OR RED SAUCE?
GREEN, PLEASE.
MMMMMM
SO, DID I EMBARRASS MYSELF LAST NIGHT?
NAH... KIND OF. LET'S SAY THAT ALCOHOL LOOSENED YOU UP, AND YOU HAD SOME PRETTY WILD IDEAS...
SORRY, I ONLY REMEMBER FLASHES. DID I SAY SOMETHING WEIRD? TELL ME WHAT HAPPENED.
ANTOJI
No2 frutal
WELL... YOU THREW UP AFTER WE RAN FROM THE COPS.
GROO
THEN WE BOUGHT SOME CHEAP WINE. WE WALKED AND WALKED...
...UNTIL WE GOT TO MY "HOUSE." YOU SAID YOU WEREN'T DRUNK, BUT YOU LOOKED ROUGH, HAHA.

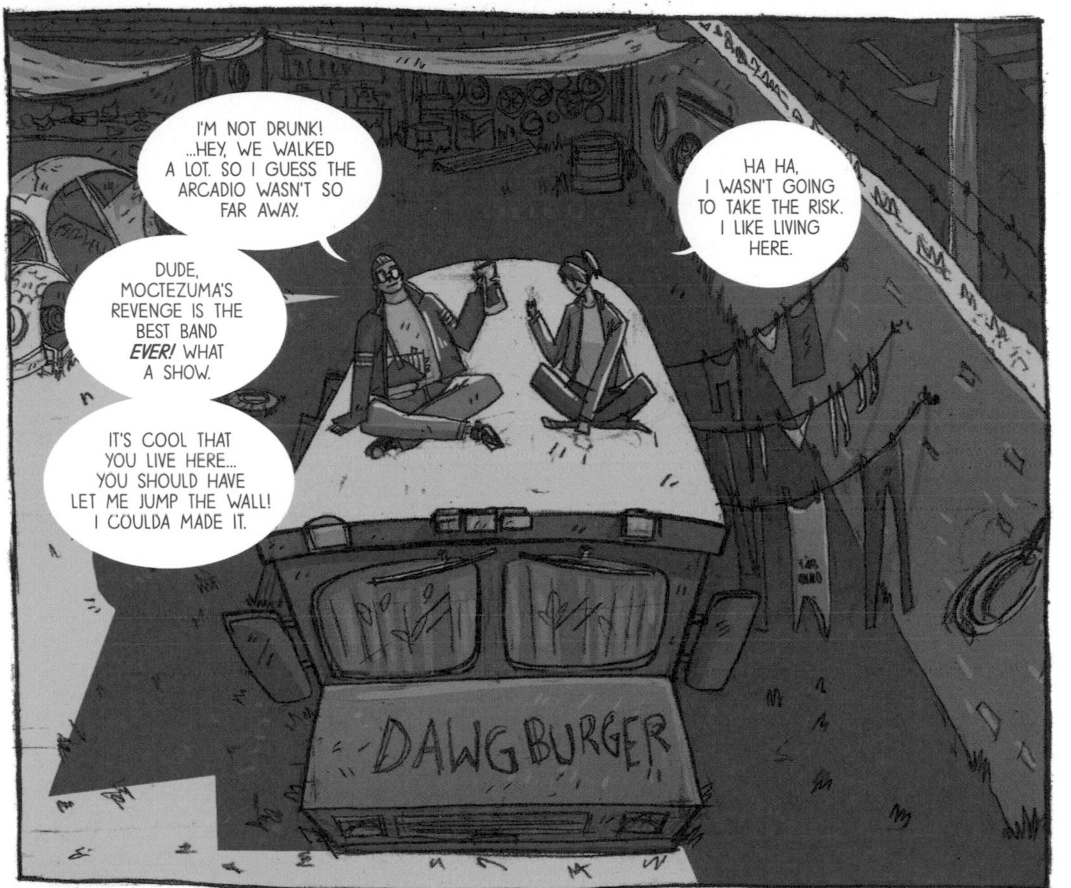
I'M NOT DRUNK! ...HEY, WE WALKED A LOT. SO I GUESS THE ARCADIO WASN'T SO FAR AWAY.
HA HA, I WASN'T GOING TO TAKE THE RISK. I LIKE LIVING HERE.
DUDE, MOCTEZUMA'S REVENGE IS THE BEST BAND *EVER!* WHAT A SHOW.
IT'S COOL THAT YOU LIVE HERE... YOU SHOULD HAVE LET ME JUMP THE WALL! I COULDA MADE IT.
DAWGBURGER

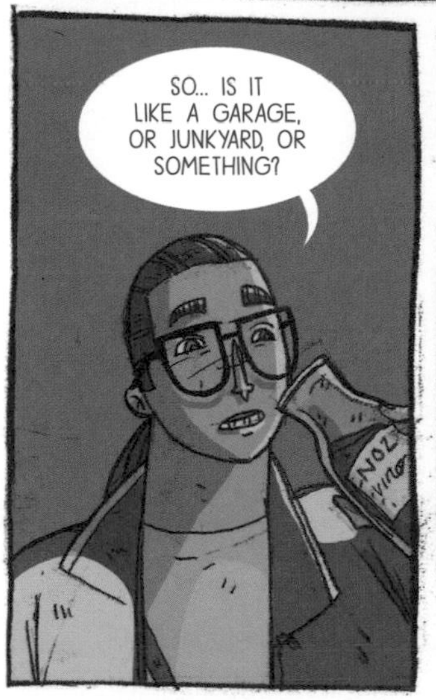
SO... IS IT LIKE A GARAGE, OR JUNKYARD, OR SOMETHING?

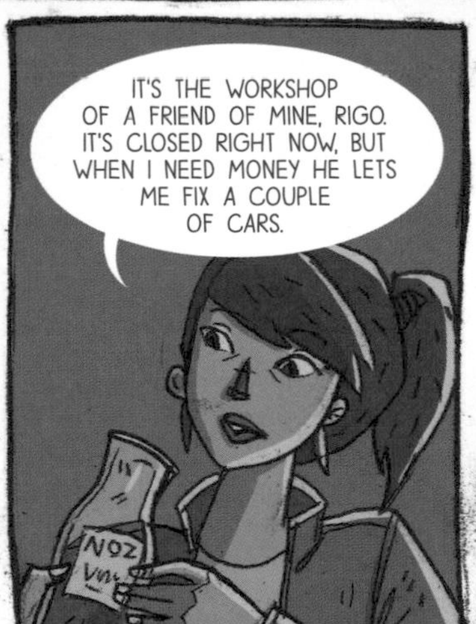
IT'S THE WORKSHOP OF A FRIEND OF MINE, RIGO. IT'S CLOSED RIGHT NOW, BUT WHEN I NEED MONEY HE LETS ME FIX A COUPLE OF CARS.

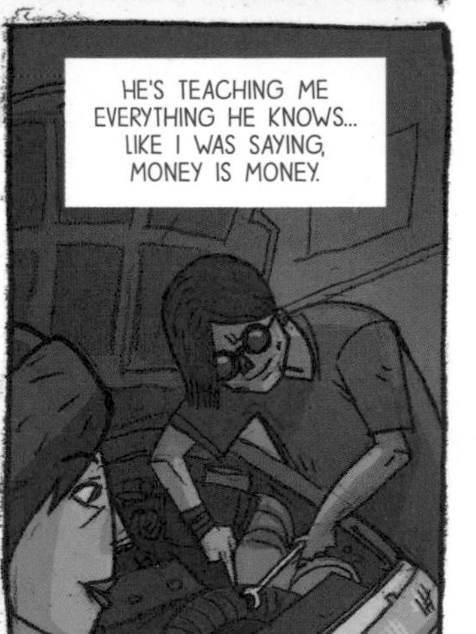
HE'S TEACHING ME EVERYTHING HE KNOWS... LIKE I WAS SAYING, MONEY IS MONEY.

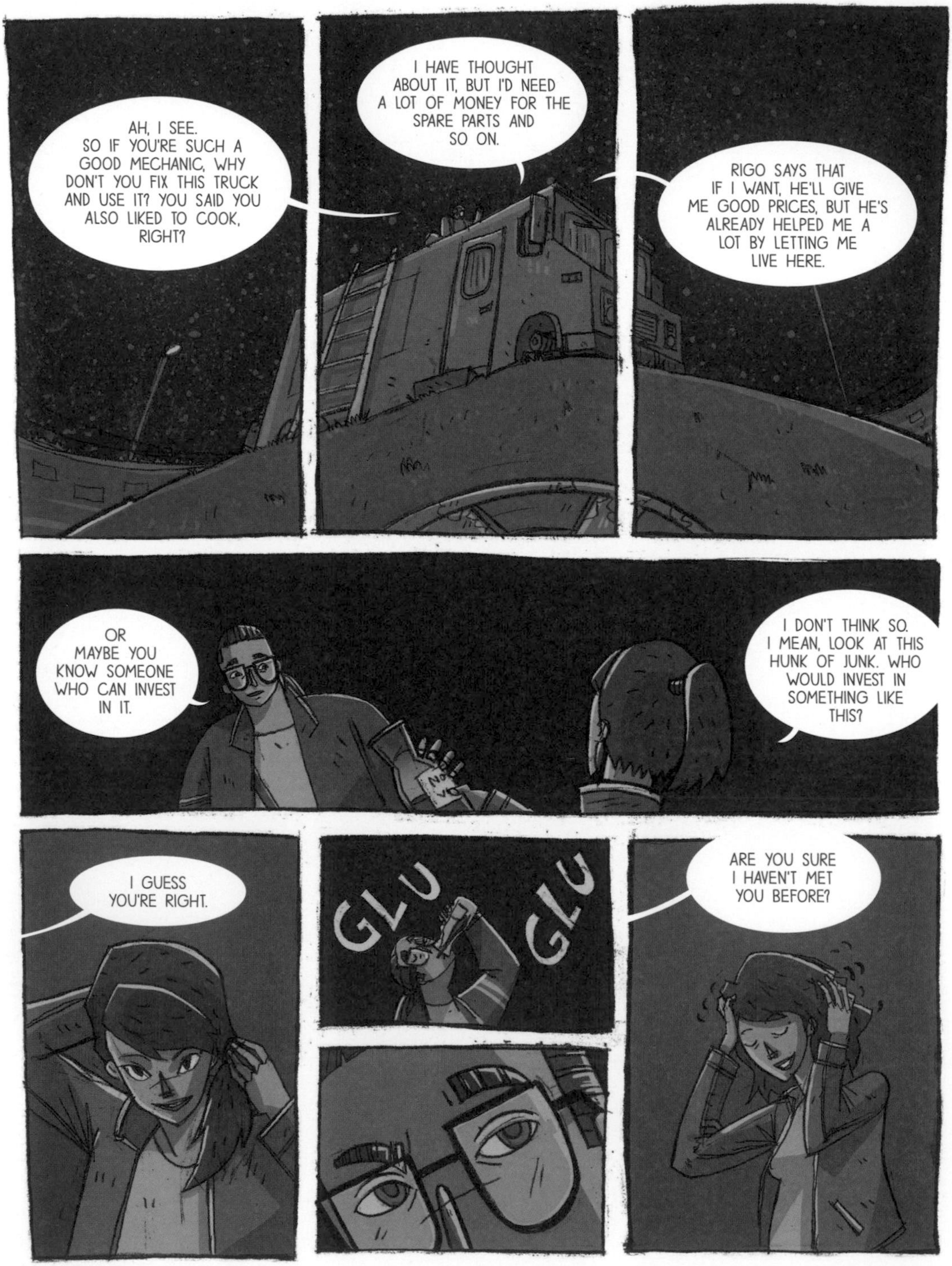
AH, I SEE. SO IF YOU'RE SUCH A GOOD MECHANIC, WHY DON'T YOU FIX THIS TRUCK AND USE IT? YOU SAID YOU ALSO LIKED TO COOK, RIGHT?
I HAVE THOUGHT ABOUT IT, BUT I'D NEED A LOT OF MONEY FOR THE SPARE PARTS AND SO ON.
RIGO SAYS THAT IF I WANT, HE'LL GIVE ME GOOD PRICES, BUT HE'S ALREADY HELPED ME A LOT BY LETTING ME LIVE HERE.
OR MAYBE YOU KNOW SOMEONE WHO CAN INVEST IN IT.
I DON'T THINK SO. I MEAN, LOOK AT THIS HUNK OF JUNK. WHO WOULD INVEST IN SOMETHING LIKE THIS?
I GUESS YOU'RE RIGHT.
GLU
GLU
ARE YOU SURE I HAVEN'T MET YOU BEFORE?

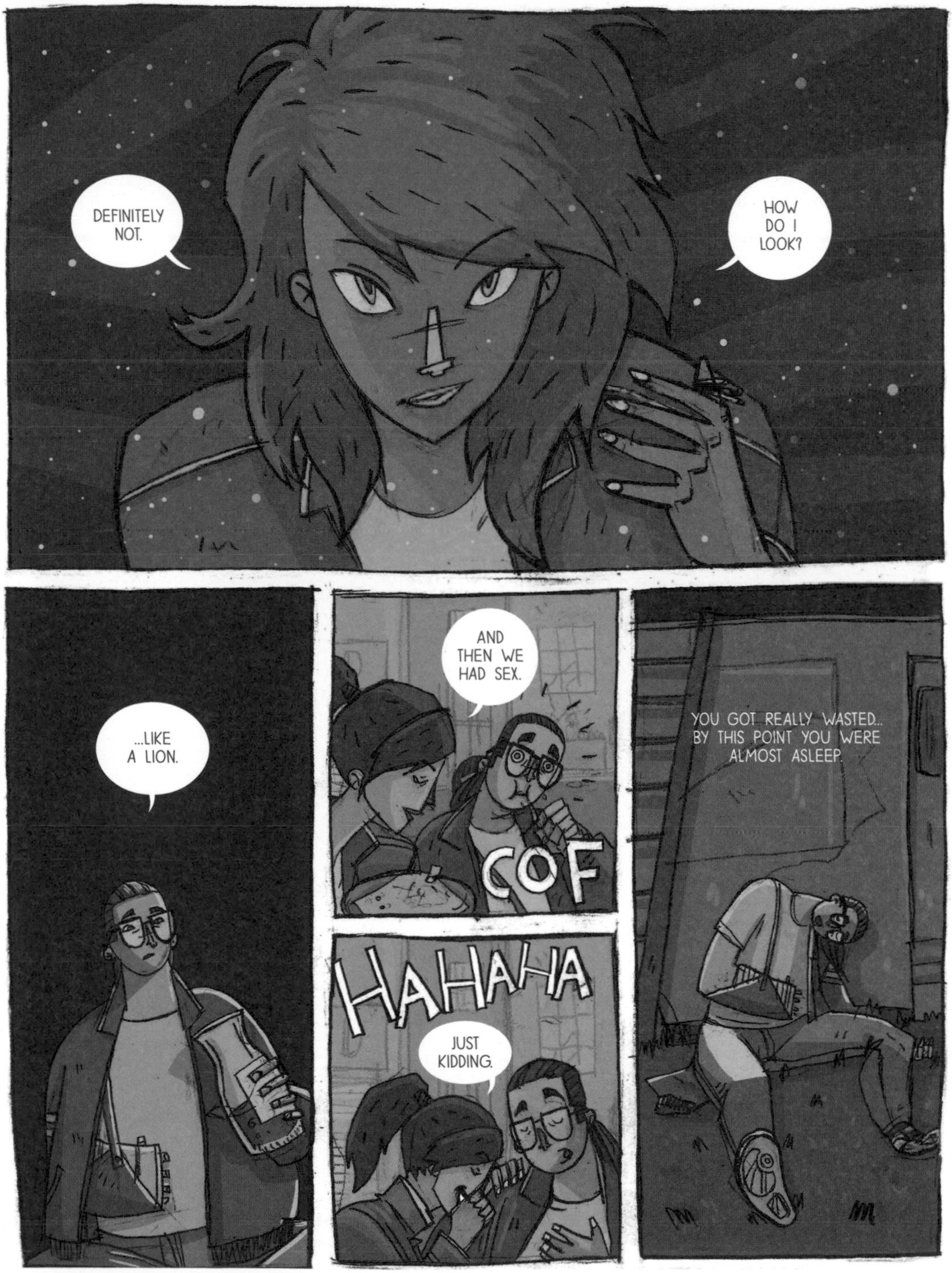

DEFINITELY NOT.
HOW DO I LOOK?
...LIKE A LION.
AND THEN WE HAD SEX.
COF
HAHAHA
JUST KIDDING.
YOU GOT REALLY WASTED... BY THIS POINT YOU WERE ALMOST ASLEEP.

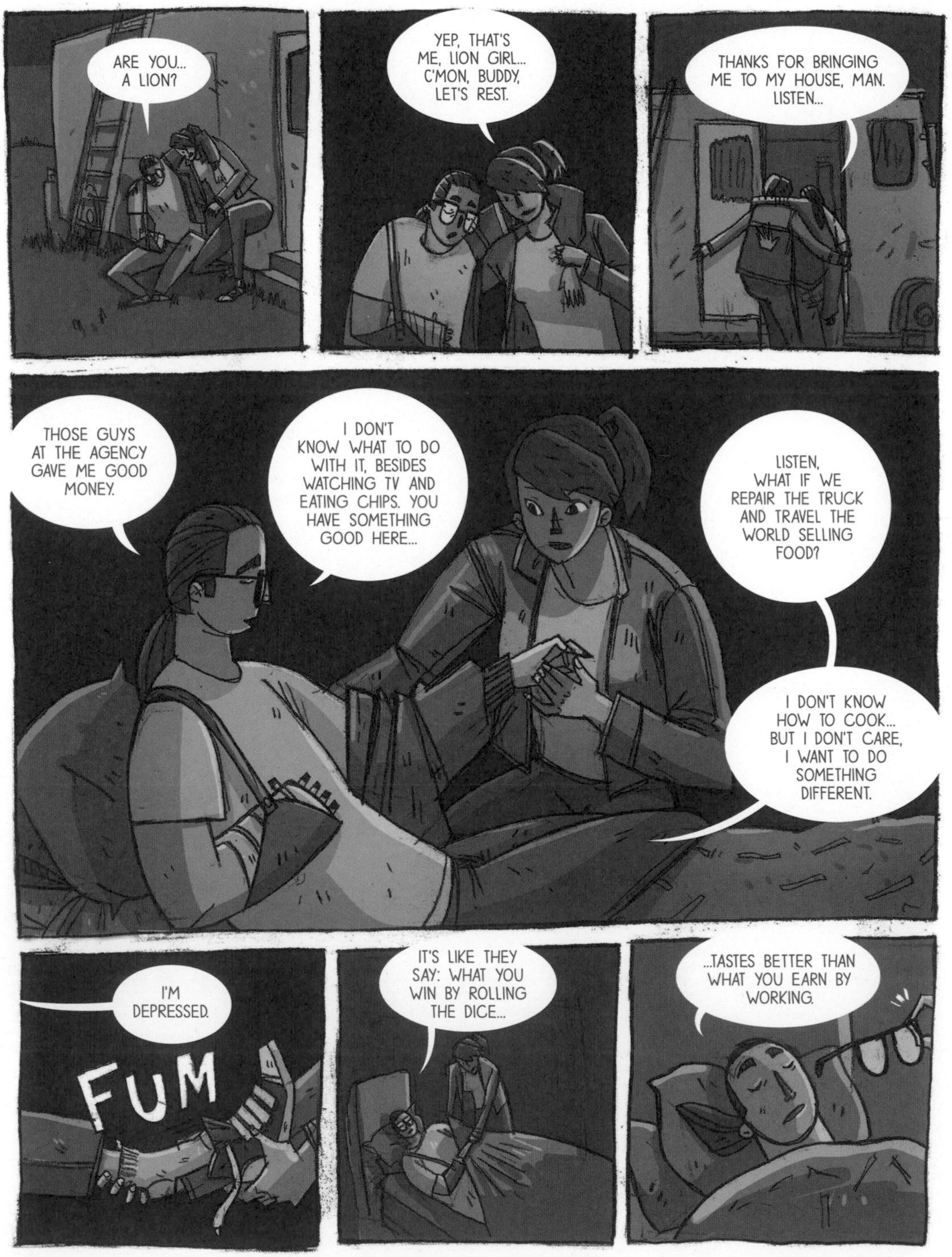
ARE YOU... A LION?
YEP, THAT'S ME, LION GIRL... C'MON, BUDDY, LET'S REST.
THANKS FOR BRINGING ME TO MY HOUSE, MAN. LISTEN...
THOSE GUYS AT THE AGENCY GAVE ME GOOD MONEY.
I DON'T KNOW WHAT TO DO WITH IT, BESIDES WATCHING TV AND EATING CHIPS. YOU HAVE SOMETHING GOOD HERE...
LISTEN, WHAT IF WE REPAIR THE TRUCK AND TRAVEL THE WORLD SELLING FOOD?
I DON'T KNOW HOW TO COOK... BUT I DON'T CARE, I WANT TO DO SOMETHING DIFFERENT.
I'M DEPRESSED.
FUM
IT'S LIKE THEY SAY: WHAT YOU WIN BY ROLLING THE DICE...
...TASTES BETTER THAN WHAT YOU EARN BY WORKING.

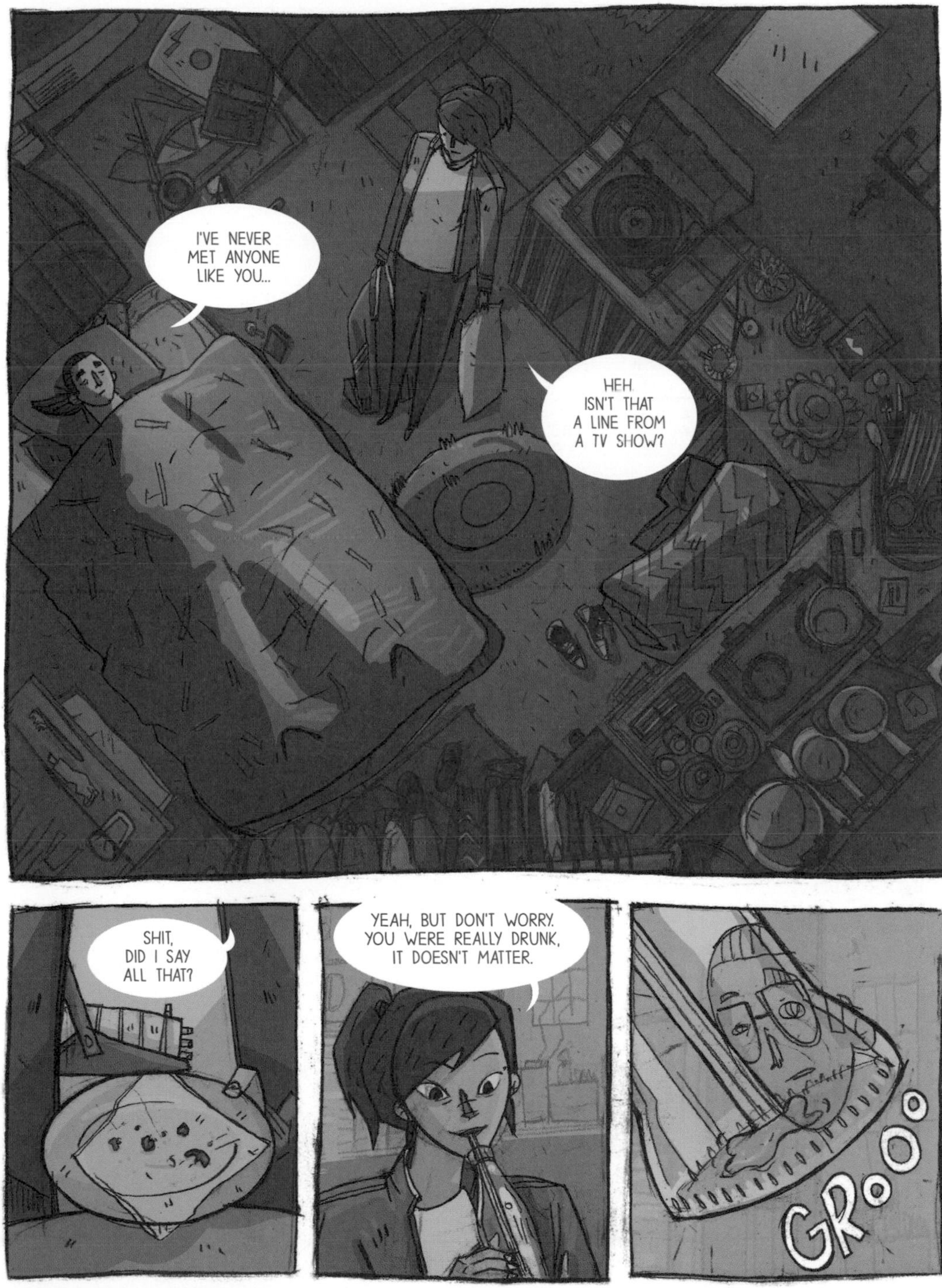
I'VE NEVER MET ANYONE LIKE YOU...
HEH. ISN'T THAT A LINE FROM A TV SHOW?
SHIT, DID I SAY ALL THAT?
YEAH, BUT DON'T WORRY. YOU WERE REALLY DRUNK, IT DOESN'T MATTER.
GROOO

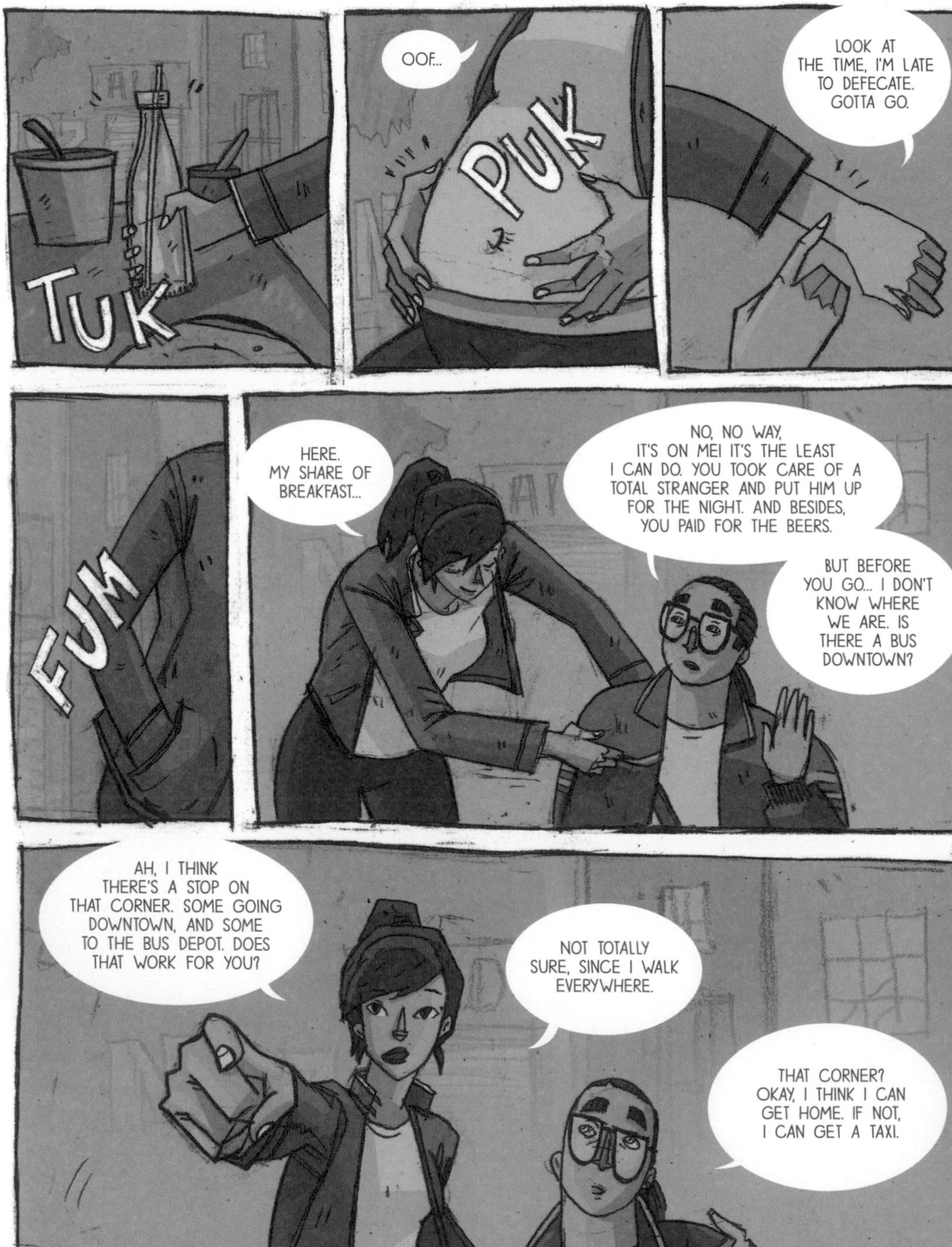
TUK
OOF...
PUK
LOOK AT THE TIME, I'M LATE TO DEFECATE. GOTTA GO.
FUM
HERE. MY SHARE OF BREAKFAST...
NO, NO WAY, IT'S ON ME! IT'S THE LEAST I CAN DO. YOU TOOK CARE OF A TOTAL STRANGER AND PUT HIM UP FOR THE NIGHT. AND BESIDES, YOU PAID FOR THE BEERS.
BUT BEFORE YOU GO... I DON'T KNOW WHERE WE ARE. IS THERE A BUS DOWNTOWN?
AH, I THINK THERE'S A STOP ON THAT CORNER. SOME GOING DOWNTOWN, AND SOME TO THE BUS DEPOT. DOES THAT WORK FOR YOU?
NOT TOTALLY SURE, SINCE I WALK EVERYWHERE.
THAT CORNER? OKAY, I THINK I CAN GET HOME. IF NOT, I CAN GET A TAXI.

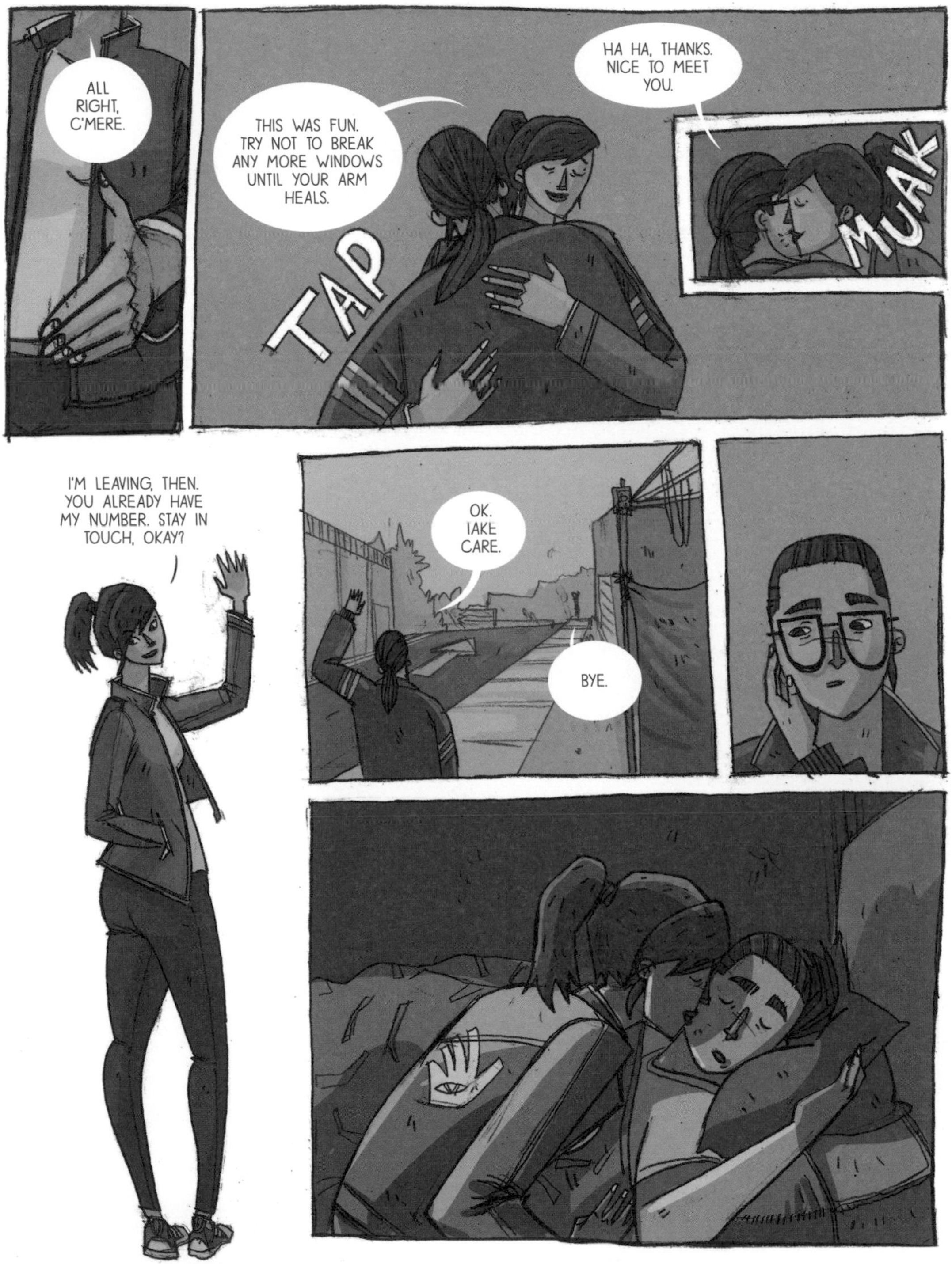
ALL RIGHT, C'MERE.
THIS WAS FUN. TRY NOT TO BREAK ANY MORE WINDOWS UNTIL YOUR ARM HEALS.
TAP
HA HA, THANKS. NICE TO MEET YOU.
MUAK
I'M LEAVING, THEN. YOU ALREADY HAVE MY NUMBER. STAY IN TOUCH, OKAY?
OK. TAKE CARE.
BYE.

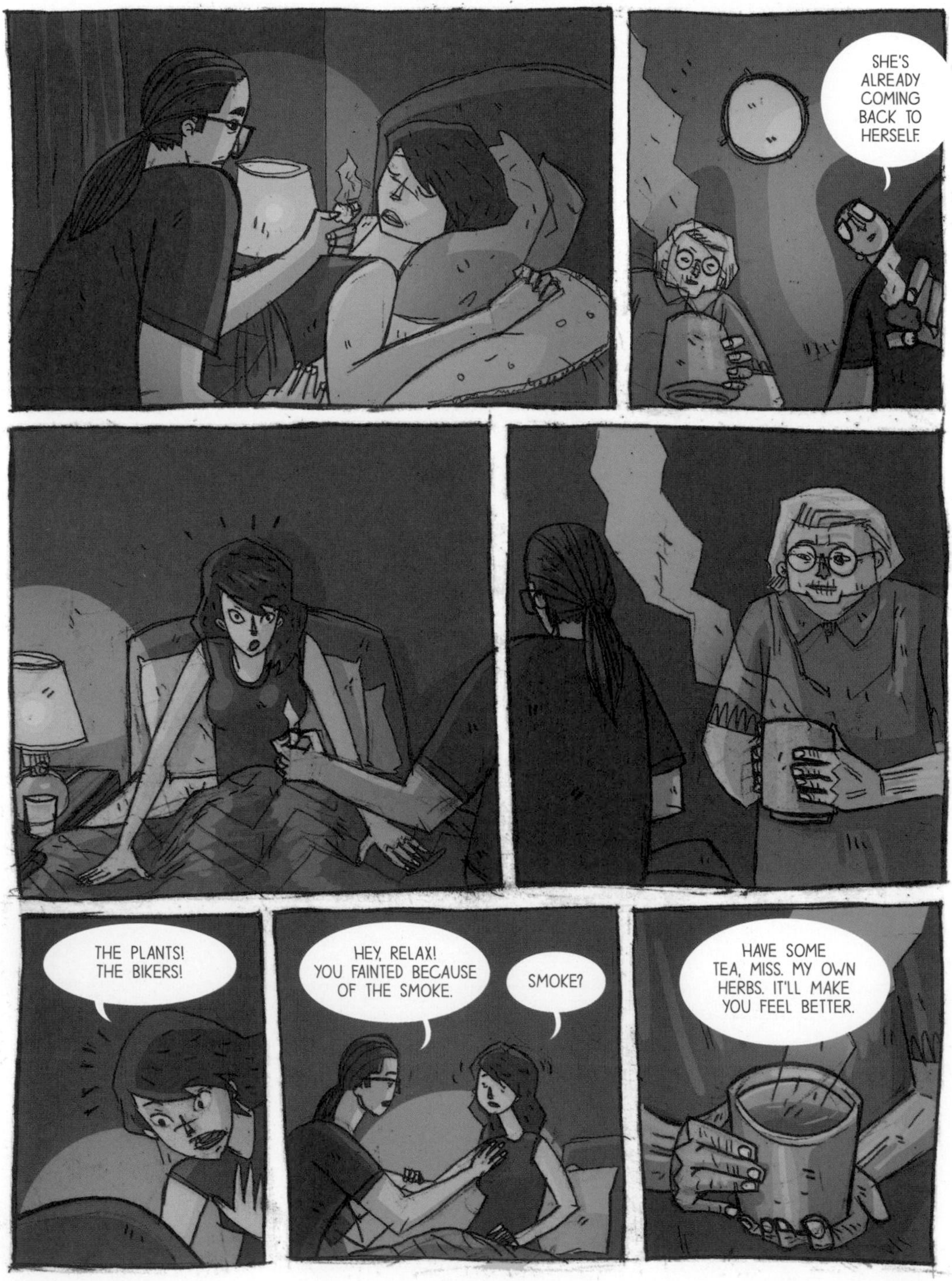
SHE'S ALREADY COMING BACK TO HERSELF.
THE PLANTS! THE BIKERS!
HEY, RELAX! YOU FAINTED BECAUSE OF THE SMOKE.
SMOKE?
HAVE SOME TEA, MISS. MY OWN HERBS. IT'LL MAKE YOU FEEL BETTER.

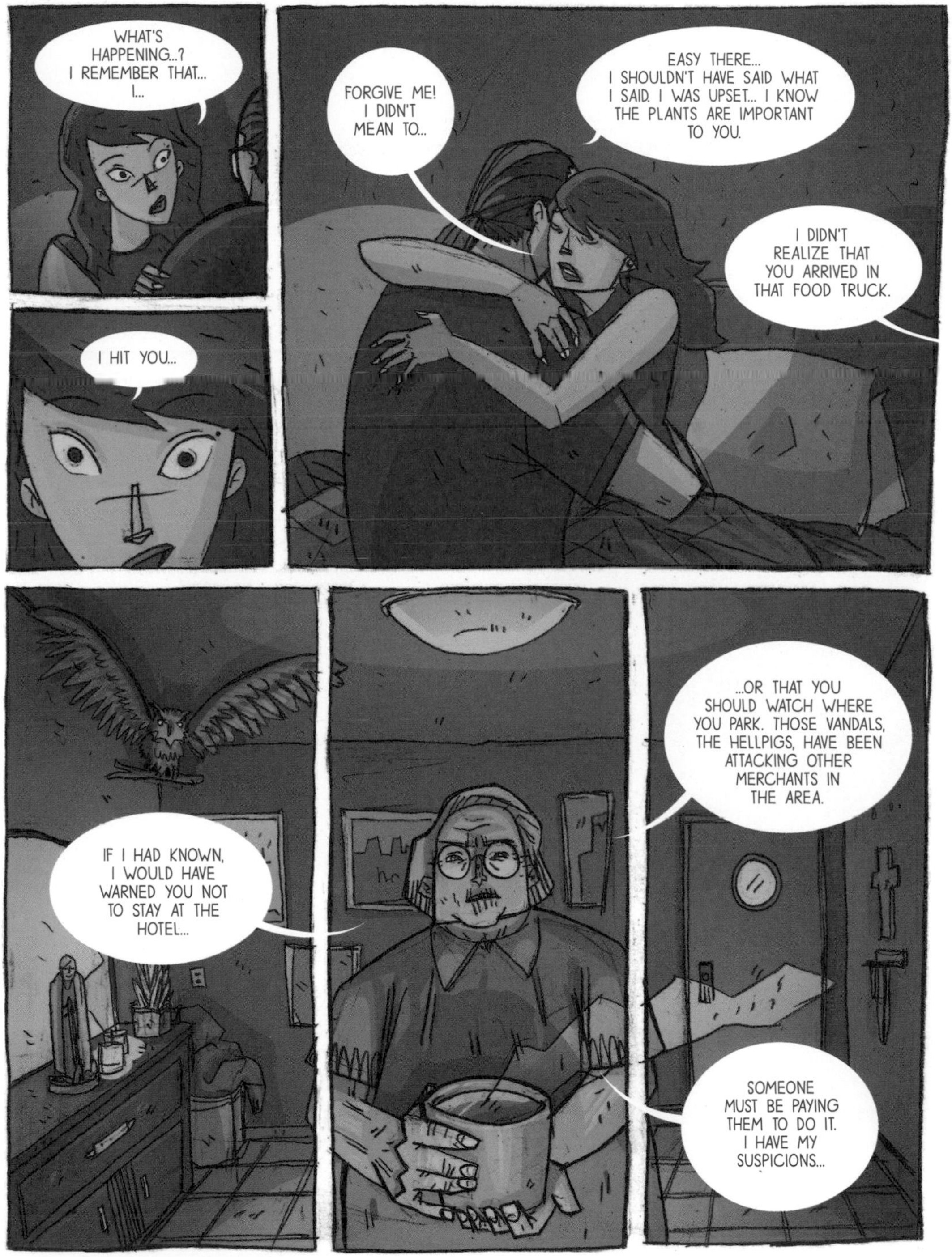
WHAT'S HAPPENING...? I REMEMBER THAT... I...
I HIT YOU...
FORGIVE ME! I DIDN'T MEAN TO...
EASY THERE... I SHOULDN'T HAVE SAID WHAT I SAID. I WAS UPSET... I KNOW THE PLANTS ARE IMPORTANT TO YOU.
I DIDN'T REALIZE THAT YOU ARRIVED IN THAT FOOD TRUCK.
IF I HAD KNOWN, I WOULD HAVE WARNED YOU NOT TO STAY AT THE HOTEL...
...OR THAT YOU SHOULD WATCH WHERE YOU PARK. THOSE VANDALS, THE HELLPIGS, HAVE BEEN ATTACKING OTHER MERCHANTS IN THE AREA.
SOMEONE MUST BE PAYING THEM TO DO IT. I HAVE MY SUSPICIONS...

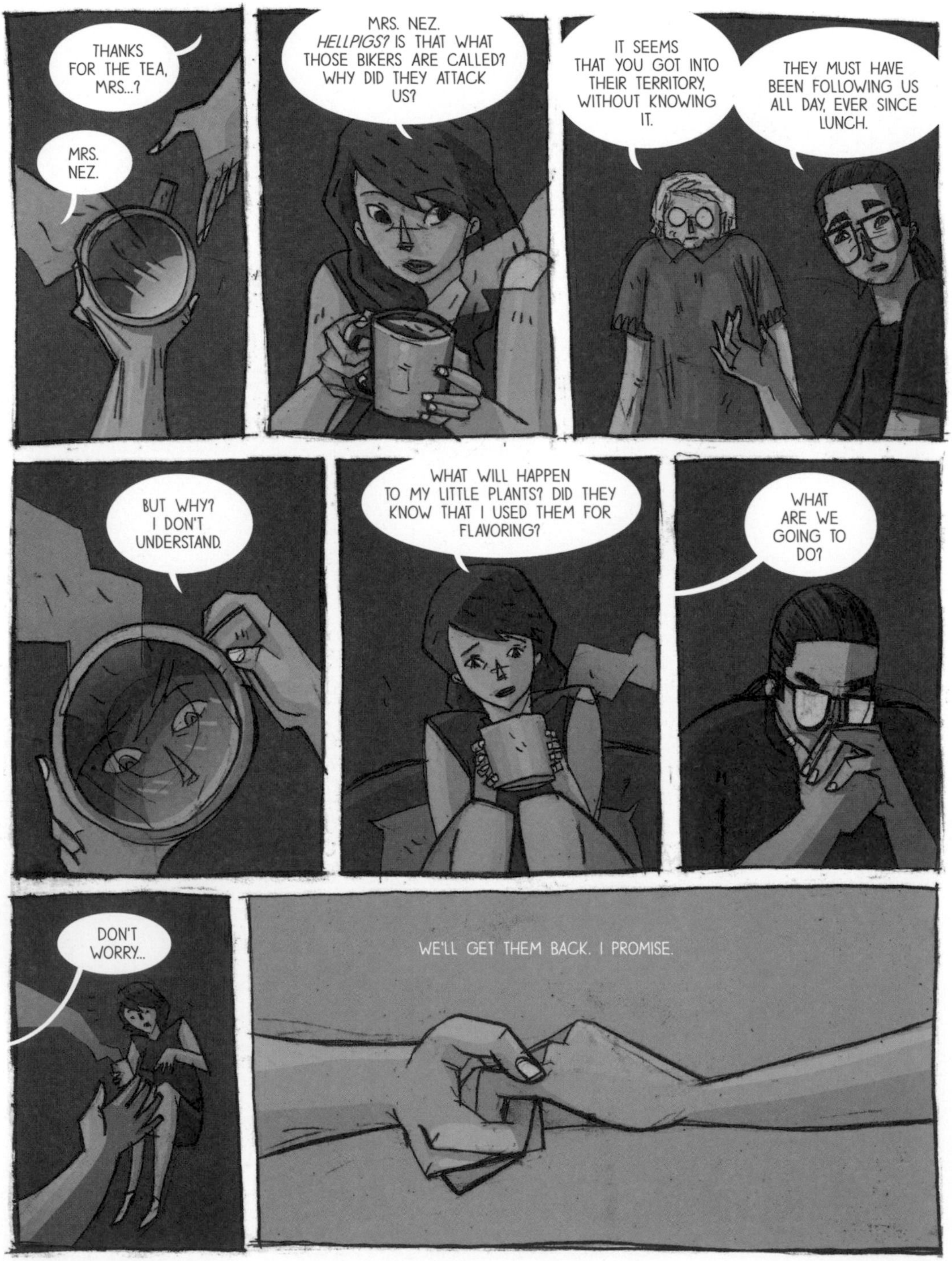
THANKS FOR THE TEA, MRS...?
MRS. NEZ.
MRS. NEZ. *HELLPIGS?* IS THAT WHAT THOSE BIKERS ARE CALLED? WHY DID THEY ATTACK US?
IT SEEMS THAT YOU GOT INTO THEIR TERRITORY, WITHOUT KNOWING IT.
THEY MUST HAVE BEEN FOLLOWING US ALL DAY, EVER SINCE LUNCH.
BUT WHY? I DON'T UNDERSTAND.
WHAT WILL HAPPEN TO MY LITTLE PLANTS? DID THEY KNOW THAT I USED THEM FOR FLAVORING?
WHAT ARE WE GOING TO DO?
DON'T WORRY...
WE'LL GET THEM BACK. I PROMISE.

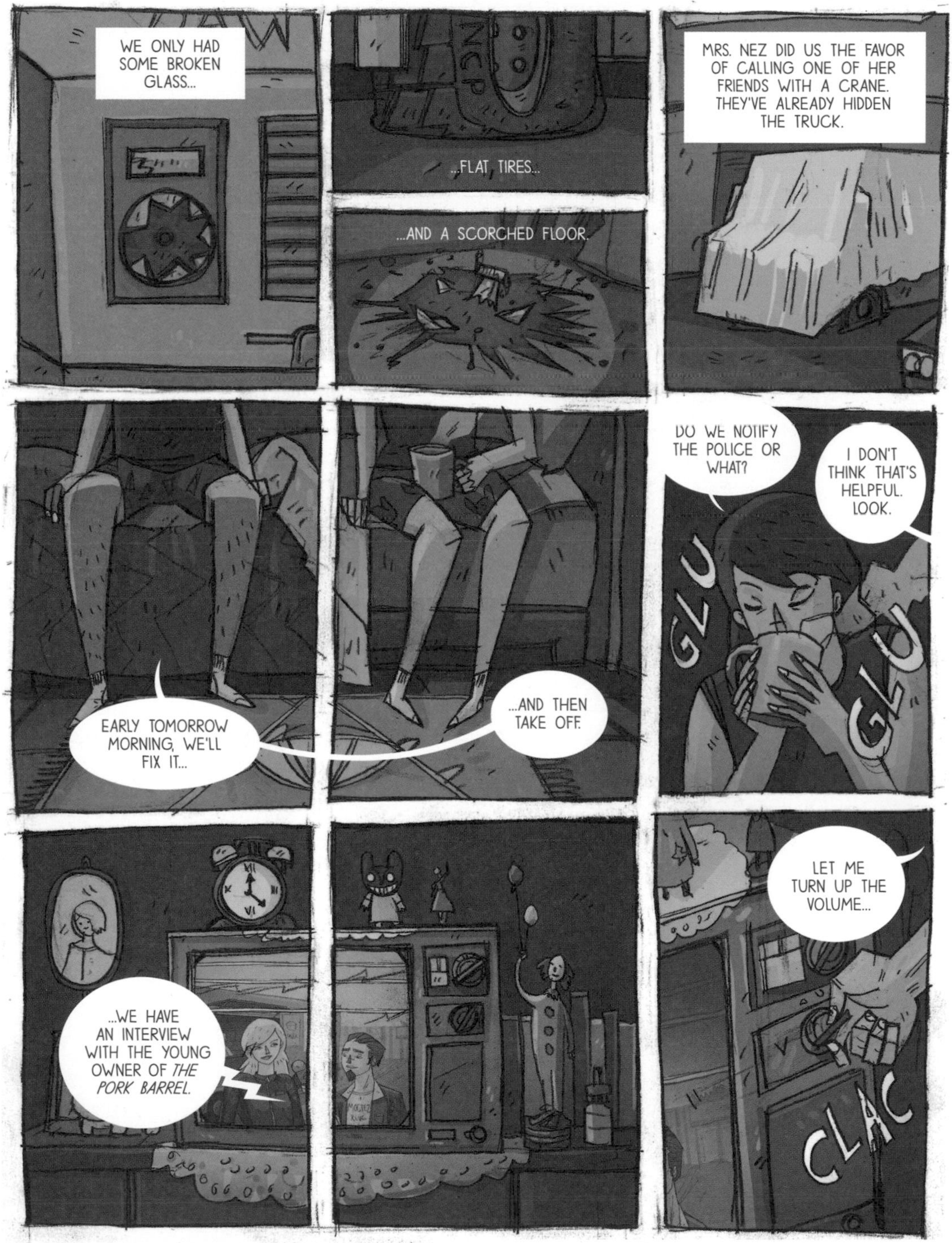
WE ONLY HAD SOME BROKEN GLASS...
...FLAT TIRES...
...AND A SCORCHED FLOOR.
MRS. NEZ DID US THE FAVOR OF CALLING ONE OF HER FRIENDS WITH A CRANE. THEY'VE ALREADY HIDDEN THE TRUCK.
EARLY TOMORROW MORNING, WE'LL FIX IT...
...AND THEN TAKE OFF.
DO WE NOTIFY THE POLICE OR WHAT?
I DON'T THINK THAT'S HELPFUL. LOOK.
GLU
GLU
...WE HAVE AN INTERVIEW WITH THE YOUNG OWNER OF *THE PORK BARREL.*
LET ME TURN UP THE VOLUME...
CLAC

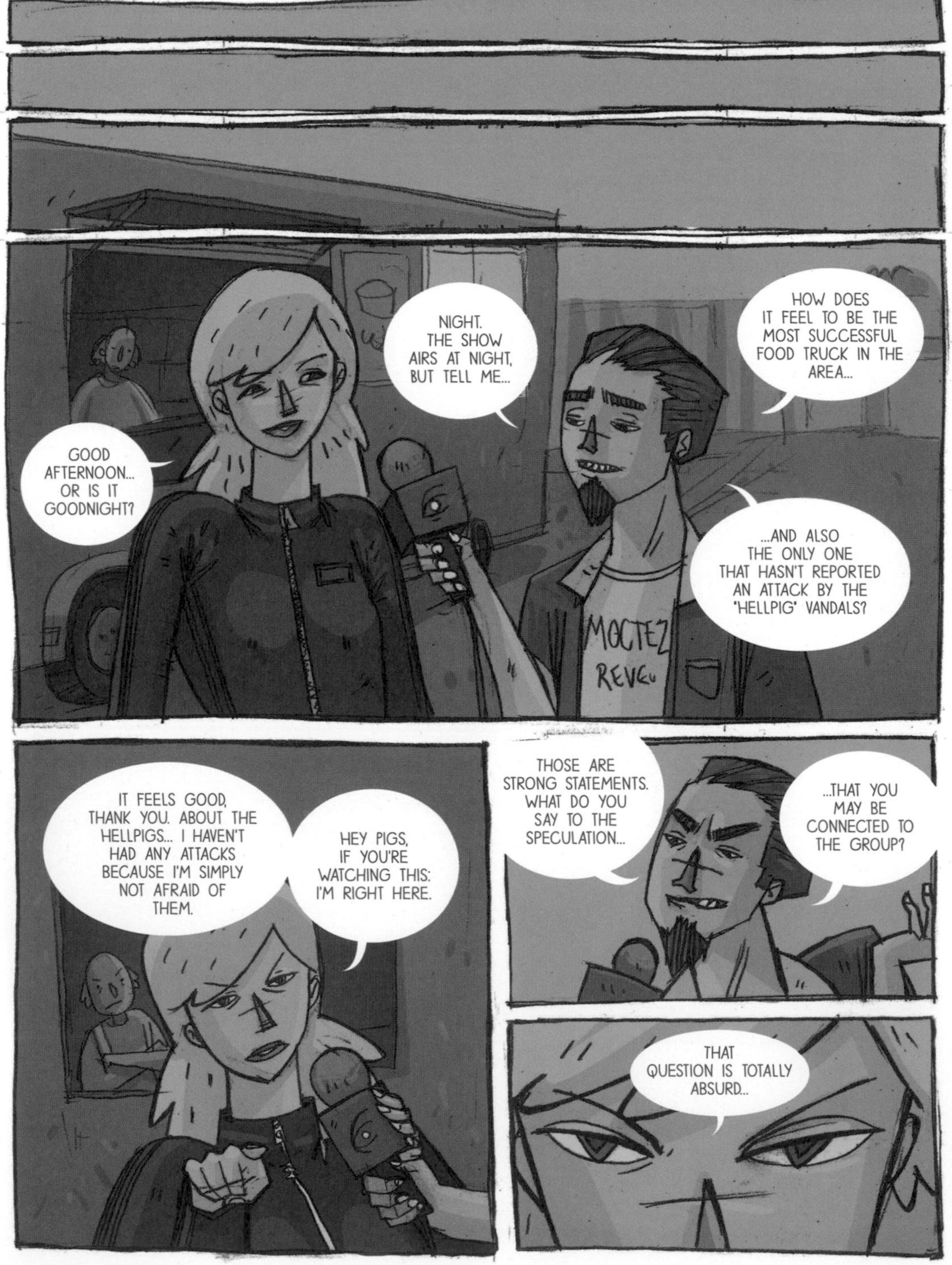
GOOD AFTERNOON... OR IS IT GOODNIGHT?
NIGHT. THE SHOW AIRS AT NIGHT, BUT TELL ME...
HOW DOES IT FEEL TO BE THE MOST SUCCESSFUL FOOD TRUCK IN THE AREA...
...AND ALSO THE ONLY ONE THAT HASN'T REPORTED AN ATTACK BY THE 'HELLPIG' VANDALS?
MOCTEZ
REVE
IT FEELS GOOD, THANK YOU. ABOUT THE HELLPIGS... I HAVEN'T HAD ANY ATTACKS BECAUSE I'M SIMPLY NOT AFRAID OF THEM.
HEY PIGS, IF YOU'RE WATCHING THIS: I'M RIGHT HERE.
THOSE ARE STRONG STATEMENTS. WHAT DO YOU SAY TO THE SPECULATION...
...THAT YOU MAY BE CONNECTED TO THE GROUP?
THAT QUESTION IS TOTALLY ABSURD...

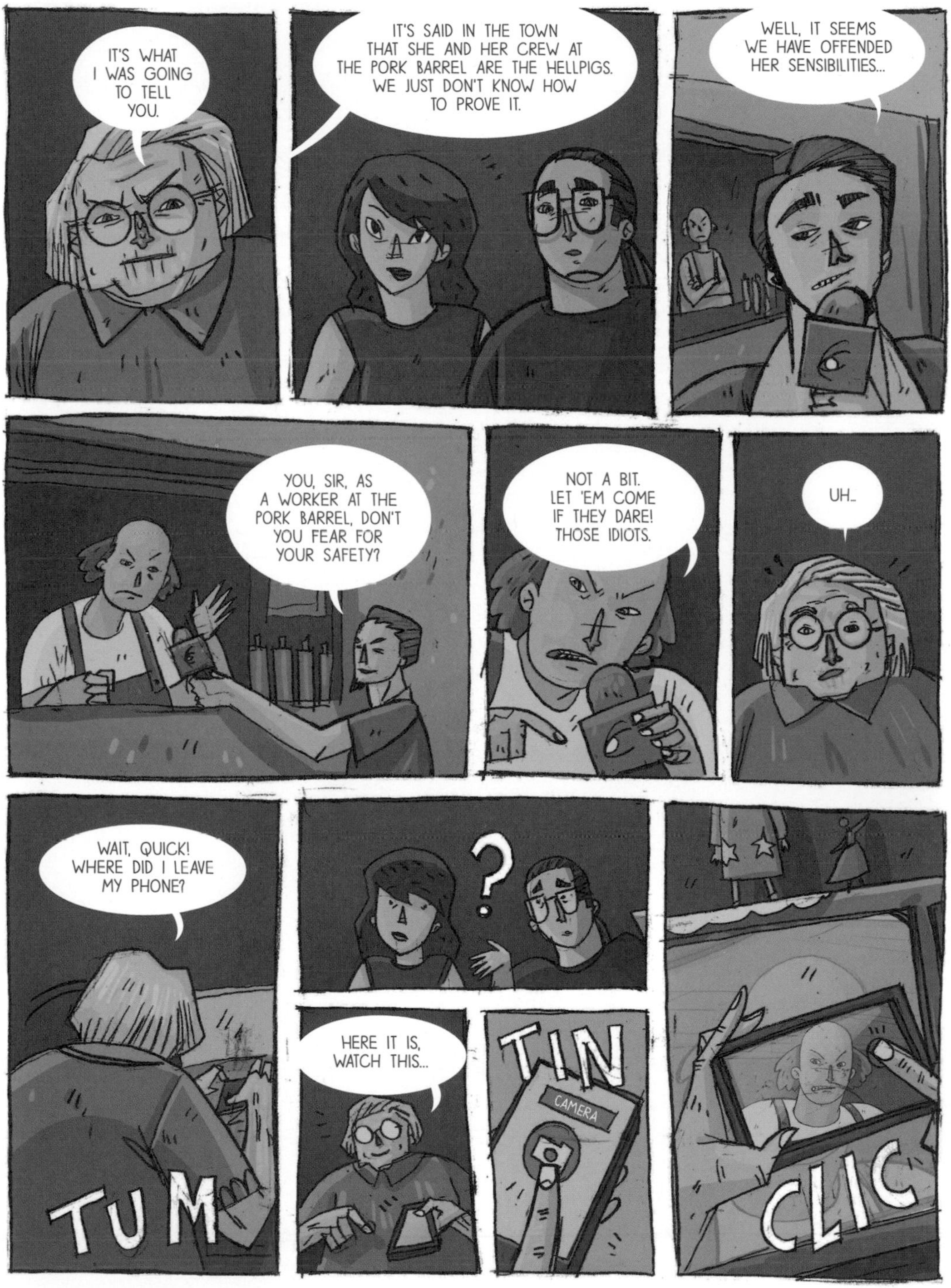
IT'S WHAT I WAS GOING TO TELL YOU.
IT'S SAID IN THE TOWN THAT SHE AND HER CREW AT THE PORK BARREL ARE THE HELLPIGS. WE JUST DON'T KNOW HOW TO PROVE IT.
WELL, IT SEEMS WE HAVE OFFENDED HER SENSIBILITIES...
YOU, SIR, AS A WORKER AT THE PORK BARREL, DON'T YOU FEAR FOR YOUR SAFETY?
NOT A BIT. LET 'EM COME IF THEY DARE! THOSE IDIOTS.
UH...
WAIT, QUICK! WHERE DID I LEAVE MY PHONE?
TUM
?
HERE IT IS, WATCH THIS...
TIN
CAMERA
CLIC

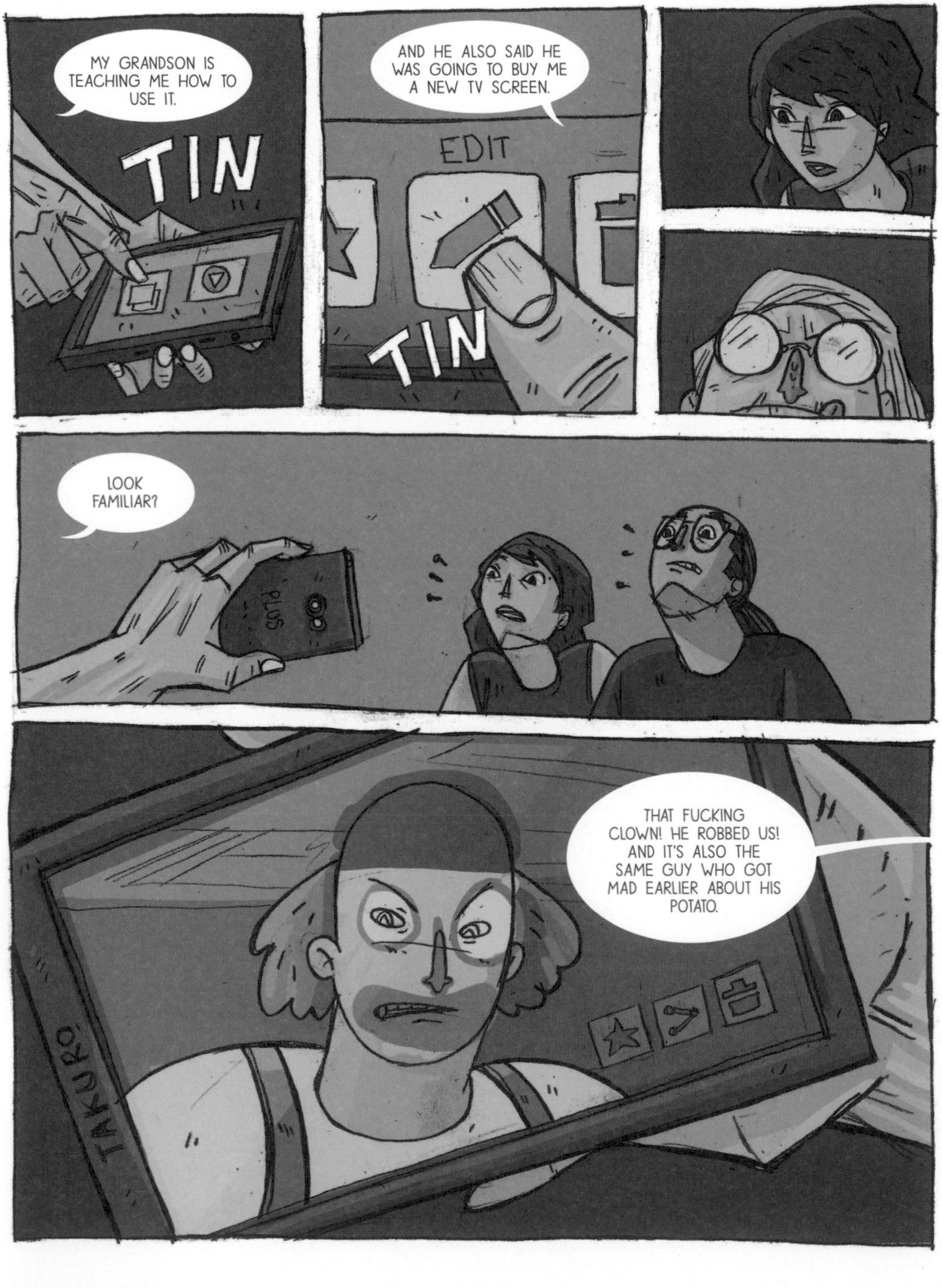
MY GRANDSON IS TEACHING ME HOW TO USE IT.
TIN
AND HE ALSO SAID HE WAS GOING TO BUY ME A NEW TV SCREEN.
EDIT
TIN
LOOK FAMILIAR?
PLUS
THAT FUCKING CLOWN! HE ROBBED US! AND IT'S ALSO THE SAME GUY WHO GOT MAD EARLIER ABOUT HIS POTATO.
TAKURO

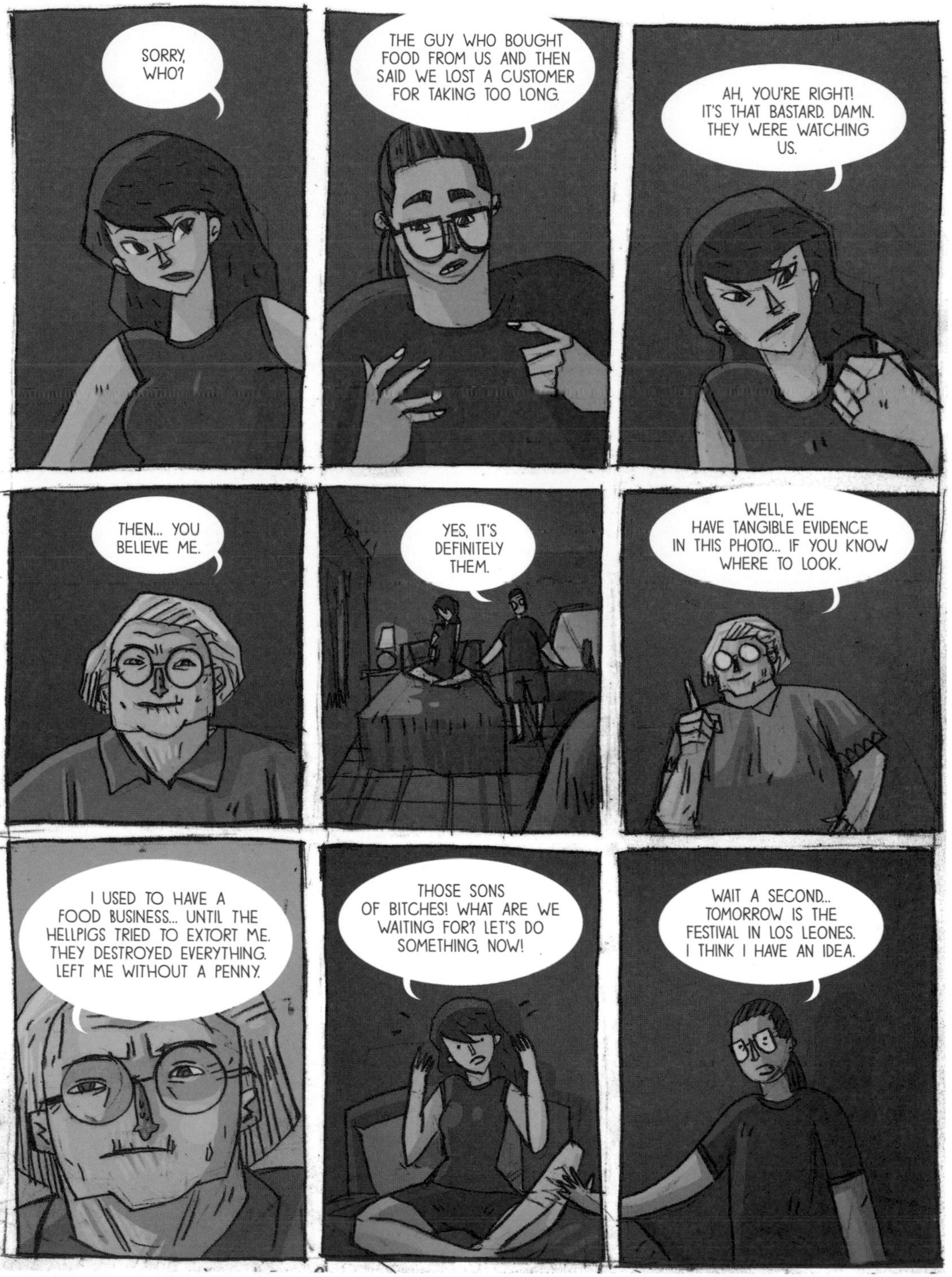
SORRY, WHO?
THE GUY WHO BOUGHT FOOD FROM US AND THEN SAID WE LOST A CUSTOMER FOR TAKING TOO LONG.
AH, YOU'RE RIGHT! IT'S THAT BASTARD. DAMN. THEY WERE WATCHING US.
THEN... YOU BELIEVE ME.
YES, IT'S DEFINITELY THEM.
WELL, WE HAVE TANGIBLE EVIDENCE IN THIS PHOTO... IF YOU KNOW WHERE TO LOOK.
I USED TO HAVE A FOOD BUSINESS... UNTIL THE HELLPIGS TRIED TO EXTORT ME. THEY DESTROYED EVERYTHING. LEFT ME WITHOUT A PENNY.
THOSE SONS OF BITCHES! WHAT ARE WE WAITING FOR? LET'S DO SOMETHING, NOW!
WAIT A SECOND... TOMORROW IS THE FESTIVAL IN LOS LEONES. I THINK I HAVE AN IDEA.

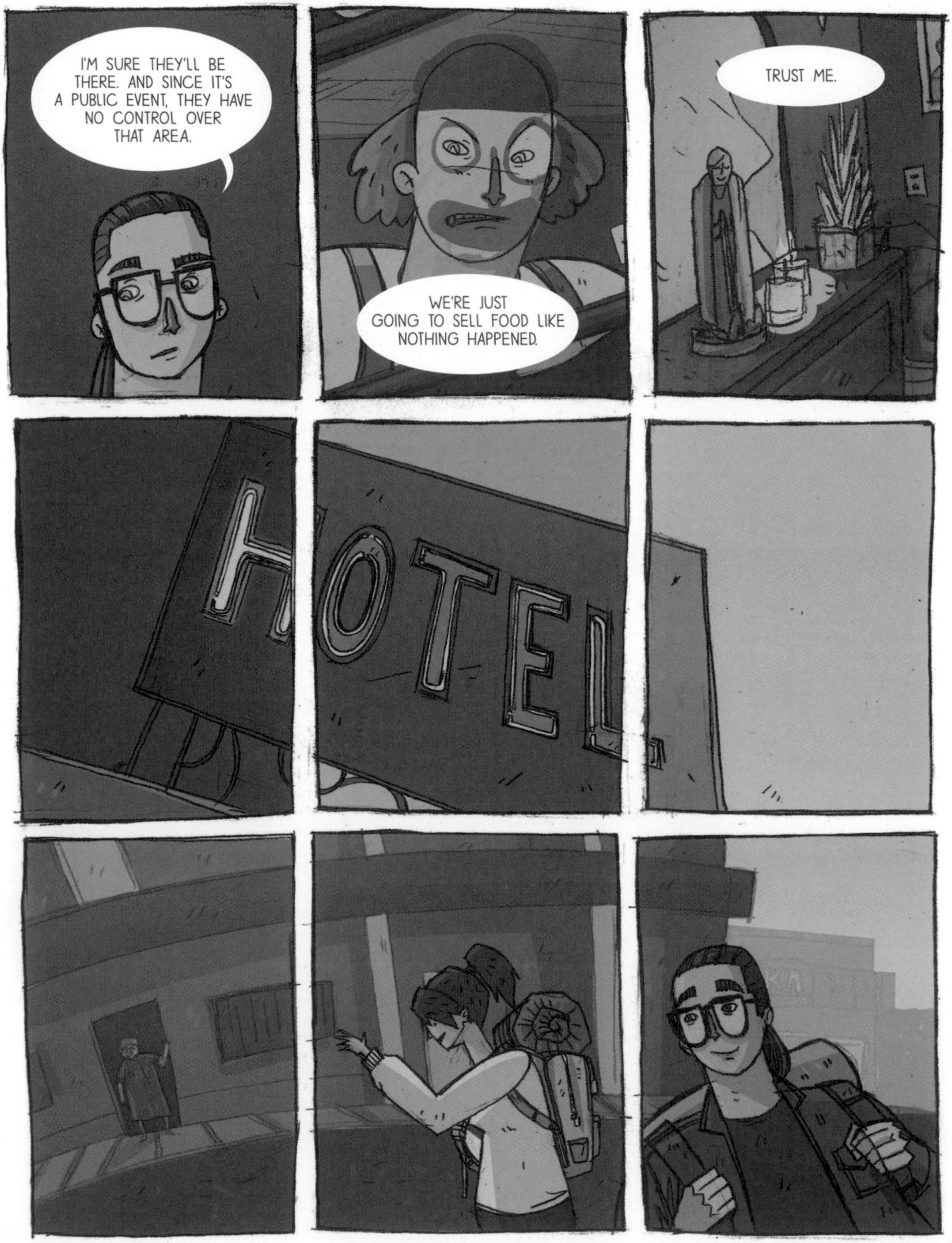
I'M SURE THEY'LL BE THERE. AND SINCE IT'S A PUBLIC EVENT, THEY HAVE NO CONTROL OVER THAT AREA.
WE'RE JUST GOING TO SELL FOOD LIKE NOTHING HAPPENED.
TRUST ME.
HOTEL

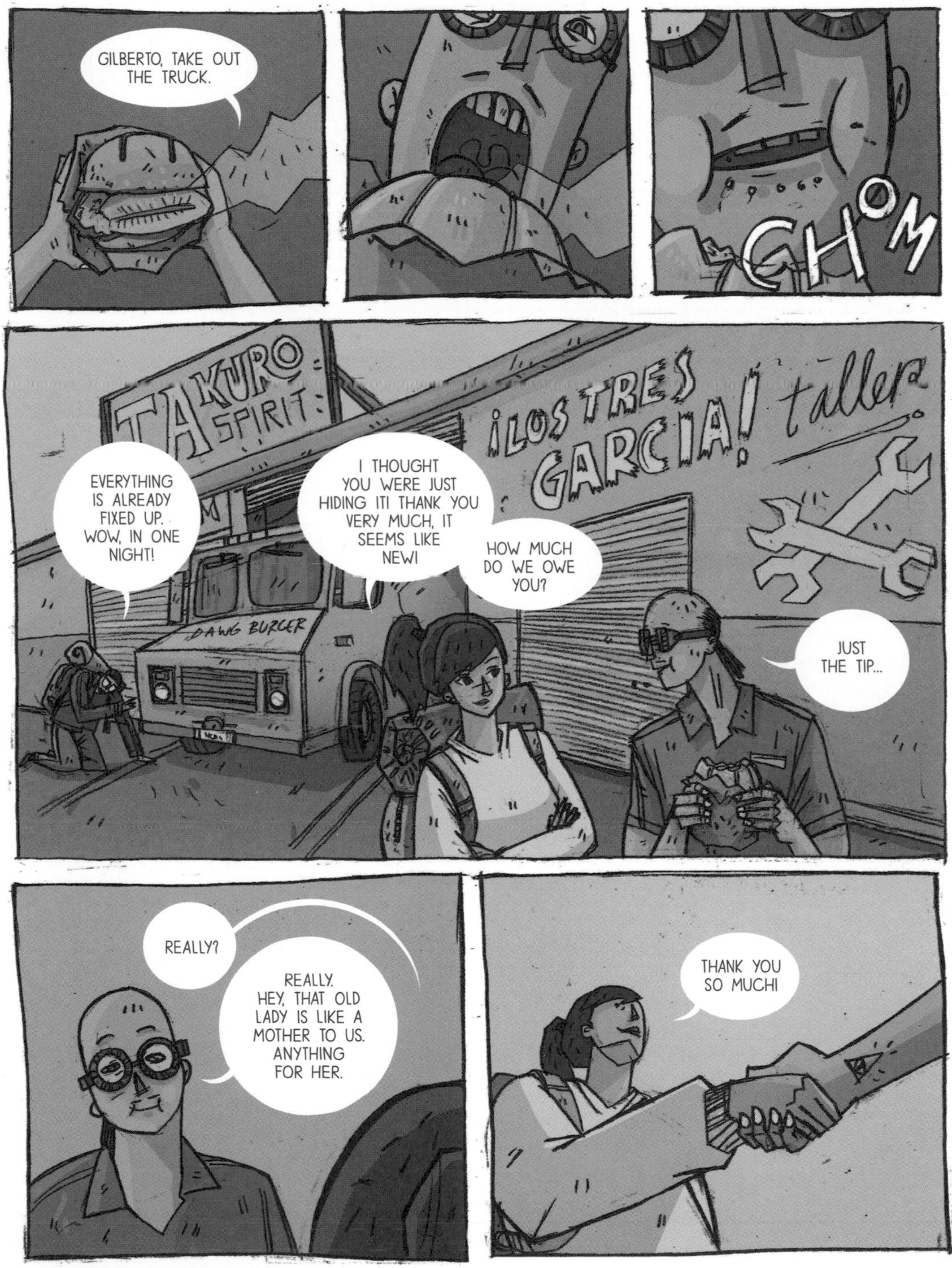
GILBERTO, TAKE OUT THE TRUCK.
CHOM
TAKURO SPIRIT
¡LOS TRES GARCIA! taller
DAWG BURGER
EVERYTHING IS ALREADY FIXED UP. WOW, IN ONE NIGHT!
I THOUGHT YOU WERE JUST HIDING IT! THANK YOU VERY MUCH, IT SEEMS LIKE NEW!
HOW MUCH DO WE OWE YOU?
JUST THE TIP...
REALLY?
REALLY. HEY, THAT OLD LADY IS LIKE A MOTHER TO US. ANYTHING FOR HER.
THANK YOU SO MUCH!

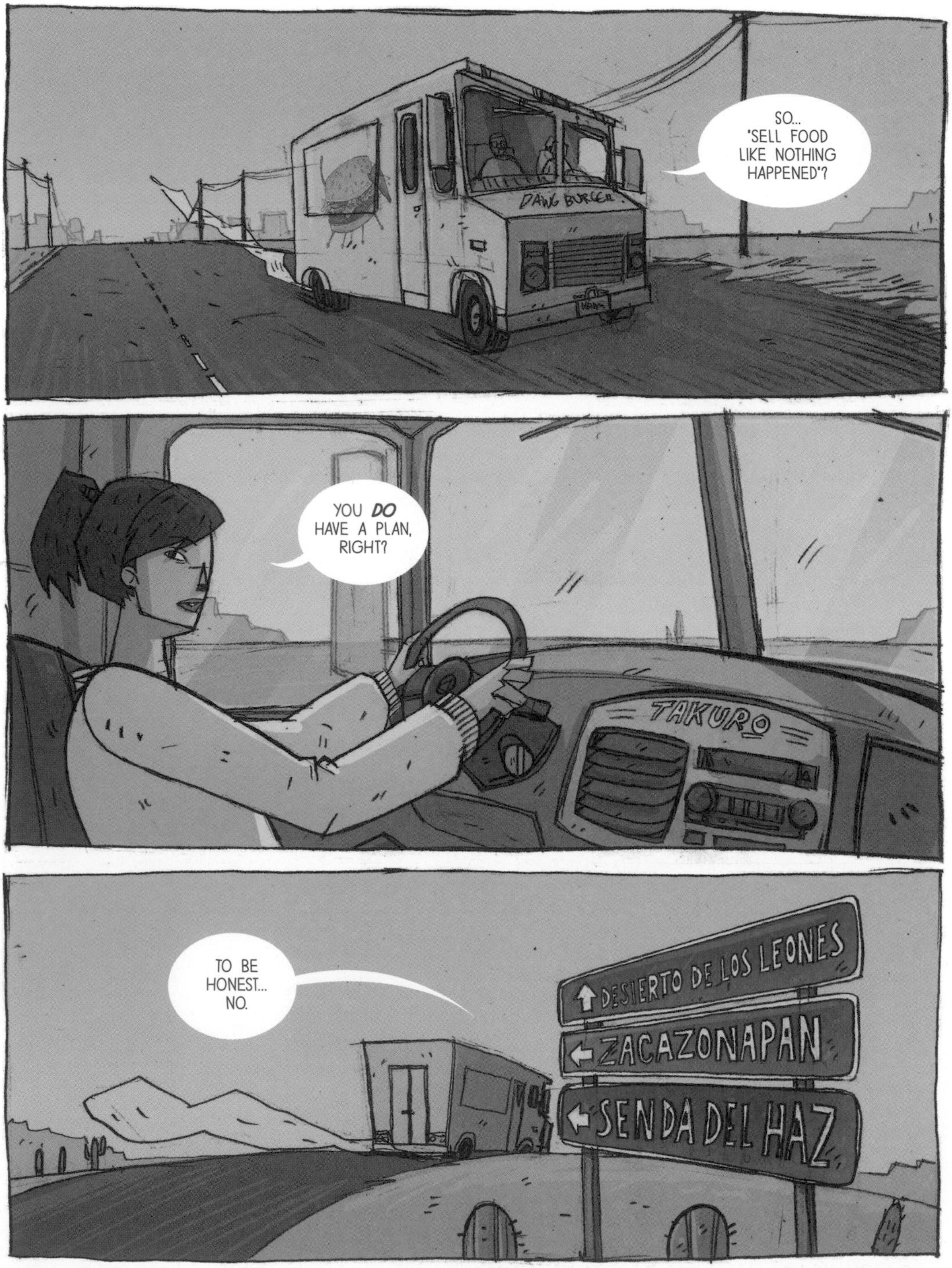

DAWG BURGER
SO... "SELL FOOD LIKE NOTHING HAPPENED"?
YOU DO HAVE A PLAN, RIGHT?
TAKURO
TO BE HONEST... NO.
DESIERTO DE LOS LEONES
ZACAZONAPAN
SENDA DEL HAZ

PART FOUR

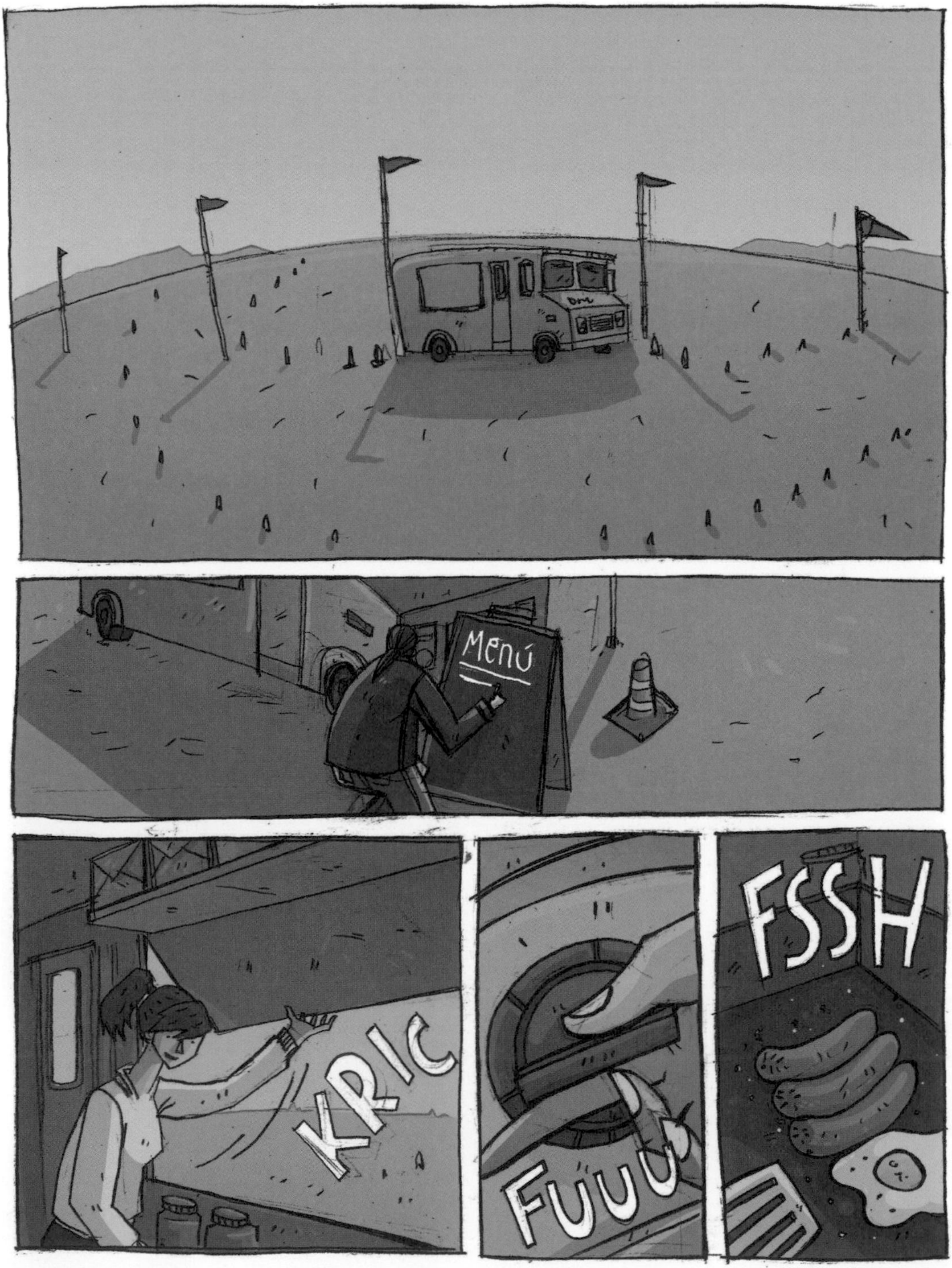
Menú
KRIC
FUUU
FSSH

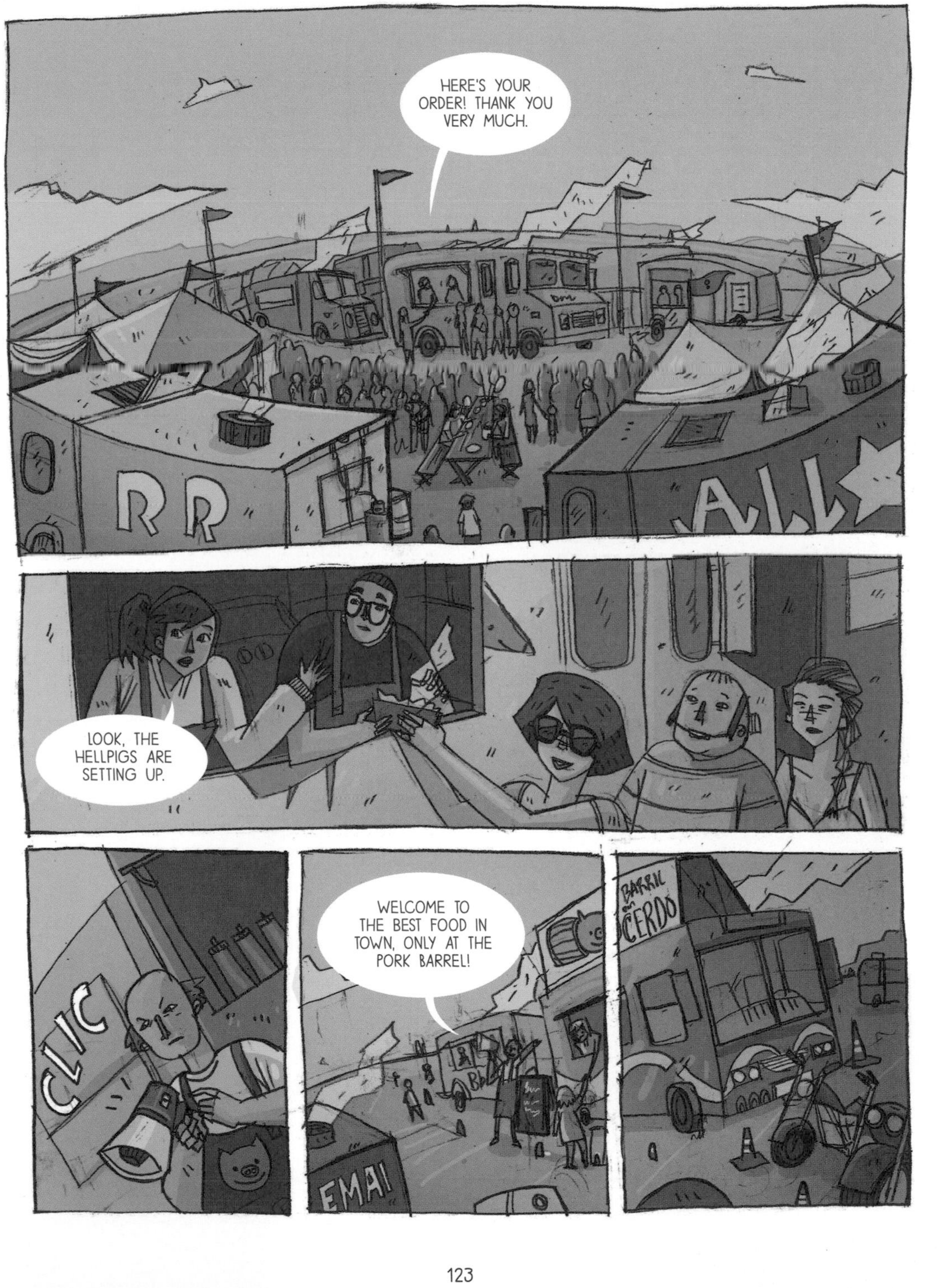
HERE'S YOUR ORDER! THANK YOU VERY MUCH.
RR
ALL
LOOK, THE HELLPIGS ARE SETTING UP.
CLIC
WELCOME TO THE BEST FOOD IN TOWN, ONLY AT THE PORK BARREL!
EMAI
BARRIL de CERDO

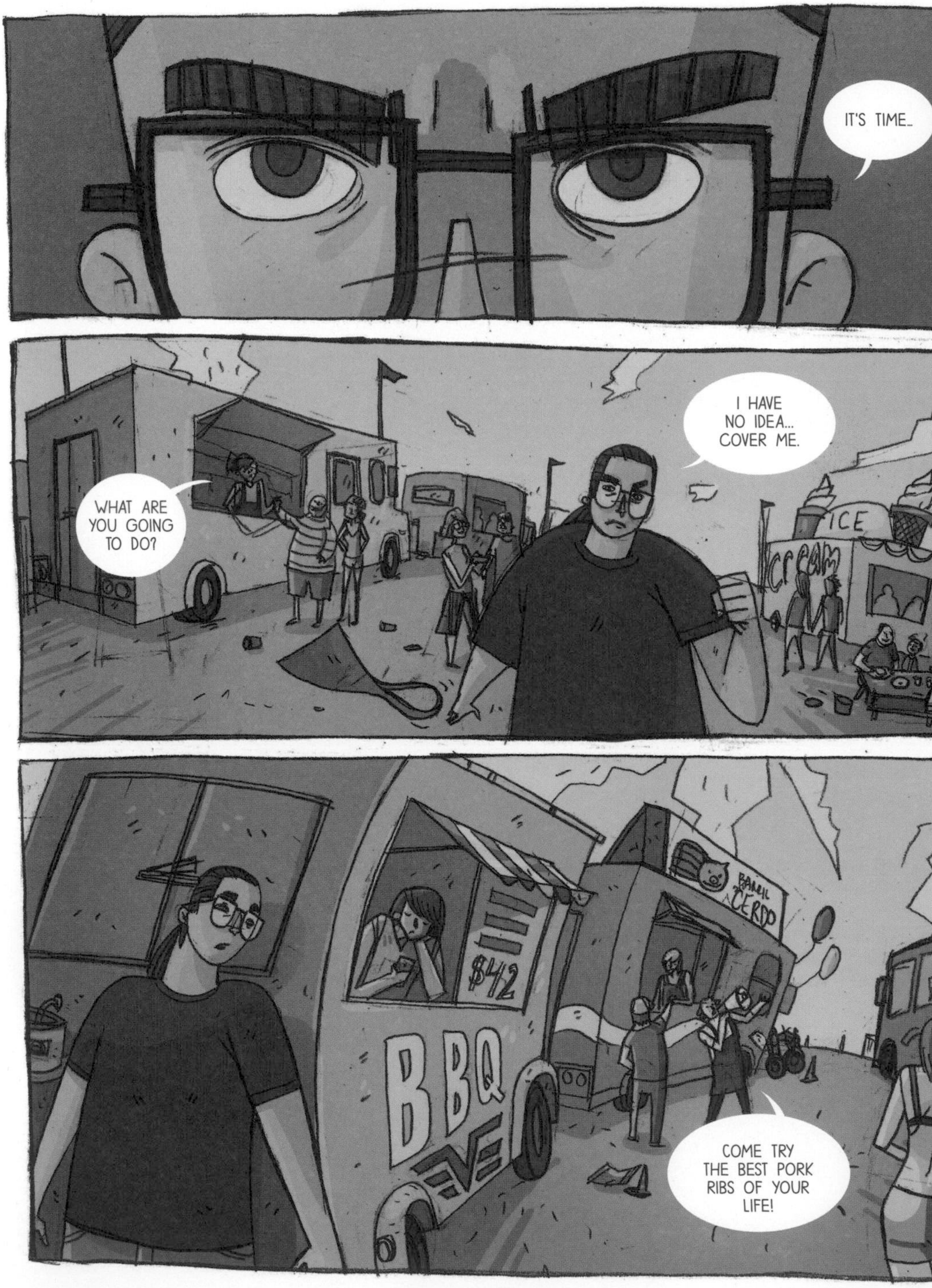
IT'S TIME...
WHAT ARE YOU GOING TO DO?
I HAVE NO IDEA... COVER ME.
ICE cream
BARRIL DE CERDO
$4.2
BBQ
COME TRY THE BEST PORK RIBS OF YOUR LIFE!

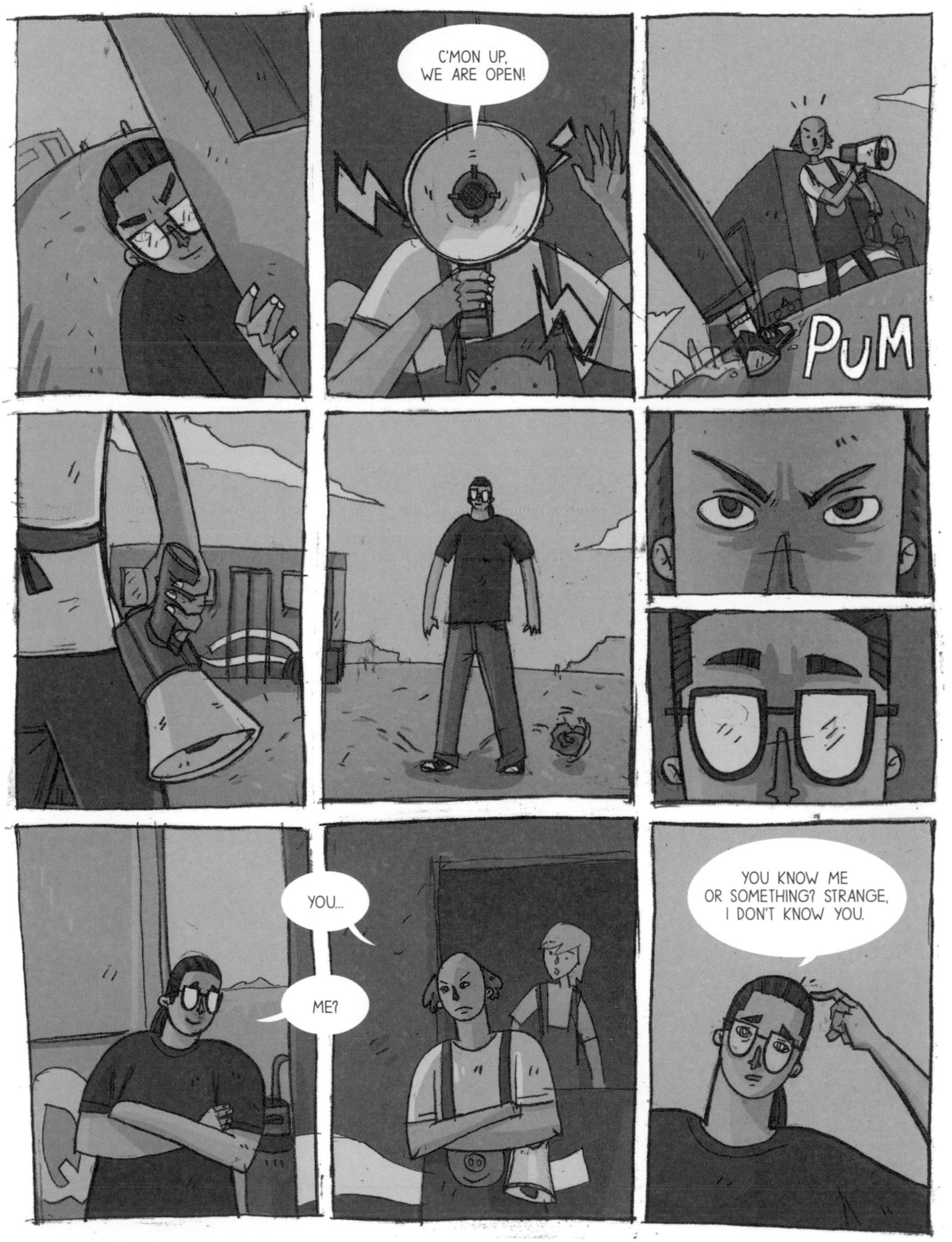
C'MON UP, WE ARE OPEN!
PUM
YOU...
ME?
YOU KNOW ME OR SOMETHING? STRANGE, I DON'T KNOW YOU.

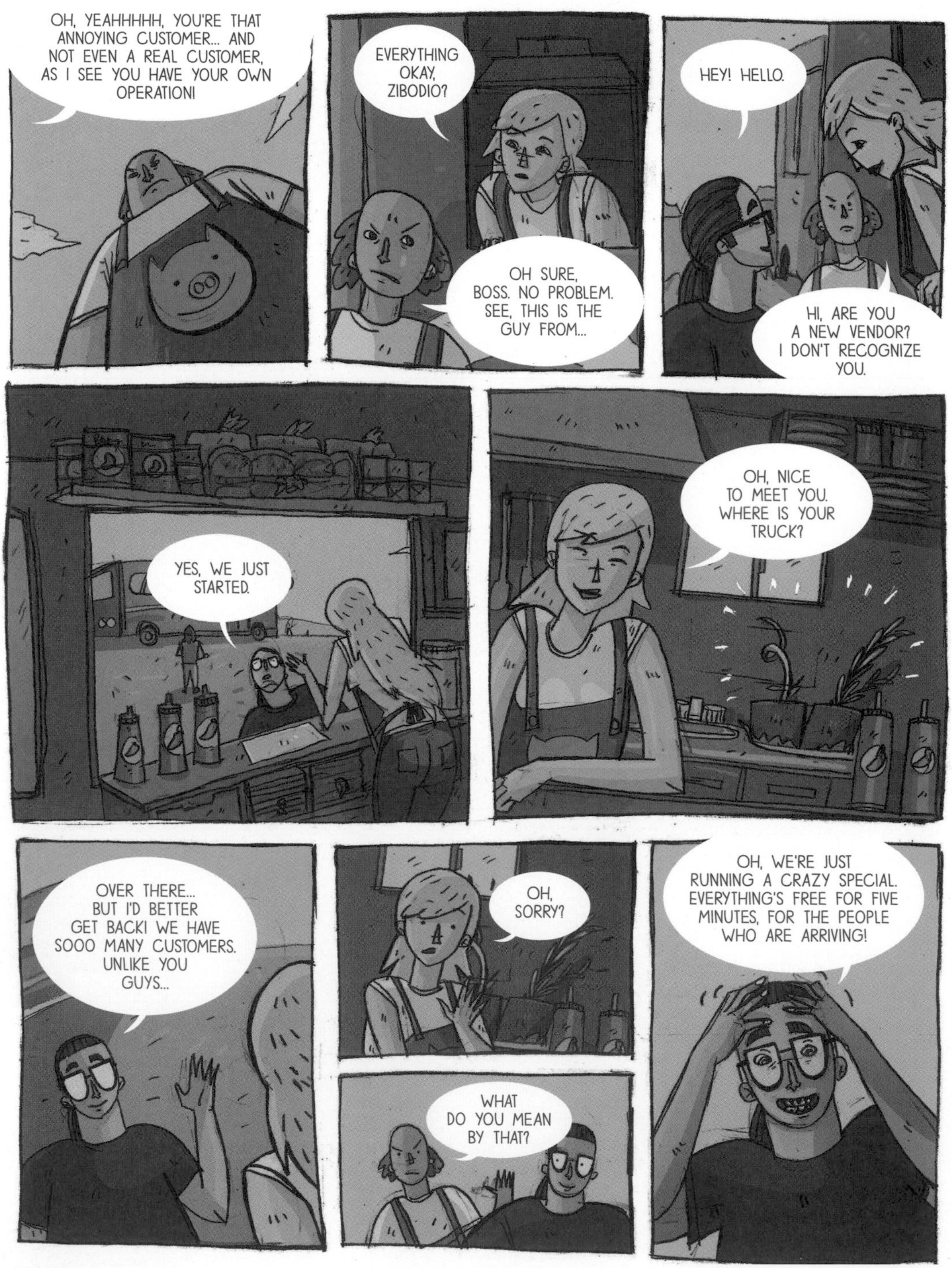
OH, YEAHHHHH, YOU'RE THAT ANNOYING CUSTOMER... AND NOT EVEN A REAL CUSTOMER, AS I SEE YOU HAVE YOUR OWN OPERATION!
EVERYTHING OKAY, ZIBODIO?
OH SURE, BOSS. NO PROBLEM. SEE, THIS IS THE GUY FROM...
HEY! HELLO.
HI, ARE YOU A NEW VENDOR? I DON'T RECOGNIZE YOU.
YES, WE JUST STARTED.
OH, NICE TO MEET YOU. WHERE IS YOUR TRUCK?
OVER THERE... BUT I'D BETTER GET BACK! WE HAVE SOOO MANY CUSTOMERS. UNLIKE YOU GUYS...
OH, SORRY?
WHAT DO YOU MEAN BY THAT?
OH, WE'RE JUST RUNNING A CRAZY SPECIAL. EVERYTHING'S FREE FOR FIVE MINUTES, FOR THE PEOPLE WHO ARE ARRIVING!

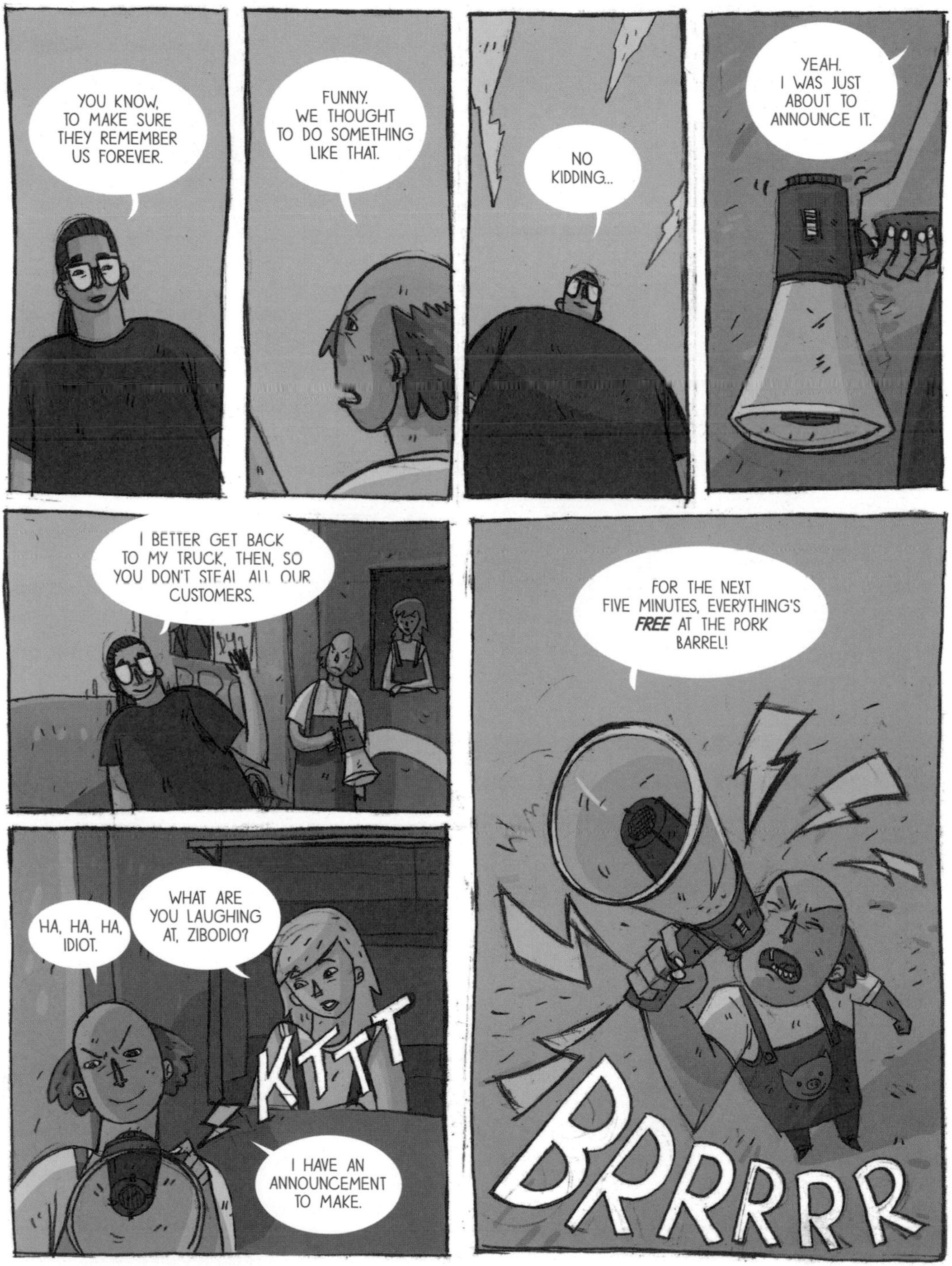
YOU KNOW, TO MAKE SURE THEY REMEMBER US FOREVER.
FUNNY. WE THOUGHT TO DO SOMETHING LIKE THAT.
NO KIDDING...
YEAH. I WAS JUST ABOUT TO ANNOUNCE IT.
I BETTER GET BACK TO MY TRUCK, THEN, SO YOU DON'T STEAL ALL OUR CUSTOMERS.
HA, HA, HA, IDIOT.
WHAT ARE YOU LAUGHING AT, ZIBODIO?
KTTT
I HAVE AN ANNOUNCEMENT TO MAKE.
FOR THE NEXT FIVE MINUTES, EVERYTHING'S ***FREE*** AT THE PORK BARREL!
BRRRRR

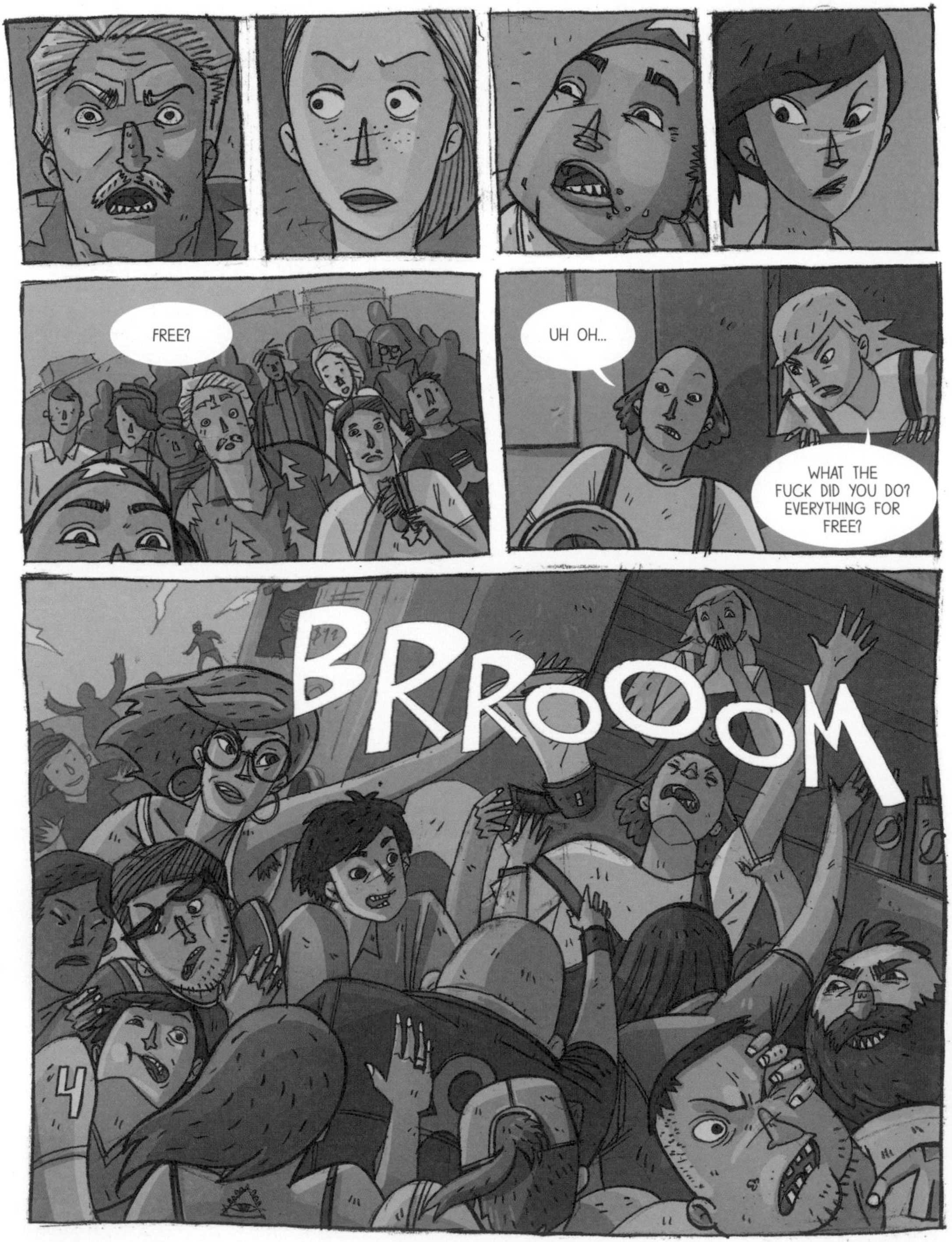
FREE?
UH OH...
WHAT THE FUCK DID YOU DO? EVERYTHING FOR FREE?
BRROOOM

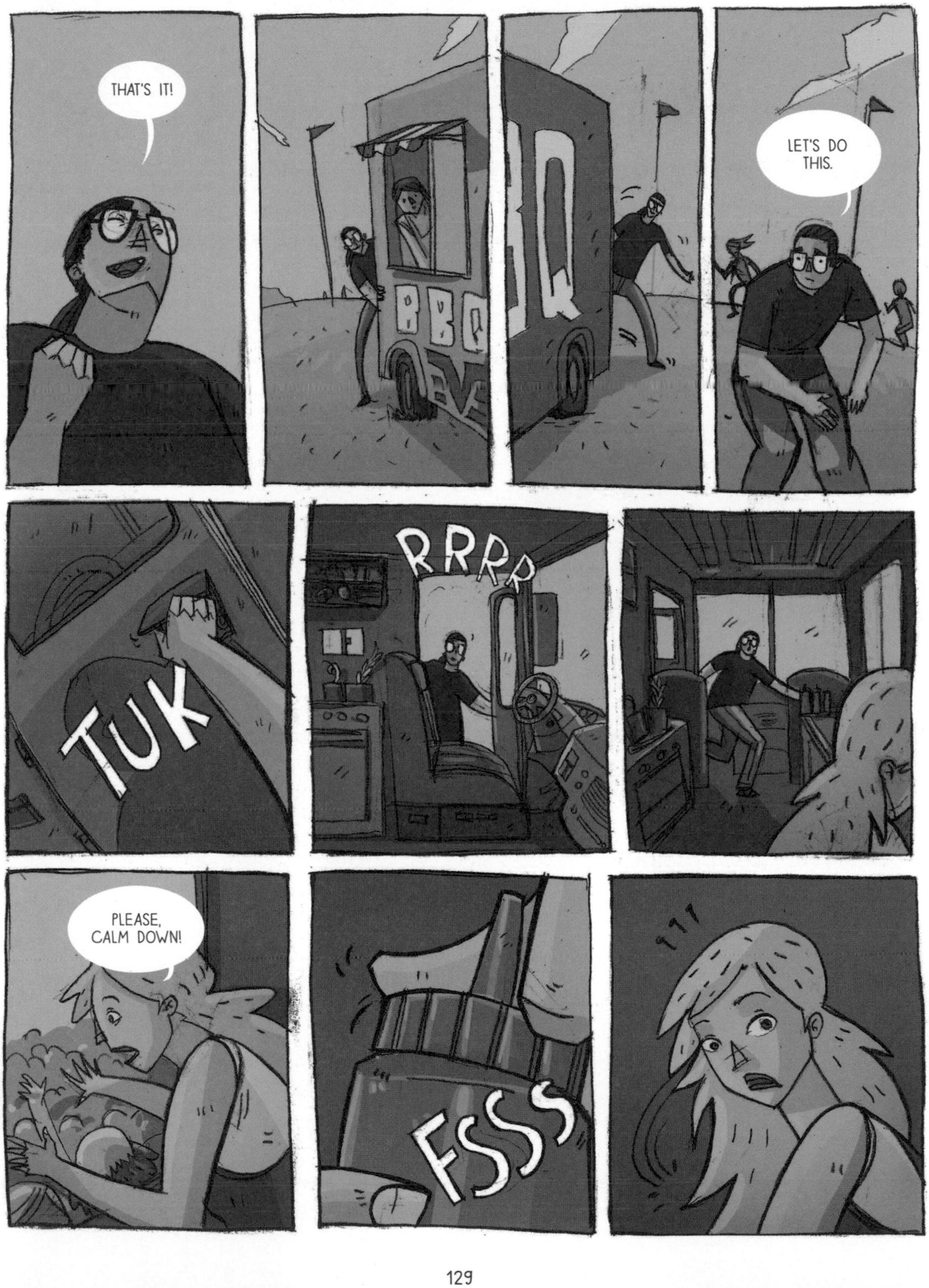
THAT'S IT!
LET'S DO THIS.
TUK
RRRR
PLEASE, CALM DOWN!
FSSS

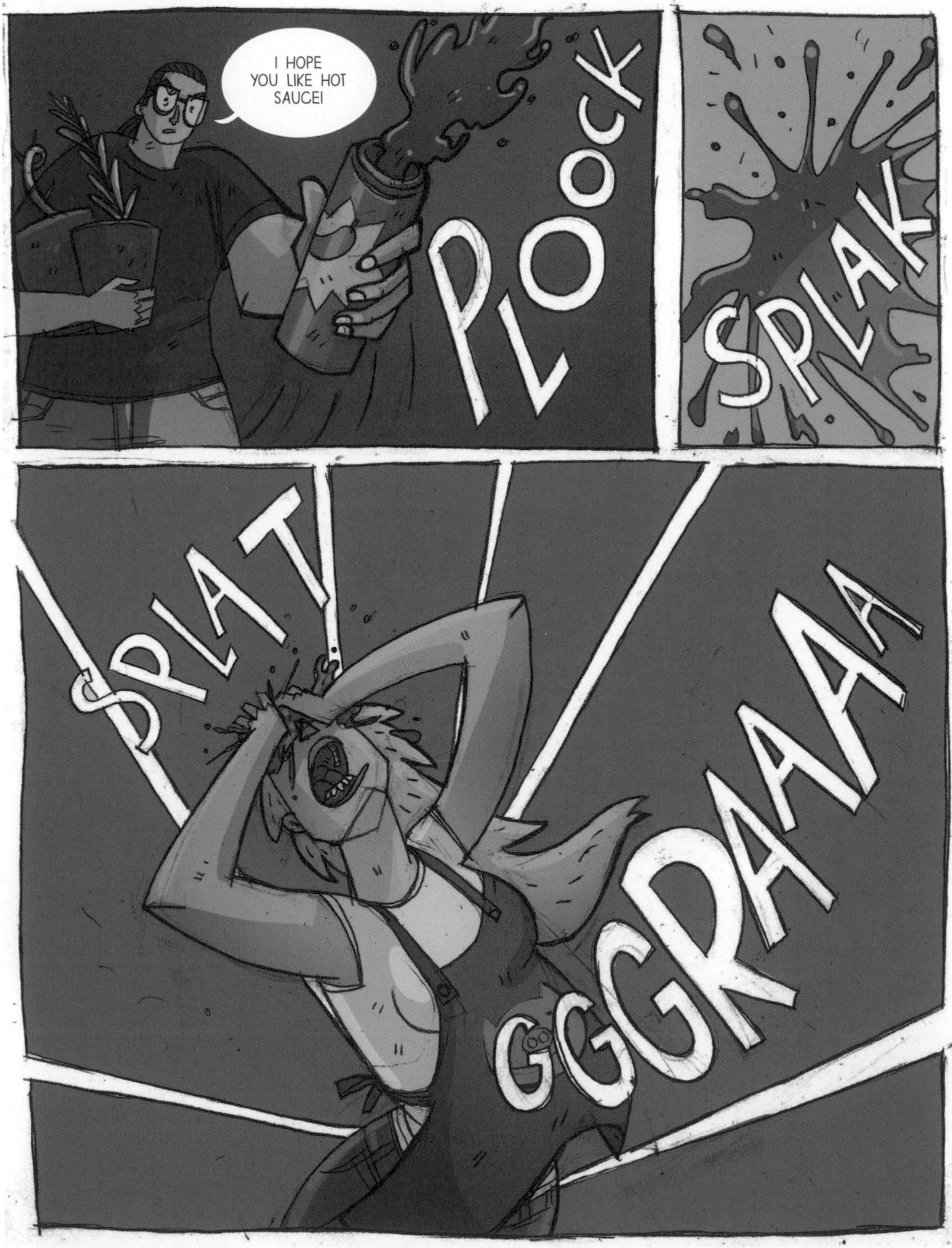

I HOPE YOU LIKE HOT SAUCE!
PLOOCK
SPLAK
SPLAT
GGGRAAAA

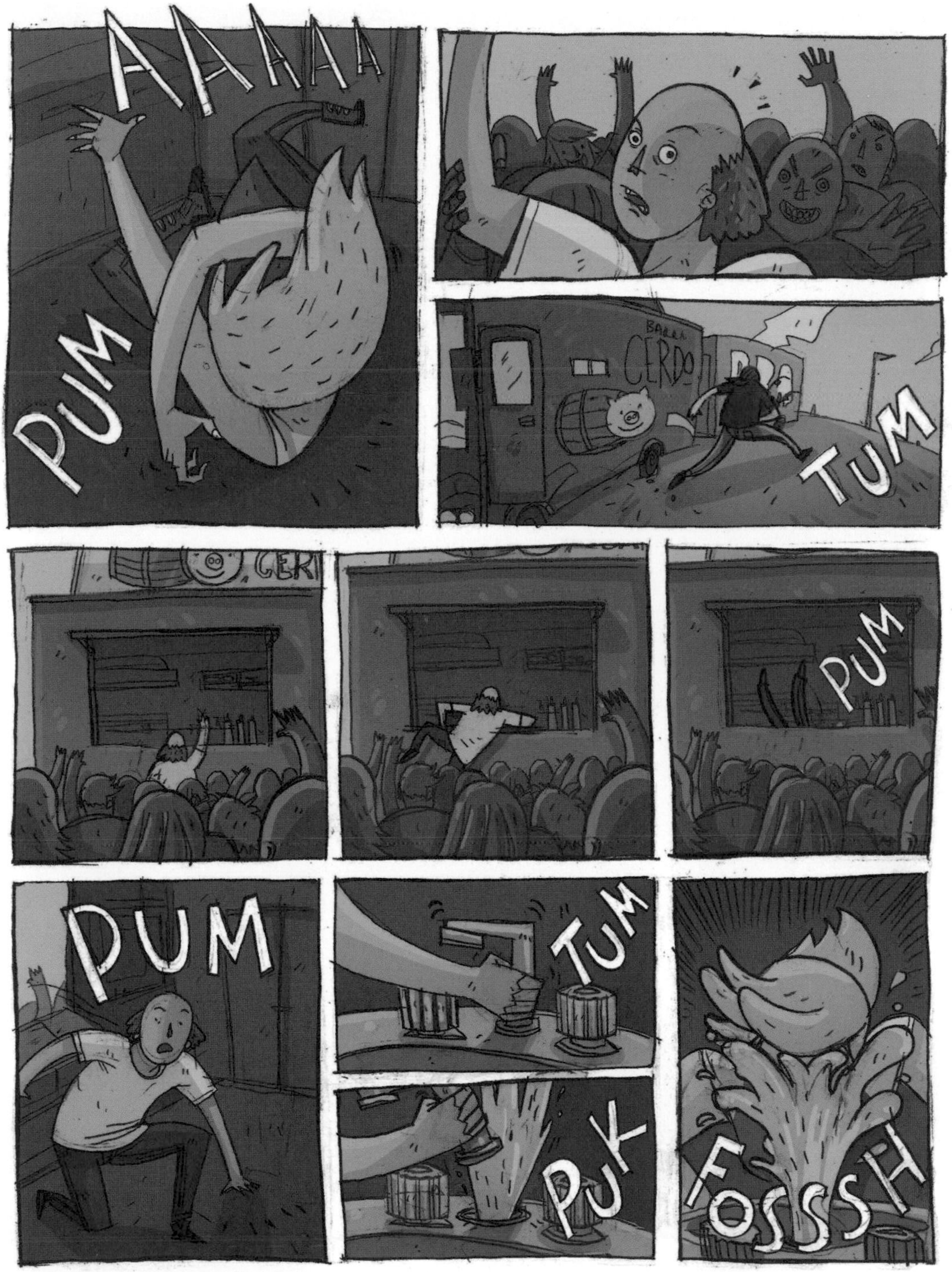
AAAAA
PUM
BARRA
CERDO
TUM
PUM
PUM
TUM
PUK
FOSSSH

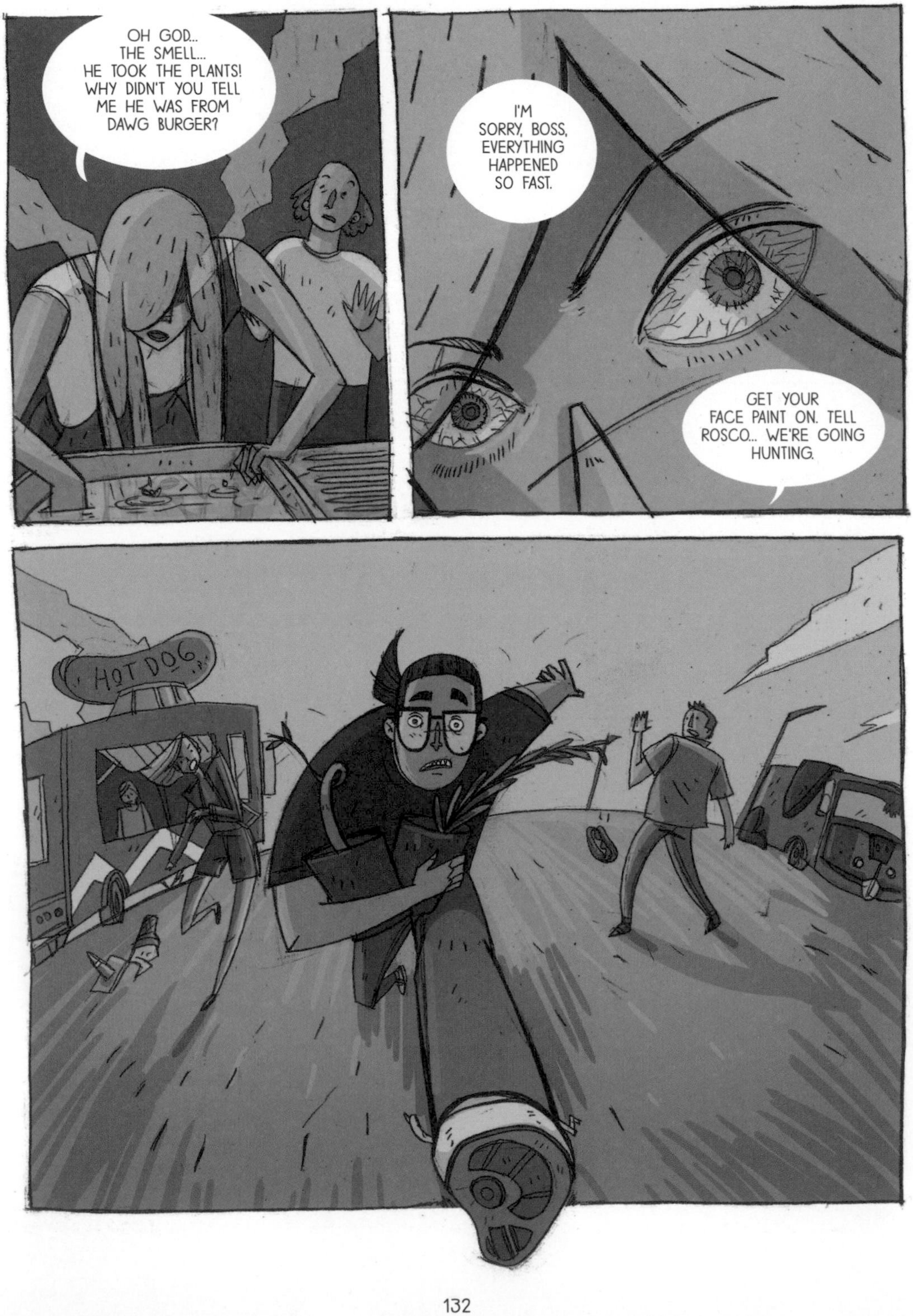
OH GOD... THE SMELL... HE TOOK THE PLANTS! WHY DIDN'T YOU TELL ME HE WAS FROM DAWG BURGER?
I'M SORRY, BOSS, EVERYTHING HAPPENED SO FAST.
GET YOUR FACE PAINT ON. TELL ROSCO... WE'RE GOING HUNTING.
HOT DOG

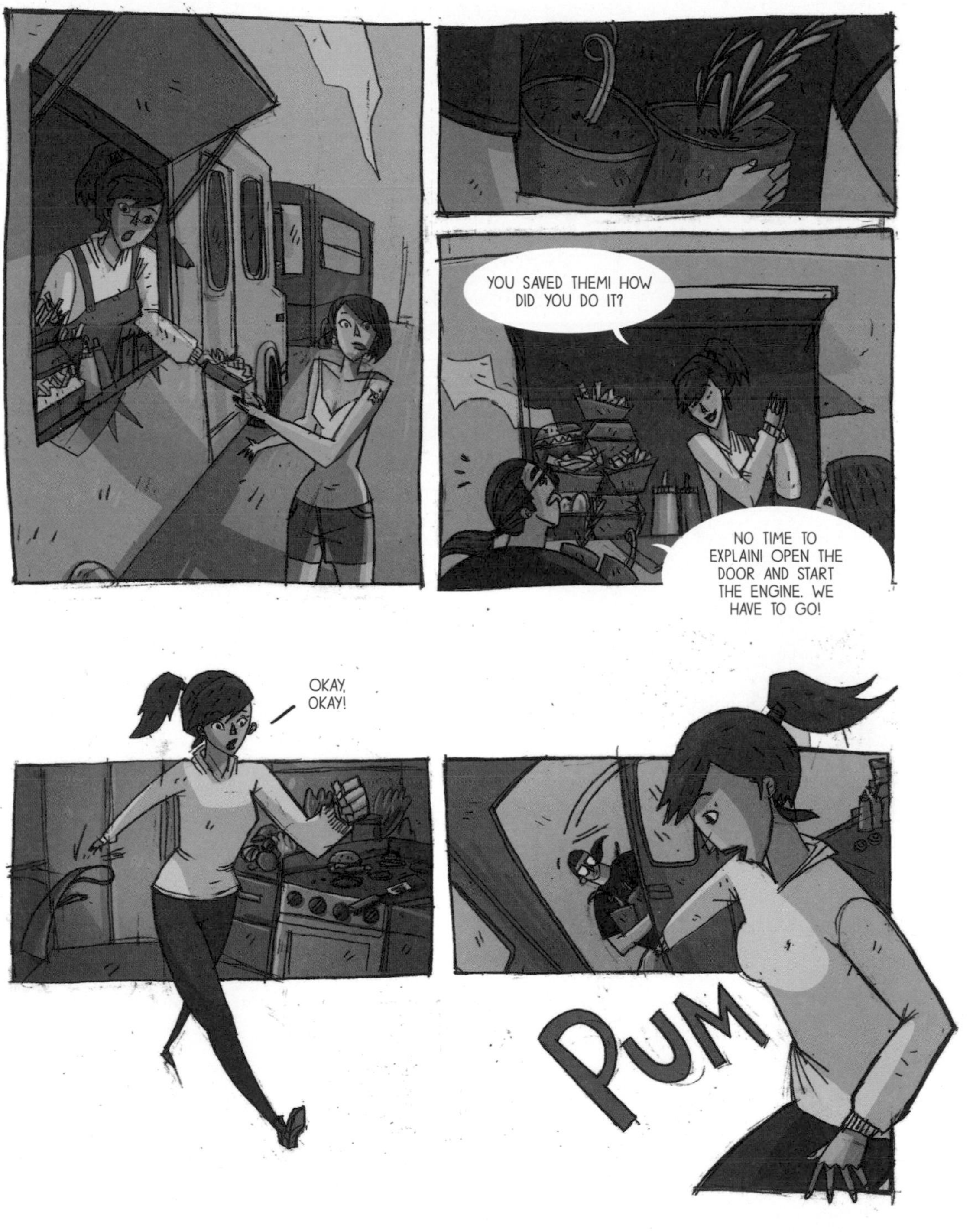
YOU SAVED THEMI HOW DID YOU DO IT?
NO TIME TO EXPLAINI OPEN THE DOOR AND START THE ENGINE. WE HAVE TO GO!
OKAY, OKAY!
PUM

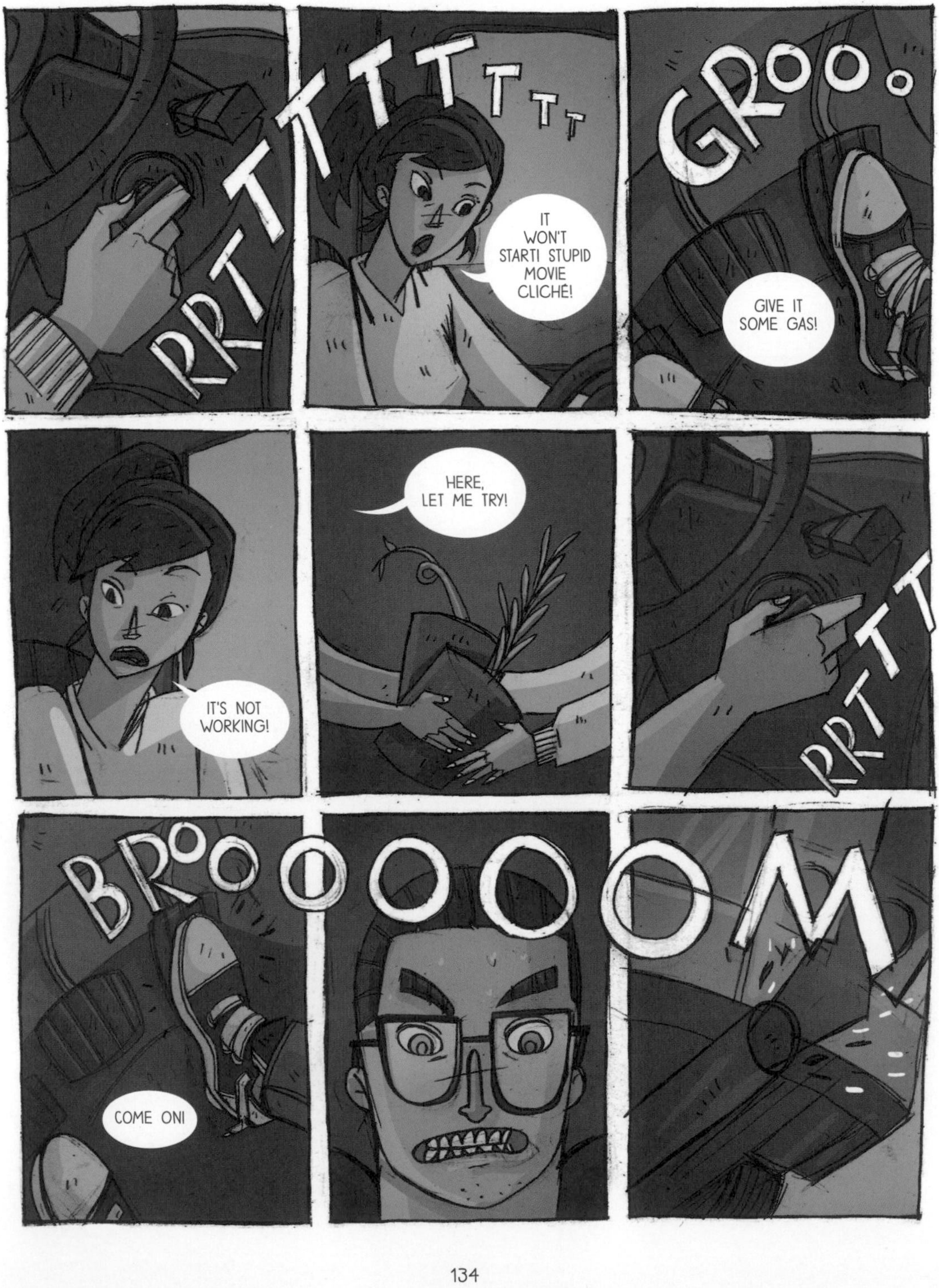

RRTTTTTTTTTT
IT WON'T START! STUPID MOVIE CLICHÉ!
GROO
GIVE IT SOME GAS!
IT'S NOT WORKING!
HERE, LET ME TRY!
RRTTT
BROOOOOOM
COME ON!

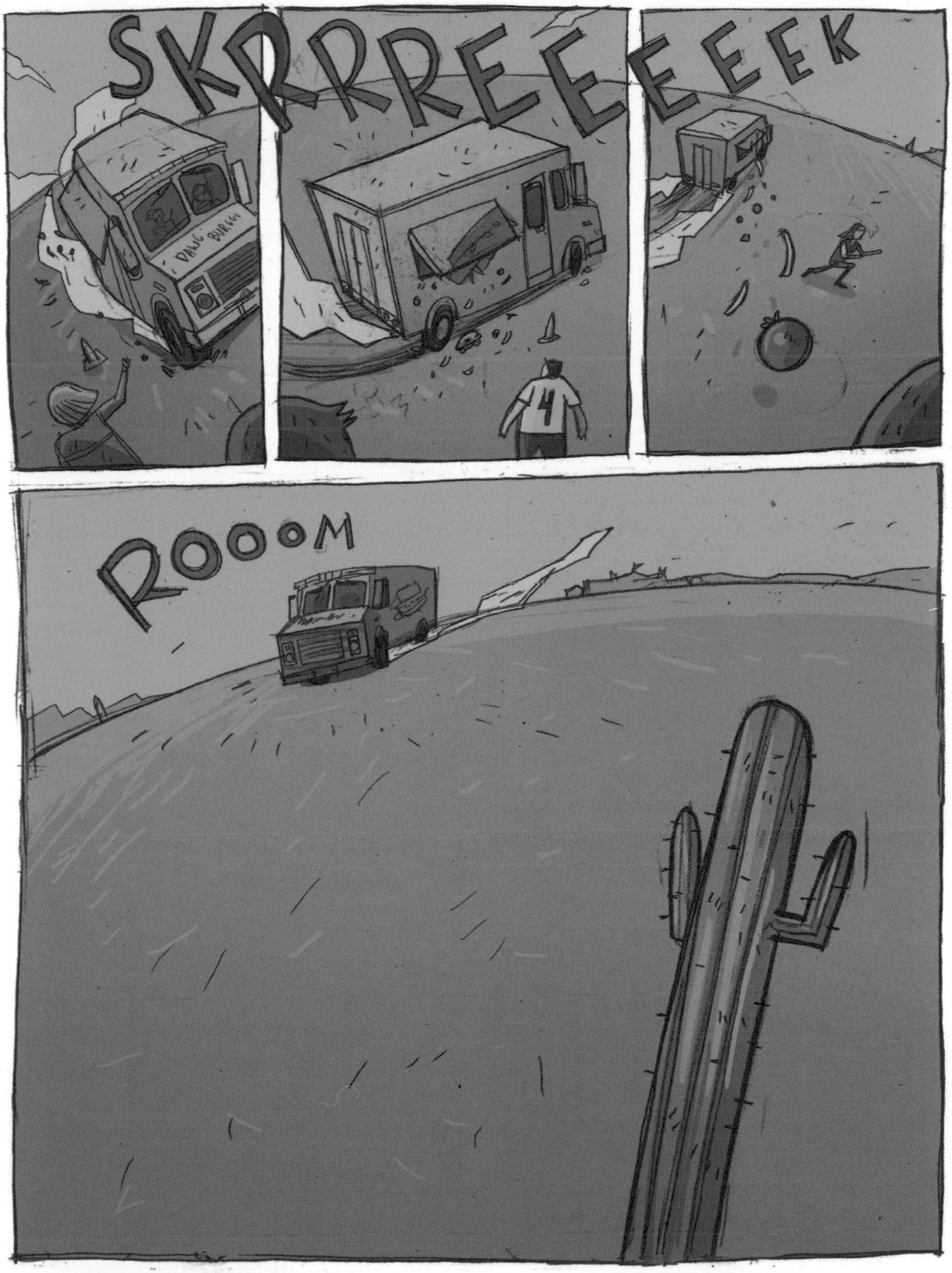
SKRRREEEEEK
ROOOM

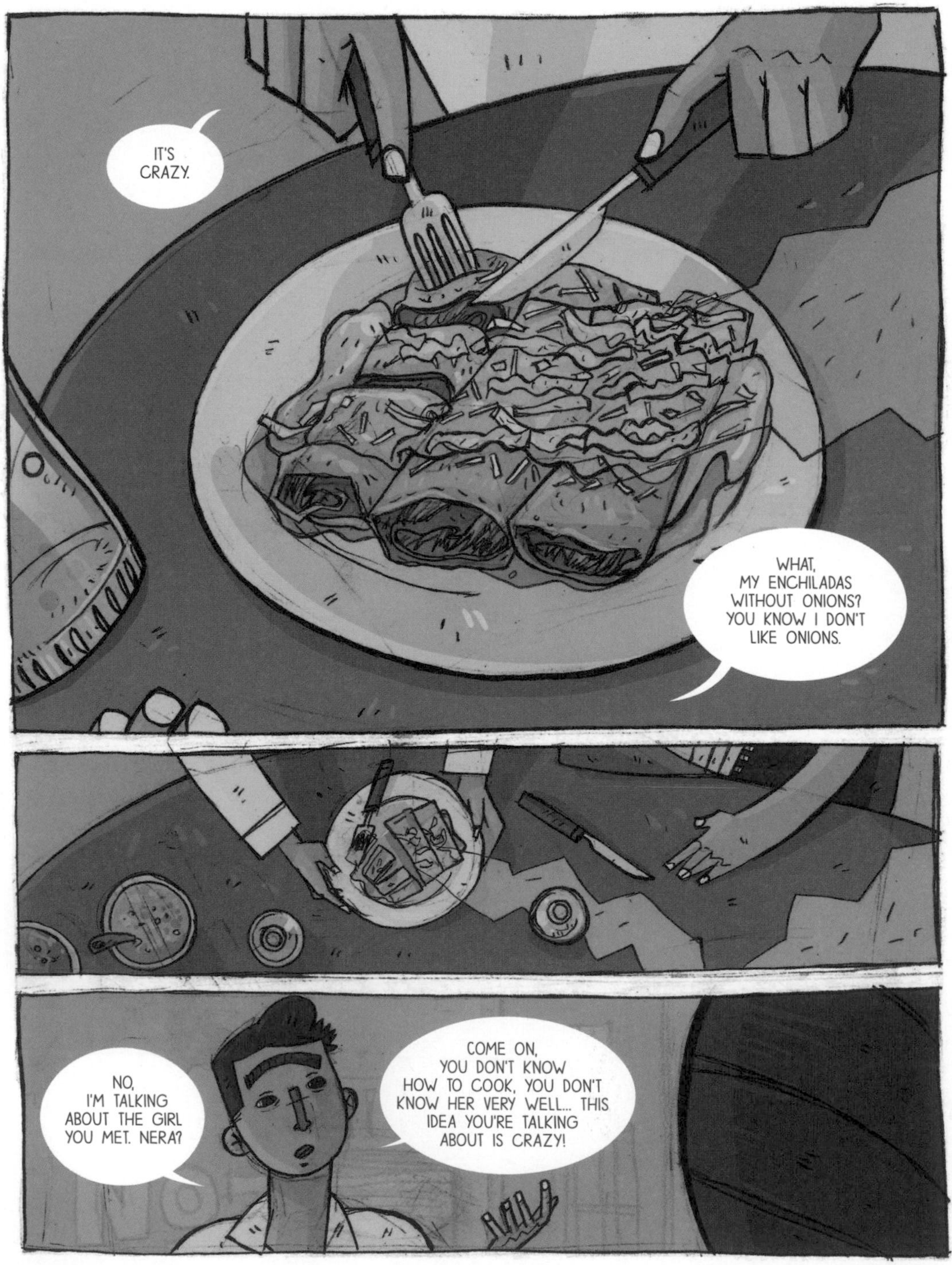
IT'S CRAZY.
WHAT, MY ENCHILADAS WITHOUT ONIONS? YOU KNOW I DON'T LIKE ONIONS.
NO, I'M TALKING ABOUT THE GIRL YOU MET. NERA?
COME ON, YOU DON'T KNOW HOW TO COOK, YOU DON'T KNOW HER VERY WELL... THIS IDEA YOU'RE TALKING ABOUT IS CRAZY!

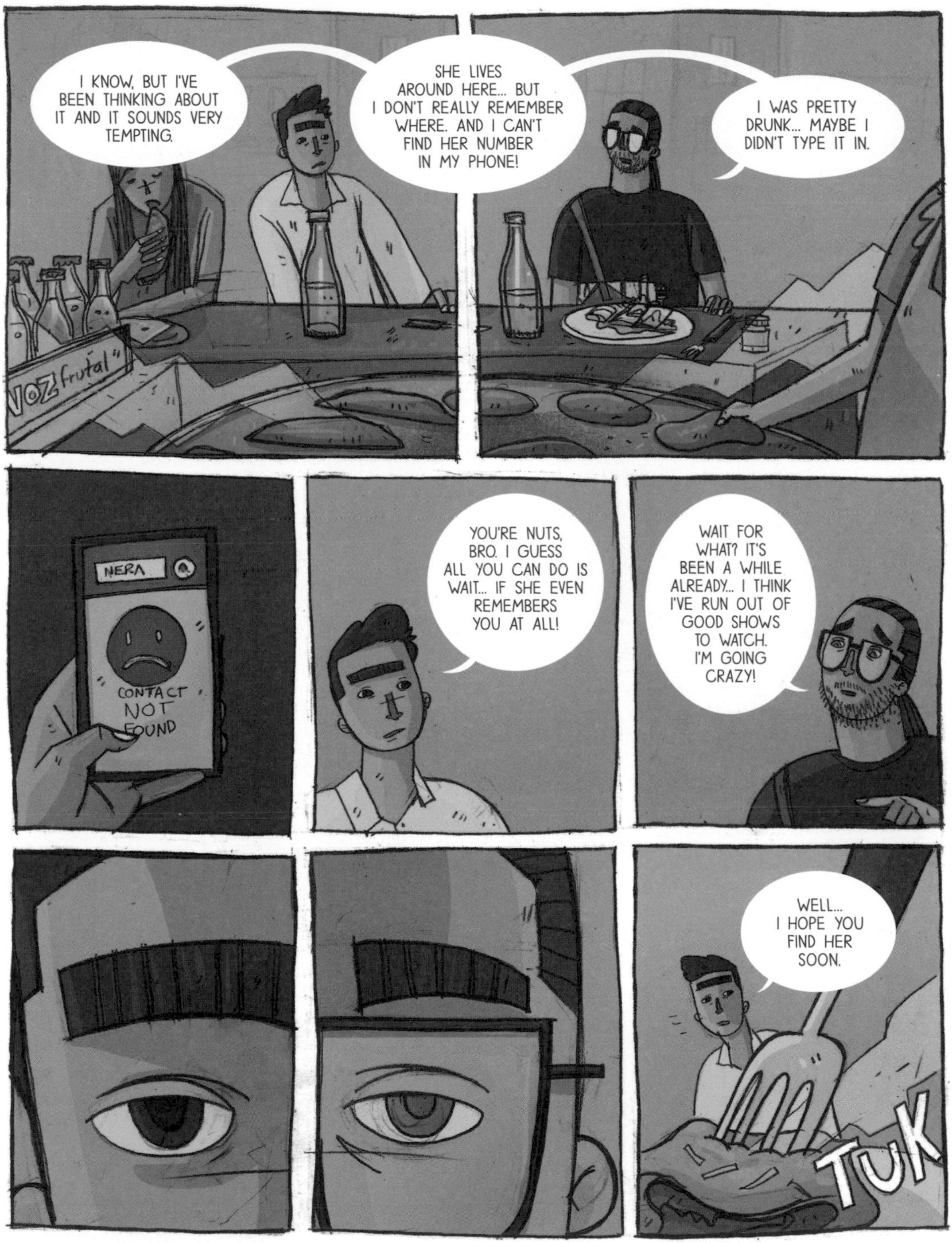
I KNOW, BUT I'VE BEEN THINKING ABOUT IT AND IT SOUNDS VERY TEMPTING.
SHE LIVES AROUND HERE... BUT I DON'T REALLY REMEMBER WHERE. AND I CAN'T FIND HER NUMBER IN MY PHONE!
I WAS PRETTY DRUNK... MAYBE I DIDN'T TYPE IT IN.
VOZ frutal
NERA
CONTACT NOT FOUND
YOU'RE NUTS, BRO. I GUESS ALL YOU CAN DO IS WAIT... IF SHE EVEN REMEMBERS YOU AT ALL!
WAIT FOR WHAT? IT'S BEEN A WHILE ALREADY... I THINK I'VE RUN OUT OF GOOD SHOWS TO WATCH. I'M GOING CRAZY!
WELL... I HOPE YOU FIND HER SOON.
TUK

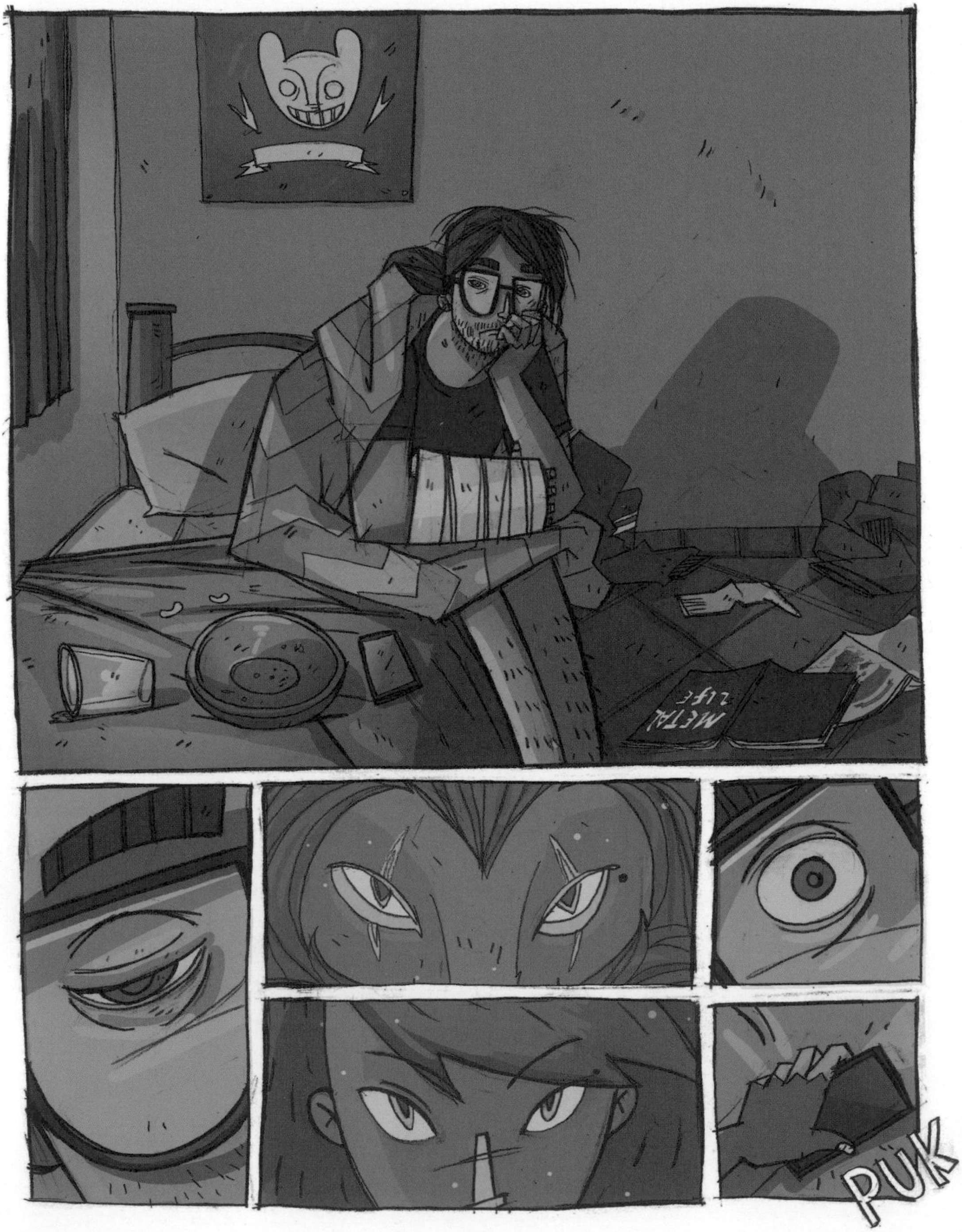
METAL LIFE
PUK

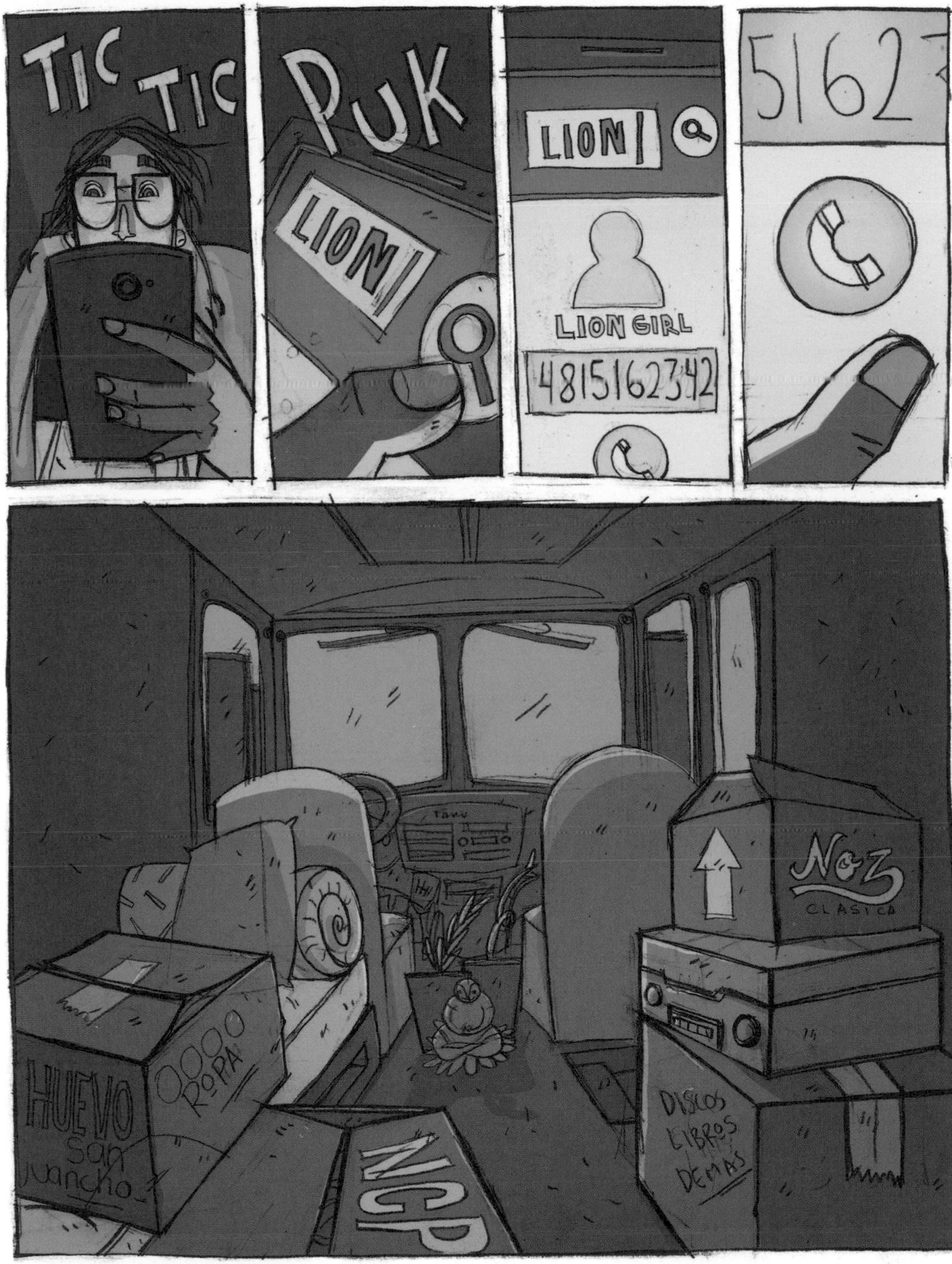
TIC TIC
PUK
LION
LION
LION GIRL
4815162342
5162
NOZ
CLASICA
HUEVO
san juancho
ROPA
NCP
DISCOS
LIBROS
DEMÁS

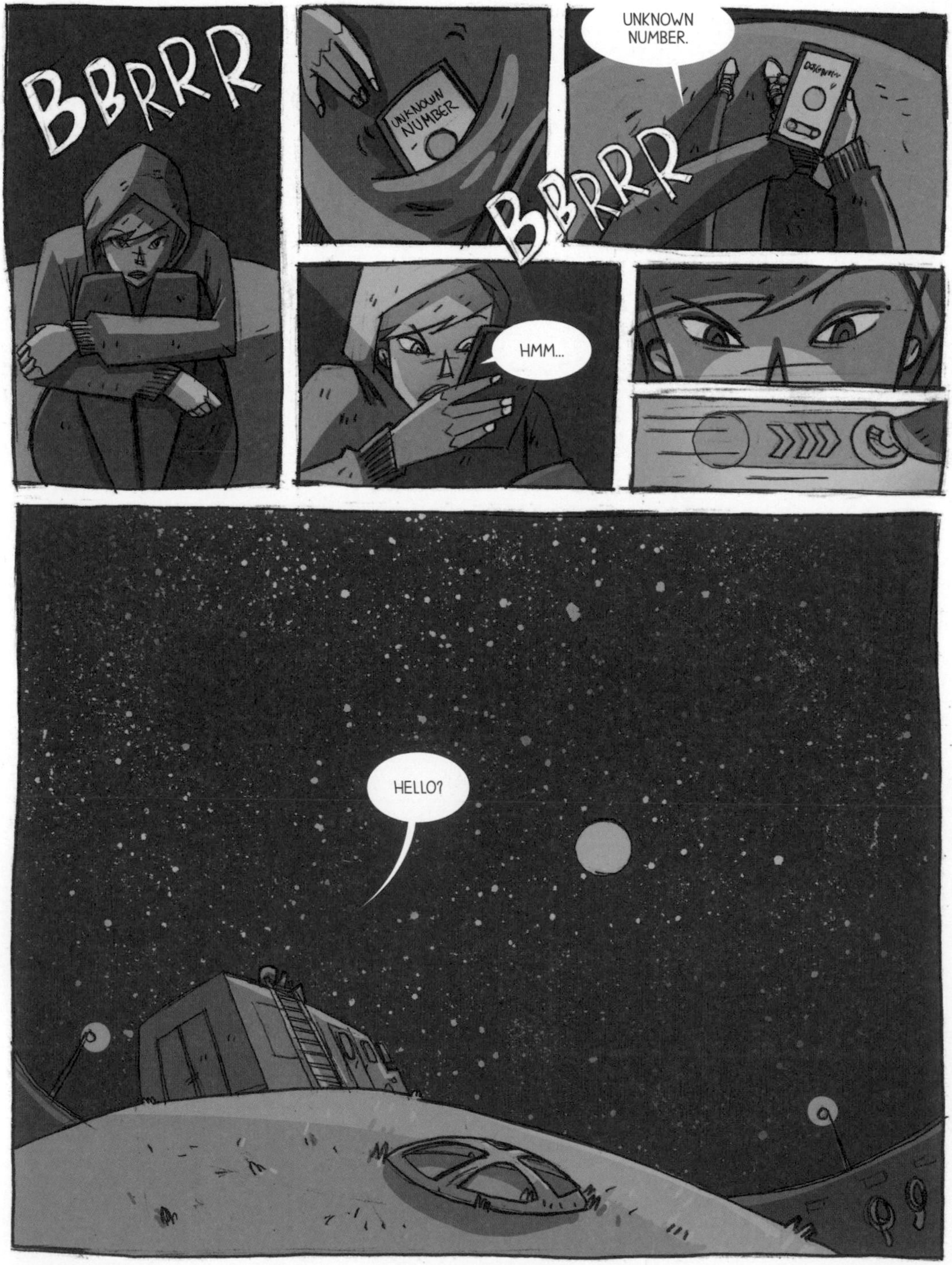
BBRRR
UNKNOWN NUMBER
UNKNOWN NUMBER.
BBRRR
HMM...
HELLO?

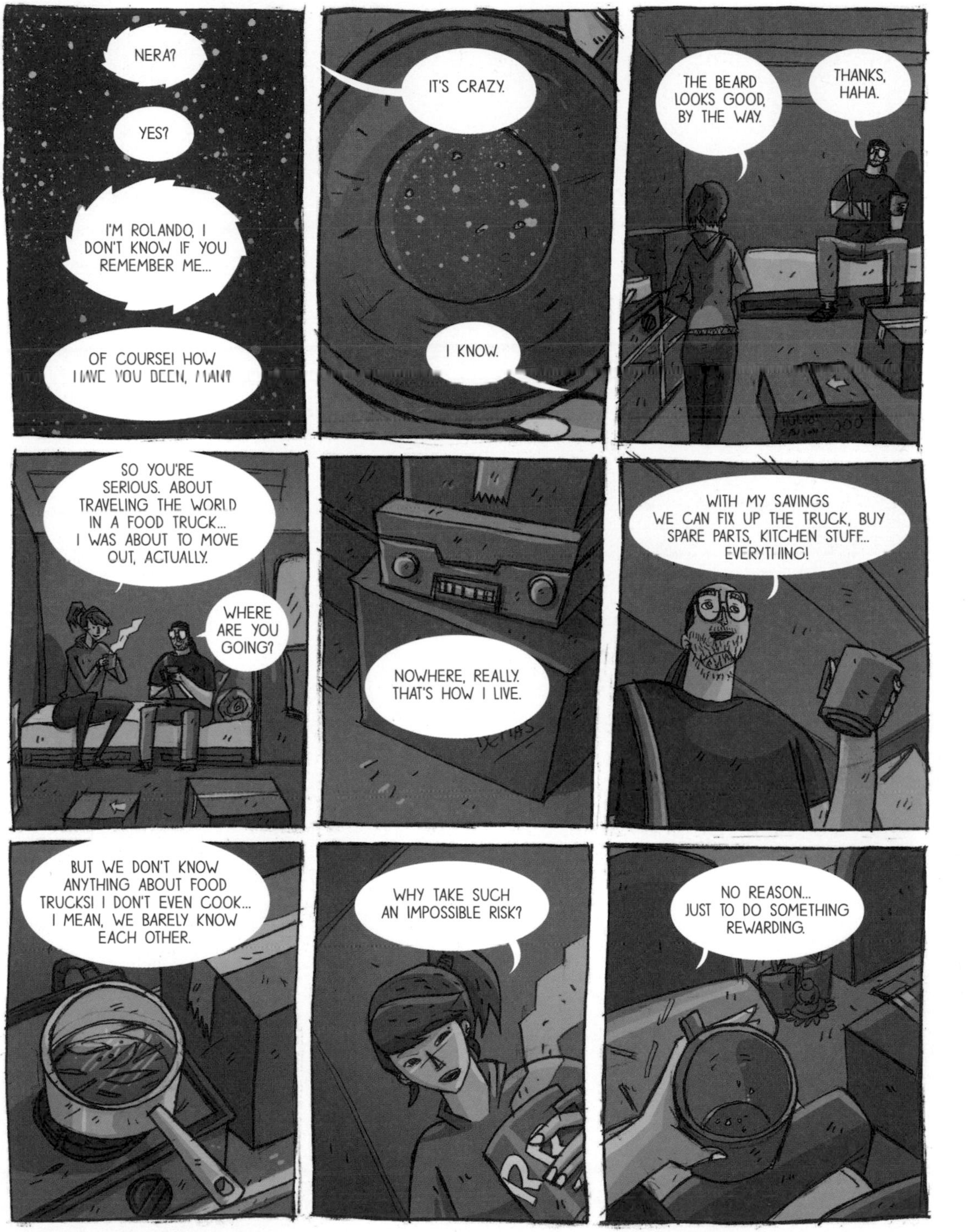
NERA?
YES?
I'M ROLANDO, I DON'T KNOW IF YOU REMEMBER ME...
OF COURSE! HOW HAVE YOU BEEN, MAN?
IT'S CRAZY.
I KNOW.
THE BEARD LOOKS GOOD, BY THE WAY.
THANKS, HAHA.
SO YOU'RE SERIOUS. ABOUT TRAVELING THE WORLD IN A FOOD TRUCK... I WAS ABOUT TO MOVE OUT, ACTUALLY.
WHERE ARE YOU GOING?
NOWHERE, REALLY. THAT'S HOW I LIVE.
WITH MY SAVINGS WE CAN FIX UP THE TRUCK, BUY SPARE PARTS, KITCHEN STUFF... EVERYTHING!
BUT WE DON'T KNOW ANYTHING ABOUT FOOD TRUCKS! I DON'T EVEN COOK... I MEAN, WE BARELY KNOW EACH OTHER.
WHY TAKE SUCH AN IMPOSSIBLE RISK?
NO REASON... JUST TO DO SOMETHING REWARDING.

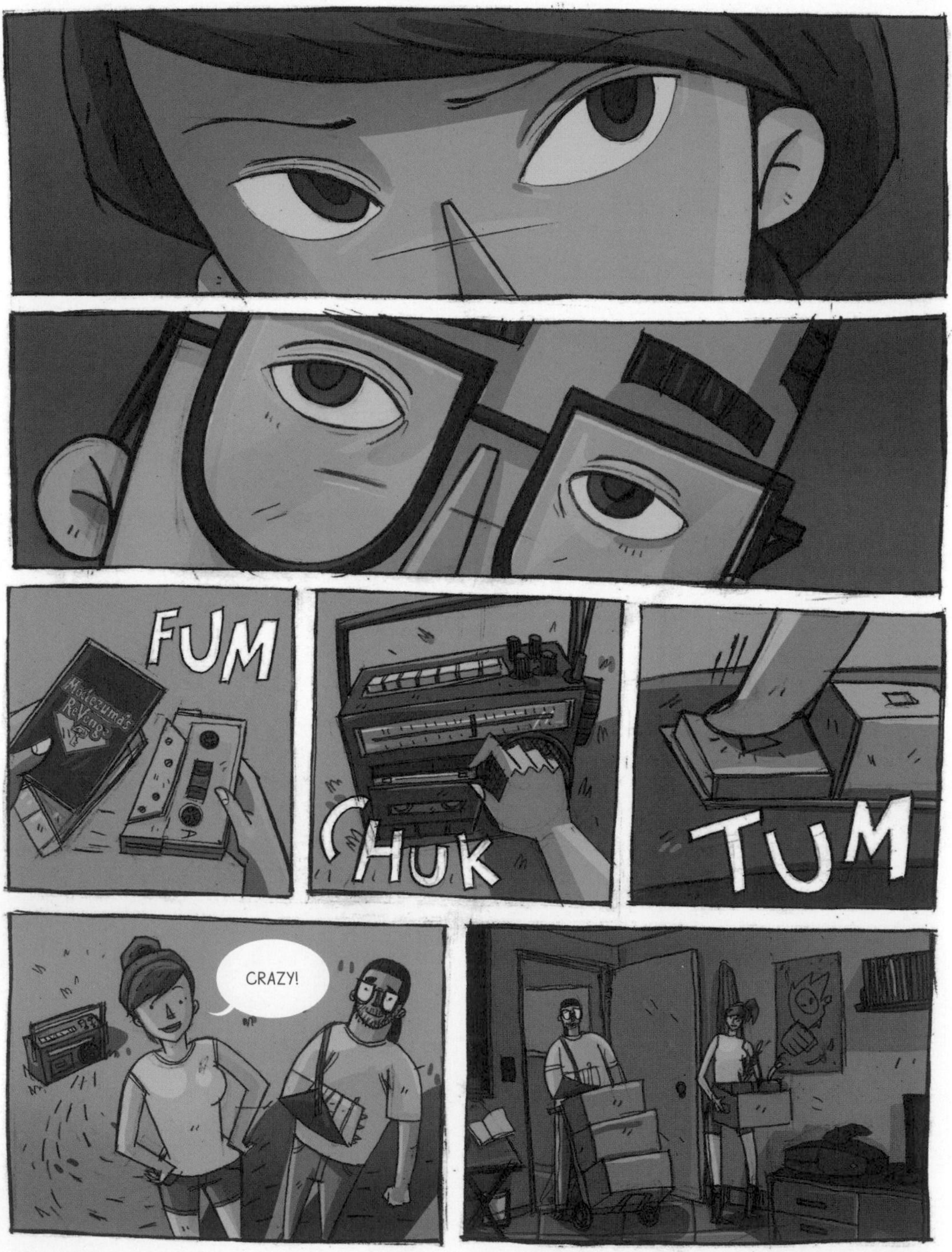
Moctezuma's Revenge
FUM
CHUK
TUM
CRAZY!

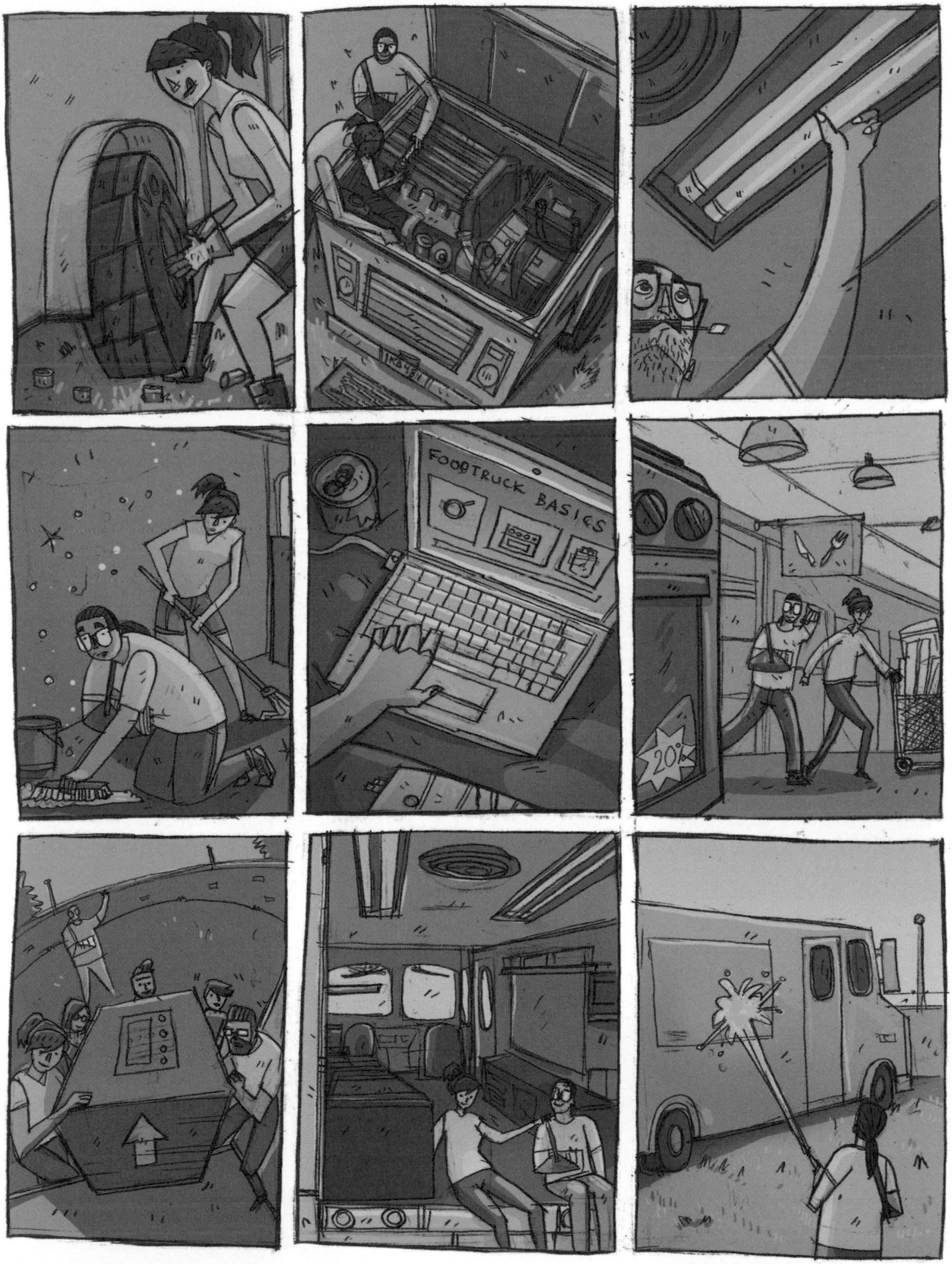
FOODTRUCK BASICS
20%

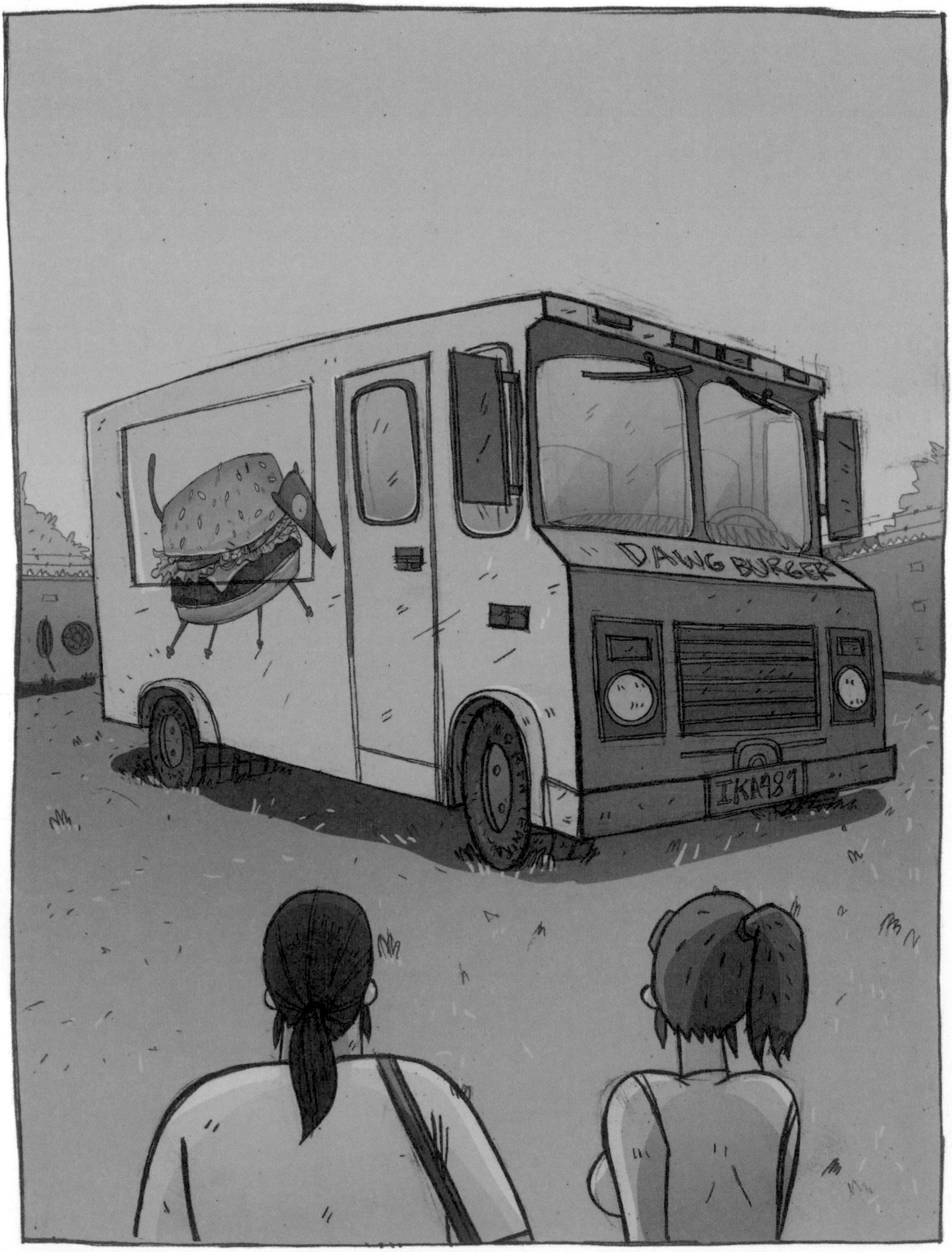
DAWG BURGER
IKA481

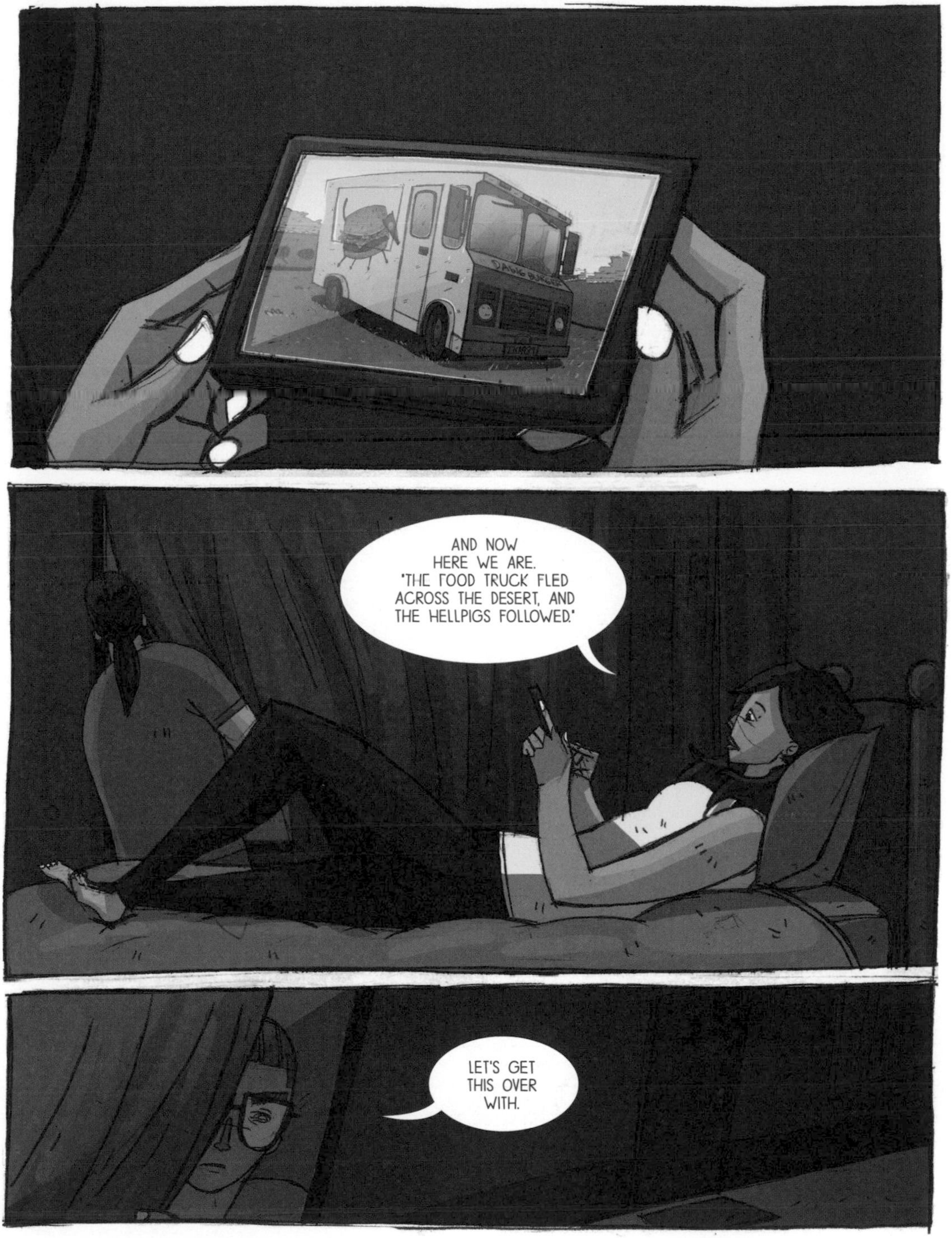
AND NOW HERE WE ARE. "THE FOOD TRUCK FLED ACROSS THE DESERT, AND THE HELLPIGS FOLLOWED."
LET'S GET THIS OVER WITH.

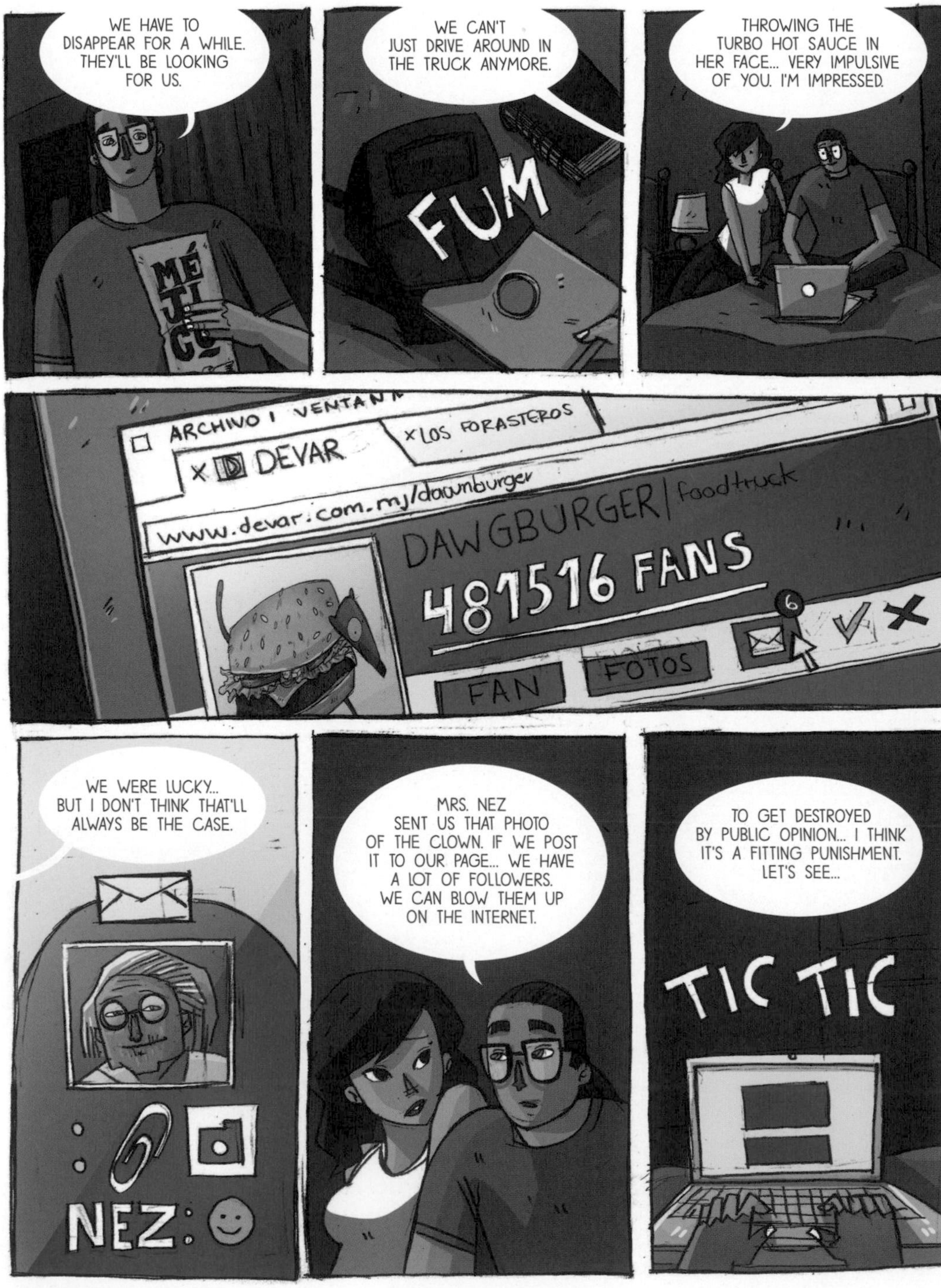
WE HAVE TO DISAPPEAR FOR A WHILE. THEY'LL BE LOOKING FOR US.
MÉJICO
WE CAN'T JUST DRIVE AROUND IN THE TRUCK ANYMORE.
FUM
THROWING THE TURBO HOT SAUCE IN HER FACE... VERY IMPULSIVE OF YOU. I'M IMPRESSED.
ARCHIVO I VENTAN
× DEVAR
×LOS FORASTEROS
www.devar.com.mj/dawnburger
DAWGBURGER | foodtruck
481516 FANS
6
FOTOS
FAN
WE WERE LUCKY... BUT I DON'T THINK THAT'LL ALWAYS BE THE CASE.
NEZ:
MRS. NEZ SENT US THAT PHOTO OF THE CLOWN. IF WE POST IT TO OUR PAGE... WE HAVE A LOT OF FOLLOWERS. WE CAN BLOW THEM UP ON THE INTERNET.
TO GET DESTROYED BY PUBLIC OPINION... I THINK IT'S A FITTING PUNISHMENT. LET'S SEE...
TIC TIC

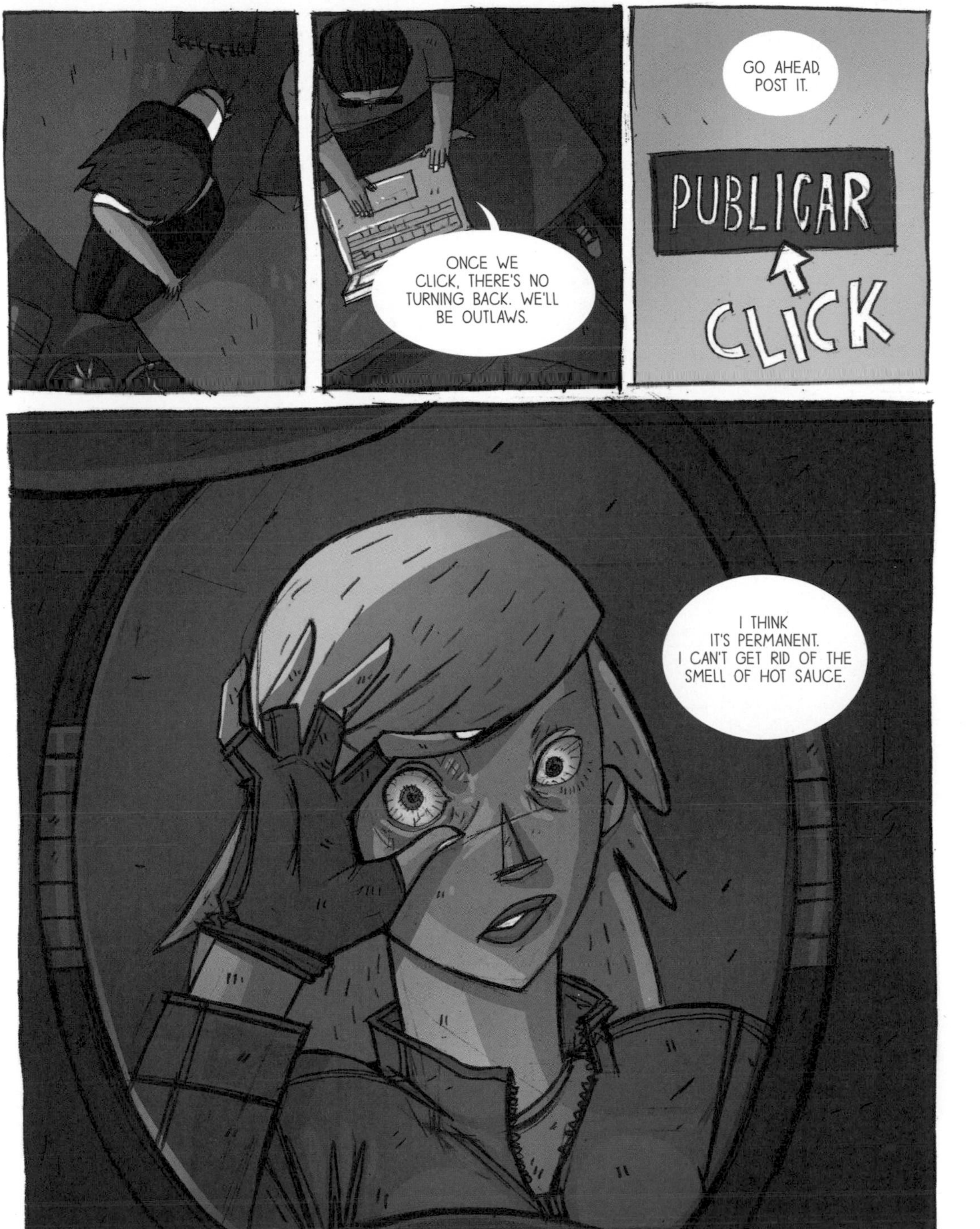
ONCE WE CLICK, THERE'S NO TURNING BACK. WE'LL BE OUTLAWS.
GO AHEAD, POST IT.
PUBLICAR
CLICK
I THINK IT'S PERMANENT. I CAN'T GET RID OF THE SMELL OF HOT SAUCE.

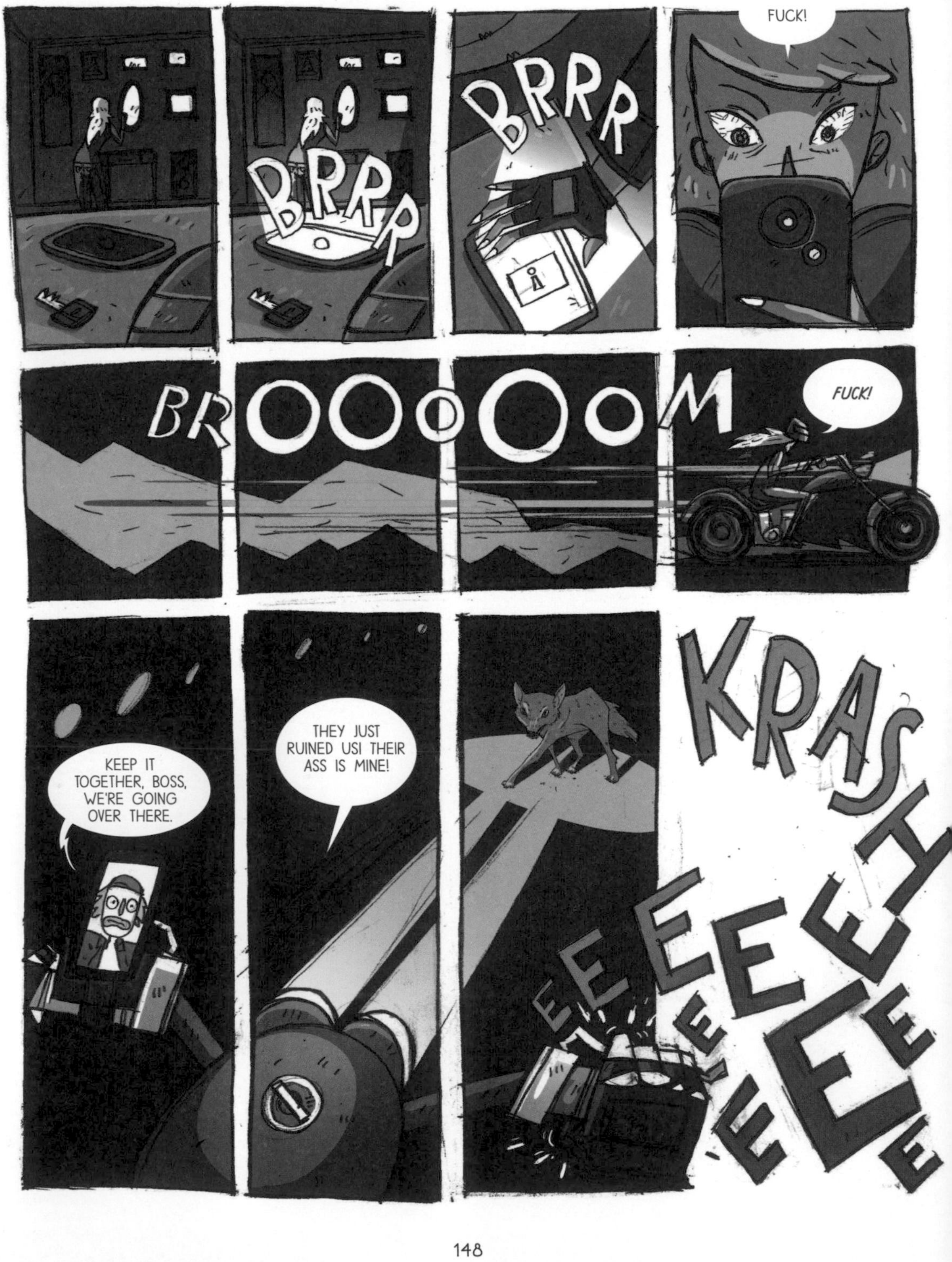
BRRRR
BRRRR
FUCK!
BROOoOOOM
FUCK!
KEEP IT TOGETHER, BOSS, WE'RE GOING OVER THERE.
THEY JUST RUINED US! THEIR ASS IS MINE!
KRASH
EEEEEEEEE

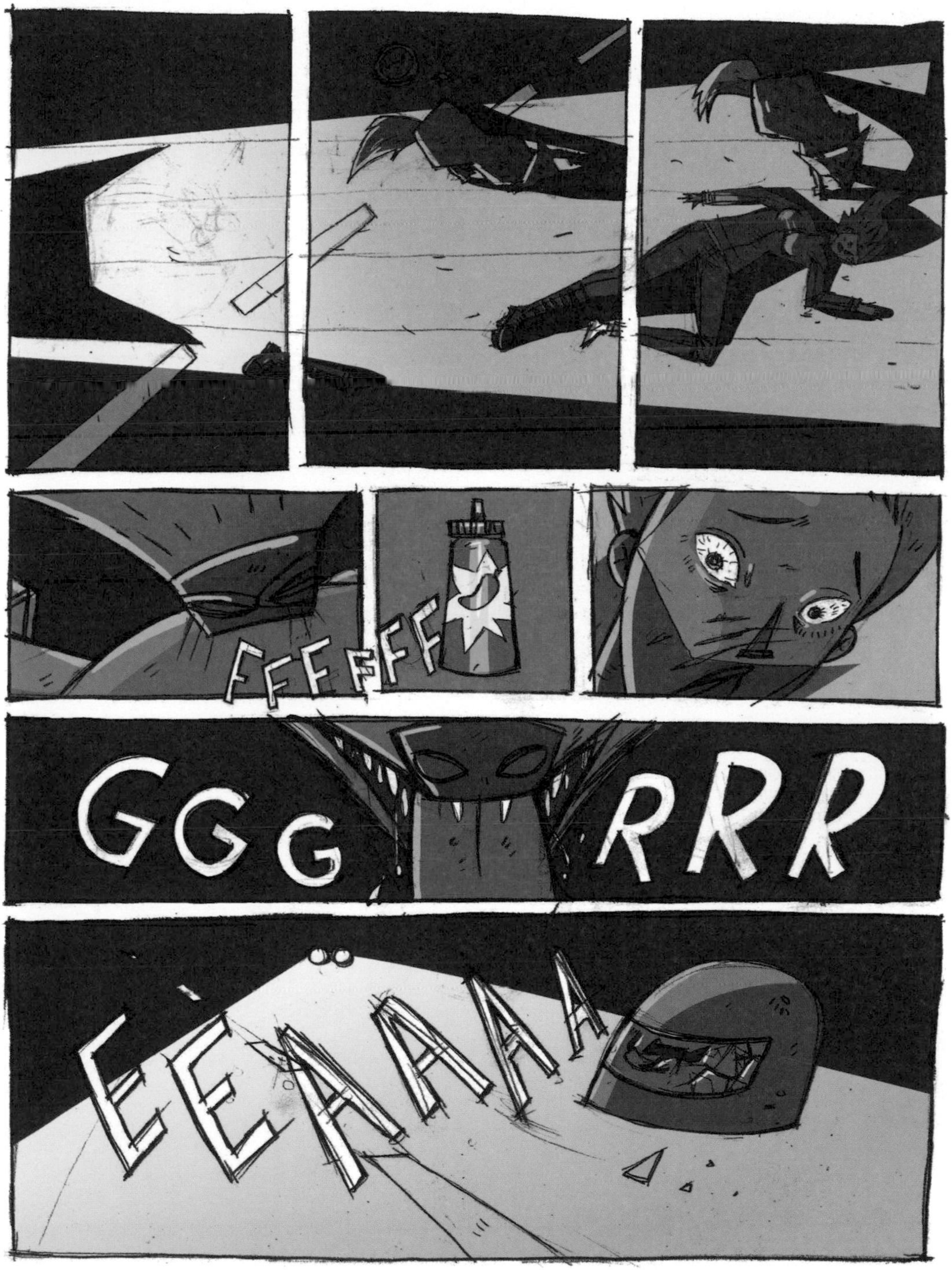
FFFFFF
GGG
RRR
EEAAAA

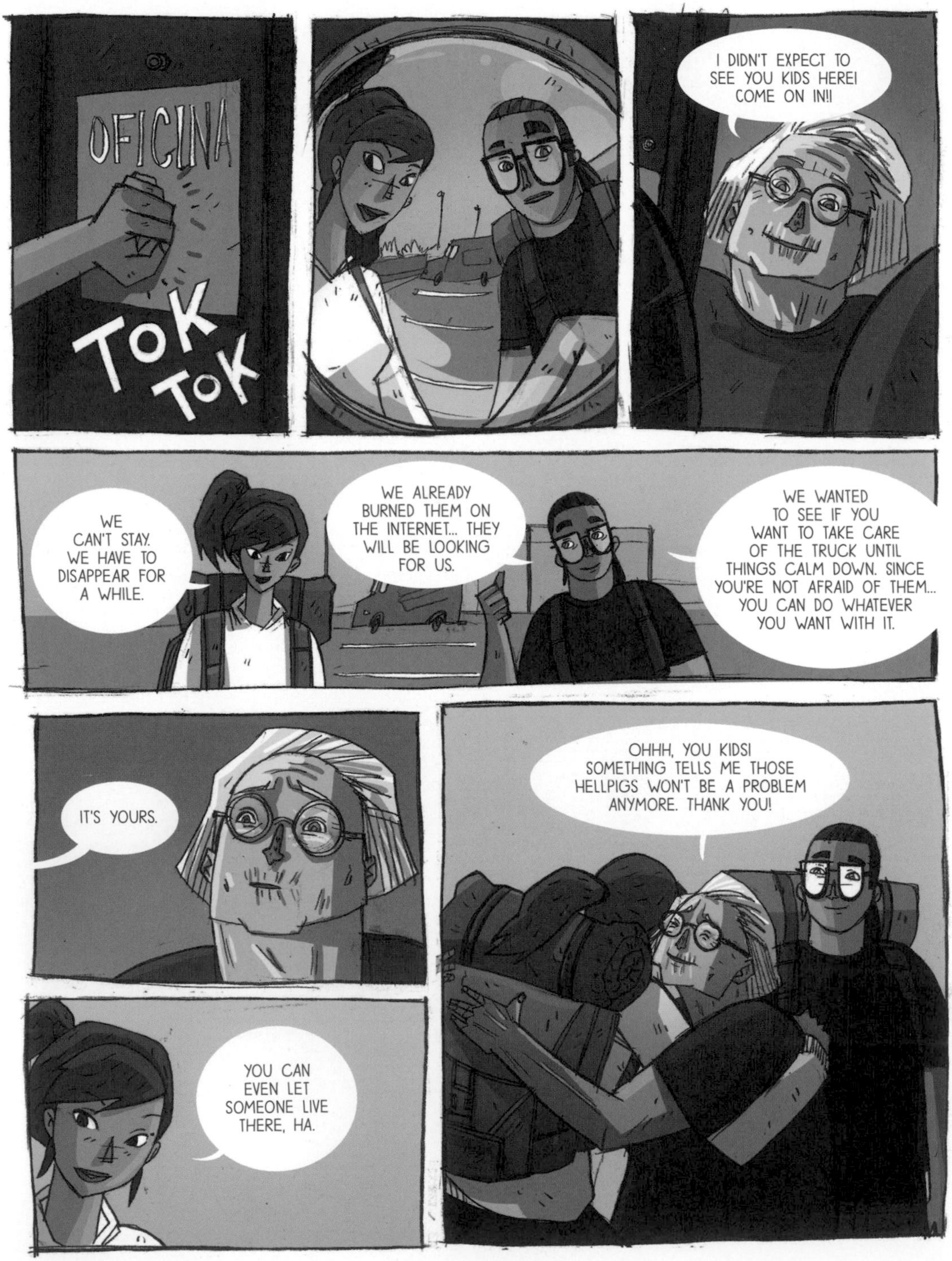
OFICINA
TOK TOK
I DIDN'T EXPECT TO SEE YOU KIDS HERE! COME ON IN!!
WE CAN'T STAY. WE HAVE TO DISAPPEAR FOR A WHILE.
WE ALREADY BURNED THEM ON THE INTERNET... THEY WILL BE LOOKING FOR US.
WE WANTED TO SEE IF YOU WANT TO TAKE CARE OF THE TRUCK UNTIL THINGS CALM DOWN. SINCE YOU'RE NOT AFRAID OF THEM... YOU CAN DO WHATEVER YOU WANT WITH IT.
IT'S YOURS.
YOU CAN EVEN LET SOMEONE LIVE THERE, HA.
OHHH, YOU KIDS! SOMETHING TELLS ME THOSE HELLPIGS WON'T BE A PROBLEM ANYMORE. THANK YOU!

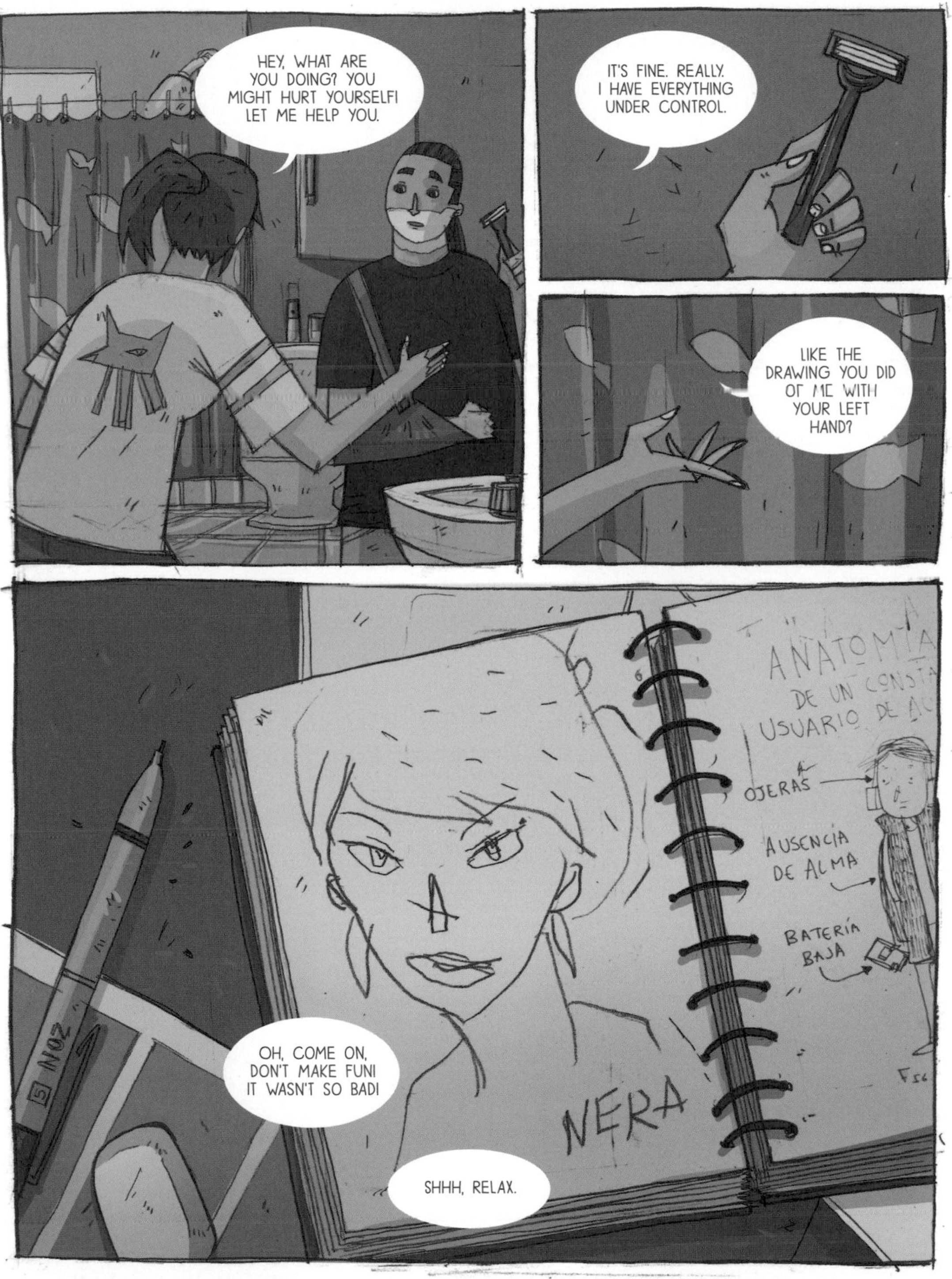

HEY, WHAT ARE YOU DOING? YOU MIGHT HURT YOURSELF! LET ME HELP YOU.
IT'S FINE. REALLY. I HAVE EVERYTHING UNDER CONTROL.
LIKE THE DRAWING YOU DID OF ME WITH YOUR LEFT HAND?
ANATOMIA
DE UN CONSTA
USUARIO DE
OJERAS
AUSENCIA DE ALMA
BATERÍA BAJA
NERA
OH, COME ON, DON'T MAKE FUN! IT WASN'T SO BAD!
SHHH, RELAX.

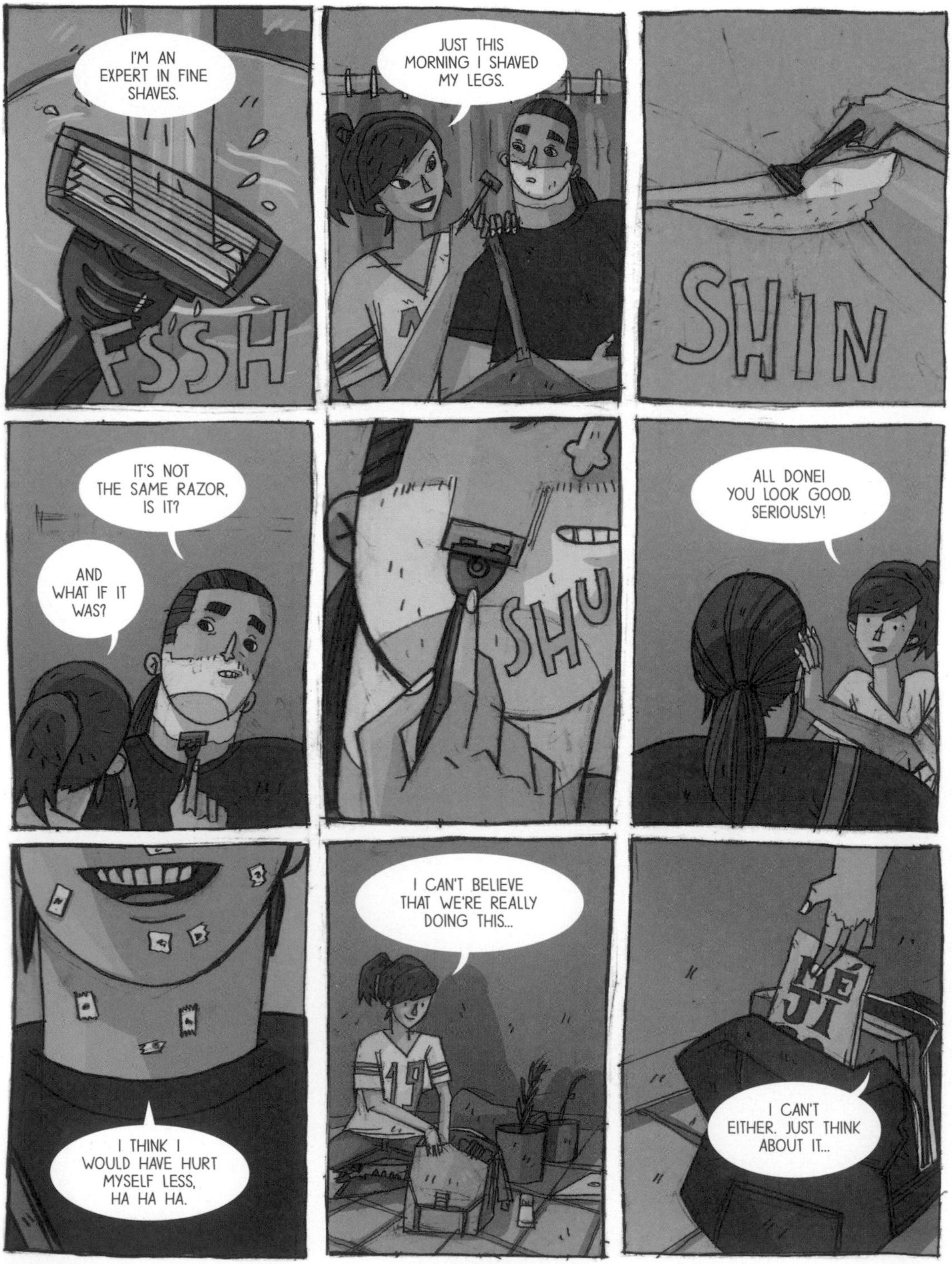
I'M AN EXPERT IN FINE SHAVES.
FSSH
JUST THIS MORNING I SHAVED MY LEGS.
SHIN
IT'S NOT THE SAME RAZOR, IS IT?
AND WHAT IF IT WAS?
SHU
ALL DONE! YOU LOOK GOOD. SERIOUSLY!
I THINK I WOULD HAVE HURT MYSELF LESS, HA HA HA.
I CAN'T BELIEVE THAT WE'RE REALLY DOING THIS...
I CAN'T EITHER. JUST THINK ABOUT IT...

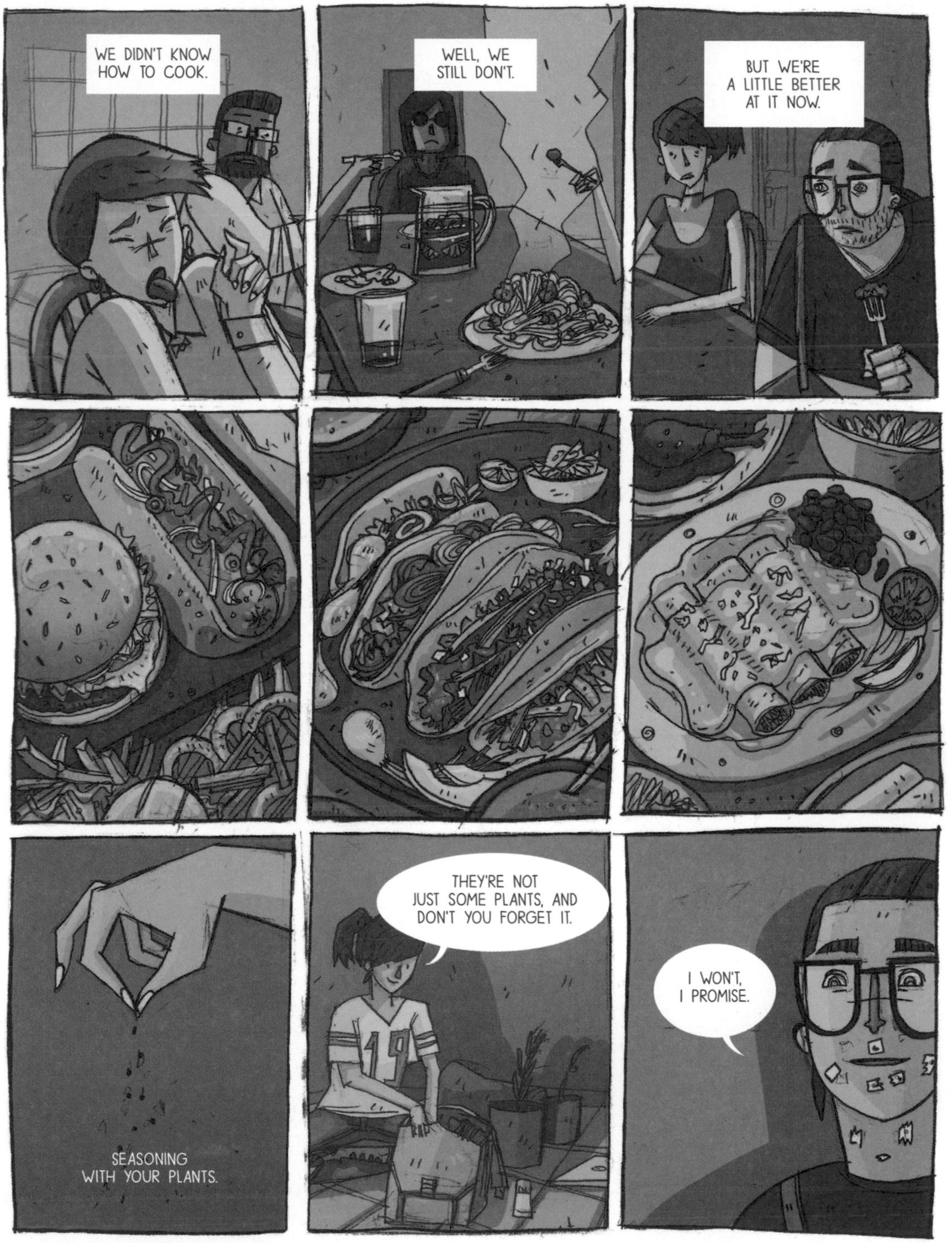
WE DIDN'T KNOW HOW TO COOK.
WELL, WE STILL DON'T.
BUT WE'RE A LITTLE BETTER AT IT NOW.
SEASONING WITH YOUR PLANTS.
THEY'RE NOT JUST SOME PLANTS, AND DON'T YOU FORGET IT.
I WON'T, I PROMISE.

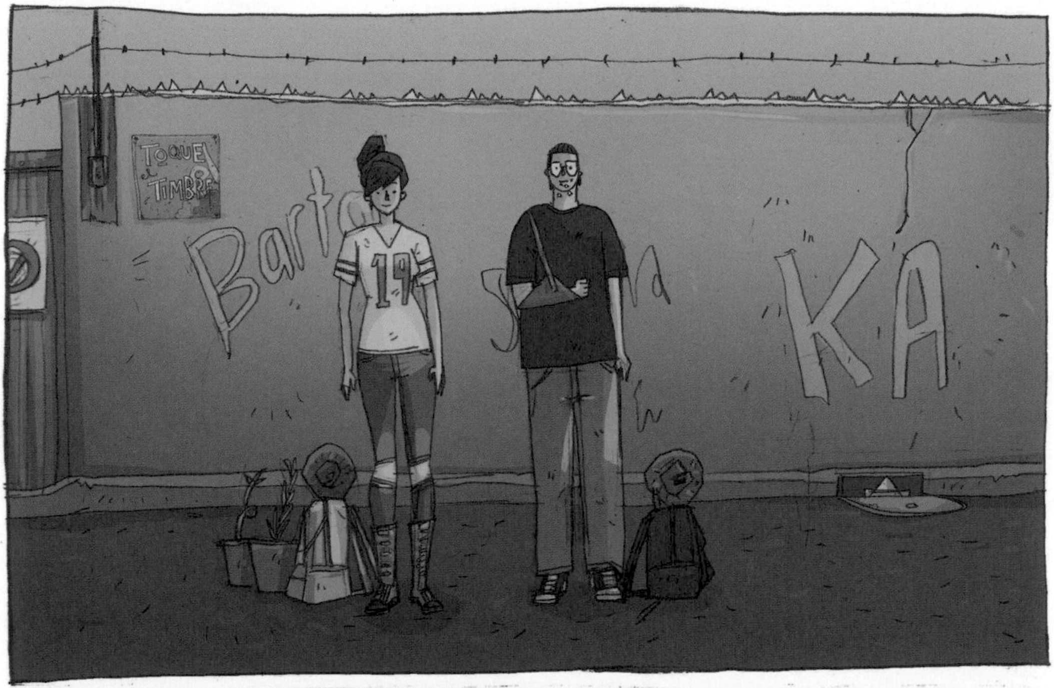
TOQUE el TIMBRE
KA

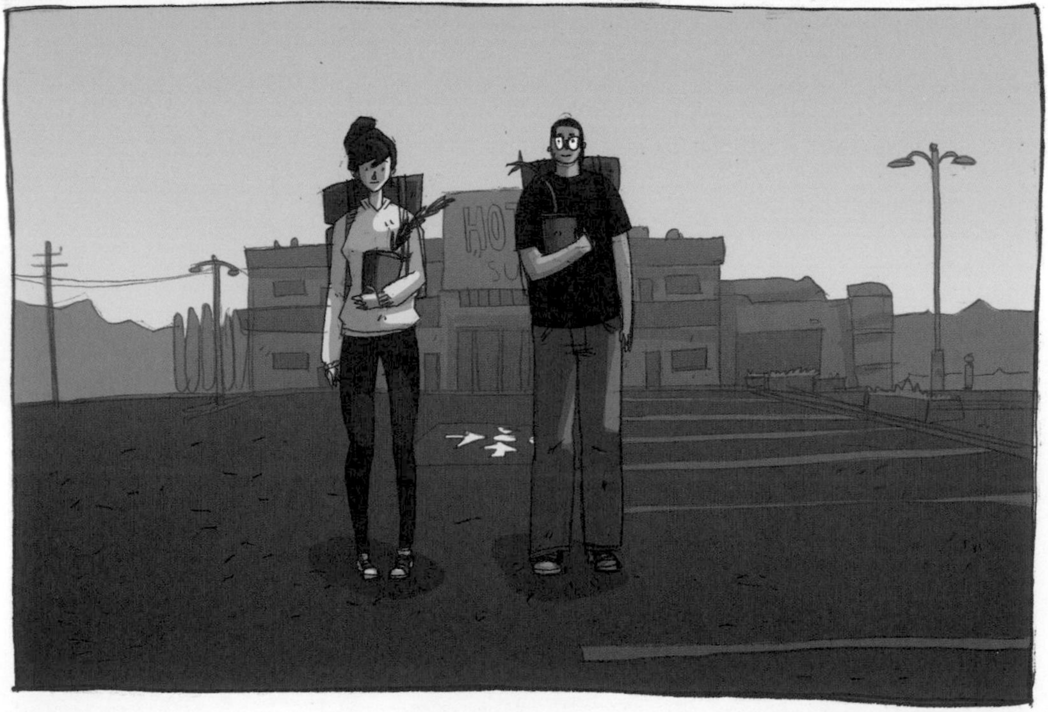

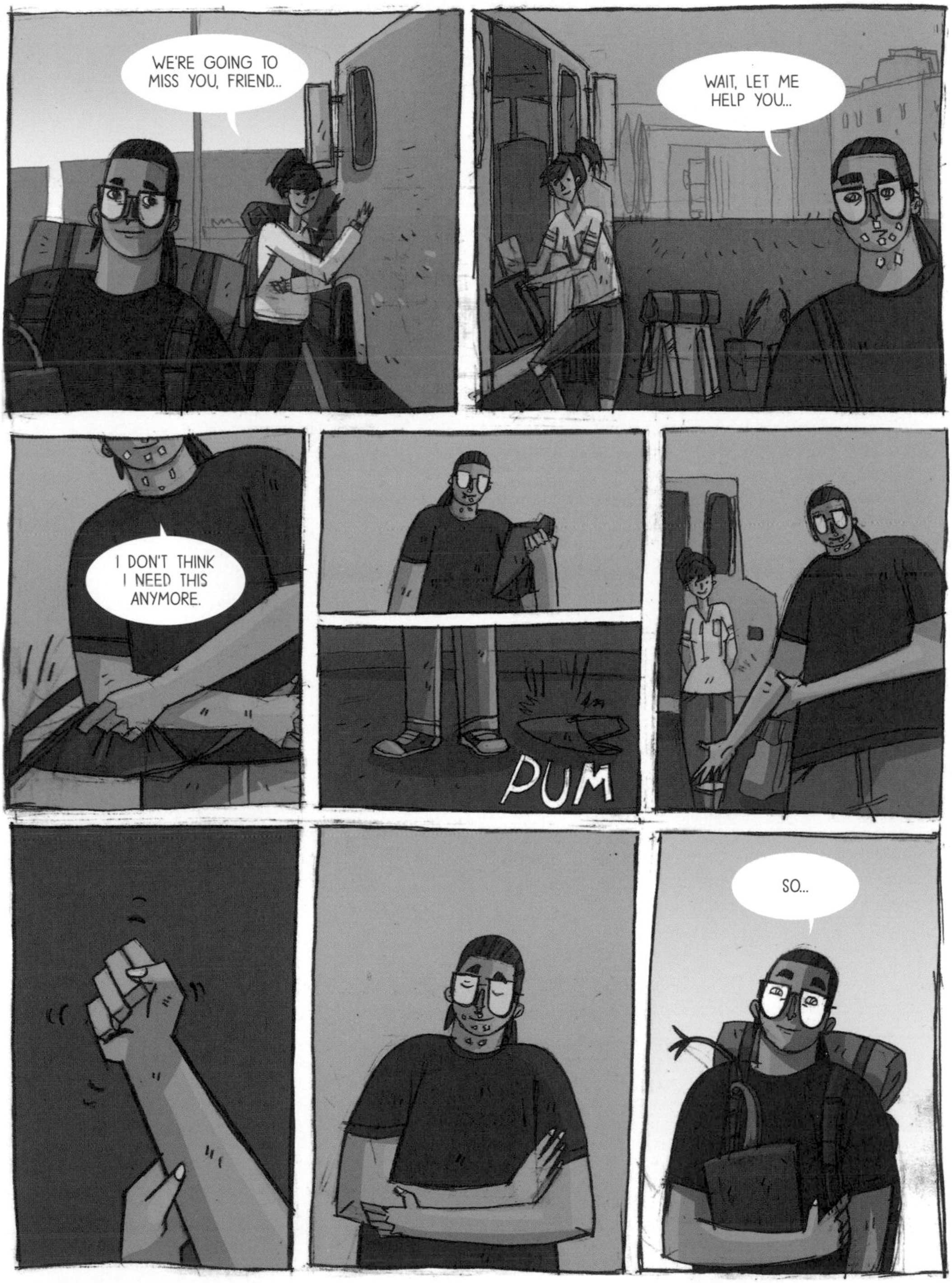
WE'RE GOING TO MISS YOU, FRIEND...
WAIT, LET ME HELP YOU...
I DON'T THINK I NEED THIS ANYMORE.
PUM
SO...

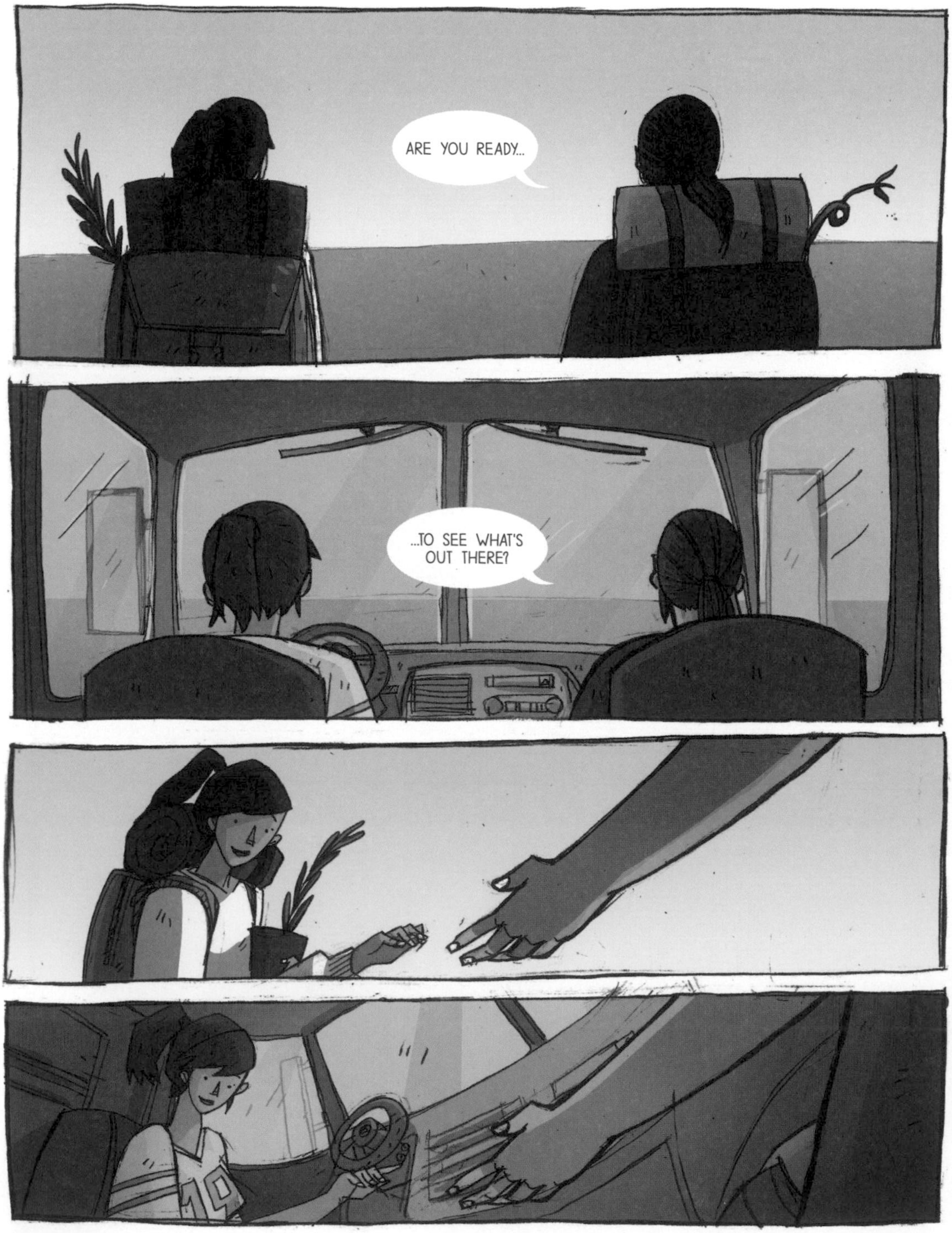
ARE YOU READY...
...TO SEE WHAT'S OUT THERE?

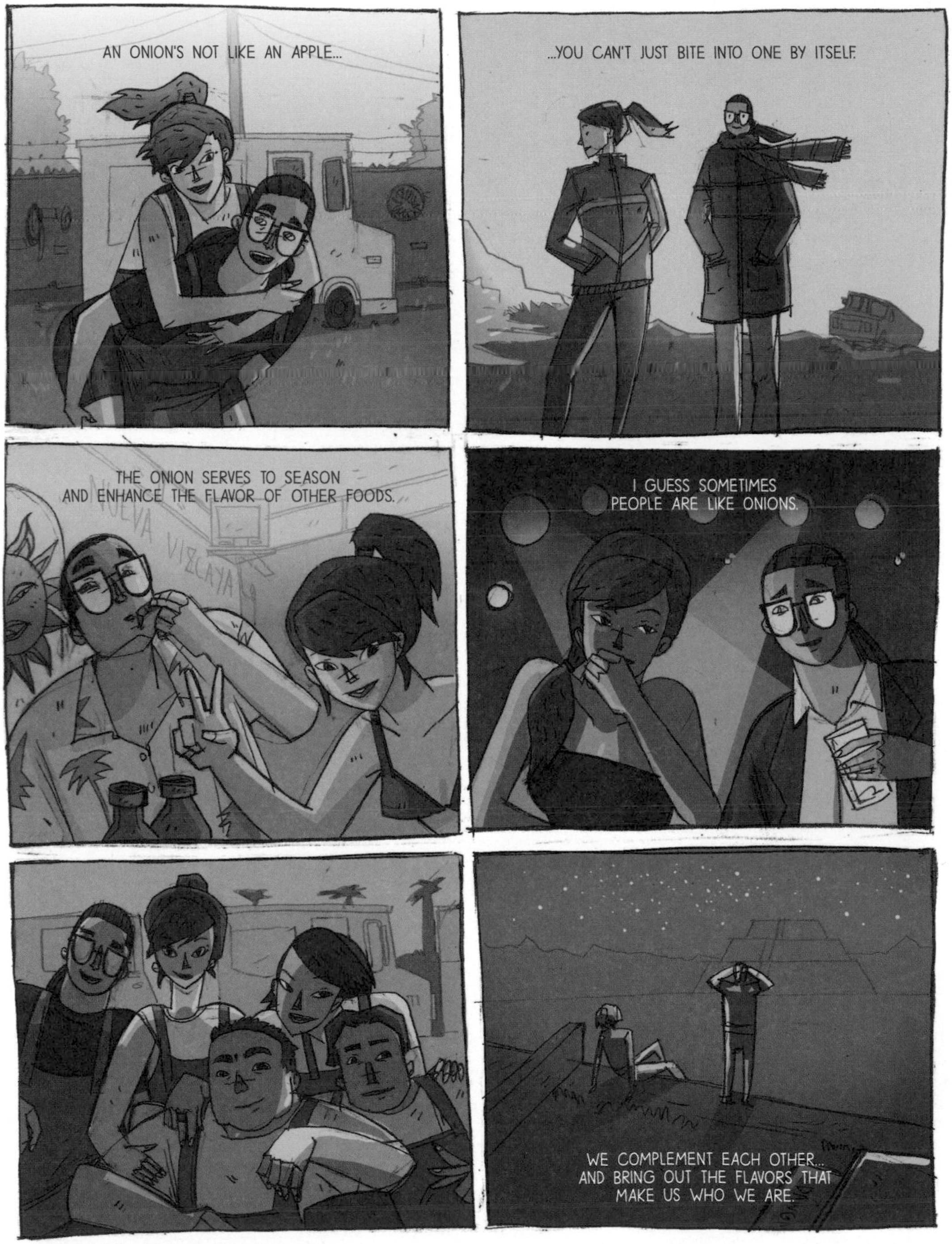
AN ONION'S NOT LIKE AN APPLE...
...YOU CAN'T JUST BITE INTO ONE BY ITSELF.
THE ONION SERVES TO SEASON AND ENHANCE THE FLAVOR OF OTHER FOODS.
NUEVA VIZCAYA
I GUESS SOMETIMES PEOPLE ARE LIKE ONIONS.
WE COMPLEMENT EACH OTHER... AND BRING OUT THE FLAVORS THAT MAKE US WHO WE ARE.

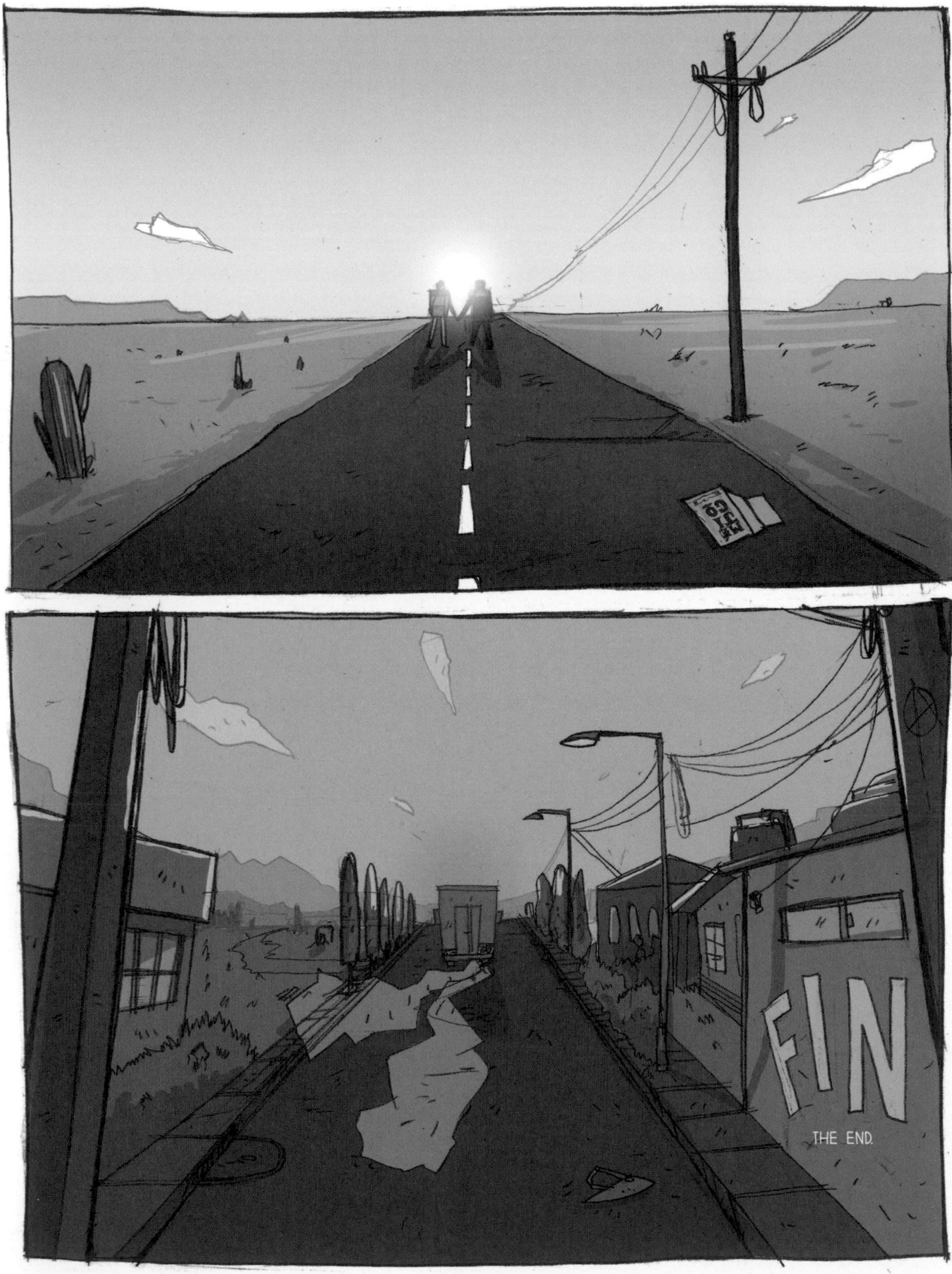
FIN
THE END.

'ONION SKIN'
WRITTEN AND DRAWN BY
EDGAR CAMACHO